THE SHADOW OF THE NORTH

A STORY OF OLD NEW YORK AND A LOST CAMPAIGN

By

JOSEPH A. ALTSHELER

Double9
Books

The Shadow Of The North
A Story Of Old New York
And A Lost Campaign

by   **Joseph A. Altsheler**

Copyright © 2023

ISBN: 978-93-57486-27-9

Published by

DOUBLE 9 BOOKS

2/13-B, Ansari Road, Daryaganj
New Delhi – 110002
info@double9books.com
www.double9books.com
Tel. 011-40042856

ABOUT THE AUTHOR

Joseph A. Altsheler was born on April 29, 1862, in Three Springs, Hart County, Kentucky, to Joseph and Louise Altsheler. He was a newspaper reporter, editor, and author of popular juvenile historical fiction. He wrote fifty novels and at least fifty-three short stories. Seven of his novels were in sequence. He worked as an editor at the Louisville Courier-Journal in 1885. In 1892, he started to work for New York World and then as the editor of the World's tri-weekly magazine. He wrote children's stories due to a lack of suitable stories. On May 30, 1880, Altsheler married Sarah Boles and had a son named Sidney. In 1914, during World War I Altsheler and his family were in Germany and they were forced to remain there. Altsheler died at the age of 57, on June 5, 1919, in New York. His wife, Sarah Boles died after 30 years. Their bodies are buried at the Cave Hill Cemetery in Louisville, Kentucky. Although each of the thirty-two novels constitutes an independent story, Altsheler suggested reading in sequence for each series (that is, he numbered the volumes). You can read the remaining eighteen novels in any order.

CONTENTS

CHAPTER I
THE ONONDAGA

Tayoga, of the Clan of the Bear, of the nation Onondaga, of the great League of the Hodenosaunee, advanced with utmost caution through a forest, so thick with undergrowth that it hid all objects twenty yards away. He was not armed with a rifle, but carried instead a heavy bow, while a quiver full of arrows hung over his shoulder. He wore less clothing than when he was in the white man's school at Albany, his arms and shoulders being bare, though not painted.

The young Indian's aspect, too, had changed. The great struggle between English and French, drawing with it the whole North American wilderness, had begun and, although the fifty sachems still sought to hold the Six Nations neutral, many of their bravest warriors were already serving with the Americans and English, ranging the forest as scouts and guides and skirmishers, bringing to the campaign an unrivaled skill, and a faith sealed by the long alliance.

Tayoga had thrown himself into the war heart and soul. Nothing could diminish by a hair his hostility to the French and the tribes allied with them. The deeds of Champlain and Frontenac were but of yesterday, and the nation to which they belonged could never be a friend of the Hodenosaunee. He trusted the Americans and the English, but his chief devotion, by the decree of nature was for his own people, and now, that fighting in the forest had occurred between the rival nations, he shed more of the white ways and became a true son of the wilderness, seeing as red men saw and thinking as red men thought.

He was bent over a little, as he walked slowly among the bushes, in the position of one poised for instant flight or pursuit as the need might be. His eyes, black and piercing, ranged about incessantly, nothing escaping a vision so keen and trained so thoroughly that he not only heard everything passing in the wilderness, but he knew the nature of the sound, and what had made it.

The kindly look that distinguished Tayoga in repose had disappeared. Unnumbered generations were speaking in him now, and the Indian, often so gentle in peace, had become his usual self, stern and unrelenting in war. His strong sharp chin was thrust forward. His cheek bones seemed to be a little higher. His tread was so light that the grass scarcely bent before his moccasins, and no leaves rustled. He was in every respect the wilderness hunter and warrior, fitted perfectly by the Supreme Hand into his setting, and if an enemy appeared now he would fight as his people had fought for centuries, and the customs and feelings of the new races that had come across the ocean would be nothing to him.

A hundred yards more, and he sat down by the trunk of a great oak, convinced that no foe was near. His own five splendid senses had told him so, and the fact had been confirmed by an unrivaled sentinel hidden among the leaves over his head, a small bird that poured forth a wonderful volume of song. Were any other coming the bird would cease his melody and fly away, but Tayoga felt that this tiny feathered being was his ally and would not leave because of him. The song had wonderful power, too, soothing his senses and casting a pleasing spell. His imaginative mind, infused with the religion and beliefs of his ancestors, filled the forest with friendly spirits. Unseen, they hovered in the air and watched over him, and the trees, alive, bent protecting boughs toward him. He saw, too, the very spot in the heavens where the great shining star on which Tododaho lived came out at night and glittered.

He remembered the time when he had gone forth in the dusk to meet Tandakora and his friends, and how Tododaho had looked down on him with approval. He had found favor in the sight of the great league's founder, and the spirit that dwelt on the shining star still watched over him. The Ojibway, whom he hated and who hated him in yet greater measure, might be somewhere in the forest, but if he came near, the feathered sentinel among the leaves over his head would give warning.

Tayoga sat nearly half an hour listening to the song of the bird. He had no object in remaining there, his errand bade him move on, but there was no hurry and he was content merely to breathe and to feel the glory and splendor of the forest about him. He knew now that the Indian nature had never been taken out of him by the schools. He loved the wilderness, the trees, the lakes, the streams and all their magnificent disorder, and war itself did not greatly trouble him, since the legends of the tribes made it the natural state of man. He knew well that he was in Tododaho's keeping, and, if by chance, the great chief should turn against him it would be for some grave fault, and he would deserve his punishment.

He sat in that absolute stillness of which the Indian by nature and training was capable, the green of his tanned and beautifully soft deerskin blending so perfectly with the emerald hue of the foliage that the bird above his head at last took him for a part of the forest itself and so, having no fear, came down within a foot of his head and sang with more ecstasy than ever. It was a little gray bird, but Tayoga knew that often the smaller a bird was, and the more sober its plumage the finer was its song. He understood those musical notes too. They expressed sheer delight, the joy of life just as he felt it then himself, and the kinship between the two was strong.

The bird at last flew away and the Onondaga heard its song dying among the distant leaves. A portion of the forest spell departed with it, and Tayoga, returning to thoughts of his task, rose and walked on, instinct rather than will causing him to keep a close watch on earth and foliage. When he saw the faint trace of a large moccasin on the earth all that was left of the spell departed suddenly and he became at once the wilderness warrior, active, alert, ready to read every sign.

He studied the imprint, which turned in, and hence had been made by an Indian. Its great size too indicated to him that it might be that of Tandakora, a belief becoming with him almost a certainty as he found other and similar traces farther on. He followed them about a mile, reaching stony ground where they vanished altogether, and then he turned to the west.

The fact that Tandakora was so near, and might approach again was not unpleasant to him, as Tayoga, having all the soul of a warrior, was anxious to match himself with the gigantic Ojibway, and since the war was now active on the border it seemed that the opportunity might come. But his attention must be occupied with something else for the present, and he went toward the west for a full hour through the primeval forest. Now and then he stopped to listen, even lying down and putting his ear to the ground, but the sounds he heard, although varied and many, were natural to the wild.

He knew them all. The steady tapping was a woodpecker at work upon an old tree. The faint musical note was another little gray bird singing the delight of his soul as he perched himself upon a twig; the light shuffling noise was the tread of a bear hunting succulent nuts; a caw-caw so distant that it was like an echo was the voice of a circling crow, and the tiny trickling noise that only the keenest ear could have heard was made by a brook a yard wide taking a terrific plunge over a precipice six inches high. The rustling, one great blended note, universal but soft, was that of the leaves moving in harmony before the gentle wind.

The young Onondaga was sure that the forest held no alien presence. The traces of Tandakora were hours old, and he must now be many miles away with his band, and, such being the case, it was fit time for him to choose a camp and call his friends.

It pleased Tayoga, zealous of mind, to do all the work before the others came, and, treading so lightly and delicately, that he would not have alarmed a rabbit in the bush, he gathered together dead sticks and heaped them in a little sunken place, clear of undergrowth. Flint and steel soon lighted a fire, and then he sent forth his call, the long penetrating whine of the wolf. The reply came from the north, and, building his fire a little higher, he awaited the result, without anxiety.

The dry wood crackled and many little flames red or yellow arose. Tayoga heaped dead leaves against the trunk of a tree and sat down comfortably, his shoulders and back resting against the bark. Presently he heard the first alien sound in the forest, a light tread approaching That he knew was Willet, and then he heard the second tread, even lighter than the first, and he knew that it was the footstep of Robert.

"All ready! It's like you, Tayoga," said Willet, as he entered the open space. "Here you are, with the house built and the fire burning on the hearth!"

"I lighted the fire," said Tayoga, rising, "but Manitou made the hearth, and built the house which is worthy of Him."

He looked with admiration at the magnificent trees spreading away on every side, and the foliage in its most splendid, new luxuriant green.

"It is worthy, Tayoga," said Robert, whose soul was like that of the Onondaga, "and it takes Manitou himself a century or more to grow trees like these."

"Some of them, I dare say, are three or four hundred years old or more," said Willet, "and the forest goes west, so I've heard the Indians say, a matter of near two thousand miles. It's pleasant to know that if all the axes in the world were at work it couldn't all be cut down in our time or in the time of our children."

Tayoga's heart swelled with indignation at the idea that the forest might be destroyed, but he said nothing, as he knew that Willet and Robert shared his feeling.

"Here's your rifle, Tayoga," said the hunter; "I suppose you didn't have an occasion to use your bow and arrows."

"No, Great Bear," replied the Onondaga, "but I might have had the chance had I come earlier."

"What do you mean by that?"

"I saw on the grass a human trace. It was made by a foot clothed in a moccasin, a large foot, a very large foot, the foot of a man whom we all have cause to hate."

"I take it you're speaking of Tandakora, the Ojibway."

"None other. I cannot be mistaken. But the trail was cold. He and his warriors have gone north. They may be thirty, forty miles from here."

"Likely enough, Tayoga. They're on their way to join the force the French are sending to the fort at the junction of the Monongahela and the Alleghany. Perhaps St. Luc—and there isn't a cleverer officer in this continent—is with them. I tell you, Tayoga, and you too, Robert, I don't like it! That young Washington ought to have been sent earlier into the Ohio country, and they should have given him a much larger force. We're sluggards and all our governors are sluggards, except maybe Shirley of Massachusetts. With the war just blazing up the French are already in possession, and we're to drive 'em out, which doubles our task. It was a great victory for us to keep the Hodenosaunee on our side, or, in the main, neutral, but it's going to be uphill work for us to win. The young French leaders are genuine kings of the wilderness. You know that, Robert, as well as I do."

"Yes," said the youth. "I know they're the men whom the English colonies have good cause to fear."

When he spoke he was thinking of St. Luc, as he had last seen him in the vale of Onondaga, defeated in the appeal to the fifty sachems, but gallant, well bred, showing nothing of chagrin, and sure to be a formidable foe on the field of battle. He was an enemy of whom one could be proud, and Robert felt an actual wish to see him again, even though in opposing ranks.

"We may come into contact with some of 'em," said the hunter. "The French are using all their influence over the Indians, and are directing their movements. I know that St. Luc, Jumonville, Beaujeu, Dumas, De Villiers, De Courcelles and all their best men are in the forest. It's likely that Tandakora, fierce and wild as he is, is acting under the direction of some Frenchman. St. Luc could control him."

Robert thought it highly probable that the chevalier was in truth with the Indians on the border, either leading some daring band or gathering the warriors to the banner of France. His influence with them would be great, as he understood their ways, adapted himself to them and showed in battle a skill and daring that always make a powerful appeal to the savage heart. The youth had matched himself against St. Luc in the test of words in the vale of Onondaga, and now he felt that he must match himself anew, but in the test of forest war.

Tayoga having lighted the fire, the hunter cooked the food over it, while the two youths reposed calmly. Robert watched Willet with interest, and he was impressed for the thousandth time by his great strength, and the lightness of his movements. When he was younger, the disparity in years had made him think of Willet as an old man, but he saw now that he was only in early middle age. There was not a gray hair on his head, and his face was free from wrinkles.

An extraordinarily vivid memory of that night in Quebec when the hunter had faced Boucher, the bully and bravo, reputed the best swordsman of France, leaped up in Robert's mind. He had found no time to think of Willet's past recently and he realized now that he knew little about it. The origin of that hunter was as obscure as his own. But the story of the past and its mysteries must wait. The present was so great and overwhelming that it blotted out everything else.

"The venison and the bacon are ready," said Willet, "and you two lads can fall on. You're not what I'd call epicures, but I've never known your appetites to fail."

"Nor will they," said Robert, as he and Tayoga helped themselves. "What's the news from Britain, Dave? You must have heard a lot when you were in Albany."

"It's vague, Robert, vague. The English are slow, just as we Americans are, too. They're going to send out troops, but the French have dispatched a fleet and regiments already. The fact that our colonies are so much larger than theirs is perhaps an advantage to them, as it gives them a bigger target to aim at, and our people who are trying to till their farms, will be struck down by their Indians from ambush."

"And you see now what a bulwark the great League of the Hodenosaunee is to the English," said Tayoga.

"A fact that I've always foreseen," said Willet warmly. "Nobody knows better than I do the power of the Six Nations, and nobody has ever been readier to admit it."

"I know, Great Bear. You have always been our true friend. If all the white men were like you no trouble would ever arise between them and the Hodenosaunee."

Robert finished his food and resumed a comfortable place against a tree. Willet put out the fire and he and Tayoga sat down in like fashion. Their trees were close together, but they did not talk now. Each was absorbed in his own thoughts and Robert had much to think about.

The war was going slowly. He had believed a great flare would come at once and that everybody would soon be in the thick of action, but since young Washington had been defeated by Coulon de Villiers at the Great Meadows the British Colonies had spent much time debating and pulling in different directions. The union for which his eager soul craved did not come, and the shadow of the French power in the north, reinforced by innumerable savages, hung heavy and black over the land. Every runner brought news of French activities. Rumor painted as impregnable the fort they had built where two rivers uniting formed the Ohio, and it was certain that many bands already ranged down in the regions the English called their own.

Spring had lingered far into summer where they were, and the foliage was not yet touched by heat. All the forest was in deep and heavy green, hiding every object a hundred yards away, but from their opening they saw a blue and speckless sky, which the three by and by watched attentively, and with the same motive. Before the dark had begun to come in the east they saw a thin dark line drawn slowly across it, the trail of smoke. It might not have been noticed by eyes less keen, but they understood at once that it was a signal. Robert noted its drifting progress across the heavens, and then he said to Willet:

"How far from here do you calculate the base of that smoke is, Dave?"

"A long distance, Robert. Several miles maybe. The fire, I've no doubt, was kindled on top of a hill. It may be French speaking to Indians, or Indians talking to Indians."

"And you don't think it's people of ours?"

"I'm sure it isn't. We've no hunters or runners in these parts, except ourselves."

"And it's not Tandakora," said the Onondaga. "He must be much farther away."

"But the signal may be intended for him," said the hunter. "It may be carried to him by relays of smoke. I wish I could read that trail across the sky."

"It's thinning out fast," said Robert. "You can hardly see it! and now it's gone entirely!"

But the hunter continued to look thoughtfully at the sky, where the smoke had been. He never underrated the activity of the French, and he believed that a movement of importance, something the nature of which they should discover was at hand.

"Lads," he said, "I expected an easy night of good sleep for all three of us, but I'm thinking instead that we'd better take to the trail, and travel toward the place where that smoke was started."

"It's what scouts would do," said Tayoga tersely.

"And such we claim to be," said Robert.

As the sun began to sink they saw far in the west another smoke, that would have been invisible had it not been outlined against a fiery red sky, across which it lay like a dark thread. It was gone in a few moments, and then the dusk began to come.

"An answer to the first signal," said Tayoga. "It is very likely that a strong force is gathering. Perhaps Tandakora has come back and is planning a blow."

"It can't be possible that they're aiming it at us," said the hunter, thoughtfully. "They don't know of our presence here, and if they did we've too small a party for such big preparations."

"Perhaps a troop of Pennsylvanians are marching westward," said Tayoga, "and the French and their allies are laying a trap for them."

"Then," said Robert, "there is but one thing for us to do. We must warn our friends and save them from the snare."

"Of course," said Willet, "but we don't know where they are, and meanwhile we'd better wait an hour or two. Perhaps something will happen that will help us to locate them."

Robert and Tayoga nodded and the three remained silent while the night came. The blazing red in the west faded rapidly and darkness swept down over the wilderness. The three, each leaning against his tree, did not move but kept their rifles across their knees ready at once for possible use. Tayoga had fastened his bow over his back by the side of his quiver, and their packs were adjusted also.

Robert was anxious not so much for himself as for the unknown others who were marching through the wilderness, and for whom the French and Indians were laying an ambush. It had been put forward first as a suggestion, but it quickly became a conviction with him, and he felt that his comrades and he must act as if it were a certainty. But no sound that would tell them which way to go came out of this black forest, and they remained silent, waiting for the word.

The night thickened and they were still uncertain what to do. Robert made a silent prayer to the God of the white man, the Manitou of the red man, for a sign, but none came, and infected strongly as he was with the Indian philosophy and religion, he felt that it must be due to some lack of virtue in himself. He searched his memory, but he could not discover in what particular he had erred, and he was forced to continue his anxious waiting, until the stars should choose to fight for him.

Tayoga too was troubled, his mind in its own way being as active as Robert's. He knew all the spirits of earth, air and water were abroad, but he hoped at least one of them would look upon him with favor, and give him a warning. He sought Tododaho's star in the heavens, but the clouds were too thick, and, eye failing, he relied upon his ear for the signal which he and his young white comrade sought so earnestly.

If Tayoga had erred either in omission or commission then the spirits that hovered about him forgave him, as when the night was thickest they gave the sign. It was but the faint fall of a foot, and, at first, he thought a bear or a deer had made it, but at the fourth or fifth fall he knew that it was a human footstep and he whispered to his comrades:

"Some one comes!"

As if by preconcerted signal the three arose and crept silently into the dense underbrush, where they crouched, their rifles thrust forward.

"It is but one man and he walks directly toward us," whispered Tayoga.

"I hear him now," said Robert. "He is wearing moccasins, as his step is too light for boots."

"Which means that he's a rover like ourselves," said Willet. "Now he's stopped. There isn't a sound. The man, whoever he is, has taken alarm, or at least he's decided that it's best for him to be more watchful. Perhaps he's caught a whiff from the ashes of our fire. He's white or he wouldn't be here alone, and he's used to the forest, or he wouldn't have suspected a presence from so little."

"The Great Bear thinks clearly," said Tayoga. "It is surely a white man and some great scout or hunter. He moved a little now to the right, because I heard his buckskin brush lightly against a bush. I think Great Bear is right about the fire. The wind has brought the ashes from it to his nostrils, and he will lie in the bush long before moving."

"Which doesn't suit our plans at all," said Willet. "There's a chance, just a chance, that I may know who he is. White men of the kind to go scouting through the wilderness are not so plenty on the border that one has to make many guesses. You lads move away a little so you won't be in line if a shot comes, and I'll give a signal."

Robert and Tayoga crept to other points in the brush, and the hunter uttered a whistle, low but very clear and musical. In a moment or two, a like answer came from a place about a hundred yards away, and Willet rising, advanced without hesitation. Robert and Tayoga followed promptly, and a tall figure, emerging from the darkness, came forward to meet them.

The stranger was a man of middle years, and of a singularly wild appearance. His eyes roved continually, and were full of suspicion, and of a sort of smoldering anger, as if he had a grievance against all the world. His hair was long and tangled, his face brown with sun and storm, and his dress more Indian than white. He was heavily armed, and, whether seen in the dusk or in the light, his whole aspect was formidable and dangerous. But Willet continued to advance without hesitation.

"Captain Jack," he said extending his hand. "We were not looking for you tonight, but no man could be more welcome. These are young friends of mine, brave warriors both, the white and the red, Robert Lennox, who is almost a son to me, and Tayoga, the Onondaga, to whom I feel nearly like a father too."

Now Robert knew him, and he felt a thrill of surprise, and of the most intense curiosity. Who along the whole border had not heard of Captain Jack, known also as the Black Hunter, the Black Rifle and by many other names? The tale had been told in every cabin in the woods how returning home, he had found his wife and children tomahawked and scalped, and how he had taken a vow of lifelong vengeance upon the Indians, a vow most terribly kept. In all the villages in the Ohio country and along the Great Lakes, the name of Black Rifle was spoken with awe and terror. No more singular and ominous figure ever crossed the pages of border story.

He swept the two youths with questing glances, but they met his gaze firmly, and while his eye had clouded at first sight of the Onondaga the threatening look soon passed.

"Friends of yours are friends of mine, Dave Willet," he said. "I know you to be a good man and true, and once when I was at Albany I heard of Robert Lennox, and of the great young warrior, Tayoga, of the clan of the Bear, of the nation Onondaga, of the great League of the Hodenosaunee."

The young Onondaga's eyes flashed with pleasure, but he was silent.

"How does it happen, Willet?" asked Black Rifle, "that we meet here in the forest at such a time?"

"We're on our way to the Ohio country to learn something about the gathering of the French and Indian forces. Just before sundown we saw smoke signals and we think our enemies are planning to cut off a force of ours, somewhere here in the forest."

Black Rifle laughed, but it was not a pleasant laugh. It had in it a quality that made Robert shudder.

"Your guesses are good, Dave," said Black Rifle. "About fifty men of the Pennsylvania militia are in camp on the banks of a little creek two miles from here. They have been sent out to guard the farthest settlements. Think of that, Dave! They're to be a guard against the French and Indians!"

His face contracted into a wry smile, and Robert understood his feeling of derision for the militia.

"As I told you, they're in camp," continued Black Rifle. "They built a fire there to cook their supper, and to show the French and Indians where they are, lest they miss 'em in the darkness. They don't know what part of the country they're in, but they're sure it's a long distance west of Philadelphia, and if the Indians will only tell 'em when they're coming they'll be ready for 'em. Oh, they're brave enough! They'll probably all die with their faces to the enemy."

He spoke with grim irony and Robert shuddered. He knew how helpless men from the older parts of the country were in the depths of the wilderness, and he was sure that the net was already being drawn about the Pennsylvanians.

"Are the French here too, Black Rifle?" asked Willet.

The strange man pointed toward the north.

"A band led by a Frenchman is there," he replied. "He is the most skillful of all their men in the forest, the one whom they call St. Luc."

"I thought so!" exclaimed Robert. "I believed all the while he would be here. I've no doubt he will direct the ambush."

"We must warn this troop," said Willet, "and save 'em if they will let us. You agree with me, don't you, Tayoga?"

"The Great Bear is right."

"And you'll back me up, of course, Robert. Will you help us too, Black Rifle?"

The singular man smiled again, but his smile was not like that of anybody else. It was sinister and full of menace. It was the smile of a man who rejoiced in sanguinary work, and it made Robert think again of his extraordinary history, around which the border had built so much of truth and legend.

"I will help, of course," he replied. "It's my trade. It was my purpose to warn 'em before I met you, but I feared they would not listen to me. Now, the words of four may sound more real to 'em than the words of one."

"Then lead the way," said Willet. "'Tis not a time to linger."

Black Rifle, without another word, threw his rifle over his shoulder and started toward the north, the others falling into Indian file behind him. A light, pleased smile played over his massive and rugged features. More than the rest he rejoiced in the prospect of combat. They did not seek battle and they fought only when they were compelled to do so, but he, with his whole nature embittered forever by that massacre of long ago, loved it for its own sake. He had ranged the border, a torch of fire, for years, and now he foresaw more of the revenge that he craved incessantly.

He led without hesitation straight toward the north. All four were accomplished trailers and the flitting figures were soundless as they made their swift march through the forest. In a half hour they reached the crest of a rather high hill and Black Rifle, stopping, pointed with a long forefinger toward a low and dim light.

"The camp of the Pennsylvanians," he said with bitter irony. "As I told you, fearing lest the savages should miss 'em in the forest they keep their fire burning as a beacon."

"Don't be too hard on 'em, Black Rifle," said Willet. "Maybe they come from Philadelphia itself, and city bred men can scarcely be expected to learn all about the wilderness in a few days."

"They'll learn, when it's too late, at the muzzles of the French and Indian rifles," rejoined Black Rifle, abating a little his tone of savage derision.

"At least they're likely to be brave men," said Willet, "and now what do you think will be our best manner of approaching 'em?"

"We'll walk directly toward their fire, the four of us abreast. They'll blaze away all fifty of 'em together, as soon as they see us, but the darkness will spoil their aim, and at least one of us will be left alive, able to walk, and able to tell 'em of their danger. We don't know who'll be the lucky man, but we'll see."

"Come, come, Captain Jack! Give 'em a chance! They may be a more likely lot than you think. You three wait here and I'll go forward and announce our coming. I dare say we'll be welcome."

Willet advanced boldly toward the fire, which he soon saw consisted of a great bed of coals, surrounded by sleepers. But the figures of men, pacing back and forth, showed that the watch had not been neglected, although in the deep forest such sentinels would be but little protection against the kind of ambush the French and Indians were able to lay.

Not caring to come within the circle of light lest he be fired upon, the hunter whistled, and when he saw that the sentinels were at attention he whistled again. Then he emerged from the bushes, and walked boldly toward the fire.

"Who are you?" a voice demanded sharply, and a young man in a fine uniform stood up in front of the fire. The hunter's quick and penetrating look noted that he was tall, built well, and that his face was frank and open.

"My name is David Willet," he replied, "and I am sometimes called by my friends, the Iroquois, the Great Bear. Behind me in the woods are three comrades, young Robert Lennox, of New York and Albany; Tayoga, a young warrior of the clan of the Bear, of the nation Onondaga, of the great League of the Hodenosaunee, and the famous hunter and border fighter, of whom everybody has heard, Captain Jack, Black Hunter, or Black Rifle as he has been called variously."

"I know the name," replied the young man, "and yours too, Mr. Willet. My own is Colden, James Colden of Philadelphia, and I am in command of this troop, sent to guard the farthest settlements against the French and Indians. Will you call your comrades, Mr. Willet? All of you are welcome."

The hunter whistled again, and Robert, Tayoga and Black Rifle, advancing from the forest, came within the area of half light cast by the glow from the coals, young Captain Colden watching them with the most intense curiosity as they approached. And well he might feel surprise. All, even Robert, wore the dress of the wilderness, and their appearance at such a time was uncommon and striking. Most of the soldiers had been awakened by the voices, and were sitting up, rubbing sleepy eyes. Robert saw at once that they were city men, singularly out of place in the vast forest and the darkness.

"We welcome you to our camp," said young Captain Colden, with dignity. "If you are hungry we have food, and if you are without blankets we can furnish them to you."

Willet and Tayoga looked at Robert and he knew they expected him to fill his usual role of spokesman. The words rushed to his lips, but they were held there by embarrassment. The soldiers who had been awakened were already going back to sleep. Captain Colden sat down on a log and waited for them to state their wants. Then Robert spoke, knowing they could not afford to delay.

"We thank you, Captain Colden," he said, "for the offer of supper and bed, but I must say to you, sir, that it's no time for either."

"I don't take your meaning, Mr. Lennox."

"Tayoga, Mr. Willet and Black Rifle, are the best scouts in the wilderness, and before sunset they saw smoke on the horizon. Then they saw smoke answering smoke, and Black Rifle has seen more. The French and Indians, sir, are in the forest, and they're led, too, by Frenchmen."

Young James Colden was a brave man, and his eyes glittered.

"We ask nothing better than to meet 'em," he said, "At the first breath of dawn we'll march against 'em, if your friends will only be so good as to show us the way."

"It's not a matter of waiting until dawn, nor even of going to meet 'em. They'll bring the battle to us. You and your force, Captain Colden, are surrounded already."

The young captain stared at Robert, but his eyes were full of incredulity. Several of the soldiers were standing near, and they too heard, but the warning found no answer in their minds. Robert looked around at the men asleep and the others ready to follow them, and, despite his instinctive liking for Colden, his anger began to rise.

"I said that you were surrounded," he repeated sharply, "and it's no time, Captain Colden, for unbelief! Mr. Willet, Tayoga and I saw the signals of the enemy, but Black Rifle here has looked upon the warriors themselves. They're led too by the French, and the best of all the French forest captains, St. Luc, is undoubtedly with them off there."

He waved his hand toward the north, and a little of the high color left Colden's face. The youth's manner was so earnest and his words were spoken with so much power of conviction that they could not fail to impress.

"You really mean that the French and Indians are here, that they're planning to attack us tonight?" said the Philadelphian.

"Beyond a doubt and we must be prepared to meet them."

Colden took a few steps back and forth, and then, like the brave young man he was, he swallowed his pride.

"I confess that I don't know much of the forest, nor do my men," he said, "and so I shall have to ask you four to help me."

"We'll do it gladly," said Robert. "What do you propose, Dave?"

"I think we'd better draw off some distance from the fire," replied the hunter. "To the right there is a low hill, covered with thick brush, and old logs thrown down by an ancient storm. It's the very place."

"Then," said Captain Colden briskly, "we'll occupy it inside of five minutes. Up, men, up!"

The sleepers were awakened rapidly, and, although they were awkward and made much more noise than was necessary, they obeyed their captain's sharp order, and marched away with all their arms and stores to the thicket on the hill, where, as Willet had predicted, they found also a network of fallen trees, affording a fine shelter and defense. Here they crouched and Willet enjoined upon them the necessity of silence.

"Not at all. It's not the Indian way, nor is it the way either of the French, who go with them. They know your men are raw—pardon me—inexperienced troops, and they'll put a cruel burden upon your patience. They may wait for hours, and they'll try in every manner to wear them out, and to provoke them at last into some rash movement. You'll have to guard most, Captain Colden, against the temper of your troop. If you'll take advice from one who's a veteran in the woods, you'd better threaten them with death for disobedience of orders."

"As I said before, I'm grateful to you for any advice or suggestion, Mr. Willet. This seems a long way from Philadelphia, and I'll confess I'm not so very much at home here."

He crawled among his men, and Willet and Robert heard him threatening them in fierce whispers, and their replies that they would be cautious and patient. It was well that Willet had given the advice, as a full hour passed without any sign from the foe. Troops even more experienced than the city men might well have concluded it was a false alarm, and that the forest contained nothing more dangerous than a bear. There was no sound, and Captain Colden himself asked if the warriors had not gone away.

"Not a chance of it," replied Willet. "They think they're certain of a victory, and they would not dream of retiring."

"And we have more long waiting in the dark to do?"

"I warned you. There is no other way to fight such enemies. We must never make the mistake of undervaluing them."

Captain Colden sighed. He had a gallant heart, and he and his troop had made a fine parade through the streets of Philadelphia, before he started for the frontier, but he had expected to meet the French in the open, perhaps with a bugle playing, and he would charge at the head of his men, waving the neat small sword, now buckled to his side. Instead he lay in a black thicket, awaiting the attack of creeping savages. Nevertheless, he put down his pride for the third time, and resolved to trust the four who had come so opportunely to his aid, and who seemed to be so thoroughly at home in the wilderness.

Another hour dragged its weary length away, and there was no sound of anything stirring in the forest. The skies lightened a little as the moon came out, casting a faint whitish tint over trees and bushes, but the brave young captain was yet unable to see any trace of the enemy.

"Do you feel quite sure that we're still besieged?" he whispered to Willet.

"Yes, Captain," replied the hunter, "and, as I said, patience is the commodity we need most. It would be fatal for us to force the action, but I don't think we have much longer to wait. Since they can't induce us to take some rash step they're likely to make a movement soon."

"I see the bushes waving again," said Tayoga. "It is proof that the warriors are approaching. It would be well for the soldiers to lie flat for a little while."

Captain Colden, adhering to his resolution to take the advice of his new friends, crept along the line, telling the men in sharp whispers to hug the earth, a command that they obeyed willingly, as the darkness, the silence and the mysterious nature of the danger had begun to weigh heavily upon their nerves.

Robert saw a bead of flame among the bushes, and heard a sharp report. A bullet cut a bough over his head, and a leaf drifted down upon his face. The soldiers shifted uneasily and began to thrust their rifles forward, but again the stern command of the young captain prompted by the hunter, held them down.

"'Twas intended merely to draw us," said Willet. "They're sure we're in this wood, but of course they don't know the exact location of our men. They're hoping for a glimpse of the bright uniforms, but, if the men keep very low, they won't get it."

It was a tremendous trial for young and raw troops, but they managed to still their nerves, and to remain crouched and motionless. A second shot was fired soon, and then a third, but like the first they were trial bullets and both went high. Black Rifle grew impatient. The memory of his murdered family began to press upon him once more. The night was black, but now it looked red to him. Lying almost flat, he slowly pulled himself forward like a great wild beast, stalking its prey. Colden looked at him, and then at Willet, who nodded.

"Don't try to stop him," whispered the hunter, "because he'll go anyhow. Besides, it's time for us to reply to their shots."

The dark form, moving forward without noise, had a singular fascination for Robert. His imagination, which colored and magnified everything, made Black Rifle sinister and supernatural. The complete absence of sound, as he advanced, heightened the effect. Not a leaf nor a blade of grass rustled. Presently he stopped and Robert saw the black muzzle of his rifle shoot forward. A stream of flame leaped forth, and then the man quickly slid into a new position.

A fierce shout came from the opposing thicket, and a half dozen shots were fired. Bullets again cut twigs and leaves over Robert's head, but all of them went too high.

"Do you think Black Rifle hit his mark?" whispered Robert to Tayoga.

"It is likely," replied the Onondaga, "but we may never know. I think it would be well, Dagaeoga, for you and me to go toward the left. They may try to creep around our flank, and we must meet them there."

Willet and Colden approved of the plan, and a half dozen of the best soldiers went with them, the movement proving to be wise, as within five minutes a scattering fire was opened upon that point. The soldiers fired two rash shots, merely aiming at the reports and the general blackness, but Robert and Tayoga quickly reduced them to control, insisting that they wait until they saw a foe, before pulling trigger again. Then they sank back among the bushes and remained quite still.

Tayoga suddenly drew a deep and very long breath, which with him was equivalent to an exclamation.

"What is it, Tayoga?" asked Robert.

"I saw a bit of a uniform, and I caught just a glimpse of a white face."

"An officer. Then we were right in our surmise that the French are here, leading the warriors."

"It was but a glimpse, but it showed the curve of his jaw and chin, and I knew him. He is one who is beginning to be important in your life, Dagaeoga."

"St. Luc."

"None other. I could not be mistaken. He is leading the attack upon us. Perhaps Tandakora is with him. The Frenchman does not like the Ojibway, but war makes strange comrades. That was close!"

A bullet whistled directly between them, and Tayoga, kneeling, fired in return. There was no doubt about his aim, as a warrior uttered the death cry, and a fierce shout of rage from a dozen throats followed. Robert, imaginative, ready to flame up in a moment, exulted, not because a warrior had fallen, but because the flank attack upon his own people had been stopped in the beginning. St. Luc himself would have admitted that the Americans, or the English, as he would have called them, were acting wisely. The soldiers, stirred by the successful shot, showed again a great desire to fire at the black woods, but Robert and the Onondaga still kept them down.

A crackling fire arose behind them, showing that the main force had engaged, and now and then the warriors uttered defiant cries. But Robert had enough power of will to watch in front, sure that Willet and Black Rifle were sufficient to guide the central defense. He observed intently the segment of the circle in front of them, and he wondered if St. Luc would appear there again, but he concluded that he would not, since the failure of the attempted surprise at that point would be likely to send him back to the main force.

"Do you think they'll go away and concentrate in front?" he asked Tayoga.

"No," replied the Onondaga. "They still think perhaps that they have only the soldiers from the city to meet, and they may attempt a rush."

Robert crept from soldier to soldier, cautioning every one to take shelter, and to have his rifle ready, and they, being good men, though without experience, obeyed the one who so obviously knew what he was doing. Meantime the combat behind them proceeded with vigor, the shots crashing in volleys, accompanied by shouts, and once by the cry of a stricken soldier. It was evident that St. Luc was now pushing the battle, and Robert was quite sure the attack on the flank would soon come again.

They did not wait much longer. The warriors suddenly leaped from the undergrowth and rushed straight toward them, a white man now in front. The light was sufficient for Robert to see that the leader was not St. Luc, and then without hesitation he raised his rifle and fired. The man fell, Tayoga stopped the rush of a warrior, and the bullets of the soldiers wounded others. But their white leader was gone, and Indians have little love for an attack upon a sheltered enemy. So the charge broke, before it was half way to the defenders, and the savages vanished in the thickets.

The soldiers began to exult, but Robert bade them reload as fast as possible, and keep well under cover. The warriors from new points would fire at every exposed head, and they could not afford to relax their caution for an instant.

But it was a difficult task for the youthful veterans of the forest to keep the older but inexperienced men from the city under cover. They had an almost overpowering desire to see the Indians who were shooting at them, and against whom they were sending their bullets. In spite of every command and entreaty a man would raise his head now and then, and one, as he did so, received a bullet between the eyes, falling back quietly, dead before he touched the ground.

"A brave lad has been lost," whispered Tayoga to Robert, "but he has been an involuntary example to the rest."

The Onondaga spoke in his precise school English, but he knew what he was saying, as the soldiers now became much more cautious, and controlled their impulse to raise up for a look, after every shot. Another man was wounded, but the hurt was not serious and he went on with his firing. Robert, seeing that the line on the flank could be held without great difficulty, left Tayoga in command, and crept back to the main force, where the bullets were coming much faster.

Two of the soldiers in the center had been slain, and three had been wounded, but Captain Colden had not given ground. He was sitting behind a rocky outcrop and at the suggestion of Willet was giving orders to his men. Oppressed at first by the ambush and weight of responsibility he was exulting now in their ability to check the savage onset. Robert was quite willing to play a little to his pride and he said in the formal military manner:

"I wish to report, sir, that all is going well on the southern flank. One of our men has been killed, but we have made it impossible for the enemy to advance there."

"Thank you, Mr. Lennox," said the young captain with dignity. "We have also had some success here, due chiefly to the good advice of Mr. Willet, and the prowess and sharpshooting of the extraordinary man whom you call Black Rifle. See him now!"

He indicated a dark figure a little distance ahead, behind a clump of bushes, and, as Robert looked, a jet of fire leaped from the muzzle of the man's rifle, followed almost immediately by a cry in the forest.

"I think he has slain more of our enemies than the rest of us combined," said Captain Colden.

Robert shuddered a little, but those who lived on the border became used to strange things. The constant struggle for existence hardened the nerves, and terrible scenes did not dwell long in the mind. He bent forward for a better look, and a bullet cut the hair upon his forehead. He started back, feeling as if he had been seared by lightning and Willet looked at him anxiously.

"The lead burned as it passed," the lad said, "but the skin is not broken. I was guilty of the same rashness, for which I have been lecturing the men on the flank."

"I caught a glimpse of the fellow who fired the shot," said Willet. "I think it was the Canadian, Dubois, whom we saw with St. Luc."

"Tayoga saw St. Luc himself on the flank," said Robert, "and so there is no doubt that he is leading the attack. The fact makes it certain that it will be carried on with persistence."

"We shall be here, still besieged, when day comes," said the hunter. "It's lucky that the cliff protects us on one side."

As if to disprove his assertion, all the firing stopped suddenly, and for a long time the forest was silent. Fortunately they had water in their canteens, and they were able to soothe the thirst of the wounded men. They talked also of victory, and, knowing that it was only two or three hours until dawn, Captain Colden's spirits rose to great heights. He was sure now that the warriors, defeated, had gone away. This Frenchman, St. Luc, of whom they talked, might be a great partisan leader, but he would know when the price he was paying became too high, and would draw off.

The men believed their captain, and, despite the earnest protest of the foresters, began to stir in the bushes shortly before dawn. A rifle shot came from the opposing thickets and one of them would stir no more. Captain Colden, appalled, was all remorse. He took the death of the man directly to himself, and told Willet with emotion that all advice of his would now be taken at once.

"Let the men lie as close as they can," said the hunter. "The day will soon be here."

Robert found shelter behind the trunk of a huge oak, and crouched there, his nerves relaxing. He did not believe any further movement of the enemy would come now. As the great tension passed for a time he was conscious of an immense weariness. The strain upon all the physical senses and upon the mind as well made him weak. It was a luxury merely to sit there with his back against the bark and rest. Near him he heard the soldiers moving softly, and now and then a wounded man asking for water. A light breeze had sprung up, and it had upon his face the freshness of the dawn. He wondered what the day would bring. The light that came with it would be cheerful and uplifting, but it would disclose their covert, at least in part, and St. Luc might lead both French and Indians in one great rush.

"Better eat a little," said Tayoga, who had returned to the center. "Remember that we have plenty of food in our knapsacks, nor are our canteens empty."

"I had forgotten it," said Robert, and he ate and drank sparingly. The breeze continued to freshen, and in the east the dawn broke, gray, turning to silver, and then to red and gold. The forest soon stood out, an infinite tracery in the dazzling light, and then a white fleck appeared against the wall of green.

"A flag of truce!" exclaimed Captain Colden. "What can they want to say to us?"

"Let the bearer of the flag appear first," suggested Willet, "and then we'll talk with 'em."

The figure of a man holding up a white handkerchief appeared and it was St. Luc himself, as neat and irreproachable as if he were attending a ball in the Intendant's palace at Quebec. Robert knew that he must have been active in the battle all through the night, but he showed no signs of it. He wore a fine close-fitting uniform of dark blue, and the handkerchief of lace was held aloft on the point of a small sword, the golden hilt of which glittered in the morning sunlight. He was a strange figure in the forest, but a most gallant one, and to Robert's eyes a chevalier without fear and without reproach.

"I know that you speak good French, Mr. Lennox," said Captain Colden. "Will you go forward and meet the Frenchman? You will perhaps know what to say to him, and, if not, you can refer to Mr. Willet and myself."

"I will do my best, sir," said Robert, glad of the chance to meet St. Luc face to face again. He did not know why his heart leaped so every time he saw the chevalier, but his friendship for him was undeniable. It seemed too that St. Luc liked him, and Robert felt sure that whatever hostility his official enemy felt for the English cause there was none for him personally.

Unconsciously he began to arrange his own attire of forest green, beautifully dyed and decorated deerskin, that he might not look less neat than the man whom he was going to meet. St. Luc was standing under the wide boughs of an oak, his gold hilted rapier returned to its sheath and his white lace handkerchief to its pocket. The smile of welcome upon his face as he saw the herald was genuine.

"I salute you, Mr. Lennox," he said, "and wish you a very good morning. I learned that you were in the force besieged by us, and it's a pleasure to see that you've escaped unhurt. When last we met the honors were yours. You fairly defeated me at the word play in the vale of Onondaga, but you will admit that the savage, Tandakora, played into your hands most opportunely. You will admit also that word play is not sword play, and that in the appeal to the sword we have the advantage of you."

"It may seem so to one who sees with your eyes and from your position," said Robert, "but being myself I'm compelled to see with my own eyes and from our side. I wish to say first, however, Chevalier de St. Luc, that since you have wished me a very good morning I even wish you a better."

St. Luc laughed gayly.

"You and I will never be enemies. It would be against nature," he said.

"No, we'll never be enemies, but why is it against nature?"

"Perhaps I was not happy in my phrase. We like each other too well, and—in a way—our temperaments resemble too much to engender a mutual hate. But we'll to business. Mine's a mission of mercy. I come to receive the surrender of your friends and yourself, since continued resistance to us will be vain!"

Robert smiled. His gift of golden speech was again making its presence felt. He had matched himself against St. Luc before the great League of the Hodenosaunee in the vale of Onondaga, and they had spoken where all might hear. Now they two alone could hear, but he felt that the test was the same in kind. He knew that his friends in the thickets behind him were watching, and he was equally sure that French and savages in the thickets before him were watching too. He had no doubt the baleful eyes of Tandakora were glaring at him at that very moment, and that the fingers of the Ojibway were eager to grasp his scalp. The idea, singularly enough, caused him amusement, because his imagination, vivid as usual, leaped far ahead, and he foresaw that his hair would never become a trophy for Tandakora.

"You smile, Mr. Lennox," said St. Luc. "Do you find my words so amusing?"

"Not amusing, chevalier! Oh, no! And if, in truth, I found them so I would not be so impolite as to smile. But there is a satisfaction in knowing that your official enemy has underrated the strength of your position. That is why my eyes expressed content—I would scarcely call it a smile."

"I see once more that you're a master of words, Mr. Lennox. You play with them as the wind sports among the leaves."

"But I don't speak in jest, Monsieur de St. Luc. I'm not in command here. I'm merely a spokesman a herald or a messenger, in whichever way you should choose to define me. Captain James Colden, a gallant young officer of Philadelphia, is our leader, but, in this instance, I don't feel the need of consulting him. I know that your offer is kindly, that it comes from a generous soul, but however much it may disappoint you I must decline it. Our resistance in the night has been quite successful, we have inflicted upon you much more damage than you have inflicted upon us, and I've no doubt the day will witness a battle continued in the same proportion."

St. Luc threw back his head and laughed, not loud, but gayly and with unction. Robert reddened, but he could not take offense, as he saw that none was meant.

"I no longer wonder at my defeat by you in the vale of Onondaga," said the chevalier, "since you're not merely a master of words, you're a master-artist. I've no doubt if I listen to you you'll persuade me it's not you but we who are besieged, and it would be wise for us to yield to you without further ado."

"Perhaps you're not so very far wrong," said Robert, recovering his assurance, which was nearly always great. "I'm sure Captain Colden would receive your surrender and treat you well."

The eyes of the two met and twinkled.

"Tandakora is with us," said St. Luc, "and I've a notion he wouldn't relish it. Perhaps he distrusts the mercy he would receive at the hands of your Onondaga, Tayoga. And at this point in our dialogue, Mr. Lennox, I want to apologize to you again, for the actions of the Ojibway before the war really began. I couldn't prevent them, but, since there is genuine war, he is our ally, and I must accord to him all the dignities and honors appertaining to his position."

"You're rather deft with words yourself, Monsieur de St. Luc. Once, at New York, I saw a juggler with balls who could keep five in the air at the same time, and in some dim and remote way you make me think of him. You'll pardon the illustration, chevalier, because I really mean it as a compliment."

"I pardon gladly enough, because I see your intentions are good. We both play with words, perhaps because the exercise tickles our fancy, but to return to the true spirit and essence of things, I warn you that it would be wise to surrender. My force is very much greater than Captain Colden's, and has him hemmed in. If my Indian allies suffer too much in the attack it will be difficult to restrain them. I'm not stating this as a threat—you know me too well for that—but to make the facts plain, and to avoid something that I should regret as much as you."

"I don't think it necessary to consult Captain Colden, and without doing so I decline your offer. We have food to eat, water to drink and bullets to shoot, and if you care to take us you must come and do so."

"And that is the final answer? You're quite sure you don't wish to consult your superior officer, Captain Colden?"

"Absolutely sure. It would waste the time of all of us."

"Then it seems there is nothing more to say, and to use your own fanciful way of putting it, we must go back from the play of words to the play of swords."

"I see no alternative."

"And yet I hope that you will survive the combat, Mr. Lennox."

"I've the same hope for you, Chevalier de St. Luc."

Each meant it, and, in the same high manner of the day, they saluted and withdrew. Robert, as he walked back to the thickets in which the defenders lay, felt that Indian eyes were upon him, and that perhaps an Indian bullet would speed toward him, despite St. Luc. Tandakora and the savages around him could not always be controlled by their French allies, as was to be shown too often in this war. His sensitive mind once more turned fancy into reality and the hair on his head lifted a little, but pride would not let him hasten his steps.

No gun was fired, and, with an immense relief, he sank down behind a fallen log, and by the side of Colden and Willet.

"What did the Frenchman want?" asked the young captain.

"Our instant and unconditional surrender. Knowing how you felt about it, I gave him your refusal at once."

"Well done, Mr. Lennox."

"He said that in case of a rush and heavy loss by his Indians he perhaps would not be able to control them in the moment of victory, which doubtless is true."

"They will know no moment of victory. We can hold them off."

"Where is Tayoga?" asked Robert of Willet.

The hunter pointed westward.

"Why, the cliff shuts off the way in that direction!" said Robert.

"Not to a good climber."

"Do you mean, then, that Tayoga is gone?"

"I saw him go. He went while you were talking with St. Luc."

"Why should Tayoga leave us?"

"He saw another smoke against the sky. It was but a faint trace. Only an extremely keen eye would have noticed it, and having much natural curiosity, Tayoga is now on his way to see who built the fire that made the smoke."

"And it may have been made by friends."

"That's our hope."

Robert drew a long breath and looked toward the west. The sky was now clear there, but he knew that Tayoga could not have made any mistake. Then, his heart high once more, he settled himself down to wait.

CHAPTER III
THE SIGNAL

The day advanced, brilliant with sunshine, and the forces of St. Luc were quiet. For a long time, not a shot was fired, and it seemed to the besieged that the forest was empty of human beings save themselves. Robert did not believe the French leader would attempt a long siege, since an engagement could not be conducted in that manner in the forest, where a result of some kind must be reached soon. Yet it was impossible to tell what plan St. Luc had in mind, and they must wait until Tayoga came.

Young Captain Colden was in good spirits. It was his first taste of wilderness warfare, and he knew that he had done well. The dead were laid decently among the bushes to receive Christian burial later, if the chance came, and the wounded, their hurts bound up, prepared to take what part they could in a new battle. Robert crept to the edge of the cliff, and looked toward the west, whence Tayoga had gone. He saw only a dazzling blue sky, unflecked by anything save little white clouds, and there was nothing to indicate whether the mission of his young Onondaga comrade would have any success. He crept back to the side of Willet.

"Have you any opinion, Dave, about the smoke that Tayoga saw," he asked.

"None, Robert, just a hope. It might have been made by another French and Indian band, most probably it was, but there is a chance, too, that friends built the fire."

"If it's a force of any size it could hardly be English. I don't think any troop of ours except Captain Colden's is in this region."

"We can't look for help from our own race."

Robert was silent, gazing intently into the west, whence Tayoga had gone. He recognized the immense difficulties of their position.

Indians, if an attack or two of theirs failed, would be likely to go away, but the French, and especially St. Luc, would increase their persistence and hold them to the task. He returned to the forest, and his attention was drawn once more by Black Rifle. The man was lying almost flat in the thicket, and evidently he had caught a glimpse of a foe, as he was writhing slowly forward like a great beast of prey, and his eyes once more had the expectant look of one who is going to strike. Robert considered him. He knew that the man's whole nature had been poisoned by the great tragedy in his life, and that it gave him a sinister pleasure to inflict blows upon those who had inflicted the great blow upon him. Yet he would be useful in the fierce war that was upon them and he was useful now.

Black Rifle crept forward two or three yards more, and, after he had lain quite still for a few moments, he suddenly thrust out his rifle and fired. A cry came from the opposing thicket and Robert heard the sharpshooter utter a deep sigh of satisfaction. He knew that St. Luc was one warrior less, which was good for the defense, but he shuddered a little. He could never bring himself to steal through the bushes and shoot an unseeing enemy. Still Black Rifle was Black Rifle, and being what he was he was not to be judged as other men were.

After a half hour's silence, the besiegers suddenly opened fire from five or six points, sending perhaps two score bullets into the wood, clipping off many twigs and leaves which fell upon the heads of the defenders. Captain Colden did not forget to be grateful to Willet for his insistence that the soldiers should always lie low, as the hostile lead, instead of striking, now merely sent a harmless shower upon them. But the fusillade was brief, Robert, in truth, judging that it had been against the commands of St. Luc, who was too wise a leader to wish ammunition to be wasted in random firing. At the advice of Willet, Captain Colden would not let his men reply, restraining their eagerness, and silence soon returned.

It was nearly noon now and a huge golden sun shone over the vast wilderness in which two little bands of men fought, mere motes in the limitless sea of green. Robert ate some venison, and drank a little water from the canteen of a friendly soldier. Then his thoughts turned again to Tayoga. The Onondaga was a peerless runner, he had been gone long now, and what would he find at the base of the smoke? If it had been the fire of an enemy then he would be back in the middle of the afternoon, and they would be in no worse case than before. They might try to escape in the night down the cliff, but it was not likely that vigilant foes would permit men, clumsy in the woods like the soldiers, to steal away in such a manner.

The earlier hours of the afternoon were passed by the sharpshooters on either side trying to stalk one another. Although Robert had no part in it, it was a savage play that alternately fascinated and repelled him. He had no way to tell exactly, but he believed that two more of the Indians had fallen, while a soldier received a wound. A bullet grazed Black Rifle's head, but instead of daunting him it seemed to give him a kind of fierce joy, and to inspire in him a greater desire to slay.

These efforts, since they achieved no positive results, soon died down, and both sides lay silent in their coverts. Robert made himself as comfortable as he could behind a log, although he longed to stand upright, and walk about once more like a human being. It was now mid-afternoon and if the smoke had meant nothing good for them it was time for Tayoga to be back. It was not conceivable that such a marvelous forester and matchless runner could have been taken, and, since he had not come, Robert's heart again beat to the tune of hope.

Willet with whom he talked a little, was of like opinion. He looked to Tayoga to bring them help, and, if he failed their case, already hard, would become harder. The hunter did not conceal from himself the prowess and skill of St. Luc and he knew too, that the savage persistency of Tandakora was not to be held lightly. Like Robert he gazed long into the blue west, which was flecked only by little clouds of white.

"A sign! A sign!" he said. "If we could only behold a sign!"

But the heavens said nothing. The sun, a huge ball of glowing copper, was already far down the Western curve, and the hunter's heart beat hard with anxiety. He felt that if help came it should come soon. But little water was left to the soldiers, although their food might last another day, and the night itself, now not far away, would bring the danger of a new attack by a creeping foe, greatly superior in numbers. He turned away from the cliff, but Robert remained, and presently the youth called in a sharp thrilling whisper:

"Dave! Dave! Come back!"

Robert had continued to watch the sky and he thought he saw a faint dark line against the sea of blue. He rubbed his eyes, fearing it was a fault of vision, but the trace was still there, and he believed it to be smoke.

"Dave! Dave! The signal! Look! Look!" he cried.

The hunter came to the edge of the cliff and stared into the west. A thread of black lay across the blue, and his heart leaped.

"Do you believe that Tayoga has anything to do with it?" asked Robert.

"I do. If it were our foes out there he'd have been back long since."

"And since it may be friends they've sent up this smoke, hoping we'll divine what they mean."

"It looks like it. Tayoga is a sharp lad, and he'll want to put heart in the soldiers. It must be the Onondaga, and I wish I knew what his smoke was saying."

Captain Colden joined them, and they pointed out to him the trace across the sky which was now broadening, explaining at the same time that it was probably a signal sent up by Tayoga, and that he might be leading a force to their aid.

"What help could he bring?" asked the captain.

Willet shook his head.

"I can't answer you there," he replied; "but the smoke has significance for us. Of that I feel sure. By sundown we'll know what it means."

"And that's only about two hours away," said Captain Colden. "Whatever happens we'll hold out to the last. I suppose, though, that St. Luc's force also will see the smoke."

"Quite likely," replied Willet, "and the Frenchman may send a runner, too, to see what it means, but however good a runner he may be he'll be no match for Tayoga."

"That's sure," said Robert.

So great was his confidence in the Onondaga that it never occurred to him that he might be killed or taken, and he awaited his certain return, either with or without a helping force. He lay now near the edge of the cliff, whence he could look toward the west, the point of hope, whenever he wished, ate another strip of venison, and took another drink of water out of a friendly canteen.

The west was now blazing with terraces of red and yellow, rising above one another, and the east was misty, gray and dim. Twilight was not far away. The thread of smoke that had lain against the sky above the forest was gone, the glittering bar of red and gold being absolutely free from any trace. St. Luc's force opened fire again, bullets clipping twigs and leaves, but the defense lay quiet, except Black Rifle, who crept back and forth, continually seeking a target, and pulling the trigger whenever he found it.

The misty gray in the east turned to darkness, in the west the sun went down the slope of the world, and the brilliant terraces of color began to fade. The firing ceased and another tense period of quiet, hard, to endure, came. At the suggestion of the hunter Colden drew in his whole troop near the cliff and waited, all, despite their weariness and strain, keeping the keenest watch they could.

But Robert, instead of looking toward the east, where St. Luc's force was, invariably looked into the sunset, because it was there that Tayoga had gone, and it was there that they had seen the smoke, of which they expected so much. The terraces of color, already grown dim, were now fading fast. At the top they were gone altogether, and they only lingered low down. But on the forest the red light yet blazed. Every twig and leaf seemed to stand individual and distinct, black against a scarlet shield. But it was for merely a few minutes. Then all the red glow disappeared, like a great light going out suddenly, and the western forest as well as the eastern, lay in a gray gloom.

It always seemed to Robert that the last going of the sunset that day was like a signal, because, when the night swept down, black and complete everywhere, there was a burst of heavy firing from the south and a long exultant yell. No bullet sped through the thickets, where the defenders lay, and Willet cried:

"Tayoga! Tayoga and help! Ah, here they come! The Mohawks!"

Tayoga, panting from exertion, sprang into the bushes among them, and he was followed by a tall figure in war paint, lofty plumes waving from his war bonnet. Behind him came many warriors, and others were already on the flanks, spreading out like a fan, filing rapidly and shouting the war whoop. Robert recognized at once the great figure that stood before them. It was Daganoweda, the young Mohawk chief of his earlier acquaintance, whom he had met both on the war path and at the great council of the fifty sachems in the vale of Onondaga. Had his been the right to choose the man who was to come to their aid, the Mohawk would have been his first choice. Robert knew his intense hatred of the French and their red allies, and he also knew his fierce courage and great ability in battle.

The soldiers looked in some alarm at the painted host that had sprung among them, but Willet and Robert assured them insistently that these were friends, and the sound of the battle they were already waging on the flank with St. Luc's force, was proof enough.

"Captain Colden," said Robert, not forgetful that an Indian likes the courtesies of life, and can take his compliments thick, "this is the great young Mohawk Chief, Daganoweda, which in our language means 'The Inexhaustible' and such he is, inexhaustible in resource and courage in battle, and in loyalty to his friends."

Daganoweda smiled and extended his hand in the white man's fashion.
Young Colden had the tact to shake it heartily at once and to say in English, which the young Mohawk chief understood perfectly:

"Daganoweda, whatever praise of you Mr. Lennox has given it's not half enough. I confess now although I would not have admitted it before, that if you had not come we should probably have been lost."

He had made a friend for life, and then, without further words the two turned to the battle. But Robert remained for a minute beside Tayoga, whose chest was still heaving with his great exertions.

"Where did you find them?" he asked.

"Many miles to the west, Lennox. After I descended the cliff I was pursued by Huron skirmishers, and I had to shake them off. Then I ran at full speed toward the point where the smoke had risen, knowing that the need was great, and I overtook Daganoweda and the Mohawks. Their first smoke was but that from a camp-fire, as being in strong force they did not care who saw them, but the last, just before the sunset, was sent up as a signal by two warriors whom we left behind for the purpose. We thought you might take it to mean that help was coming."

"And so we did. How many warriors has Daganoweda?"

"Fifty, and that is enough. Already they push the Frenchman and his force before them. Come, we must join them, Dagaeoga. The breath has come back into my body and I am a strong man again!"

The two now quickly took their places in the battle in the night and the forest, the position of the two forces being reversed. The soldiers and the Mohawks were pushing the combat at every point, and the agile warriors extending themselves on the flanks had already driven in St. Luc's skirmishers. Black Rifle, uttering fierce shouts, was leading a strong attack in the center. The firing was now rapid and much heavier than it had been at any time before. Flashes of flame appeared everywhere in the thicket. Above the crackle of rifles and muskets swelled the long thrilling war cry of the Mohawks, and back in fierce defiance came the yells of the Hurons and Abenakis.

Willet joined Robert and the two, with Tayoga, saw that the soldiers fought well under cover. The young Philadelphians, in the excitement of battle and of a sudden and triumphant reversal of fortune, were likely to expose themselves rashly, and the advice of the forest veterans was timely. Captain Colden saw that it was taken, although two more of his men were slain as they advanced and several were wounded. But the issue was no longer doubtful. The weight that the Mohawks had suddenly thrown into the battle was too great. The force of St. Luc was steadily driven northward, and Daganoweda's alert skirmishers on the flanks kept it compressed together.

Robert knew how bitter the defeat would be to St. Luc, but the knowledge did not keep his exultation from mounting to a high pitch. St. Luc might strive with all his might to keep his men in the battle, but the Frenchmen could not be numerous, and it was the custom of Indians, once a combat seemed lost, to melt away like a mist. They believed thoroughly that it was best to run away and fight another day, and there was no disgrace in escaping from a stricken field.

"They run! They run! And the Frenchmen must run with them!" exclaimed Black Rifle. As he spoke, a bullet grazed his side and struck a soldier behind him, but the force pressed on with the ardor fed by victory. Willet did not try any longer to restrain them, although he understood full well the danger of a battle in the dark. But he knew that Daganoweda and his Mohawks, experienced in every forest wile, would guard them against surprise, and he deemed it best now that they should strike with all their might.

Robert seldom saw any of the warriors before him, and he did not once catch a glimpse of a Frenchman. Whenever his rifle was loaded he fired at a flitting form, never knowing whether or not his bullet struck true, and glad of his ignorance. His sensitive and imaginative mind became greatly excited. The flashes of flame in the thickets were multiplied a hundred fold, a thousand little pulses beat heavily in his temples, and the shouts of the savages seemed to fill the forest. But he pressed on, conscious that the enemy was disappearing before them.

In his eagerness he passed ahead of Willet and Tayoga and came very near to St. Luc's retreating line. His foot became entangled in trailing vines and he fell, but he was up in an instant, and he fired at a shadowy figure not more than twenty feet in advance. In his haste he missed, and the figure, turning, raised a rifle. There was a fair moonlight and Robert saw the muzzle of the weapon bearing directly upon him, and he knew too that the rifle was held by firm hands. His vivid and sensitive imagination at once leaped into intense life. His own weapon was empty and his last moment had come. He saw the strong brown hands holding the rifle, and then his gaze passed on to the face of St. Luc. He saw the blue eyes of the Frenchman, as they looked down the sights, open wide in a kind of horror. Then he abruptly dropped the muzzle, waved one hand to Robert, and vanished in the thickets and the darkness.

The battle was over. There were a few dying shots, scattered beads of flame, an occasional shout of triumph from the Mohawks, a defiant yell or two in reply from the Hurons and the Abenakis, and then the trail of the combat swept out of the sight and hearing of Robert, who stood dazed and yet with a heart full of gratitude. St. Luc had held his life upon the pressure of a trigger, and the trigger would have been pulled had he not seen before it was too late who stood before the muzzle of his rifle. The moonlight was enough for Robert to see that look of horror in his eyes when he recognized the target. And then the weapon had been turned away and he had gone like a flash! Why? For what reason had St. Luc spared him in the heat and fury of a desperate and losing battle? It must have been a powerful motive for a man to stay his bullet at such a time!

"Wake up, lad! Wake up! The battle has been won!"

Willet's heavy but friendly hand fell upon his shoulder, and Robert came out of his daze. He decided at once that he would say nothing about the meeting with St. Luc, and merely remarked in a cryptic manner:

"I was stunned for a moment by a bullet that did not hit me. Yes, we've won, Dave, thanks to the Mohawks."

"Thanks to Daganoweda and his brave Mohawks, and to Tayoga, and to the gallant Captain Colden and his gallant men. All of us together have made the triumph possible. I understand that the bodies of only two Frenchmen have been found and that neither was that of St. Luc. Well, I'm glad. That Frenchman will do us great damage in this war, but he's an honorable foe, and a man of heart, and I like him."

A man of heart! Yes, truly! None knew it better than Robert, but again he kept his own counsel. He too was glad that his had not been one of the two French bodies found, but there was still danger from the pursuing Mohawks, who would hang on tenaciously, and he felt a sudden thrill of alarm. But it passed, as he remembered that the chevalier was a woodsman of experience and surpassing skill.

Tayoga came back to them somewhat blown. He had followed the fleeing French and Indian force two or three miles. But there was a limit even to his nerves and sinews of wrought steel. He had already run thirty miles before joining in the combat, and now it was time to rest.

"Come, Tayoga," said the hunter, "we'll go back to the ground our lads have defended so well, and eat, drink and sleep. The Mohawks will attend to all the work that's left, which isn't much. We've earned our repose."

Captain Colden, slightly wounded in the arm, appeared and Willet gave him the high compliments that he and his soldiers deserved. He told him it was seldom that men unused to the woods bore themselves so well in an Indian fight, but the young captain modestly disclaimed the chief merit, replying that he and his detachment would surely have been lost, had it not been for Willet and his comrades.

Then they went back to the ground near the cliff, where they had made their great fight, and Willet although the night was warm, wisely had a large fire built. He knew the psychological and stimulating effect of heat and light upon the lads of the city, who had passed through such a fearful ordeal in the dark and Indian-haunted forest. He encouraged them to throw on more dead boughs, until the blaze leaped higher and higher and sparkled and roared, sending up myriads of joyous sparks that glowed for their brief lives among the trees and then died. No fear of St. Luc and the Indians now! That fierce fringe of Mohawks was a barrier that they could never pass, even should they choose to return, and no such choice could possibly be theirs! The fire crackled and blazed in increasing volume, and the Philadelphia lads, recovering from the collapse that had followed tremendous exertions and excitement, began to appreciate the extent of their victory and to talk eagerly with one another.

But the period of full rest had not yet come. Captain Colden made them dig with their bayonets shallow graves for their dead, six in number. Fluent of speech, his sensitive mind again fitting into the deep gravity of the situation, Robert said a few words above them, words that he felt, words that moved those who heard. Then the earth was thrown in and stones and heavy boughs were placed over all to keep away the digging wolves or other wild animals.

The wounded were made as comfortable as possible before the fire, and in the light of the brilliant flames the awe created by the dead quickly passed. Food was served and fresh water was drunk, the canteens being refilled from a spring that Tayoga found a quarter of a mile away. Then the soldiers, save six who had been posted as guard, stretched themselves on grass or leaves, and fell asleep, one by one. Tayoga who had made the greatest physical effort followed them to the land of slumber, but Captain Colden sat and talked with Robert and Willet, although it was now far past midnight.

The bushes parted and a dark figure, making no sound as it came, stepped into the circle of light. It was Black Rifle and his eyes still glittered, but he said nothing. Robert thought he saw upon his face a look of intense satisfaction and once more he shuddered a little. The man lay down with his rifle beside him, and fell asleep, his hands still clutching his weapon.

Before dawn Daganoweda and the Mohawks came back also, and Robert in behalf of them all thanked the young chief in the purest Mohawk, and with the fine phrasing and apt allegory so dear to the Indian heart. Daganoweda made a fitting reply, saying that the merit did not belong to him but to Manitou, and then, leaving a half dozen of his warriors to join in the watch, he and the others slept before the fire.

"It was well that you played so strongly upon the feelings of the Mohawks at that test in the vale of Onondaga, Robert," said Willet. "If you had not said over and over again that the Quebec of the French was once the Stadacona of the Mohawks they would not have been here tonight to save us. They say that deeds speak louder than words, but when the same man speaks with both words and deeds people have got to hear."

"You give me too much credit, Dave. The time was ripe for a Mohawk attack upon the French."

"Aye, lad, but one had to see a chance and use it. Now, join all those fellows in sleep. We won't move before noon."

But Robert's brain was too active for sleep just yet. While his imaginative power made him see things before other people saw them, he also continued to see them after they were gone. The wilderness battle passed once more before him, and when he brushed his eyes to thrust it away, he looked at the sleeping Mohawks and thought what splendid savages they were. The other tribes of the Hodenosaunee were still holding to their neutrality — all that was asked of them — but the Mohawks, with the memories of their ancient wrongs burning in their hearts, had openly taken the side of the English, and tonight their valor and skill had undoubtedly saved the American force. Daganoweda was a hero! And so was Tayoga, the Onondaga, always the first of red men to Robert.

His heated brain began to grow cool at last. The vivid pictures that had been passing so fast before his eyes faded. He saw only reality, the blazing fire, the dusky figures lying motionless before it, and the circling wall of dark woods. Then he slept.

Willet was the only white man who remained awake. He saw the great fire die, and the dawn come in its place. He felt then for the first time in all that long encounter the strangeness of his own position. The wilderness, savages and forest battle had become natural to him, and yet his life had once been far different. There was a taste of a distant past in that fierce duel at Quebec when he slew the bravo, Boucher, a deed for which he had never felt a moment's regret, and yet when he balanced the old times against the present, he could not say which had the advantage. He had found true friends in the woods, men who would and did risk their own lives to save his.

The dawn came swiftly, flooding the earth with light. Daganoweda and many of the Mohawk warriors awoke, but the young Philadelphia captain and his men slept on, plunged in the utter stupor of exhaustion. Tayoga, who had made a supreme effort, both physical and mental, also continued to sleep, and Robert, lying with his feet to the coals, never stirred.

Daganoweda shook himself, and, so shaking, shook the last shred of sleep from his eyes. Then he looked with pride at his warriors, those who yet lay upon the ground and those who had arisen. He was a young chief, not yet thirty years of age, and he was the bloom and flower of Mohawk courage and daring. His name, Daganoweda, the Inexhaustible, was fully deserved, as his bravery and resource were unlimited. But unlike Tayoga, he had in him none of the priestly quality. He had not drunk or even sipped at the white man's civilization. The spirituality so often to be found in the Onondagas was unknown to him. He was a warrior first, last and all the time. He was Daganoweda of the Clan of the Turtle, of the Nation Ganeagaono, the Keepers of the Eastern Gate, of the great League of the Hodenosaunee, and he craved no glory save that to be won in battle, which he craved all the time.

Daganoweda, as he looked at his men, felt intense satisfaction, because the achievement of his Mohawks the night before had been brilliant and successful, but he concealed it from all save himself. It was not for a chief who wished to win not one victory, but a hundred to show undue elation. But he turned and for a few moments gazed directly into the sun with unwinking eyes, and when he shifted his gaze away, a great tide of life leaped in his veins.

Then he gave silent thanks. Like all the other Indians in North America the Mohawks personified and worshipped the sun, which to them was the mighty Dweller in Heaven, almost the same as Manitou, a great spirit to whom sacrifices and thanksgivings were to be made. The sun, an immortal being, had risen that morning and from his seat in the highest of the high heavens he had looked down with his invincible eye which no man could face more than a few seconds, upon his favorite children, the Mohawks, to whom he had given the victory. Daganoweda bowed a head naturally haughty and under his breath murmured thanks for the triumph given and prayers for others to come.

The warriors built the fire anew and cooked their breakfasts. They had venison and hominy of three kinds according to the corn of which it was made, *Onaogaant* or the white corn, *Ticne* or the red corn, and *Hagowa* or the white flint corn. They also had bear meat and dried beans. So their breakfast was abundant, and they ate with the appetite of warriors who had done mighty deeds.

Daganoweda and Willet, as became great men, sat together on a log and were served by a warrior who took honor from the task. Black Rifle sat alone a little distance away. He would have been welcome in the company of the Mohawk chief and the hunter, but, brooding and solitary in mind, he wished to be alone and they knew and respected his wish. Daganoweda glanced at him more than once as he remained in silence, and always there was pity in his looks. And there was admiration too, because Black Rifle was a great warrior. The woods held none greater.

When Robert awoke it was well on toward noon and he sprang up, refreshed and strong.

"You've had quite a nap, Robert," said Willet, who had not slept at all, "but some of the soldiers are still sleeping, and Tayoga has just gone down to the spring to bathe his face."

"Which I also will do," said Robert.

"And when you come back food will be ready for you."

Robert found Tayoga at the spring, flexing his muscles, and taking short steps back and forth. "It was a great run you made," said the white youth, "and it saved us. There's no stiffness, I hope?"

"There was a little, Dagaeoga, but I have worked it out of my body. Now all my muscles are as they were. I am ready to make another and equal run."

"It's not needed, and for that I'm thankful. St. Luc will not come back, nor will Tandakora, I think, linger in the woods, hoping for a shot. He knows that the Mohawk skirmishers will be too vigilant."

As they went back to the fire for their food they heard a droning song and the regular beat of feet. Some of the Mohawks were dancing the Buffalo Dance, a dance named after an animal never found in their country, but which they knew well. It was a tribute to the vast energy and daring of the nations of the Hodenosaunee that they should range in such remote regions as Kentucky and Tennessee and hunt the buffalo with the Cherokees, who came up from the south.

They called the dance Dageyagooanno, and it was always danced by men only. One warrior beat upon the drum, *ganojoo*, and another used *gusdawasa* or the rattle made of the shell of a squash. A dozen warriors danced, and players and dancers alike sang. It was a most singular dance and Robert, as he ate and drank, watched it with curious interest.

The warriors capered back and forth, and often they bent themselves far over, until their hands touched the ground. Then they would arch their backs, until they formed a kind of hump, and they leaped to and fro, bellowing all the time. The imitation was that of a buffalo, recognizable at once, and, while it was rude and monotonous, both dancing and singing preserved a rhythm, and as one listened continuously it soon crept into the blood. Robert, with that singular temperament of his, so receptive to all impressions, began to feel it. Their chant was of war and victory and he stirred to both. He was on the warpath with them, and he passed with them through the thick of battle.

They danced for a long time, quitting only when exhaustion compelled. By that time all the soldiers were awake and Captain Colden talked with the other leaders, red and white. His instructions took him farther west, where he was to build a fort for the defense of the border, and, staunch and true, he did not mean to turn back because he had been in desperate battle with the French and their Indian allies.

"I was sent to protect a section of the frontier," he said to Willet, "and while I've found it hard to protect my men and myself, yet I must go on. I could never return to Philadelphia and face our people there."

"It's a just view you take, Captain Colden," said Willet.

"I feel, though, that my men and I are but children in the woods. Yesterday and last night proved it. If you and your friends continue with us our march may not be in vain."

Willet glanced at Robert, and then at Tayoga.

"Ours for the present, at least, is a roving commission," said young Lennox. "It seems to me that the best we can do is to go with Captain Colden."

"I am not called back to the vale of Onondaga," said Tayoga, "I would see the building of this fort that Captain Colden has planned."

"Then we three are agreed," said the hunter. "It's best not to speak to Black Rifle, because he'll follow his own notions anyway, and as for Daganoweda and his Mohawks I think they're likely to resume their march northward against the French border."

"I'm grateful to you three," said Captain Colden, "and, now that it's settled, we'll start as soon as we can."

"Better give them all a good rest, and wait until the morning," said the hunter.

Again Captain Colden agreed with him.

CHAPTER IV
THE PERILOUS PATH

After a long night of sleep and rest, the little troop resumed its march the next morning. The wounded fortunately were not hurt so badly that they could not limp along with the others, and, while the surgery of the soldiers was rude, it was effective nevertheless. Daganoweda, as they had expected, prepared to leave them for a raid toward the St. Lawrence. But he said rather grimly that he might return, in a month perhaps. He knew where they were going to build their fort, and unless Corlear and all the other British governors awoke much earlier in the morning it was more than likely that the young captain from Philadelphia would need the help of the Mohawks again.

Then Daganoweda said farewell to Robert, Tayoga, Willet and Black Rifle, addressing each according to his quality. Them he trusted. He knew them to be great warriors and daring rovers of the wilderness. He had no advice for them, because he knew they did not need it, but he expected them to be his comrades often in the great war, and he wished them well. To Tayoga he said:

"You and I, oh, young chief of the Onondagas, have hearts that beat alike. The Onondagas do well to keep aloof from the white man's quarrels for the present, and to sit at peace, though watchful, in the vale of Onondaga, but your hopes are with our friends the English and you in person fight for them. We Mohawks know whom to hate. We know that the French have robbed us more than any others. We know, that their Quebec is our Stadacona. So we have dug up the tomahawk and last night we showed to Sharp Sword and his men and Tandakora the Ojibway how we could use it."

Sharp Sword was the Iroquois name for St. Luc, who had already proved his great ability and daring as a forest leader.

"The Ganeagaono are now the chief barrier against the French and their tribes," said Tayoga.

The brilliant eyes of Daganoweda glittered in his dark face. He knew that Tayoga would not pay the Mohawks so high a compliment unless he meant it.

"Tayoga," he said, "we belong to the leading nations of the great League of the Hodenosaunee, you to the Onundahgaono and I to the Ganeagaono. You are first in the council and we are first on the warpath. It was Tododaho, the Onondaga, who first formed the great League and it was Hayowentha, the Mohawk, who combed the snakes out of his hair and who strengthened it and who helped him to build it so firmly that it shall last forever. Brothers are we, and always shall be."

He touched his forehead in salute, and the Onondaga touched his in reply.

"Aye, brothers are we," he said, "Mohawk and Onondaga, Onondaga and Mohawk. The great war of the white kings which draws us in it has come, but I know that Hayowentha watches over his people, and Tododaho over his. In the spring when I went forth in the night to fight the Hurons I gazed off there in the west where shines the great star on which Tododaho makes his home, and I saw him looking down upon me, and casting about me the veil of his protection."

Daganoweda looked up at the gleaming blue of the heavens, and his eyes glittered again. He believed every word that Tayoga said.

"As Tododaho watches over you, so Hayowentha watches over me," he said, "and he will bring me back in safety and victory from the St. Lawrence. Farewell again, my brother."

"Farewell once more, Daganoweda!"

The Mohawk chief plunged into the forest, and his fifty warriors followed him. Like a shadow they were gone, and the waving bushes gave back no sign that they had ever been. Captain Colden rubbed his eyes and then laughed.

"I never knew men to vanish so swiftly before," he said, "but last night was good proof that they were here, and that they came in time. I suppose it's about the only victory of which we can make boast."

He spoke the full truth. From the St. Lawrence to the Ohio the border was already ravaged with fire and sword. Appeals for help were pouring in from the distant settlements, and the governors of New York, Pennsylvania and Massachusetts scarcely knew what to do. France had struck the first blow, and she had struck hard. Young Washington, defeated by overwhelming numbers, was going back to Virginia, and Duquesne, the fort of the French at the junction of the Monongahela and Allegheny, was a powerful rallying place for their own forces and the swarming Indian bands, pouring out of the wilderness, drawn by the tales of unlimited scalps and plunder.

The task before Captain Colden's slender force was full of danger. His numbers might have been five times as great and then they would not have been too many to build and hold the fort he was sent to build and hold. But he had no thought of turning back, and, as soon as Daganoweda and the Mohawks were gone, they started, bending their course somewhat farther toward the south. At the ford of a river twenty men with horses carrying food, ammunition and other supplies were to meet them, and they reckoned that they could reach it by midnight.

The men with the horses had been sent from another point, and it was not thought then that there was any danger of French and Indian attack before the junction was made, but the colonial authorities had reckoned without the vigor and daring of St. Luc. Now the most cruel fears assailed young Captain Colden, and Robert and the hunter could not find much argument to remove them. It was possible that the second force had been ambushed also, and, if so, it had certainly been destroyed, being capable of no such resistance as that made by Colden's men, and without the aid of the three friends and the Mohawks. And if the supplies were gone the expedition would be useless.

"Don't be downhearted about it, captain," said Willet. "You say there's not a man in the party who knows anything about the wilderness, and that they've got just enough woods sense to take them to the ford. Well, that has its saving grace, because now and then, the Lord seems to watch over fool men. The best of hunters are trapped sometimes in the forest, when fellows who don't know a deer from a beaver, go through 'em without harm."

"Didn't I tell you, lads," he said, "there wasn't an Indian nearer than Fort Duquesne, and that's a long way from here! We've come a great distance and not a foe has appeared anywhere. It may be that the French vanish when they hear this valiant Quaker troop is coming, but it's my own personal opinion they'll stay pretty well back in the west with their red allies."

The youth, although he called himself so, did not look much like a Quaker to Robert. He had a frank face and merry eyes, and manner and voice indicated a tendency to gayety. Judging from his words he had no cares and Indians and ambush were far from his thoughts. Proof of this was the absence of sentinels. The men, scattered about the fire, were eating their suppers and the horses, forty in number, were grazing in an open space. It all looked like a great picnic, and the effect was heightened by the youth of the soldiers.

"As the Great Bear truly said," whispered Tayoga, "Manitou has watched over them. The forest does not hold easier game for the taking, and had Tandakora known that they were here he would have come seeking revenge for his loss in the attack upon Captain Colden's troop."

"You're right as usual, Tayoga, and now we'd better hail them. But don't you come forward just yet. They don't know the difference between Indians and likely your welcome would be a bullet."

"I will wait," said Tayoga.

"I tell you, Carson," the young lieutenant was saying in an oratorical manner, "that they magnify the dangers of the wilderness. The ford at which we were to meet Colden is just ahead, and we've come straight to it without the slightest mishap. Colden is no sluggard, and he should be here in the morning at the latest. Do you find anything wrong with my reasoning, Hugh?"

"Naught, William," replied the other, who seemed to be second in command. "Your logic is both precise and beautiful. The dangers of the border are greatly exaggerated, and as soon as we get together a good force all these French and Indians will flee back to Canada. Ah, who is this?"

Both he and his chief turned and faced the woods in astonishment. A youth had stepped forth, and stood in full view. He was taller than either, but younger, dressed completely in deerskin, although superior

"Then if there's any virtue in what you say we'll pray that these men are the biggest fools who ever lived."

"Smoke! smoke again!" called Robert cheerily, pointing straight ahead.

Sure enough, that long dark thread appeared once more, now against the western sky. Willet laughed.

"They're the biggest fools in the forest, just as you hoped, Captain," he said, "and they've taken no more harm than if they had built their fires in a Philadelphia street. They've set themselves down for the night, as peaceful and happy as you please. If that isn't the campfire of your men with the pack horses then I'll eat my cap."

Captain Colden laughed, but it was the slightly hysterical laugh of relief. He was bent upon doing his task, and, since the Lord had carried him so far through a mighty danger, the disappointment of losing the supplies would have been almost too much to bear.

"You're sure it's they, Mr. Willet?" he said.

"Of course. Didn't I tell you it wasn't possible for another such party of fools to be here in the wilderness, and that the God of the white man and the Manitou of the red man taking pity on their simplicity and innocence have protected them?"

"I like to think what you say is true, Mr. Willet."

"It's true. Be not afraid that it isn't. Now, I think we'd better stop here, and let Robert and Tayoga go ahead, spy 'em out and make signals. It would be just like 'em to blaze away at us the moment they saw the bushes move with our coming."

Captain Colden was glad to take his advice, and the white youth and the red went forward silently through the forest, hearing the sound of cheerful voices, as they drew near to the campfire which was a large one blazing brightly. They also heard the sound of horses moving and they knew that the detachment had taken no harm. Tayoga parted the bushes and peered forth.

"Look!" he said. "Surely they are watched over by Manitou!"

About twenty men, or rather boys, for all of them were very young, were standing or lying about a fire. A tall, very ruddy youth in the uniform of a colonial lieutenant was speaking to them.

in cut and quality to that of the ordinary borderer, his complexion fair beneath his tan, and his hair light. He gazed at them steadily with bright blue eyes, and both the first lieutenant and the second lieutenant of the Quaker troop saw that he was no common person.

"Who are you?" repeated William Wilton, who was the first lieutenant.

"Who are you?" repeated Hugh Carson, who was the second lieutenant.

"My name is Robert Lennox," replied the young stranger in a mellow voice of amazing quality, "and you, I suppose, are Lieutenant William Wilton, the commander of this little troop."

He spoke directly to the first lieutenant, who replied, impressed as much by the youth's voice as he was by his appearance:

"Yes, such is my name. But how did you know it? I don't recall ever having met you before, which doubtless is my loss."

"I heard it from an associate of yours, your chief in command, Captain James Colden, and I am here with a message from him."

"And so Colden is coming up? Well, we beat him to the place of meeting. We've triumphed with ease over the hardships of the wilderness." "Yes, you arrived first, but he was delayed by a matter of importance, a problem that had to be solved before he could resume his march."

"You speak in riddles, sir."

"Perhaps I do for the present, but I shall soon make full explanations. I wish to call first a friend of mine, an Indian—although you say there are no Indians in the forest—a most excellent friend of ours. Tayoga, come!"

The Onondaga appeared silently in the circle of light, a splendid primeval figure, drawn to the uttermost of his great height, his lofty gaze meeting that of Wilton, half in challenge and half in greeting. Robert had been an impressive figure, but Tayoga, owing to the difference in race, was even more so. The hands of several of the soldiers moved towards their weapons.

"Did I not tell you that he was a friend, a most excellent friend of ours?" said Robert sharply. "Who raises a hand against him raises a hand against me also, and above all raises a hand against our cause.

Lieutenant Wilton, this is Tayoga, of the Clan of the Bear, of the nation Onondaga, of the great League of the Hodenosaunee. He is a prince, as much a prince as any in Europe. His mind and his valor have both been expended freely in our service, and they will be expended with equal freedom again."

Robert's tone was so sharp and commanding that Wilton, impressed by it, saluted the Onondaga with the greatest courtesy, and Tayoga bowed gravely in reply.

"You're correct in assuming that my name is Wilton," said the young lieutenant. "I'm William Wilton, of Philadelphia, and I beg to present my second in command, Hugh Carson, of the same city."

He looked questioningly at Robert, who promptly responded:

"My name is Lennox, Robert Lennox, and I can claim either Albany or New York as a home."

"I think I've heard of you," said Wilton. "A rumor came to Philadelphia about a man of that name going to Quebec on an errand for the governor of New York."

"I was the messenger," said Robert, "but since the mission was a failure it may as well be forgotten."

"But it will not be forgotten. I've heard that you bore yourself with great judgment and address. Nevertheless, if your modesty forbids the subject we'll come back to another more pressing. What did you mean when you said Captain Colden's delay was due to the solution of a vexing problem?"

"It had to do with Indians, who you say are not to be found in these forests. I could not help overhearing you, as I approached your camp."

Wilton reddened and then his generous impulse and sense of truth came to his aid.

"I'll admit that I'm careless and that my knowledge may be small!" he exclaimed. "But tell me the facts, Mr. Lennox. I judge by your face that events of grave importance have occurred."

"Captain Colden, far east of this point, was attacked by a strong force of French and Indians under the renowned partisan leader, St. Luc. Tayoga, David Willet, the hunter, the famous ranger Black Rifle and I were able to warn him and give him some help, but even then we should have been overborne and destroyed had not a Mohawk chief, Daganoweda, and a formidable band come to our aid. United, we defeated St. Luc and drove him northward. Captain Colden lost several of his men, but with the rest he is now marching to the junction with you."

Wilton's face turned gray, but in a moment or two his eyes brightened.

"Then a special Providence has been watching over us," he said. "We haven't seen or heard of an Indian."

His tone was one of mingled relief and humor, and Robert could not keep from laughing.

"At all events," he said, "you are safe for the present. I'll remain with you while Tayoga goes back for Captain Colden."

"If you'll be so good," said Wilton, who did not forget his manners, despite the circumstances. "I've begun to feel that we have more eyes, or at least better ones, with you among us. Where is that Indian? You don't mean to say he's gone?"

Robert laughed again. Tayoga, after his fashion, had vanished in silence.

"He's well on his way to Captain Colden now," he said, exaggerating a little for the sake of effect. "He'll be a great chief some day, and meanwhile he's the fastest runner in the whole Six Nations."

Colden and his troop arrived soon, and the two little commands were united, to the great joy of all. Lieutenant Wilton had passed from the extreme of confidence to the utmost distrust. Where it had not been possible for an Indian to exist he now saw a scalplock in every bush.

"On my honor," he said to Colden, "James, I was never before in my life so happy to see you. I'm glad you have the entire command now. As Mr. Lennox said, Providence saved me so far, but perhaps it wouldn't lend a helping hand any longer."

The pack horses carried surgical supplies for the wounded, and Willet and Black Rifle were skillful in using them. All of the hurt, they were sure would be well again within a week, and there was little to mar the general feeling of high spirits that prevailed in the camp. Wilton and Carson were lads of mettle, full of talk of Philadelphia, then the greatest city in the British Colonies, and related to most of its leading families, as was Colden too, his family being a branch of the New York family of that name. Robert was at home with them at once, and they were eager to hear from him about Quebec and the latest fashions of the French, already the arbiters of fashion, and recognized as such, despite the war between them, by English and Americans.

"I had hoped to go to Quebec myself," said Wilton reflectively, "but I suppose it's a visit that's delayed for a long time now."

"How does it happen that you, a Quaker, are second in command here?" asked Robert.

"It must be the belligerency repressed through three or four generations and breaking out at last in me," replied Wilton, his eyes twinkling. "I suppose there's just so much fighting in every family, and if three or four generations in succession are peaceful the next that follows is likely to be full of warlike fury. So, as soon as the war began I started for it. It's not inherent in me. As I said, it's the confined ardor of generations bursting forth suddenly in my person. I'm not an active agent. I'm merely an instrument."

"It was the same warlike fury that caused you to come here, build your fire and set no watch, expecting the woods to be as peaceful as Philadelphia?" said Colden.

Wilton colored.

"I didn't dream the French and Indians were so near," he replied apologetically.

"If comparisons are valuable you needn't feel any mortification about it, Will," said Colden. "I was just about as careless myself, and all of us would have lost our scalps, if Willet, Lennox and Tayoga hadn't come along."

Wilton was consoled. But both he and Colden after the severe lesson the latter had received were now all for vigilance. Many sentinels had been posted, and since Colden was glad to follow the advice of Willet and Tayoga they were put in the best places. They let the fire die early, as the weather had now become very warm, and all of them, save the watch soon slept. The night brought little coolness with it, and the wind that blew was warm and drying. Under its touch the leaves began to crinkle up at the edge and turn brown, the grass showed signs of withering and Willet, who had taken charge of the guard that night, noticed that summer was passing into the brown leaf. It caused him a pang of disappointment.

Great Britain and the Colonies had not yet begun to move. The Provincial legislatures still wrangled, and the government at London was provokingly slow. There was still no plan of campaign, the great resources of the Anglo-Saxons had not yet been brought together for use against the quick and daring French, and while their slow, patient courage might win in the end, Willet foresaw a long and terrible war with many disasters at the beginning.

He was depressed for the moment. He knew what an impression the early French successes would make on the Indian tribes, and he knew, too, as he heard the wind rustling through the dry leaves, that there would be no English campaign that year. One might lead an army in winter on the good roads and through the open fields of Europe, but then only borderers could make way through the vast North American wilderness in the deep snows and bitter cold, where Indian trails alone existed. The hunter foresaw a long delay before the British and Colonial forces moved, and meanwhile the French and Indians would be more strongly planted in the territory claimed by the rival nations, and, while in law possession was often nine points, it seemed in war to be ten points and all.

As he walked back and forth Black Rifle touched him on the arm.

"I'm going, Dave," he said. "They don't need me here any longer. Daganoweda and his Mohawks, likely enough, will follow the French and Indians, and have another brush with 'em. At any rate, it's sure that St. Luc and Tandakora won't come back, and these young men can go on without being attacked again and build their fort. But they'll be threatened there later on, and I'll come again with a warning."

"I know you will," said Willet. "Wherever danger appears on the border, Black Rifle, there you are. I see great and terrible days ahead for us all."

"And so do I," said Black Rifle. "This continent is on fire."

The two shook hands, and the somber figure of Black Rifle disappeared in the forest. Willet looked after him thoughtfully, and then resumed his pacing to and fro.

They made an early start at dawn of a bright hot day, crossed the ford, and resumed their long march through the forest which under the light wind now rustled continually with the increasing dryness.

But the company was joyous. The wounded were put upon the pack horses, and the others, young, strong and refreshed by abundant rest, went forward with springing steps. Robert and Tayoga walked with the three Philadelphians. Colden already knew the quality of the Onondaga, and respected and admired him, and Wilton and Carson, surprised at first at his excellent English education, soon saw that he was no ordinary youth. The five, each a type of his own, were fast friends before the day's march was over. Wilton, the Quaker, was the greatest talker of them all, which he declared was due to suppression in childhood.

"It's something like the battle fever which will come out along about the fourth or fifth generation," he said. "I suppose there's a certain amount of talk that every man must do in his lifetime, and, having been kept in a state of silence by my parents all through my youth, I'm now letting myself loose in the woods."

"Don't apologize, Will," said Colden. "Your chatter is harmless, and it lightens the spirits of us all."

"The talker has his uses," said Tayoga gravely. "My friend Lennox, known to the Hodenosaunee as Dagaeoga, is golden-mouthed. The gift of great speech descends upon him when time and place are fitting."

"And so you're an orator, are you?" said Carson, looking at Robert.

Young Lennox blushed.

"Tayoga is my very good friend," he replied, "and he gives me praise I don't deserve."

"When one has a gift direct from Manitou," said the Onondaga, gravely, "it is not well to deny it. It is a sign of great favor, and you must not show ingratitude, Dagaeoga."

"He has you, Lennox," laughed Wilton, "but you needn't say more. I know that Tayoga is right, and I'm waiting to hear you talk in a crisis."

Robert blushed once more, but was silent. He knew that if he protested again the young Philadelphians would chaff him without mercy, and he knew at heart also that Tayoga's statement about him was true. He remembered with pride his defeat of St. Luc in the great test of words in the vale of Onondaga. But Wilton's mind quickly turned to another subject. He seemed to exemplify the truth of his own declaration that all the impulses bottled up in four or five generations of Quaker ancestors were at last bursting out in him. He talked more than all the others combined, and he rejoiced in the freedom of the wilderness.

"I'm a spirit released," he said. "That's why I chatter so."

"Perhaps it's just as well, Will, that while you have the chance you should chatter to your heart's content, because at any time an Indian arrow may cut short your chance for chattering," said Carson.

"I can't believe it, Hugh," said Wilton, "because if Providence was willing to preserve us, when we camped squarely among the Indians, put out no guards, and fairly asked them to come and shoot at us, then it was for a purpose and we'll be preserved through greater and continuous dangers."

"There may be something in it, Will. I notice that those who deserve it least are often the chosen favorites of fortune."

"Which seems to be a hit at your superior officer, but I'll pass it over, Hugh, as you're always right at heart though often wrong in the head."

Although the young officers talked much and with apparent lightness, the troop marched with vigilance now. Willet and Tayoga, and Colden, who had profited by bitter experience, saw to it. The hunter and the Onondaga, often assisted by Robert, scouted on the flanks, and three or four soldiers, who developed rapid skill in the woods, were soon able to help. But Tayoga and Willet were the main reliance, and they found no further trace of Indians. Nevertheless the guard was never relaxed for an instant.

Robert found the march not only pleasant but exhilarating. It appealed to his imaginative and sensitive mind, which magnified everything, and made the tints more vivid and brilliant. To him the forests were larger and grander than they were to the others, and the rivers were wider and deeper. The hours were more intense, he lived every second of them, and the future had a scope and brilliancy that few others would foresee. In company with youths of his own age coming from the largest city of the British colonies, the one that had the richest social traditions, his whole nature expanded, and he cast away much of his reserve. Around the campfires in the evening he became one of the most industrious talkers, and now and then he was carried away so much by his own impulse that all the rest would cease and listen to the mellow, golden voice merely for the pleasure of hearing. Then Tayoga and Willet would look at each other and smile, knowing that Dagaeoga, though all unconsciously, held the center of the stage, and the others were more than willing for him to hold it.

The friendships of the young ripen fast, and under such circumstances they ripen faster than ever. Robert soon felt that he had known the three young Philadelphians for years, and a warm friendship, destined to last all their lives, in which Tayoga was included, was soon formed. Robert saw that his new comrades, although they did not know much of the forest, were intelligent, staunch and brave, and they saw in him all that Tayoga and Willet saw, which was a great deal.

The heat and dryness increased, and the brown of leaf and grass deepened. Nearly all the green was gone now, and autumn would soon come. The forest was full of game, and Willet and Tayoga kept them well supplied, yet their progress became slower. Those who had been wounded severely approached the critical stage, and once they stopped two days until all danger had passed.

Three days later a fierce summer storm burst upon them. Tayoga had foreseen it, and the whole troop was gathered in the lee of a hill, with all their ammunition protected by blankets, canvas and the skins of deer that they had killed. But the young Philadelphians, unaccustomed to the fury of the elements in the wilderness, looked upon it with awe.

In the west the lightning blazed and the thunder crashed for a long time. Often the forest seemed to swim in a red glare, and Robert himself was forced to shut his eyes before the rapid flashes of dazzling brightness. Then came a great rushing of wind with a mighty rain on its edge, and, when the wind died, the rain fell straight down in torrents more than an hour.

Although they kept their ammunition and other supplies dry the men themselves were drenched to the bone, but the storm passed more suddenly than it had come. The clouds parted on the horizon, then all fled away. The last raindrop fell and a shining sun came out in a hot blue sky. As the men resumed a drooping march their clothes dried fast in the fiery rays and their spirits revived.

When night came they were dry again, and youth had taken no harm. The next day they struck an Indian trail, but both Willet and Tayoga said it had been made by less than a dozen warriors, and that they were going north.

"It's my belief," said Willet, "that they were warriors from the Ohio country on their way to join the French along the Canadian border."

"And they're not staying to meet us," said Colden. "I'm afraid, Will, it'll be some time before you have a chance to show your unbottled Quaker valor."

"Perhaps not so long as you think," replied Wilton, who had plenty of penetration. "I don't claim to be any great forest rover, although I do think I've learned something since I left Philadelphia, but I imagine that our building of a fort in the woods will draw 'em. The Indian runners will soon be carrying the news of it, and then they'll cluster around us like flies seeking sugar."

"You're right, Mr. Wilton," said Willet. "After we build this fort it's as sure as the sun is in the heavens that we'll have to fight for it."

Two days later they reached the site for their little fortress which they named Fort Refuge, because they intended it as a place in which harried settlers might find shelter. It was a hill near a large creek, and the source of a small brook lay within the grounds they intended to occupy, securing to them an unfailing supply of good water in case of siege.

Now, the young soldiers entered upon one of the most arduous tasks of the war, to build a fort, which was even more trying to them than battle. Arms and backs ached as Colden, Wilton and Carson, advised by Willet, drove them hard. A strong log blockhouse was erected, and then a stout palisade, enclosing the house and about an acre of ground, including the precious spring which spouted from under a ledge of stone at the very wall of the blockhouse itself. Behind the building they raised a shed in which the horses could be sheltered, as all of them foresaw a long stay, dragging into winter with its sleet and snow, and it was important to save the animals.

Robert, Willet and Tayoga had a roving commission, and, as they could stay with Colden and his command as long as they chose, they chose accordingly to remain where they thought they could do the most good. Robert took little part in the hunting, but labored with the soldiers on the building, although it was not the kind of work to which his mind turned.

The blockhouse itself, was divided into a number of rooms, in which the soldiers who were not on guard could sleep, and they had blankets and the skins of the larger animals the hunters killed for beds. Venison jerked in great quantities was stored away in case of siege, and the whole forest was made to contribute to their larder. The work was hard, but it toughened the sinews of the young soldiers, and gave them an occupation in which they were interested. Before it was finished they were joined by another small detachment with loaded pack horses, which by the same kind of miracle had come safely through the wilderness. Colden now had a hundred men, fifty horses and powder and lead for all the needs of which one could think.

"If we only had a cannon!" he said, looking proudly at their new blockhouse, "I think I'd build a platform for it there on the roof, and then we could sweep the forest in every direction. Eh, Will, my lad?"

"But as we haven't," said Wilton, "we'll have to do the sweeping with our rifles."

"And our men are good marksmen, as they showed in that fight with St. Luc. But it seems a world away from Philadelphia, doesn't it, Will? I wonder what they're doing there!"

"Counting their gains in the West India trade, looking at the latest fashions from England that have come on the ships up the Delaware, building new houses out Germantown way, none of them thinking much of the war, except old Ben Franklin, who pegs forever at the governor of the Province, the Legislature, and every influential man to take action before the French and Indians seize the whole border."

"I hope Franklin will stir 'em up, and that they won't forget us out here in the woods. For us at least the French and Indians are a reality."

Meanwhile summer had turned into autumn, and autumn itself was passing.

CHAPTER V
THE RUNNER

Fort Refuge, the stronghold raised by young arms, was the most distant point in the wilderness held by the Anglo-American forces, and for a long time it was cut off entirely from the world. No message came out of the great forest that rimmed it round, but Colden had been told to build it and hold it until he had orders to leave it, and he and his men waited patiently, until word of some kind should come or they should be attacked by the French and Indian forces that were gathering continually in the north.

They saw the autumn reach its full glory. The wilderness glowed in intense yellows and reds. The days grew cool, and the nights cold, the air was crisp and fresh like the breath of life, the young men felt their muscles expand and their courage rise, and they longed for the appearance of the enemy, sure that behind their stout palisade they would be able to defeat whatever numbers came.

Tayoga left them early one morning for a visit to his people. The leaves were falling then under a sharp west wind, and the sky had a cold, hard tint of blue steel. Winter was not far away, but the day suited a runner like Tayoga who wished to make speed through the wilderness. He stood for a moment or two at the edge of the forest, a strong, slender figure outlined against the brown, waved his hand to his friends watching on the palisade, and then disappeared.

"A great Indian," said young Wilton thoughtfully. "I confess that I never knew much about the red men or thought much about them until I met him. I don't recall having come into contact with a finer mind of its kind."

"Most of the white people make the mistake of undervaluing the Indians," said Robert, "but we'll learn in this war what a power they are. If the Hodenosaunee had turned against us we'd have been beaten already."

"At any rate, Tayoga is a noble type. Since I had to come into the forest I'm glad to meet such fellows as he. Do you think, Lennox, that he'll get through safely?"

Robert laughed.

"Get through safely?" he repeated. "Why, Tayoga is the fastest runner among the Indian nations, and they train for speed. He goes like the wind, he never tires, night and day are the same to him, he's so light of foot that he could pass through a band of his own comrades and they would never know he was there, and yet his own ears are so keen that he can hear the leaves falling a hundred yards away. The path from here to the vale of Onondaga may be lined on either side with the French and the hostile tribes, standing as thick as trees in the forest, but he will flit between them as safely and easily as you and I would ride along a highroad into Philadelphia. He will arrive at the vale of Onondaga, unharmed, at the exact minute he intends to arrive, and he will return, reaching Fort Refuge also on the exact day, and at the exact hour and minute he has already selected."

The young Quaker surveyed Robert with admiration and then laughed.

"What they tell of you is true," he said. "In truth that was a most gorgeous and rounded speech you made about your friend. I don't recall finer and more flowing periods! What vividness! What imagery! I'm proud to know you, Lennox!"

Robert reddened and then laughed.

"I do grow enthusiastic when I talk about Tayoga," he said, "but you'll see that what I predict will come to pass. He's probably told Willet just when he'll be back at Fort Refuge. We'll ask him."

The hunter informed them that Tayoga intended to take exactly ten days.

"This is Monday," he said. "He'll be here a week from next Thursday at noon."

"But suppose something happens to detain him," said Wilton, "suppose the weather is too bad for traveling, or suppose a lot of other things that can happen easily."

Willet shrugged his shoulders.

"In such a case as this where Tayoga is concerned," he said, "we don't suppose anything, we go by certainties. Before he left, Tayoga settled the day and the hour when he would return and it's not now a problem or a question. He has disposed of the subject."

"I can't quite see it that way," said Wilton tenaciously. "I admit that Tayoga is a wonderful fellow, but he cannot possibly tell the exact hour of his return from such a journey as the one he has undertaken."

"You wait and see," said the hunter in the utmost good nature. "You think you know Tayoga, but you don't yet know him fully."

"If I were not a Quaker I'd wager a small sum of money that he does not come at the time appointed," said Wilton.

"Then it's lucky for your pocket that you're a Quaker," laughed Willet.

It turned much colder that very afternoon, and the raw edge of winter showed. The wind from the northwest was bitter and the dead leaves fell in showers. At dusk a chilling rain began, and the young soldiers, shivering, were glad enough to seek the shelter of the blockhouse, where a great fire was blazing on the broad hearth. They had made many rude camp stools and sitting down on one before the blaze Wilton let the pleasant warmth fall upon his face.

"I'm sorry for Tayoga," he said to Robert. "Just when you and Willet were boasting most about him this winter rain had to come and he was no more than fairly started. He'll have to hunt a den somewhere in the forest and crouch in it wrapped in his blanket."

Robert smiled serenely.

"Den! Crouch! Wrapped in his blanket! What do you mean?" he asked in his mellow, golden voice. "Are you speaking of my friend, Tayoga, of the Clan of the Bear, of the nation Onondaga, of the great League of the Hodenosaunee? Can it be possible, Wilton, that you are referring to him, when you talk of such humiliating subterfuges?"

"I refer to him and none other, Lennox. I see him now, stumbling about in the deep forest, looking for shelter."

"No, Wilton, you don't see Tayoga. You merely see an idle figment of a brain that does not yet fully know my friend, the great young Onondaga. But *I* see him, and I see him clearly. I behold a tall, strong figure, head slightly bent against the rain, eyes that see in the dark as well as yours see in the brightest sunlight, feet that move surely and steadily in the path, never stumbling and never veering, tireless muscles that carry him on without slackening."

"Dithyrambic again, Lennox. You are certainly loyal to your friend. As for me, I'm glad I'm not out there in the black and wet forest. No human being can keep to his pace at such a time."

Robert again smiled serenely, but he said nothing more. His confidence was unlimited. Presently he wrapped around his body a rude but serviceable overcoat of beaver skin that he had made for himself, and went out. The cold, drizzling icy rain that creeps into one's veins was still falling, and he shivered despite his furs. He looked toward the northeast whither Tayoga's course took him, and he felt sorry for his red comrade, but he never doubted that he was speeding on his way with sure and unfaltering step.

The sentinels, mounted on the broad plank that ran behind the palisade, were walking to and fro, wrapped to their eyes. A month or two earlier they might have left everything on such a night to take care of itself, but now they knew far better. Captain Colden, with the terrible lesson of the battle in the bush, had become a strict disciplinarian, and Willet was always at his elbow with unobtrusive but valuable advice which the young Philadelphian had the good sense to welcome.

Robert spoke to them, and one or two referred to the Indian runner who had gone east, saying that he might have had a better night for his start. The repetition of Wilton's words depressed Robert for a moment, but his heart came back with a bound. Nothing could defeat Tayoga. Did he not know his red comrade? The wilderness was like a trimmed garden to him, and neither rain, nor hail, nor snow could stop him.

As he said the word "hail" to himself it came, pattering upon the dead leaves and the palisade in a whirlwind of white pellets. Again he shivered, and knowing it was no use to linger there returned inside, where most of the men had already gone to sleep. He stretched himself on his blanket and followed them in slumber. When he awoke the next morning it was still hailing, and Wilton said in a serious tone that he hoped Tayoga would give up the journey and come back to Fort Refuge.

"I like that Onondaga," he said, "and I don't want him to freeze to death in the forest. Why, the earth and all the trees are coated with ice now, and even if a man lives he is able to make no progress."

Once more Robert smiled serenely.

"You're thinking of the men you knew in Philadelphia, Will," he said. "They, of course, couldn't make such a flight through a white forest, but Tayoga is an altogether different kind of fellow. He'll merely exert himself a little more, and go on as fast as ever."

Wilton looked at the vast expanse of glittering ice, and then drew the folds of a heavy cloak more closely about his body.

"I rejoice," he said, "that it's the Onondaga and not myself who has to make the great journey. I rejoice, too, that we have built this fort. It's not Philadelphia, that fine, true, comfortable city, but it's shelter against the hard winter that I see coming so fast."

Colden, still following the advice of Willet, kept his men busy, knowing that idleness bred discontent and destroyed discipline. At least a dozen soldiers, taught by Willet and Robert, had developed into excellent hunters, and as the game was abundant, owing to the absence of Indians, they had killed deer, bear, panther and all the other kinds of animals that ranged these forests. The flesh of such as were edible was cured and stored, as they foresaw the day when many people might be in Fort Refuge and the food would be needed. The skins also were dressed and were put upon the floor or hung upon the walls. The young men working hard were happy nevertheless, as they were continually learning new arts. And the life was healthy to an extraordinary degree. All the wounded were as whole as before, and everybody acquired new and stronger muscles.

Their content would have been yet greater in degree had they been able to learn what was going on outside, in that vast world where France and Britain and their colonies contended so fiercely for the mastery. But they looked at the wall of the forest, and it was a blank. They were shut away from all things as completely as Crusoe on his island. Nor would they hear a single whisper until Tayoga came back—if he came back.

On the second day after the Onondaga's departure the air softened, but became darker. The glittering white of the forest assumed a more somber tinge, clouds marched up in solemn procession from the southwest, and mobilized in the center of the heavens, a wind, touched with damp, blew. Robert knew very well what the elements portended and again he was sorry for Tayoga, but as before, after the first few moments of discouragement his courage leaped up higher than ever. His brilliant imagination at once painted a picture in which every detail was vivid and full of life, and this picture was of a vast forest, trees and bushes alike clothed in ice, and in the center of it a slender figure, but straight, tall and strong, Tayoga himself speeding on like the arrow from the bow, never wavering, never weary. Then his mind allowed the picture to fade. Wilton might not believe Tayoga could succeed, but how could this young Quaker know Tayoga as he knew him?

The clouds, having finished their mobilization in the center of the heavens, soon spread to the horizon on every side. Then a single great white flake dropped slowly and gracefully from the zenith, fell within the palisade, and melted before the eyes of Robert and Wilton. But it was merely a herald of its fellows which, descending at first like skirmishers, soon thickened into companies, regiments, brigades, divisions and armies. Then all the air was filled with the flakes, and they were so thick they could not see the forest.

"The first snow of the winter and a big one," said Wilton, "and again I give thanks for our well furnished fort. There may be greater fortresses in Europe, and of a certainty there are many more famous, but there is none finer to me than this with its' stout log walls, its strong, broad roofs, and its abundance of supplies. Once more, though, I'm sorry for your friend, Tayoga. A runner may go fast over ice, if he's extremely sure of foot and his moccasins are good, but I know of no way in which he can speed like the gull in its flight through deep snow."

"Not through the snow, but he may be on it," said Robert.

"And how on it, wise but cryptic young sir?"

"Snow shoes."

"But he took none with him and had none to take."

"Which proves nothing. The Indians often hide in the forest articles they'll need at some far day. A canoe may be concealed in a thicket at the creek's edge, a bow and arrows may be thrust away under a ledge, all awaiting the coming of their owner when he needs them most."

"The chance seems too small to me, Lennox. I can't think a pair of snow shoes will rise out of the forest just when Tayoga wants 'em, walk up to him and say: 'Please strap us on your feet.' I make concession freely that the Onondaga is a most wonderful fellow, but he can't work miracles. He does not hold such complete mastery over the wilderness that it will obey his lightest whisper. I read fairy tales in my youth and they pleased me much, but alas! they were fairy tales! The impossible doesn't happen!"

"Who's the great talker now? Your words were flowing then like the trickling of water from a spout. But you're wrong, Will, about the impossible. The impossible often happens. Great spirits like Tayoga love the impossible. It draws them on, it arouses their energy, they think it worth while. I've seen Tayoga more than once since he started, as plainly as I see you, Will. Now, I shut my eyes and I behold him once more. He's in the forest. The snow is pouring down. It lies a foot deep on the ground, the boughs bend with it, and sometimes they crack under it with a report like that of a rifle. The tops of the bushes crowned with white bend their weight toward the ground, the panthers, the wolves, and the wildcats all lie snug in their dens. It's a dead world save for one figure. Squarely in the center of it I see Tayoga, bent over a little, but flying straight forward at a speed that neither you nor I could match, Will. His feet do not sink in the snow. He skims upon it like a swallow through the air. His feet are encased in something long and narrow. He has on snow shoes and he goes like the wind!"

"You do have supreme confidence in the Onondaga, Lennox!"

"So would you if you knew him as I do, Will, a truth I've told you several times already."

"But he can't provide for every emergency!"

"Must I tell you for the twentieth time that you don't know Tayoga as I know him?"

"No, Lennox, but I'll wait and see what happens."

The fall of snow lasted the entire day and the following night. The wilderness was singularly beautiful, but it was also inaccessible, comfortable for those in the fort, but outside the snow lay nearly two feet deep.

"I hope that vision of yours comes true," said Wilton to Robert, as they looked at the forest. "They say the Highland Scotch can go into trances or something of that kind, and look into the future, and I believe the Indians claim the gift, but I've never heard that English and Americans assumed the possession of such powers."

"I'm no seer," laughed Robert. "I merely use my imagination and produce for myself a picture of things two or three days ahead."

"Which comes to the same thing. Well, we'll see. I take so great an interest in the journey of your Onondaga friend that somehow I feel myself traveling along with him."

"I know I'm going with him or I wouldn't have seen him flying ahead on his snow shoes. But come, Will, I've promised to teach you how to sew buckskin with tendons and sinews, and I'm going to see that you do it."

The snow despite its great depth was premature, because on the fourth day soft winds began to blow, and all the following night a warm rain fell. It came down so fast that the whole earth was flooded, and the air was all fog and mist. The creek rose far beyond its banks, and the water stood in pools and lakes in the forest.

"Now, in very truth, our friend Tayoga has been compelled to seek a lair," said Wilton emphatically. "His snow shoes would be the sorriest of drags upon his feet in mud and water, and without them he will sink to his knees. The wilderness has become impassable."

Robert laughed.

"I see no way out of it for him," said Wilton.

"But I do."

"Then what, in Heaven's name, is it?"

"I not only see the way for Tayoga, but I shut my eyes once more and I see him using it. He has put away his snow shoes, and, going to the thick bushes at the edge of a creek, he has taken out his hidden canoe. He has been in it some time, and with mighty sweeps of the paddle, that he knows so well how to use, it flies like a wild duck over the water. Now he passes from the creek into a river flowing eastward, and swollen by the floods to a vast width. The rain has poured upon him, but he does not mind it. The powerful exercise with the paddles dries his body, and sends the pleasant warmth through every vein. His feet and ankles rest, after his long flight on the snow shoes, and his heart swells with pleasure, because it is one of the easiest parts of his journey. His rifle is lying by his side, and he could seize it in a moment should an enemy appear, but the forest on either side of the stream is deserted, and he speeds on unhindered. There may be better canoemen in the world than Tayoga, but I doubt it."

"Come, come, Lennox! You go too far! I can admit the possibility of the snow shoes and their appearance at the very moment they're needed, but the evocation of a river and a canoe at the opportune instant puts too high a strain upon credibility."

"Then don't believe it unless you wish to do so," laughed Robert, "but as for me I'm not only believing it, but I'm almost at the stage of knowing it."

The flood was so great that all hunting ceased for the time, and the men stayed under shelter in the fort, while the fires were kept burning for the sake of both warmth and cheer. But they were on the edge of the great Ohio Valley, where changes in temperature are often rapid and violent. The warm rain ceased, the wind came out of the southwest cold and then colder. The logs of the buildings popped with the contracting cold all through the following night and the next dawn came bright, clear and still, but far below zero. The ice was thick on the creek, and every new pool and lake was covered. The trees and bushes that had been dripping the day before were sheathed in silver mail. Breath curled away like smoke from the lips.

"If Tayoga stayed in his canoe," said Wilton, "he's frozen solidly in the middle of the river, and he won't be able to move it until a thaw comes."

Robert laughed with genuine amusement and also with a certain scorn.

"I've told you many times, Will," he said, "that you didn't know all about Tayoga, but now it seems that you know nothing about him."

"Well, then, wherein am I wrong, Sir Robert the Omniscient?" asked Wilton.

"In your assumption that Tayoga would not foresee what was coming. Having spent nearly all his life with nature he has naturally been forced to observe all of its manifestations, even the most delicate. And when you add to these necessities the powers of an exceedingly strong and penetrating mind you have developed faculties that can cope with almost anything. Tayoga foresaw this big freeze, and I can tell you exactly what he did as accurately as if I had been there and had seen it. He kept to the river and his canoe almost until the first thin skim of ice began to show. Then he paddled to land, and hid the canoe again among thick bushes. He raised it up a little on low boughs in such a manner that it would not touch the water. Thus it was safe from the ice, and so leaving it well hidden and in proper condition, and situation, he sped on."

"Of course you're a master with words, Robert, and the longer they are the better you seem to like 'em, but how is the Onondaga to make speed over the ice which now covers the earth? Snow shoes, I take it, would not be available upon such a smooth and tricky surface, and, at any rate, he has left them far behind."

"In part of your assumption you're right, Will. Tayoga hasn't the snow shoes now, and he wouldn't use 'em if he had 'em. He foresaw the possibility of the freeze, and took with him in his pack a pair of heavy moose skin moccasins with the hair on the outside. They're so rough they do not slip on the ice, especially when they inclose the feet of a runner, so wiry, so agile and so experienced as Tayoga. Once more I close my eyes and I see his brown figure shooting through the white forest. He goes even faster than he did when he had on the snow shoes, because whenever he comes to a slope he throws himself back upon his heels and lets himself slide down the ice almost at the speed of a bird darting through the air."

"If you're right, Lennox, your red friend is not merely a marvel, but a series of marvels."

"I'm right, Will. I do not doubt it. At the conclusion of the tenth day when Tayoga arrives on the return from the vale of Onondaga you will gladly admit the truth."

"There can be no doubt about my gladness, Lennox, if it should come true, but the elements seem to have conspired against him, and I've learned that in the wilderness the elements count very heavily."

"Earth, fire and water may all join against him, but at the time appointed he will come. I know it."

The great cold, and it was hard, fierce and bitter, lasted two days. At night the popping of the contracting timbers sounded like a continuous pistol fire, but Willet had foreseen everything. At his instance, Colden had made the young soldiers gather vast quantities of fuel long ago from a forest which was filled everywhere with dead boughs and fallen timber, the accumulation of scores of years.

Then another great thaw came, and the fickle climate proceeded to show what it could do. When the thaw had been going on for a day and a night a terrific winter hurricane broke over the forest. Trees were shattered as if their trunks had been shot through by huge cannon balls. Here and there long windrows were piled up, and vast areas were a litter of broken boughs.

"As I reckon, and allowing for the marvels you say he can perform, Tayoga is now in the vale of Onondaga, Lennox," said Wilton. "It's lucky that he's there in the comfortable log houses of his own people, because a man could scarcely live in the forest in such a storm as this, as he would be beaten to death by flying timbers."

"This time, Will, you're wrong in both assumptions. Tayoga has already been to the vale of Onondaga. He has spent there the half day that he allowed to himself, and now on the return journey has left the vale far behind him. I told you how sensitive he was to the changes of the weather, and he knew it was coming several hours before it arrived. He sought at once protection, probably a cleft in the rock, or an opening of two or three feet under a stony ledge. He is lying there now, just as snug and safe as you please, while this storm, which covers a vast area, rages over his head. There is much that is primeval in Tayoga, and his comfort and safety make him fairly enjoy the storm. As he lies under the ledge with his blanket drawn around him, he is warm and dry and his sense of comfort, contrasting his pleasant little den with the fierce storm without, becomes one of luxury."

"I suppose of course, Lennox, that you can shut your eyes and see him once more without any trouble."

"In all truth and certainty I can, Will. He is lying on a stone shelf with a stone ledge above him. His blanket takes away the hardness of the stone that supports him. He sees boughs and sticks whirled past by the storm, but none of them touches him. He hears the wind whistling and screaming at a pitch so fierce that it would terrify one unused to the forest, but it is only a song in the ears of Tayoga. It soothes him, it lulls him, and knowing that he can't use the period of the storm for traveling, he uses it for sleep, thus enabling him to take less later on when the storm has ceased. So, after all, he loses nothing so far as his journey is concerned. Now his lids droop, his eyes close, and he slumbers while the storm thunders past, unable to touch him."

"You do have the gift, Lennox. I believe that sometimes your words are music in your own ears, and inspire you to greater efforts. When the war is over you must surely become a public man—one who is often called upon to address the people."

"We'll fight the war first," laughed Robert.

The storm in its rise, its zenith and its decline lasted several hours, and, when it was over, the forest looked like a wreck, but Robert knew that nature would soon restore everything. The foliage of next spring would cover up the ruin and new growth would take the place of the old and broken. The wilderness, forever restoring what was lost, always took care of itself.

A day or two of fine, clear winter weather, not too cold, followed, and Willet went forth to scout. He was gone until the next morning and when he returned his face was very grave.

"There are Indians in the forest," he said, "not friendly warriors of the Hodenosaunee, but those allied with the enemy. I think a formidable Ojibway band under Tandakora is there, and also other Indians from the region of the Great Lakes. They may have started against us some time back, but were probably halted by the bad weather. They're in different bodies now, scattered perhaps for hunting, but they'll reunite before long."

"Did you see signs of any white men, Dave?" asked Robert.

"Yes, French officers and some soldiers are with 'em, but I don't think St. Luc is in the number. More likely it's De Courcelles and Jumonville, whom we have such good cause to remember."

"I hope so, Dave, I'd rather fight against those two than against St. Luc."

"So would I, and for several reasons. St. Luc is a better leader than they are. They're able, but he's the best of all the French."

That afternoon two men who ventured a short distance from Fort Refuge were shot at, and one was wounded slightly, but both were able to regain the little fortress. Willet slipped out again, and reported the forest swarming with Indians, although there was yet no indication of a preconcerted attack. Still, it was well for the garrison to keep close and take every precaution.

"And this shuts out Tayoga," said Wilton regretfully to Robert. "He may make his way through rain and flood and sleet and snow and hurricane, but he can never pass those watchful hordes of Indians in the woods."

Once more the Onondaga's loyal friend laughed. "The warriors turn Tayoga back, Will?" he said. "He will pass through 'em just as if they were not there. The time will be up day after tomorrow at noon, and then he will be here."

"Even if the Indians move up and besiege us in regular form?"

"Even that, and even anything else. At noon day after tomorrow Tayoga will be here."

Another man who went out to bring in a horse that had been left grazing near the fort was fired upon, not with rifles or muskets but with arrows, and grazed in the shoulder. He had, however, the presence of mind to spring upon the animal's back and gallop for Fort Refuge, where the watchful Willet threw open the gate to the stockade, let him in, then quickly closed and barred it fast. A long fierce whining cry, the war whoop, came from the forest.

"The siege has closed in already," said Robert, "and it's well that we have no other men outside."

"Except Tayoga," said Wilton.

"The barrier of the red army doesn't count so far as Tayoga is concerned. How many times must I tell you, Will, that Tayoga will come at the time appointed?"

After the shout from the woods there was a long silence that weighed upon the young soldiers, isolated thus in the wintry and desolate wilderness. They were city men, used to the streets and the sounds of people, and their situation had many aspects that were weird and appalling. They were hundreds of miles from civilization, and around them everywhere stretched a black forest, hiding a tenacious and cruel foe. But on the other hand their stockade was stout, they had plenty of ammunition, water and provisions, and one victory already to their credit. After the first moments of depression they recalled their courage and eagerly awaited an attack.

But the attack did not come and Robert knew it would not be made, at least not yet. The Indians were too wary to batter themselves to pieces against the palisade, and the Frenchmen with them, skilled in forest war, would hold them back.

"Perhaps they've gone away, realizing that we're too strong for 'em," said Wilton.

"That's just what we must guard against," said Robert. "The Indian fights with trick and stratagem. He always has more time than the white man, and he is wholly willing to wait. They want us to think they've left, and then they'll cut off the incautious."

The afternoon wore on, and the silence which had grown oppressive persisted. A light pleasant wind blew through the forest, which was now dry, and the dead bark and wintry branches rustled. To many of the youths it became a forest of gloom and threat, and they asked impatiently why the warriors did not come out and show themselves like men. Certainly, it did not become Frenchmen, if they were there to lurk in the woods and seek ambush.

Willet was the pervading spirit of the defense. Deft in word and action, acknowledging at all times that Colden was the commander, thus saving the young Philadelphian's pride in the presence of his men, he contrived in an unobtrusive way to direct everything. The guards were placed at suitable intervals about the palisade, and were instructed to fire at anything suspicious, the others were compelled to stay in the blockhouse and take their ease, in order that their nerves might be steady and true, when the time for battle came. The cooks were also instructed to prepare an unusually bountiful supper for them.

Robert was Willet's right hand. Next to the hunter he knew most about the wilderness, and the ways of its red people. There was no possibility that the Indians had gone. Even if they did not undertake to storm the fort they would linger near it, in the hope of cutting off men who came forth incautiously, and at night, especially if it happened to be dark, they would be sure to come very close.

The palisade was about eight feet high, and the men stood on a horizontal plank three feet from the ground, leaving only the head to project above the shelter, and Willet warned them to be exceedingly careful when the twilight came, since the besiegers would undoubtedly use the darkness as a cover for sharp-shooting. Then both he and Robert looked anxiously at the sun, which was just setting behind the black waste.

"The night will be dark," said the hunter, "and that's bad. I'm afraid some of our sentinels will be picked off. Robert, you and I must not sleep until tomorrow. We must stay on watch here all the while."

As he predicted, the night came down black and grim. Vast banks of darkness rolled up close to the palisade, and the forest showed but dimly. Then the warriors proved to the most incredulous that they had not gone far away. Scattered shots were fired from the woods, and one sentinel who in spite of warnings thrust his head too high above the palisade, received a bullet through it falling back dead. It was a terrible lesson, but afterwards the others took no risks, although they were anxious to fire on hostile figures that their fancy saw for them among the trees. Willet, Robert and Colden compelled them to withhold their fire until a real and tangible enemy appeared.

Later in the night burning arrows were discharged in showers and fell within the palisade, some on the buildings. But they had pails, and an unfailing spring, and they easily put out the flames, although one man was struck and suffered both a burn and a bruise.

Toward midnight a terrific succession of war whoops came, and a great number of warriors charged in the darkness against the palisade. The garrison was ready, and, despite the darkness, poured forth such a fierce fire that in a few minutes the horde vanished, leaving behind several still forms which they stole away later. Another of the young Philadelphians was killed, and before dawn he and his comrade who had been slain earlier in the evening were buried behind the blockhouse.

At intervals in the remainder of the night the warriors fired either arrows or bullets, doing no farther damage except the slight wounding of one man, and when day came Willet and Robert, worn to the bone, sought a little rest and sleep in the blockhouse. They knew that Golden could not be surprised while the sun was shining, and that the savages were not likely to attempt anything serious until the following night So they felt they were not needed for the present.

Robert slept until nearly noon, when he ate heartily of the abundant food one of the young cooks had prepared, and learned that beyond an occasional arrow or bullet the forest had given forth no threat. His own spirits rose high with the day, which was uncommonly brilliant, with a great sun shining in the center of the heavens, and not a cloud in the sky. Wilton was near the blockhouse and was confident about the siege, but worried about Tayoga.

"You tell me that the Indians won't go away," he said, "and if you're right, and I think you are, the Onondaga is surely shut off from Fort Refuge."

Robert smiled.

"I tell you for the last time that he will come at the appointed hour," he said.

A long day began. Hours that seemed days in themselves passed, and quiet prevailed in the forest, although the young soldiers no longer had any belief that the warriors had gone away.

CHAPTER VI
THE RETURN

It was near the close of a day that had been marked by little demonstration from the enemy, and the young officers, growing used to the siege, attained a philosophical state of mind. They felt sure they could hold the palisade against any number of enemies, and the foresight of Willet, Robert and Tayoga had been so great that by no possibility could they be starved out. They began now to have a certain exultation. They were inside comfortable walls, with plenty to eat and drink, while the enemy was outside and must forage for game.

"If it were not for Tayoga," said Wilton to Robert, "I should feel more than satisfied with the situation. But the fate of your Onondaga friend sticks in my mind. Mr. Willet, who knows everything, says we're surrounded completely, and I don't wish him to lose his life in an attempt to get through at a certain time, merely on a point of honor."

"It's no point of honor, Will. It's just the completion of a plan at the time and place chosen. Do you see anything in that tall tree to the east of the palisade?"

"Something appears to be moving up the trunk, but as it's on the far side, I catch only a glimpse of it."

"That's an Indian warrior, seeking a place for a shot at us. He'll reach the high fork, but he'll always keep well behind the body of the tree. It's really too far for a bullet, but I think it would be wise for us to slip back under cover."

The sharpshooter reached his desired station and fired, but his bullet fell short. He tried three more, all without avail, and then Willet picked him off with his long and deadly rifle. Robert shut his eyes when he saw the body begin its fall, but his vivid imagination, so easily excited, made him hear its thump when it struck the earth.

"And so ends that attempt!" he said.

An hour later he saw a white flag among the trees, and when Willet mounted the palisade two French officers came forward. Robert saw at once that they were De Courcelles and Jumonville, and his heart beat hard. They linked him with Quebec, in which he had spent some momentous days, and despite their treachery to him he did not feel hatred of them at that moment.

"Will you stay with me, Mr. Willet, and you also, Mr. Lennox, while I talk to them?" asked Captain Colden. "You know these Frenchmen better than I do, and their experience is so much greater than mine that I need your help."

Robert and the hunter assented gladly. Robert, in truth, was very curious to hear what these old friends and enemies of his had to say, and he felt a thrill when the two recognized and saluted him in the most friendly fashion, just as if they had never meant him any harm.

"Chance brings about strange meetings between us, Mr. Lennox," said De Courcelles. "It gives me pleasure to note that you have not yet taken any personal harm from our siege."

"Nor you nor Monsieur de Jumonville, from our successful defense," replied Robert in the same spirit.

"You have us there. The points so far are in your favor, although only superficially so, as I shall make clear to you presently."

Then De Courcelles turned his attention to Colden, who he saw was the nominal leader of the garrison.

"My name," he said, "is Auguste de Courcelles, a colonel in the service of His Majesty, King Louis of France. My friend is Captain Francois de Jumonville, and we have the honor to lead the numerous and powerful force of French and Indians now besieging you."

"And my name is Colden, Captain James Colden," replied the young officer. "I've heard of you from my friends, Mr. Lennox and Mr. Willet, and I have the honor of asking you what I can do for you."

"You cannot do for us more than you can do for yourself, Captain Colden. We ask the surrender of your little fort, and of your little garrison, which we freely admit has defended itself most gallantly.

It's not necessary for us to make an assault. You're deep in the wilderness, we can hold you here all winter, and help cannot possibly come to you. We guarantee you good treatment in Canada, where you will be held until the war is over."

Young Colden smiled. They were standing before the single gate in the palisade, and he looked back at the solid buildings, erected by the hands of his own men, with the comfortable smoke curling up against the cold sky. And he looked also at the wintry forest that curved in every direction.

"Colonel de Courcelles," he said, "it seems to me that we are in and you are out. If it comes to holding us here all winter we who have good houses can stand it much better than you who merely have the forest as a home, where you will be rained upon, snowed upon, hailed upon, and maybe frozen. Why should we exchange our warm house for your cold forest?"

Colonel de Courcelles frowned. There was a humorous inflection in Colden's tone that did not please him, and the young officer's words also had a strong element of truth.

"It's not a time to talk about houses and forests," he said, somewhat haughtily. "We have here a formidable force capable of carrying your fort, and, for that reason, we demand your surrender. Indians are always inflamed by a long and desperate resistance and while Captain de Jumonville and I will do our best to restrain them, it's possible that they may escape from our control in the hour of victory."

Young Colden smiled again. With Willet at his right hand and Robert at his left, he acquired lightness of spirit.

"A demand and a threat together," he replied. "For the threat we don't care. We don't believe you'll ever see that hour of victory in which you can't control your Indians, and there'll be no need for you, Colonel de Courcelles, to apologize for a massacre committed by your allies, and which you couldn't help. We're also growing used to requests of surrender.

"There was your countryman, St. Luc, a very brave and skillful man, who asked it of us, but we declined, and in the end we defeated him. And if we beat St. Luc without the aid of a strong fort, why shouldn't we beat you with it, Colonel de Courcelles?"

Colonel de Courcelles frowned once more, and Captain de Jumonville frowned with him.

"You don't know the wilderness, Captain Colden," he said, "and you don't give our demand the serious consideration to which it is entitled. Later on, the truth of what I tell you may bear heavily upon you."

"I may not know the forest as you do, Colonel de Courcelles, but I have with me masters of woodcraft, Mr. Lennox and Mr. Willet, with whom you're already acquainted."

"We've had passages of various kinds with Colonel de Courcelles, both in the forest and at Quebec," said Robert, quietly.

Both De Courcelles and Jumonville flushed, and it became apparent that they were anxious to end the interview.

"This, I take it, is your final answer," the French Colonel said to the young Philadelphia captain.

"It is, sir."

"Then what may occur rests upon the knees of the gods."

"It does, sir, and I'm as willing as you to abide by the result."

"And I have the honor of bidding you good day."

"An equally great honor is mine."

The two French officers were ceremonious. They lifted their fine, three-cornered hats, and bowed politely, and Colden, Willet and Robert were not inferior in courtesy. Then the Frenchmen walked away into the forest, while the three Americans went inside the palisade, where the heavy gate was quickly shut behind them and fastened securely. But before he turned back Robert thought he saw the huge figure of Tandakora in the forest.

When the French officers disappeared several shots were fired and the savages uttered a long and menacing war whoop, but the young soldiers had grown used to such manifestations, and, instead of being frightened, they felt a certain defiant pleasure.

"Yells don't hurt us," said Wilton to Robert. "Instead I feel my Quaker blood rising in anger, and I'd rejoice if they were to attack now. A very heavy responsibility rests upon me, Robert, since I've to fight not only for myself but for my ancestors who wouldn't fight at all. It rests upon me, one humble youth, to bring up the warlike average of the family."

"You're one, Will, but you're not humble," laughed Robert. "I believe that jest of yours about the still, blood of generations bursting forth in you at last is not a jest wholly. When it comes to a pitched battle I expect to see you perform prodigies of valor."

"If I do it won't be Will Wilton, myself, and I won't be entitled to any credit. I'll be merely an instrument in the hands of fate, working out the law of averages. But what do you think those French officers and their savage allies will do now, Robert, since Colden, so to speak, has thrown a very hard glove in their faces?"

"Draw the lines tighter about Fort Refuge. It's cold in the forest, but they can live there for a while at least. They'll build fires and throw up a few tepees, maybe for the French. But their anger and their desire to take us will make them watch all the more closely. They'll draw tight lines around this snug little, strong little fort of ours."

"Which removes all possibility that your friend Tayoga will come at the appointed time."

Robert glared at him.

"Will," he said, "I've discovered that you have a double nature, although the two are never struggling for you at the same time."

"That is I march tandem with my two natures, so to speak?"

"They alternate. At times you're a sensible boy."

"Boy? I'm older than you are!"

"One wouldn't think it. But a well bred Quaker never interrupts. As I said, you're quite sensible at times and you ought to thank me for saying so. At other times your mind loves folly. It fairly swims and dives in the foolish pool, and it dives deepest when you're talking about Tayoga. I trust, foolish young, sir, that I've heard the last word of folly from you about the arrival of Tayoga, or rather what you conceive will be his failure to arrive. Peace, not a word!"

"At least let me say this," protested Wilton. "I wish that I could feel the absolute confidence in any human being that you so obviously have in the Onondaga."

The night came, white and beautiful. It was white, because the Milky Way was at its brightest, which was uncommonly bright, and every star that ever showed itself in that latitude came out and danced. The heavens were full of them, disporting themselves in clusters on spangled seas, and the forest was all in light, paler than that of day, but almost as vivid.

The Indians lighted several fires, well beyond rifle shot, and the sentinels on the palisade distinctly saw their figures passing back and forth before the blaze Robert also noticed the uniforms of Frenchmen, and he thought it likely that De Courcelles and Jumonville had with them more soldiers than he had supposed at first. The fires burned at different points of the compass, and thus the fort was encircled completely by them. Both young Lennox and Willet knew they had been lighted that way purposely, that is in order to show to the defenders that a belt of fire and steel was drawn close about them.

To Wilton at least the Indian circle seemed impassable, and despite the enormous confidence of Robert he now had none at all himself. It was impossible for Tayoga, even if he had triumphed over sleet and snow and flood and storm, to pass so close a siege. He would not speak of it again, but Robert had allowed himself to be deluded by friendship. He felt sorry for his new friend, and he did not wish to see his disappointment on the morrow.

Wilton was in charge of the guard until midnight, and then he slept soundly until dawn, awakening to a brilliant day, the fit successor of such a brilliant night. The Indian fires were still burning and he could see the warriors beside them sleeping or eating at leisure. They still formed a complete circle about the fort, and while the young Quaker felt safe inside the palisade, he saw no chance for a friend outside. Robert joined him presently but, respecting his feelings, the Philadelphian said nothing about Tayoga.

The winter, it seemed, was exerting itself to show how fine a day it could produce. It was cold but dazzling. A gorgeous sun, all red and gold, was rising, and the light was so vivid and intense that they could see far in the forest, bare of leaf. Robert clearly discerned both De Courcelles and Jumonville about six hundred yards away, standing by one of the fires. Then he saw the gigantic figure of Tandakora, as the Ojibway joined them. Despite the cold, Tandakora wore little but the breechcloth, and his mighty chest and shoulders were painted with many hideous devices. In the distance and in the glow of the flames his size was exaggerated until he looked like one of the giants of ancient mythology.

Robert was quite sure the siege would never be raised if the voice of the Ojibway prevailed in the allied French and Indian councils. Tandakora had been wounded twice, once by the hunter and once by the Onondaga, and a mind already inflamed against the Americans and the Hodenosaunee cherished a bitter personal hate. Robert knew that Willet, Tayoga and he must be eternally on guard against his murderous attacks.

The savages built their fires higher, as if in defiance and triumph. They could defend themselves against cold, because the forest furnished unending fuel, but rain or hail, sleet or snow would bring severe hardship. The day, however, favored them to the utmost. It had seemed at dawn that it could not be more brilliant, but as the morning advanced the world fairly glowed with color. The sky was golden save in the east, where it burned in red, and the trunks and black boughs of the forest, to the last and least little twig, were touched with it until they too were clothed in a luminous glow.

The besiegers seemed lazy, but Robert knew that the watch upon the fort and its approaches was never neglected for an instant. A fox could not steal through their lines, unseen, and yet he never doubted. Tayoga would come, and moreover he would come at the time appointed. Toward the middle of the morning the Indians shot some arrows that fell inside the palisade, and uttered a shout or two of defiance, but nobody was hurt, and nobody was stirred to action. The demonstration passed unanswered, and, after a while, Wilton called Robert's attention to the fact that it was only two hours until noon. Robert did not reply, but he knew that the conditions could not be more unfavorable. Rain or hail, sleet or snow might cover the passage of a warrior, but the dazzling sunlight that enlarged twigs two hundred yards away into boughs, seemed to make all such efforts vain. Yet he knew Tayoga, and he still believed.

Soon a stir came in the forest, and they heard a long, droning chant. A dozen warriors appeared coming out of the north, and they were welcomed with shouts by the others.

"Hurons, I think," said Willet. "Yes, I'm sure of it. They've undoubtedly sent away for help, and it's probable that other bands will come about this time." He reckoned right, as in half an hour a detachment of Abenakis came, and they too were received with approving shouts, after which food was given to them and they sat luxuriously before the fires. Then three runners arrived, one from the north, one from the west, and one from the east, and a great shout of welcome was uttered for each.

"What does it mean?" Wilton asked Robert.

"The runners were sent out by De Courcelles and Tandakora to rally more strength for our siege. They've returned with the news that fresh forces are coming, as the exultant shout from the warriors proves."

The young Philadelphian's heart sank. He knew that it was only a half hour until noon, and noon was the appointed time. Nor did the heavens give any favoring sign. The whole mighty vault was a blaze of gold and blue. Nothing could stir in such a light and remain hidden from the warriors. Wilton looked at his comrade and he caught a sudden glitter in his eyes. It was not the look of one who despaired. Instead it was a flash of triumph, and the young Philadelphian wondered. Had Robert seen a sign, a sign that had escaped all others? He searched the forest everywhere with his own eyes, but he could detect nothing unusual. There were the French, and there were the Indians. There were the new warriors, and there were the three runners resting by the fires.

The runners rose presently, and the one who had come out of the north talked with Tandakora, the one who had come out of the west stood near the edge of the forest with an Abenaki chief and looked at the fort. The one who had come out of the east joined De Courcelles himself and they came nearer to the fort than any of the others, although they remained just beyond rifle shot. Evidently De Courcelles was explaining something to the Indian as once he pointed toward the blockhouse.

Wilton heard Robert beside him draw a deep breath, and he turned in surprise. The face of young Lennox was tense and his eyes fairly blazed as he gazed at De Courcelles and the warrior. Then looking back at the forest Robert uttered a sudden sharp, Ah! the release of uncontrollable emotion, snapping like a pistol shot.

"Did you see it, Will? Did you see it?" he exclaimed. "It was quicker than lightning!"

The Indian runner stooped, snatched the pistol from the belt of De Courcelles, struck him such a heavy blow on the head with the butt of it that he fell without a sound, and then his brown body shot forward like an arrow for the fort.

"Open the gate! Open the gate!" thundered Willet, and strong arms unbarred it and flung it back in an instant. The brown body of Tayoga flashed through, and, in another instant, it was closed and barred again.

"He is here with five minutes to spare!" said Robert as he left the palisade with Wilton, and went toward the blockhouse to greet his friend.

Tayoga, painted like a Micmac and stooping somewhat hitherto, drew himself to his full height, held out his hand in the white man's fashion to Robert, while his eyes, usually so calm, showed a passing gleam of triumph.

"I said, Tayoga, that you would be back on time, that is by noon today," said Robert, "and though the task has been hard you're with us and you have a few minutes to spare. How did you deceive the sharp eyes of Tandakora?"

"I did not let him see me, knowing he would look through my disguise, but I asked the French colonel to come forward with me at once and inspect the fort, knowing that it was my only chance to enter here, and he agreed to do so. You saw the rest, and thus I have come. It is not pleasant to those who besiege us, as your ears tell you."

Fierce yells of anger and disappointment were rising in the forest. Jumonville and two French soldiers had rushed forward, seized the reviving De Courcelles and were carrying him to one of the fires, where they would bind up his injured head. But inside the fort there was only exultation at the arrival of Tayoga and admiration for his skill. He insisted first on being allowed to wash off the Micmac paint, enabling him to return to his true character. Then he took food and drink.

"Tayoga," said Wilton, "I believed you could not come. I said so often to Lennox. You would never have known my belief, because Lennox would not have told it to you, but I feel that I must apologize to you for the thought. I underrated you, but I underrated you because I did not believe any human being could do what you have done."

Tayoga smiled, showing his splendid white teeth. "Your thoughts did me no wrong," he said in his precise school English, "because the elements and chance itself seemed to have conspired against me."

Later he told what he had heard in the vale of Onondaga where the sachems and chiefs kept themselves well informed concerning the movements of the belligerent nations. The French were still the more active of the rival powers, and their energy and conquests were bringing the western tribes in great numbers to their flag. Throughout the Ohio country the warriors were on the side of the French who were continuing the construction of the powerful fortress at the junction of the Alleghany and the Monongahela. The French were far down in the province of New York, and they held control of Lake Champlain and of Lake George also. More settlements had been cut off, and more women and children had been taken prisoners into Canada.

But the British colonies and Great Britain too would move, so Tayoga said. They were slow, much slower than Canada, but they had the greater strength and the fifty sachems in the vale of Onondaga knew it. They could not be moved from their attitude of friendliness toward the English, and the Mohawks openly espoused the English side. The American, Franklin, was very active, and a great movement against Fort Duquesne would be begun, although it might not start until next spring. An English force under an English general was coming across the sea, and the might of England was gathering for a great blow.

The Onondaga had few changes in the situation to report, but he at least brought news of the outside world, driving away from the young soldiers the feeling that they were cut off from the human race. Wilton was present when he was telling of these things and when he had finished Robert asked:

"How did you make your way through the great snow, Tayoga?"

"It is well to think long before of difficulties," he replied. "Last year when the winter was finished I hid a pair of snow shoes in this part of the forest, and when the deep snow came I found them and used them."

Robert glanced at Wilton, whose eyes were widening.

"And the great rain and flood, how did you meet that obstacle?" asked Robert.

"That, too, was forethought. I have two canoes hidden in this region, and it was easy to reach one of them, in which I traveled with speed and comfort, until I could use it no longer. Then I hid it away again that it might help me another time."

"And what did you do when the hurricane came, tearing up the bushes, cutting down the trees, and making the forest as dangerous as if it were being showered by cannon balls?"

"I crept under a wide ledge of stone in the side of a hill, where I lay snug, dry and safe."

Wilton looked at Tayoga and Robert, and then back at the Onondaga.

"Is this wizardry?" he cried.

"No," replied Robert.

"Then it's singular chance."

"Nor that either. It was the necessities that confronted Tayoga in the face of varied dangers, and my knowledge of what he would be likely to do in either case. Merely a rather fortunate use of the reasoning faculties, Will."

Willet, who had come in, smiled.

"Don't let 'em make game of you, Mr. Wilton," he said, "but there's truth in what Robert tells you. He understands Tayoga so thoroughly that he knows pretty well what he'll do in every crisis."

After the Onondaga had eaten he wrapped himself in blankets, went to sleep in one of the rooms of the blockhouse and slept twenty-four hours. When he awoke he showed no signs of his tremendous journey and infinite dangers. He was once more the lithe and powerful Tayoga of the Clan of the Bear, of the nation Onondaga of the great League of the Hodenosaunee.

The besiegers meanwhile undertook no movement, but, as if in defiance, they increased the fires in the red ring around the fort and they showed themselves ostentatiously. Robert several times saw De Courcelles with a thick bandage about his head, and he knew that the Frenchman's mortification and rage at being tricked so by the Onondaga must be intense.

Now the weather began to grow very cold again, and Robert saw the number of tepees in the forest increase. The Indians, not content with the fires, were providing themselves with good shelters, and to every one it indicated a long siege. There was neither snow, nor hail, but clear, bitter, intense cold, and again the timbers of the blockhouse and outbuildings popped as they contracted under the lower temperature.

The horses were pretty well sheltered from the cold, and Willet, with his usual foresight, had suggested before the siege closed in that a great deal of grass be cut for them, though should the French and Indians hang on for a month or two, they would certainly become a problem. Food for the men would last indefinitely, but a time might arrive when none would be left for the horses.

"If the pinch comes," said Willet, "we know how to relieve it."

"How?" asked Colden.

"We'll eat the horses."

Colden made a wry face.

"It's often been done in Europe," said the hunter. "At the famous sieges of Leyden and Haarlem, when the Dutch held out so long against the Spanish, they'd have been glad enough to have had horseflesh."

"I look ahead again," said Robert, hiding a humorous gleam in his eyes from Colden, "and I see a number of young men behind a palisade which they have held gallantly for months. They come mostly from Philadelphia and they call themselves Quakers. They are thin, awfully thin, terribly thin, so thin that there is scarcely enough to make a circle for their belts. They have not eaten for four days, and they are about to kill their last horse. When he is gone they will have to live on fresh air and scenery."

"Now I know Lennox that you're drawing on your imagination and that you're a false prophet," said Colden.

"I hope my prediction won't come true, and I don't believe it will," said Robert cheerfully.

Several nights later when there was no moon, and no stars, Willet and Tayoga slipped out of the fort. Colden was much opposed to their going, fearing for their lives, and knowing, too, how great a loss they would be if they were taken or slain, but the hunter and the Onondaga showed the utmost confidence, assuring him they would return in safety.

Colden became quite uneasy for them after they had been gone some hours, and Robert, although he refused to show it, felt a trace of apprehension. He knew their great skill in the forest, but Tandakora was a master of woodcraft too, and the Frenchmen also were experienced and alert. As he, Colden, Wilton and Carson watched at the palisade he was in fear lest a triumphant shout from the Indian lines would show that the hunter and the Onondaga had been trapped.

But the long hours passed without an alarm and about three o'clock in the morning two shadows appeared at the palisade and whispered to them. Robert felt great relief as Willet and Tayoga climbed silently over.

"We're half frozen," said the hunter. "Take us into the blockhouse and over the fire we'll tell you all we've seen."

They always kept a bed of live coals on the hearth in the main building, and the two who had returned bent over the grateful heat, warming their hands and faces. Not until they were in a normal physical condition did Colden or Robert ask them any questions and then Willet said:

"Their ring about the fort is complete, but in the darkness we were able to slip through and then back again. I should judge that they have at least three hundred warriors and Tandakora is first among them. There are about thirty Frenchmen. De Courcelles has taken off his bandage, but he still has a bruise where Tayoga struck him. Peeping from the bushes I saw him and his face has grown more evil. It was evident to me that the blow of Tayoga has inflamed his mind. He feels mortified and humiliated at the way in which he was outwitted, and, as Tandakora also nurses a personal hatred against us, it's likely that they'll keep up the siege all winter, if they think in the end they can get us.

"Their camp, too, shows increasing signs of permanency. They've built a dozen bark huts in which all the French, all the chiefs and some of the warriors sleep, and there are skin lodges for the rest. Oh, it's quite a village! And they've accumulated game, too, for a long time."

Colden looked depressed.

"We're not fulfilling our mission," he said. "We've come out here to protect the settlers on the border, and give them a place of refuge. Instead, it looks as if we'd pass the winter fighting for our own lives."

"I think I have a plan," said Robert, who had been very thoughtful.

"What is it?" asked Colden.

"I remember something I read in our Roman history in the school at Albany. It was an event that happened a tremendously long time ago, but I fancy it's still useful as an example. Scipio took his army over to Africa to meet Hannibal, and one night his men set fire to the tents of the Carthaginians. They destroyed their camp, created a terrible tumult, and inflicted great losses."

Tayoga's eyes glistened.

"Then you mean," he said, "that we are to burn the camp of the French and their allies?"

"No less."

"It is a good plan. If Great Bear and the captain agree to it we will do it."

"It's fearfully risky," said Colden.

"If Great Bear and I can go out once and come back safely," said Tayoga, "we can do it twice."

The young captain looked at Willet.

"It's the best plan," said the hunter. "Robert hasn't read his Roman history in vain."

"Then it's agreed," said Colden, "and as soon as another night as dark as this comes we'll try it."

The plan being formed, they waited a week before a night, pitchy black, arrived.

CHAPTER VII
THE RED WEAPON

The night was admirably suited to their purpose—otherwise they would not have dared to leave Fort Refuge—and Willet, Tayoga and Robert alone undertook the task. Wilton, Carson and others were anxious to go, but, as an enterprise of such great danger required surpassing skill, the three promptly ruled them out. The hunter and young Lennox would have disguised themselves as Indians, but as they did not have any paint in the fort they were compelled to go forth in their own garb.

The cold had softened greatly, and, as heavy clouds had come with it, there was promise of snow, which in truth the three hoped would fall, since it would be an admirable cloak for their purpose. But in any event theirs was to be a perilous path, and Colden shook hands with the three as they lowered themselves softly from the palisade.

"Come back," he whispered. "If you find the task too dangerous let it go and return at once. We need you here in the fort."

"We'll come back as victors," Robert replied with confidence. Then he and his comrades crouched, close against the palisade and listened. The Indian fires showed dimly in the heavy dusk, and they knew that sentinels were on watch in the woods, but still keeping in the shadow of the palisade they went to the far side, where the Indian line was thinner. Then they dropped to hand and knee and crept toward the forest.

They stopped at intervals, lying flat upon the ground, looking with all their eyes and listening with all their ears. They saw ahead but one fire, apparently about four hundred yards away, and they heard only a light damp wind rustling the dry boughs and bushes. But they knew they could not afford to relax their caution by a hair, and they continued a slow creeping progress until they reached the woods.

Then they rested on their elbows in a thicket, and took long breaths of relief. They had been a quarter of an hour in crossing the open and it was an immense relief to sit up again. They kept very close together, while their muscles recovered elasticity, and still used their eyes and ears to the utmost. It was impossible to say that a warrior was not near crouching in the thicket as they were, and they did not intend to run any useless risk. Moreover, if the alarm were raised now, they would escape into the fort, and await another chance.

But they neither heard nor saw a hostile presence. In truth, they saw nothing that betokened a siege, save the dim light flickering several hundred yards ahead of them, and they resumed their advance, bent so low that they could drop flat at the first menace. Their eyes looked continually for a sentinel, but they saw none.

"Don't you think the wind is rising a bit, Tayoga?" whispered the hunter.

"Yes," replied the Onondaga.

"And it feels damper to the face?"

"Yes, Great Bear."

"And it doesn't mean rain, because the air's too cold, but it does mean snow, for which the air is just right, and I think it's coming, as the clouds grow thicker and thicker all the time."

"Which proves that we are favored. Tododaho from his great and shining star, that we cannot see tonight, looks down upon us and will help us, since we have tried to do the things that are right. We wish the snow to come, because we wish a veil about us, while we confound our enemies, and Tododaho will send it."

He spoke devoutly and Robert admired and respected his faith, the center of which was Manitou, and Manitou in the mind of the Christian boy was the same as God. He also shared the faith of Tayoga that Tododaho would wrap the snow like a white robe about them to hide them from their enemies. Meanwhile the three crept slowly toward the fire, and Robert felt something damp brush his face. It was the first flake of snow, and Tododaho, on his shining star, was keeping his unspoken promise.

Tayoga looked up toward the point in the heavens where the great chief's star shone on clear nights, and, even in the dark, Robert saw the spiritual exaltation on his face. The Onondaga never doubted for an instant. The mighty chief who had gone away four centuries ago had answered the prayer made to him by one of his loyal children, and was sending the snow that it might be a veil before them while they destroyed the camp of their enemies. The soul of Tayoga leaped up. They had received a sign. They were in the care of Tododaho and they could not fail.

Another flake fell on Robert's face and a third followed, and then they came down in a white and gentle stream that soon covered him, Willet and Tayoga and hung like a curtain before them. He looked back toward the fort, but the veil there also hung between and he could not see it. Then he looked again, and the dim fire had disappeared in the white mist.

"Will it keep their huts and lodges from burning?" he whispered to the hunter.

Willet shook his head.

"If we get a fire started well," he said, "the snow will seem to feed it rather than put it out. It's going to help us in more ways than one, too. I'd expected that we'd have to use flint and steel to touch off our blaze, but as they're likely to leave their own fire and seek shelter, maybe we can get a torch there. Now, you two boys keep close to me and we'll approach that fire, or the place where it was."

They continued a cautious advance, their moccasins making no sound in the soft snow, all objects invisible at a distance of twelve or fifteen feet. Yet they saw one Indian warrior on watch, although he did not see or hear them. He was under the boughs of a small tree and was crouched against the trunk, protecting himself as well as he could from the tumbling flakes. He was a Huron, a capable warrior with his five senses developed well, and in normal times he was ambitious and eager for distinction in his wilderness world, but just now he did not dream that any one from the fort could be near. So the three passed him, unsuspected, and drew close to the fire, which now showed as a white glow through the dusk, sufficient proof that it was still burning. Further progress proved that the warriors had abandoned it for shelter, and they left the next task to Tayoga.

The Onondaga lay down in the snow and crept forward until he reached the fire, where he paused and waited two or three minutes to see that his presence was not detected. Then he took three burning sticks and passed them back swiftly to his comrades. Willet had already discerned the outline of a bark hut on his right and Robert had made out another on his left. Just beyond were skin tepees. They must now act quickly, and each went upon his chosen way.

Robert approached the hut on the left from the rear, and applied the torch to the wall which was made of dry and seasoned bark. Despite the snow, it ignited at once and burned with extraordinary speed. The roar of flames from the right showed that the hunter had done as well, and a light flash among the skin tepees was proof that Tayoga was not behind them.

The besieging force was taken completely by surprise. The three had imitated to perfection the classic example of Scipio's soldiers in the Carthaginian camp. The confusion was terrible as French and Indians rushed for their lives from the burning huts and lodges into the blinding snow, where they saw little, and, for the present, understood less. Tayoga who, in the white dusk readily passed for one of their own, slipped here and there, continually setting new fires, traveling in a circle about the fort, while Robert and Willet kept near him, but on the inner side of the circle and well behind the veil of snow.

The huts and lodges burned fiercely. Where they stood thickest each became a lofty pyramid of fire and then blended into a mighty mass of flames, forming an intense red core in the white cloud of falling snow. French soldiers and Indian warriors ran about, seeking to save their arms, ammunition and stores, but they were not always successful. Several explosions showed that the flames had reached powder, and Robert laughed to himself in pleasure. The destruction of their powder was a better result than he had hoped or foreseen.

The hunter uttered a low whistle and Tayoga throwing down his torch, at once joined him and Robert who had already cast theirs far from them.

"Back to the fort!" said Willet. "We've already done 'em damage they can't repair in a long time, and maybe we've broken up their camp for the winter! What a godsend the snow was!"

"It was Tododaho who sent it," said Tayoga, reverently. "They almost make a red ring around our fort. We have succeeded because the mighty chief, the founder of the great League of the Hodenosaunee, who went away to his star four centuries ago, willed for us to succeed. How splendidly the fires burn! Not a hut, not a lodge will be left!"

"And it's time for us to be going," said the hunter. "Men like De Courcelles, Jumonville and Tandakora will soon bring order out of all that tumult, and they'll be looking for those who set the torch. The snow is coming down heavier and heavier and it hides our flight, although it is not able to put out the fires. You're right, Tayoga, about Tododaho pouring his favor upon us."

It was easy for the three to regain the palisade, and they were not afraid of mistaken bullets fired at them for enemies, since Colden and Wilton had warned the soldiers that they might expect the return of the three. Tododaho continued to watch over, them as they reached the palisade, at the point where the young Philadelphia captain himself stood upon the raised plank behind it.

"Captain Colden! Captain Colden!" called Willet through the white cloud.

"Is it you, Mr. Willet?" exclaimed Colden. "Thank God you've come. I've been in great fear for you! I knew that you had set the fires, because my own eyes tell me so, but I didn't know what had become of you."

"I'm here, safe and well."

"And Mr. Lennox?"

"Here, unhurt, too," replied Robert.

"And the Onondaga?"

"All right and rejoicing that we have done even more than we hoped to do," said Tayoga, in his measured and scholastic English.

The three, coated with snow until they looked like white bears, quickly scaled the wall, and received the joyous welcome, given to those who have done a great deed, and who return unhurt to their comrades. Colden, Wilton and Carson shook their hands again and again and Robert knew that it was due as much to pleasure at the return as at the destruction of the besieging camp.

The entire population of Fort Refuge was at the palisade, heedless of the snow, watching the burning huts and lodges. There was no wind, but cinders and ashes fell near them, to be covered quickly with white. Fierce yells now came from the forest and arrows and bullets were fired at the fort, but they were harmless and the defenders did not reply.

The flames began to decline by and by, then they sank fast, and after a while the snow which still came down as if it meant never to stop covered everything. The circling white wall enveloped the stronghold completely, and Robert knew that the disaster to the French and Indians had been overwhelming. Probably all of them had saved their lives, but they had lost ammunition—the explosions had told him that—much of their stores, and doubtless all of their food. They would have to withdraw, for the present at least.

Robert felt immense exultation. They had struck a great blow, and it was he who had suggested the plan. His pride increased, although he hid it, when Willet put his large hand on his shoulder and said:

"'Twas well done, Robert, my lad, and 'twould not have been done at all had it not been for you. Your mind bred the idea, from which the action flowed."

"And you think the French and Indians have gone away now?"

"Surely, lad! Surely! Indians can stand a lot, and so can French, but neither can stand still in the middle of a snow that bids fair to be two feet deep and live. They may have to travel until they reach some Indian village farther west and north."

"Such being the case, there can be no pressing need for me just at present, and I think I shall sleep. I feel now as if I were bound to relax."

"The best thing you could do, and I'll take a turn between the blankets myself."

Robert had a great sleep. Some of the rooms in the blockhouse offered a high degree of frontier comfort, and he lay down upon a soft couch of skins. A fine fire blazing upon a stone hearth dried his deerskin garments, and, when he awoke about noon, he was strong and thoroughly refreshed. The snow was still falling heavily. The wilderness in its white blanket was beautiful, but it did not look like a possible home to Robert now. His vivid imagination leaped up at once and pictured the difficulties of any one struggling for life, even in that vast white silence.

Willet and Tayoga were up before him, and they were talking of another expedition to see how far the besieging force had gone, but while they were discussing it a figure appeared at the edge of the forest.

"It's a white man," exclaimed Wilton, "and so it must be one of the Frenchmen. He's a bold fellow walking directly within our range. What on earth can he want?"

One of the guards on the palisade raised his rifle, but Willet promptly pushed down the muzzle.

"That's no Frenchman," he said.

"Then who is it?" asked Wilton.

"He's clothed in white, as any one walking in this snow is bound to be, but I could tell at the first glimpse that it was none other than our friend, Black Rifle."

"Coming to us for refuge, and so our fort is well named."

"Not for refuge. Black Rifle has taken care of himself too long in the wilderness to be at a loss at any time. I suspect that he has something of importance to tell us or he would not come at all."

At the command of Colden the great gate was thrown open that the strange rover might enter in all honor, and as he came in, apparently oblivious of the storm, his eyes gleamed a little at the sight of Willet, his friend.

"You've come to tell us something," said the hunter.

"So I have," said Black Rifle.

"Brush off the snow, warm yourself by the fire, and then we'll listen."

"I can tell it now. I don't mind the snow. I saw from a distance the great fire last night, when the camp of the French and Indians burned. It was clever to destroy their huts and lodges, and I knew at once who did it. Such a thing as that could not have happened without you having a hand in it, Dave Willet. I watched to see what the French and Indians would do, and I followed them in their hurried retreat into the north. I hid in the snowy bushes, and heard some of their talk, too. They will not stop until they reach a village a full hundred miles from here. The Frenchmen, De Courcelles and Jumonville are mad with anger and disappointment, and so is the Indian chief Tandakora."

"And well they may be!" jubilantly exclaimed Captain Colden, off whose mind a great weight seemed to have slid. "It was splendid tactics to burn their home over their heads. I wouldn't have thought of it myself, but since others have thought of it, and, it has succeeded so admirably, we can now do the work we were sent here to do."

Tayoga and Willet made snow-shoes and went out on them a few days later, confirming the report of Black Rifle. Then small parties were sent forth to search the forest for settlers and their families. Robert had a large share in this work, and sometimes he looked upon terrible things. In more than one place, torch and tomahawk had already done their dreadful work, but in others they found the people alive and well, still clinging to their homes. It was often difficult, even in the face of imminent danger, to persuade them to leave, and when they finally went, under mild compulsion, it was with the resolve to return to their log cabins in the spring.

Fort Refuge now deserved its name. There were many axes, with plenty of strong and skillful arms to wield them, and new buildings were erected within the palisade, the smoke rising from a half dozen chimneys. They were rude structures, but the people who occupied them, used all their lives to hardships, did not ask much, and they seemed snug and comfortable enough to them. Fires always blazed on the broad stone hearths and the voices of children were heard within the log walls. The hands of women furnished the rooms, and made new clothes of deerskin.

The note of life at Fort Refuge was comfort and good cheer. They felt that they could hold the little fortress against any force that might come. The hunters, Willet, Tayoga and Black Rifle at their head, brought in an abundance of game. There was no ill health. The little children grew mightily, and, thus thrown together in a group, they had the happiest time they had ever known. Robert was their hero. No other could tell such glorious tales. He had read fairy stories at Albany, and he not only brought them all from the store of his memory but he embroidered and enlarged them. He had a manner with him, too. His musical, golden voice, his vivid eyes and his intense earnestness of tone, the same that had impressed so greatly the fifty sachems in the vale of Onondaga, carried conviction. If one telling a tale believed in it so thoroughly himself then those who heard it must believe in it too.

Robert fulfilled a great mission. He was not the orator, the golden mouthed, for nothing. If the winter came down a little too fiercely, his vivid eyes and gay voice were sufficient to lift the depression.

Even the somber face of Black Rifle would light up when he came near. Nor was the young Quaker, Wilton, far behind him. He was a spontaneously happy youth, always bubbling with good nature, and he formed an able second for Lennox.

"Will," said Robert, "I believe it actually gives you joy to be here in this log fortress in the snow and wilderness. You do not miss the great capital, Philadelphia, to which you have been used all your life."

"No, I don't, Robert. I like Fort Refuge, because I'm free from restraints. It's the first time my true nature has had a chance to come out, and I'm making the most of the opportunity. Oh, I'm developing! In the spring you'll see me the gayest and most reckless blade that ever came into the forest."

The deep snow lasted a long time. More snowshoes were made, but only six or eight of the soldiers learned to use them well. There were sufficient, however, as Willet, Robert, Tayoga and Black Rifle were already adepts, and they ranged the forest far in all directions. They saw no further sign of French or Indians, but they steadily increased their supply of game.

Christmas came, January passed and then the big snow began to melt. New stirrings entered Robert's mind. He felt that their work at Fort Refuge was done. They had gathered into it all the outlying settlers who could be reached, and Colden, Wilton and Carson were now entirely competent to guard it and hold it. Robert felt that he and Willet should return to Albany, and get into the main current of the great war. Tayoga, of course, would go with them.

He talked it over with Willet and Tayoga, and they agreed with him at once. Black Rifle also decided to depart about the same time, and Colden, although grieved to see them go, could say nothing against it. When the four left they received an ovation that would have warmed the heart of any man. As they stood at the edge of the forest with their packs on their backs, Captain Colden gave a sharp command. Sixty rifles turned their muzzles upward, and sixty fingers pulled sixty triggers. Sixty weapons roared as one, and the four with dew in their eyes, lifted their caps to the splendid salute. Then a long, shrill cheer followed. Every child in the fort had been lifted above the palisade, and they sent the best wishes of their hearts with those who were going.

"That cheer of the little ones was mostly for you, Robert," said Willet, when the forest hid them.

"It was for all of us equally," said Robert modestly.

"No, I'm right and it must help us to have the good wishes of little children go with us. If they and Tododaho watch over us we can't come to much harm."

"It is a good omen," said Tayoga soberly. "When I lie down to sleep tonight I shall hear their voices in my ear."

Black Rifle now left them, going on one of his solitary expeditions into the wilderness and the others traveled diligently all the day, but owing to the condition of the earth did not make their usual progress. Most of the snow had melted and everything was dripping with water. It fell from every bough and twig, and in every ravine and gully a rivulet was running, while ponds stood in every depression. Many swollen brooks and creeks had to be forded, and when night came they were wet and soaked to the waist.

But Tayoga then achieved a great triumph. In the face of difficulties that seemed insuperable, he coaxed a fire in the lee of a hill, and the three fed it, until it threw out a great circle of heat in which they warmed and dried themselves. When they had eaten and rested a long time they put out the fire, waited for the coals and ashes to cool, and then spread over them their blankets, thus securing a dry base upon which to sleep. They were so thoroughly exhausted, and they were so sure that the forest contained no hostile presence that all three went to sleep at the same time and remained buried in slumber throughout the night.

Tayoga was the first to awake, and he saw the dawn of a new winter day, the earth reeking with cold damp and the thawing snow. He unrolled himself from his blankets and arose a little stiffly, but with a few movements of the limbs all his flexibility returned. The air was chill and the scene in the black forest of winter was desolate, but Tayoga was happy. Tododaho on his great shining star had watched over him and showered him with favors, and he had no doubt that he would remain under the protection of the mighty chief who had gone away so long ago.

Tayoga looked down at his comrades, who still slept soundly, and smiled. The three were bound together by powerful ties, and the events of recent months had made them stronger than ever. In the school at Albany he had absorbed much of the white man's education, and, while his Indian nature remained unchanged, he understood also the white point of view. He could meet both Robert and Willet on common ground, and theirs was a friendship that could not be severed.

Now he made a circle about their camp, and, being assured that no enemy was near, came back to the point where Robert and Willet yet slept. Then he took his flint and steel, and, withdrawing a little, kindled a fire, doing so as quietly as he could, in order that the two awaking might have a pleasant surprise. When the little flames were licking the wood, and the sparks began to fly upwards, he shook Robert by the shoulder.

"Arise, sluggard," he said. "Did not our teacher in Albany tell us it was proof of a lazy nature to sleep while the sun was rising? The fire even has grown impatient and has lighted itself while you abode with Tarenyawagon (the sender of dreams). Get up and cook our breakfast, Oh, Heavy Head!"

Robert sat up and so did Willet. Then Robert drew his blankets about his body and lay down again.

"You've done so well with the fire, Tayoga, and you've shown such a spirit," he said, "that it would be a pity to interfere with your activity. Go ahead, and awake me again when breakfast is ready."

Tayoga made a rush, seized the edge of his blanket and unrolled it, depositing Robert in the ashes. Then he darted away among the bushes, avoiding the white youth's pursuit. Willet meanwhile warmed himself by the fire and laughed.

"Come back, you two," he said. "You think you're little lads again at your school in Albany, but you're not. You're here in the wilderness, confronted by many difficulties, all of which you can overcome, and subject to many perils, all of which you know how to avoid."

"I'll come," said Robert, "if you promise to protect me from this fierce Onondaga chief who is trying to secure my scalp."

"Tayoga, return to the fire and cook these strips of venison. Here is the sharp stick left from last night. Robert, take our canteens, find a spring and fill them with fresh water. By right of seniority I'm in command this morning, and I intend to subject my army to extremely severe discipline, because it's good for it. Obey at once!"

Tayoga obediently took the sharpened stick and began to fry strips of venison. Robert, the canteens over his shoulder, found a spring near by and refilled them. Like Tayoga, the raw chill of the morning and the desolate forest of winter had no effect upon him. He too, was happy, uplifted, and he sang to himself the song he had heard De Galissonnière sing:

"Hier sur le pont d'Avignon
J'ai oui chanter la belle,
    Lon, la,
J'ai oui chanter la belle,
Elle chantait d'un ton si doux
    Comme une demoiselle,
    Lon, la,
Comme une demoiselle."

All that seemed far away now, yet the words of the song brought it back, and his extraordinary imagination made the scenes at Bigot's ball pass before his eyes again, almost as vivid as reality. Once more he saw the Intendant, his portly figure swaying in the dance, his red face beaming, and once more he beheld the fiery duel in the garden when the hunter dealt with Boucher, the bully and bravo.

Quebec was far away. He had been glad to go to it, and he had been glad to come away, too. He would be glad to go to it again, and he felt that he would do so some day, though the torrent of battle now rolled between. He was still humming the air when he came back to the fire, and saluting Willet politely, tendered a canteen each to him and Tayoga.

"Sir David Willet, baronet and general," he said, "I have the honor to report to you that in accordance with your command I have found the water, spring water, fine, fresh, pure, as good as any the northern wilderness can furnish, and that is the best in the world. Shall I tender it to you, sir, on my bended knee!"

"No, Mr. Lennox, we can dispense with the bended knee, but I am glad, young sir, to note in your voice the tone of deep respect for your elders which sometimes and sadly is lacking."

"If Dagaeoga works well, and always does as he is bidden," said Tayoga, "perhaps I'll let him look on at the ceremonies when I take my place as one of the fifteen sachems of the Onondaga nation."

While they ate their venison and some bread they had also brought with them, they discussed the next stage of their journey, and Tayoga made a suggestion. Traveling would remain difficult for several days, and instead of going directly to Albany, their original purpose, they might take a canoe, and visit Mount Johnson, the seat of Colonel William Johnson, who was such a power with the Hodenosaunee, and who was in his person a center of important affairs in North America. For a while, Mount Johnson might, in truth, suit their purpose better than Albany.

The idea appealed at once to both Robert and Willet. Colonel Johnson, more than any one else could tell them what to do, and owing to his strong alliance, marital and otherwise, with the Mohawks, they were likely to find chiefs of the Ganeagaono at his house or in the neighborhood.

"It is agreed," said Willet, after a brief discussion. "If my calculations be correct we can reach Mount Johnson in four days, and I don't think we're likely to cross the trail of an enemy, unless St. Luc is making some daring expedition."

"In any event, he's a nobler foe than De Courcelles or Jumonville," said Robert.

"I grant you that, readily," said the hunter. "Still, I don't think we're likely to encounter him on our way to Mount Johnson."

But on the second day they did cross a trail which they attributed to a hostile force. It contained, however, no white footsteps, and not pausing to investigate, they continued their course toward their destination. As all the snow was now gone, and the earth was drying fast, they were able almost to double their speed and they pressed forward, eager to see the celebrated Colonel William Johnson, who was now filling and who was destined to fill for so long a time so large a place in the affairs of North America.

CHAPTER VIII
WARAIYAGEH

Now, a few pleasant days of winter came. The ground dried under comparatively warm winds, and the forest awoke. They heard everywhere the ripple of running water, and wild animals came out of their dens. Tayoga shot a young bear which made a welcome addition to their supplies.

"I hold that there's nothing better in the woods than young bear," said Willet, as he ate a juicy steak Robert had broiled over the coals. "Venison is mighty good, especially so when you're hungry, but you can get tired of it. What say you, Tayoga?"

"It is true," replied the Onondaga. "Fat young bear is very fine. None of us wants one thing all the time, and we want something besides meat, too. The nations of the Hodenosaunee are great and civilized, much ahead of the other red people, because they plant gardens and orchards and fields, and have grain and vegetables, corn, beans, squash and many other things good for the table."

"And the Iroquois, while they grow more particular about the table, remain the most valiant of all the forest people. I see your point, Tayoga. Civilization doesn't take anything from a man's courage and tenacity. Rather it adds to them. There are our enemies, the French, who are as brave and enduring as anybody, and yet they're the best cooks in the world, and more particular about their food than any other nation."

"You always speak of the French with a kind of affection, Dave," said Robert.

"I suppose I do," said the hunter. "I have reasons."

"As I know now, Dave, you've been in Paris, can't you tell us something about the city?"

"It's the finest town in the world, Robert, and they've the brightest, gayest life there, at least a part of 'em have, but things are not going right at home with the French. They say a whole nation's fortune has been sunk in the palace at Versailles, and the people are growing poorer all the time, but the government hopes to dazzle 'em by waging a successful and brilliant war over here. I repeat, though, Robert, that I like the French. A great nation, sound at the core, splendid soldiers as we're seeing, and as we're likely to see for a long time to come."

They pushed on with all speed toward Mount Johnson, the weather still favoring them, making their last camp in a fine oak grove, and reckoning that they would achieve their journey's end before noon the next day. They did not build any fire that night, but when they rose at dawn they saw the smoke of somebody else's fire on the eastern horizon.

"It couldn't be the enemy," said Willet. "He wouldn't let his smoke go up here for all the world to see, so near to the home of Colonel William Johnson and within the range of the Mohawks."

"That is so," said Tayoga. "It is likely to be some force of Colonel Johnson himself, and we can advance with certainty."

Looking well to their arms in the possible contingency of a foe, they pushed forward through the woodland, the smoke growing meanwhile as if those who had built the fire either felt sure of friendly territory, or were ready to challenge the world. The Onondaga presently held up a hand and the three stopped.

"What is it, Tayoga?" asked the hunter.

"I wish to sing a song."

"Then sing it, Tayoga."

A bird suddenly gave forth a long, musical, thrilling note. It rose in a series of trills, singularly penetrating, and died away in a haunting echo. A few moments of silence and then from a point in the forest in front of them another bird sang a like song.

"They are friends," said Tayoga, who was the first bird, "and it may be, since we are within the range of the Mohawks, that it is our friend, the great young chief Daganoweda, who replied. I do not think any one else could sing a song so like my own."

"I'm wagering that it's Daganoweda and nobody else," said Willet confidently, and scorning cover now they advanced at increased speed toward the fire.

A splendid figure, tall, heroic, the nose lofty and beaked like that of an ancient Roman, the feather headdress brilliant and defiant like that of Tayoga, came forward to meet them, and Robert saw with intense pleasure that it was none other than Daganoweda himself. Nor was the delight of the young Mohawk chieftain any less—the taciturnity and blank faces of Indians disappeared among their friends—and he came forward, smiling and uttering words of welcome.

"Daganoweda," said Willet, "the sight of you is balm to the eyes. Your name means in our language, 'The Inexhaustible' and you're an inexhaustible friend. You're always appearing when we need you most, and that's the very finest kind of a friend."

"Great Bear, Tayoga and Dagaeoga come out of the great wilderness," said Daganoweda, smiling.

"So we do, Daganoweda. We've been there a long time, but we were not so idle."

"I have heard of the fort that was built in the forest and how the young white soldiers with the help of Great Bear, Tayoga and Dagaeoga beat off the French and the savage tribes."

"I supposed that runners of the Hodenosaunee would keep you informed. Well, the fort is there and our people still hold it, and we are here, anxious to get back into the main stream of big events. Who are at the fire, Daganoweda?"

"Waraiyageh (Colonel William Johnson) himself is there. He was fishing yesterday, it being an idle time for a few days, and with ten of my warriors I joined him last night. He will be glad to see you, Great Bear, whom he knows. And he will be glad to meet Tayoga and Dagaeoga who are to bear great names."

"Easy, Daganoweda, easy!" laughed Willet.

"These are fine lads, but don't flatter 'em too much just yet. They've done brave deeds, but before this war is over they'll have to do a lot more. We'll go with you and meet Colonel Johnson."

As they walked toward the fire a tall, strongly built man, of middle years, dressed in the uniform of an English officer, came forward to meet them. His face, with a distinct Irish cast, was frank, open and resolute.

"Ah, Willet, my friend," he said, extending his hand. "So you and I meet again, and glad I am to hold your fingers in mine once more. A faithful report has come to us of what you did in Quebec, and it seems the Willet of old has not changed much."

The hunter reddened under his tan.

"It was forced upon me, colonel," he said.

Colonel William Johnson laughed heartily.

"And he who forced it did not live to regret it," he said. "I've heard that French officers themselves did not blame you, but as for me, knowing you as I do, I'd have expected no less of David Willet."

He laughed again, and his laugh was deep and hearty. Robert, looking closely at him, thought him a fine, strong man, and he was quite sure he would like him. The colonel glanced at him and Tayoga, and the hunter said:

"Colonel Johnson, I wish to present Tayoga, who is of the most ancient blood of the Onondagas, a member of the Clan of the Bear, and destined to be a great chief. A most valiant and noble youth, too, I assure you, and the white lad is Robert Lennox, to whom I stand in the place of a father."

"I have heard of Tayoga," said Colonel Johnson, "and his people and mine are friends."

"It is true," said Tayoga, "Waraiyageh has been the best friend among the white people that the nations of the Hodenosaunee have ever had. He has never tricked us. He has never lied to us, and often he has incurred great hardship and danger to help us."

"It is pleasant in my ears to hear you say so, Tayoga," said Colonel Johnson, "and as for Mr. Lennox, who, my eyes tell me is also a noble and gallant youth, it seems to me I've heard some report of him too. You carried the private letters from the Governor of New York to the Marquis Duquesne, Governor General of Canada?"

"I did, sir," replied Robert.

"And of course you were there with Willet. Your mission, I believe, was kept as secret as possible, but I learned at Albany that you bore yourself well, and that you also gave an exhibition with the sword."

It was Robert's turn to flush.

"I'm a poor swordsman, sir," he said, "by the side of Mr. Willet."

"Good enough though, for the occasion. But come, I'll make an end to badinage. You must be on your way to Mount Johnson."

"That was our destination," said Willet.

"Then right welcome guests you'll be. I have a little camp but a short distance away. Molly is there, and so is that young eagle, her brother, Joseph Brant. Molly will see that you're well served with food, and after that you shall stay at Mount Johnson as long as you like, and the longer you'll stay the better it will please Molly and me. You shall tell us of your adventures, Mr. Lennox, and about that Quebec in which you and Mr. Willet seem to have cut so wide a swath with your rapiers."

"We did but meet the difficulties that were forced upon us," protested Willet.

Colonel Johnson laughed once more, and most heartily.

"If all people met in like fashion the difficulties that were forced upon them," he said, "it would be a wondrous efficient world, so much superior to the world that now is that one would never dream they had been the same. But just beyond the hill is our little camp which, for want of a better name, I'll call a bower. Here is Joseph, now, coming to meet us."

An Indian lad of about eleven years, but large and uncommonly strong for his age, was walking down the hill toward them. He was dressed partly in civilized clothing, and his manner was such that he would have drawn the notice of the observing anywhere. His face was open and strong, with great width between the eyes, and his gaze was direct and firm. Robert knew at once that here was an unusual boy, one destined if he lived to do great things. His prevision was more than fulfilled. It was Joseph Brant, the renowned Thayendanegea, the most famous and probably the ablest Indian chief with whom the white men ever came into contact.

"This is Joseph Brant, the brother of Molly, my wife, and hence my young brother-in-law," said Colonel Johnson. "Joseph, our new friends are David Willet, known to the Hodenosaunee as the Great Bear, Robert Lennox, who seems to be in some sort a ward of Mr. Willet, and Tayoga, of the Clan of the Bear, of your great brother nation, Onondaga."

Young Thayendanegea saluted them all in a friendly but dignified way. He, like Tayoga, had a white education, and spoke perfect, but measured English.

"We welcome you," he said. "Colonel Johnson, sir, my sister has already seen the strangers from the hill, and is anxious to greet them."

"Molly, for all her dignity, has her fair share of curiosity," laughed Colonel Johnson, "and since it's our duty to gratify it, we'll go forward."

Robert had heard often of Molly Brant, the famous Mohawk wife of Colonel, afterward Sir William Johnson, a great figure in that region in her time, and he was eager to see her. He beheld a woman, young, tall, a face decidedly Iroquois, but handsome and lofty. She wore the dress of the white people, and it was of fine material. She obviously had some of the distinguished character that had already set its seal upon her young brother, then known as Keghneghtada, his famous name of Thayendanegea to come later. Her husband presented the three, and she received them in turn in a manner that was quiet and dignified, although Robert could see her examining them with swift Indian eyes that missed nothing. And with his knowledge of both white heart and red heart, of white manner and red manner, he was aware that he stood in the presence of a great lady, a great lady who fitted into her setting of the vast New York wilderness. So, with the ornate manner of the day, he bent over and kissed her hand as he was presented.

"Madam," he said, "it is a great pleasure to us to meet Colonel Johnson here in the forest, but we have the unexpected and still greater pleasure of meeting his lady also."

Colonel Johnson laughed, and patted Robert on the shoulder.

"Mr. Willet has been whispering to me something about you," he said. "He has been telling me of your gift of speech, and by my faith, he has not told all of it. You do address the ladies in a most graceful fashion, and Molly likes it. I can see that."

"Assuredly I do, sir," said she who had been Molly Brant, the Mohawk, but who was now the wife of the greatest man in the north country. "Tis a goodly youth and he speaks well. I like him, and he shall have the best our house can offer."

Colonel Johnson's mellow laugh rang out again.

"Spoken like a woman of spirit, Molly," he said. "I expected none the less of you. It's in the blood of the Ganeagaono and had you answered otherwise you would have been unworthy of your cousin, Daganoweda, here."

The young Mohawk chieftain smiled. Johnson, who had married a girl of their race, could jest with the Mohawks almost as he pleased, and among themselves and among those whom they trusted the Indians were fond of joking and laughter.

"The wife of Waraiyageh not only has a great chief for a husband," he said, "but she is a great chief herself. Among the Wyandots she would be one of the rulers."

The women were the governing power in the valiant Wyandot nation, and
Daganoweda could pay his cousin no higher compliment.

"We talk much," said Colonel Johnson, "but we must remember that our friends are tired. They've come afar in bad weather. We must let them rest now and give them refreshment."

He led the way to the light summer house that he had called a bower. It was built of poles and thatch, and was open on the eastern side, where it faced a fine creek running with a strong current. A fire was burning in one corner, and a heavy curtain of tanned skins could be draped over the wide doorway. Articles of women's apparel hung on the walls, and others indicating woman's work stood about. There were also chairs of wicker, and a lounge covered with haircloth. It was a comfortable place, the most attractive that Robert had seen in a long time, and his eyes responded to it with a glitter that Colonel Johnson noticed.

"I don't wonder that you like it, lad," he said. "I've spent some happy hours here myself, when I came in weary or worn from hunting or fishing. But sit you down, all three of you. I'll warrant me that you're weary enough, tramping through this wintry forest. Blunt, shove the faggots closer together and make up a better fire."

The command was to a white servant who obeyed promptly, but Madame Johnson herself had already shifted the chairs for the guests, and had taken their deerskin cloaks. Without ceasing to be the great lady she moved, nevertheless, with a lightness of foot and a celerity that was all a daughter of the forest. Robert watched her with fascinated eyes as she put the summer house in order and made it ready for the comfort of her guests. Here was one who had acquired civilization without losing the spirit of the wild. She was an educated and well bred woman, the wife of the most powerful man in the colonies, and she was at the same time a true Mohawk. Robert knew as he looked at her that if left alone in the wilderness she could take care of herself almost as well as her cousin, Daganoweda, the young chief.

Then his gaze shifted from Molly Brant to her brother. Despite his youth all his actions showed pride and unlimited confidence in himself. He stood near the door, and addressed Robert in English, asking him questions about himself, and he also spoke to Tayoga, showing him the greatest friendliness.

"We be of the mighty brother nations, Onondaga and Mohawk, the first of the great League," he said, "and some day we will sit together in the councils of the fifty sachems in the vale of Onondaga."

"It is so," said Tayoga gravely, speaking to the young lad as man to man. "We will ever serve the Hodenosaunee as our fathers before us have done."

"Leave the subject of the Hodenosaunee," said Colonel Johnson cheerily. "I know that you lads are prouder of your birth than the old Roman patricians ever were, but Mr. Willet, Mr. Lennox and I were not fortunate enough to be born into the great League, and you will perhaps arouse our jealousy or envy. Come, gentlemen, sit you down and eat and drink."

His Mohawk wife seconded the request and food and drink were served. Robert saw that the bower was divided into two rooms the one beyond them evidently being a sleeping chamber, but the evidences of comfort, even luxury, were numerous, making the place an oasis in the wilderness. Colonel Johnson had wine, which Robert did not touch, nor did Tayoga nor Daganoweda, and there were dishes of china or silver brought from England. He noticed also, and it was an unusual sight in a lodge in the forest, about twenty books upon two shelves. From his chair he read the titles, Le Brun's "Battles of Alexander," a bound volume of *The Gentleman's Magazine*, "Roderick Random," and several others. Colonel Johnson's eyes followed him.

"I see that you are a reader," he said. "I know it because your eyes linger upon my books. I have packages brought from time to time from England, and, before I came upon this expedition, I had these sent ahead of me to the bower that I might dip into them in the evenings if I felt so inclined. Reading gives us a wider horizon, and, at the same time, takes us away from the day's troubles."

"I agree with you heartily, sir," said Robert, "but, unfortunately, we have little time for reading now."

"That is true," sighed Colonel Johnson. "I fear it's going to be a long and terrible war. What do you see, Joseph?"

Young Brant was sitting with his face to the door, and he had risen suddenly.

"A runner comes," he replied. "He is in the forest beyond the creek, but I see that he is one of our own people. He comes fast."

Colonel Johnson also arose.

"Can it be some trouble among the Ganeagaono?" he said.

"I think not," said the Indian boy.

The runner emerged from the wood, crossed the creek and stood in the doorway of the bower. He was a tall, thin young Mohawk, and he panted as if he had come fast and long.

"What is it, Oagowa?" asked Colonel Johnson.

"A hostile band, Hurons, Abenakis, Caughnawagas, and others, has entered the territory of the Ganeagaono on the west," replied the warrior. "They are led by an Ojibway chief, a giant, called Tandakora."

Robert uttered an exclamation.

"The name of the Ojibway attracts your attention," said Colonel Johnson.

"We've had many encounters with him," replied the youth. "Besides hating the Hodenosaunee and all the white people, I think he also has a personal grievance against Mr. Willet, Tayoga and myself. He is the most bitter and persistent of all our enemies."

"Then this man must be dealt with. I can't go against him myself. Other affairs press too much, but I can raise a force with speed."

"Let me go, sir, against Tandakora!" exclaimed young Brant eagerly and in English.

Colonel Johnson looked at him a moment, his eyes glistening, and then he laughed, not with irony but gently and with approval.

"Truly 'tis a young eagle," he said, "but, Joseph, you must remember that your years are yet short of twelve, and you still have much time to spend over the books in which you have done so well. If I let you be cut off at such an early age you can never become the great chief you are destined to be. Bide a while, Joseph, and your cousin, Daganoweda, will attend to this Ojibway who has wandered so far from his own country."

Young Brant made no protest. Trained in the wonderful discipline of the Hodenosaunee he knew that he must obey before he could command. He resumed his seat quietly, but his eager eyes watched his tall cousin, the young Mohawk chieftain, as Colonel Johnson gave him orders.

"Take with you the warriors that you have now, Daganoweda," he said. "Gather the fifty who are now encamped at Teugega. Take thirty more from Talaquega, and I think that will be enough. I don't know you, Daganoweda, and I don't know your valiant Mohawk warriors, if you are not able to account thoroughly for the Ojibway and his men. Don't come back until you've destroyed them or driven them out of your country."

Colonel Johnson's tone was at once urgent and complimentary. It intimated that the work was important and that Daganoweda would be sure to do it. The Mohawk's eyes glittered in his dark face. He lifted his hand in a salute, glided from the bower, and a moment later he and his warriors passed from sight in the forest.

"That cousin of yours, Molly, deserves his rank of chief," said Colonel Johnson. "The task that he is to do I consider as good as done already. Tandakora was too daring, when he ventured into the lands of the Ganeagaono. Now, if you gentlemen will be so good as to be our guests we'll pass the night here, and tomorrow we'll go to Mount Johnson."

It was agreeable to Robert, Willet and Tayoga, and they spent the remainder of the day most pleasantly at the bower. Colonel Johnson, feeling that they were three whom he could trust, talked freely and unveiled a mind fitted for great affairs.

"I tell you three," he said, "that this will be one of the most important wars the world has known. To London and Paris we seem lost in the woods out here, and perhaps at the courts they think little of us or they do not think at all, but the time must come when the New World will react upon the Old. Consider what a country it is, with its lakes, its forests, its rivers, and its fertile lands, which extend beyond the reckoning of man. The day will arrive when there will be a power here greater than either England or France. Such a land cannot help but nourish it."

He seemed to be much moved, and spoke a long time in the same vein, but his Indian wife never said a word. She moved about now and then, and, as before, her footsteps making no noise, being as light as those of any animal of the forest.

The dusk came up to the door. They heard the ripple of the creek, but could not see its waters. Madam Johnson lighted a wax candle, and Colonel Johnson stopped suddenly.

"I have talked too much. I weary you," he said.

"Oh, no, sir!" protested Robert eagerly. "Go on! We would gladly listen to you all night."

"That I think would be too great a weight upon us all," laughed Colonel Johnson. "You are weary. You must be so from your long marching and my heavy disquisitions. We'll have beds made for you three and Joseph here. Molly and I sleep in the next room."

Robert was glad to have soft furs and a floor beneath him, and when he lay down it was with a feeling of intense satisfaction. He liked Colonel William Johnson, and knew that he had a friend in him. He was anxious for advancement in the great world, and he understood what it was to have powerful support. Already he stood high with the Hodenosaunee, and now he had found favor with the famous Waraiyageh.

They left in the morning for Mount Johnson, and there were horses for all except the Indians, although one was offered to Tayoga. But he declined to ride—the nations of the Hodenosaunee were not horsemen, and kept pace with them at the long easy gait used by the Indian runner. Robert himself was not used to the saddle, but he was glad enough to accept it, after their great march through the wilderness.

The weather continued fine for winter, crisp, clear, sparkling with life and the spirits of all were high. Colonel Johnson beckoned to Robert to ride by the side of him and the two led the way. Kegneghtada, despite his extreme youth, had refused a horse also, and was swinging along by the side of Tayoga, stride for stride. A perfect understanding and friendship had already been established between the Onondaga and the Mohawk, and as they walked they talked together earnestly, young Brant bearing himself as if he were on an equal footing with his brother warrior, Tayoga. Colonel Johnson looked at them, smiled approval and said to Robert:

"I have called my young brother-in-law an eagle, and an eagle he truly is. We're apt to think, Mr. Lennox, that we white people alone gather our forces and prepare for some aim distant but great. But the Indian intellect is often keen and powerful, as I have had good cause to know. Many of their chiefs have an acuteness and penetration not surpassed in the councils of white men. The great Mohawk whom we call King Hendrick probably has more intellect than most of the sovereigns on their thrones in Europe. And as for Joseph, the lad there who so gallantly keeps step with the Onondaga, where will you find a white boy who can excel him? He absorbs the learning of our schools as fast as any boy of our race whom I have ever known, and, at the same time, he retains and improves all the lore and craft of the red people."

"You have found the Mohawks a brave and loyal race," said Robert, knowing the colonel was upon a favorite theme of his.

"That I have, Mr. Lennox. I came among them a boy. I was a trader then, and I settled first only a few miles from their largest town, Dyiondarogon. I tried to keep faith with them and as a result I found them always keeping faith with me. Then, when I went to Oghkwaga, I had the same experience. The Indians were defrauded in the fur trade by white swindlers, but dishonesty, besides being bad in itself, does not pay, Mr. Lennox. Bear that in mind. You may cheat for a while with success, but in time nobody will do business with you. Though you, I take it, will never be a merchant."

"It is not because I frown upon the merchant's calling, sir. I esteem it a high and noble one. But my mind does not turn to it."

"So I gather from what I have seen of you, and from what Mr. Willet tells me. I've been hearing of your gift of oratory. You need not blush, my lad. If we have a gift we should accept it thankfully, and make the best use of it we can. You, I take it, will be a lawyer, then a public man, and you will sway the public mind. There should be grand occasions for such as you in a country like this, with its unlimited future."

They came presently into a region of cultivation, fields which would be green with grain in the spring, showing here and there, and the smoke from the chimney of a stout log house rising now and then. Where a creek broke into a swift white fall stood a grist mill, and from a wood the sound of axes was heard.

Robert's vivid imagination, which responded to all changes, kindled at once. He liked the wilderness, and it always made a great impression upon him, and he also took the keenest interest and delight in everything that civilization could offer. Now his spirit leaped up to meet what lay before him.

He found at Mount Johnson comfort and luxury that he had not expected, an abundance of all that the wilderness furnished, mingled with importations from Europe. He slept in a fine bed, he looked into more books, he saw on the walls reproductions of Titian and Watteau, and also pictures of race horses that had made themselves famous at Newmarket, he wrote letters to Albany on good paper, he could seal them with either black or red wax, and there were musical instruments upon one or two of which he could play.

Robert found all these things congenial. The luxury or what might have seemed luxury on the border, had in it nothing of decadence. There was an air of vigor, and Colonel Johnson, although he did not neglect his guests, plunged at once and deeply into business. A little village, dependent upon him and his affairs had grown up about him, and there were white men more or less in his service, some of whom he sent at once on missions for the war. Through it all his Indian wife glided quietly, but Robert saw that she was a wonderful help, managing with ease, and smoothing away many a difficulty.

Despite the restraint of manner, the people at Mount Johnson were full of excitement. The news from Canada and also from the west became steadily more ominous. The French power was growing fast and the warriors of the wild tribes were crowding in thousands to the Bourbon banner. Robert heard again of St. Luc and of some daring achievement of his, and despite himself he felt as always a thrill at the name, and a runner also brought the news that more French troops had gone into the Ohio country.

The fourth night of their stay at Mount Johnson Robert remained awake late. He and young Brant, the great Thayendanegea that was to be, had already formed a great friendship, the beginning of which was made easier by Robert's knowledge of Indian nature and sympathy with it. The two wrapped in fur cloaks had gone a little distance from the house, because Brant said that a bear driven by hunger had come to the edge of the village, and they were looking for its tracks. But Robert was more interested in observing the Indian boy than in finding the foot prints of the bear.

"Joseph," he said, "you expect, of course, to be a great warrior and chief some day."

The boy's eyes glittered.

"There is nothing else for which I would care," he replied. "Hark, Dagaeoga, did you hear the cry of a night bird?"

"I did, Joseph, but like you I don't think it's the voice of a real bird. It's a signal."

"So it is, and unless I reckon ill it's the signal of my cousin Daganoweda, returning from the great war trail that he has trod against the wild Ojibway, Tandakora."

The song of a bird trilled from his own throat in reply, and then from the forest came Daganoweda and his warriors in a dusky file. Robert and young Brant fell in with them and walked toward the house. Not a word was spoken, but the eyes of the Mohawk chieftain were gleaming, and his bearing expressed the very concentrated essence of haughty pride. At the house they stopped, and, young Brant going in, brought forth Colonel Johnson.

"Well, Daganoweda," said the white man.

"I met Tandakora two days' journey north of Mount Johnson," replied the Mohawk. "His numbers were equal to our own, but his warriors were not the warriors of the Hodenosaunee. Six of the Ganeagaono are gone, Waraiyageh, and sixteen more have wounds, from which they will recover, but when Tandakora began his flight toward Canada eighteen of his men lay dead, eight more fell in the pursuit, which was so fast that we bring back with us forty muskets and rifles."

"Well done, Daganoweda," said Colonel Johnson. "You have proved yourself anew a great warrior and chief, but you did not have to prove it to me. I knew it long ago. Fine new rifles, and blankets of blue or red or green have just come from Albany, half of which shall be distributed among your men in the morning."

"Waraiyageh never forgets his friends," said the appreciative Mohawk.

He withdrew with his warriors, knowing that the promise would be kept.

"Why was I not allowed to go with them?" mourned young Brant.

Colonel Johnson laughed and patted his shiny black head.

"Never mind, young fire-eater," he said. "We'll all of us soon have our fill of war—and more."

Robert was present at the distribution of rifles and blankets the next morning, and he knew that Colonel Johnson had bound the Mohawks to him and the English and American cause with another tie. Daganoweda and his warriors, gratified beyond expression, took the war path again.

"They'll remain a barrier between us and the French and their allies," said Colonel Johnson, "and faith we'll need 'em. The other nations of the Hodenosaunee wish to keep out of the war, but the Mohawks will be with us to the last. Their great chief, King Hendrick, is our devoted friend, and so is his brother, Abraham. This, too, in spite of the bad treatment of the Ganeagaono by the Dutch at Albany. O, I have nothing to say against the Dutch, a brave and tenacious people, but they have their faults, like other races, and sometimes they let avarice overcome them! I wish they could understand the nations of the Hodenosaunee better. Do what you can at Albany, Mr. Lennox, with that facile tongue of yours, to persuade the Dutch—and the others too—that the danger from the French and Indians is great, and that we must keep the friendship of the Six Nations."

"I will do my best, sir," promised Robert modestly. "I at least ought to know the power and loyalty of the Hodenosaunee, since I have been adopted into the great League and Tayoga, an Onondaga, is my brother, in all but blood."

"And I stand in the same position," said Willet firmly. "We understand, sir, your great attachment for the Six Nations, and the vast service you have done for the English among them. If we can supplement it even in some small degree we shall spare no effort to do so."

"I know it, Mr. Willet, and yet my heart is heavy to see the land I love devastated by fire and sword."

Colonel Johnson loaned them horses, and an escort of two of his own soldiers who would bring back the horses, and they started for Albany amid many hospitable farewells.

"You and I shall meet again," said young Brant to Robert.

"I hope so," said Robert.

"It will be as allies and comrades on the battle field."

"But you are too young, Joseph, yet to take part in war."

"I shall not be next year, and the war will not be over then, so my brother, Colonel William Johnson says, and he knows."

Robert looked at the sturdy young figure and the eager eyes, and he knew that the Indian lad would not be denied.

Then the little party rode into the woods, and proceeded without event to Albany.

CHAPTER IX
THE WATCHER

It was with emotion that Robert came to Albany, an emotion that was shared by his Onondaga comrade, Tayoga, who had spent a long time in a white school there. The staid Dutch town was the great outpost of the Province of New York in the wilderness, and although his temperament was unlike that of the Dutch burghers he had innumerable pleasant memories of it, and many friends there. It was, in his esteem, too, a fine town, on its hills over-looking that noble river, the Hudson, and as the little group rode on he noted that despite the war its appearance was still peaceful and safe.

Their way led along the main street which was broad and with grass on either side. The solid Dutch houses, with their gable ends to the street, stood every one on its own lawn, with a garden behind it. Every house also had a portico in front of it, on which the people sat in summer evenings, or where they visited with one another. Except that it was hills where the old country was flat, it was much like Holland, and the people, keen and thrifty, had preserved their national customs even unto the third and fourth generations. Robert understood them as he understood the Hodenosaunce, and, with his adaptable temperament, and with his mind that could understand so readily the minds of others, he was able to meet them on common ground. As they rode into the city he looked questioningly at Willet, and the hunter, understanding the voiceless query, smiled.

"We couldn't think of going to any other place," he said. "If we did we could never secure his forgiveness."

"I shall be more than glad to see him. A right good friend of ours, isn't he, Tayoga?"

"Though his tongue lashes us his heart is with us," replied the Onondaga. "He is a great white chief, three hundred pounds of greatness."

They stopped before one of the largest of the brick houses, standing on one of the widest and neatest of the lawns, and Robert and Tayoga, entering the portico, knocked upon the door with a heavy brass knocker. They heard presently the rattle of chains inside, and the rumble of a deep, grumbling voice. Then the two lads looked at each other and laughed, laughed in the careless, joyous way in which youth alone can laugh.

"It is he, Mynheer Jacobus himself, come to let us in," said Robert.

"And he has not changed at all," said Tayoga. "We can tell that by the character of his voice on the other side of the door."

"And I would not have him changed."

"Nor would I."

The door was thrown open, but as all the windows were closed there was yet gloom inside. Presently something large, red and shining emerged from the dusk and two beams of light in the center of the redness played upon them. Then the outlines of a gigantic human figure, a man tall and immensely stout, were disclosed. He wore a black suit with knee breeches, thick stockings and buckled shoes, and his powdered hair was tied in a queue. His eyes, dazzled at first by the light from without, began to twinkle as he looked. Then a great blaze of joy swept over his face, and he held out two fat hands, one to the white youth and one to the red.

"Ah, it iss you, Robert, you scapegrace, and it iss you, Tayoga, you wild Onondaga! It iss a glad day for me that you haf come, but I thought you both dead, und well you might be, reckless, thoughtless lads who haf not the thought uf the future in your minds."

Robert shook the fat hand in both of his and laughed.

"You are the same as of old, Mynheer Jacobus," he said, "and before Tayoga and I saw you, but while we heard you, we agreed that there had been no change, and that we did not want any."

"And why should I change, you two young rascals? Am I not goot enough as I am? Haf I not in the past given the punishment to both uf you und am I not able to do it again, tall and strong as the two uf you haf grown? Ah, such foolish lads! Perhaps you haf been spared because pity wass taken on your foolishness. But iss it Mynheer Willet beyond you? That iss a man of sense."

"It's none other than Dave, Mynheer Jacobus," said Robert.

"Then why doesn't he come in?" exclaimed Mynheer Jacobus Huysman. "He iss welcome here, doubly, triply welcome, und he knows it."

"Dave! Dave! Hurry!" called Robert, "or Mynheer Jacobus will chastise you. He's so anxious to fall on your neck and welcome you that he can't wait!"

Willet came swiftly up the brick walk, and the hands of the two big men met in a warm clasp.

"You see I've brought the boys back to you again, Jacob," said the hunter.

"But what reckless lads they've become," grumbled Mynheer Huysman. "I can see the mischief in their eyes now. They wass bad enough when they went to school here und lived with me, but since they've run wild in the forests this house iss not able to hold them."

"Don't you worry, Jacob, old friend. These arms and shoulders of mine are still strong, and if they make you trouble I will deal with them. But we just stopped a minute to inquire into the state of your health. Can you tell us which is now the best inn in Albany?"

The face of Mynheer Jacobus Huysman flamed, and his eyes blazed in the center of it, two great red lights.

"Inn! Inn!" he roared in his queer mixture of English, Dutch and German accent "Iss it that your head hass been struck by lightning und you haf gone crazy? If there wass a thousand inns at Albany you und Robert und Tayoga could not stop at one uf them. Iss not the house uf Jacobus Huysman good enough for you?"

Robert, Tayoga and the hunter laughed aloud.

"He did but make game of you, Mynheer Jacobus," said Robert. "We will alter your statement and say if there were a thousand inns in Albany you could not make us stay at any one of them. Despite your commands we would come directly to your house."

Mynheer Jacobus Huysman permitted himself to smile. But his voice renewed its grumbling tone.

"Ever the same," he said. "You must stay here, although only the good Lord himself knows in what condition my house will be when you leave. You are two wild lads. It iss not so strange uf you, Robert Lennox, who are white, but I would expect better uf Tayoga, who is to be a great Onondaga chief some day."

"You make a great mistake, Mynheer Jacobus," said Robert. "Tayoga is far worse than I am. All the mischief that I have ever done was due to his example and persuasion. It is my misfortune that I have a weak nature, and I am easily led into evil by my associates."

"It iss not so. You are equally bad. Bring in your baggage und I will see if Caterina, der cook, cannot find enough for you three, who always eat like raging lions."

The soldiers, who were to return immediately to Colonel William Johnson, rode away with their horses, and Robert, Tayoga and Willet took their packs into the house of Mynheer Huysman, who grumbled incessantly while he and a manservant and a maidservant made them as comfortable as possible.

"Would you und Tayoga like to haf your old room on the second floor?" he said to Robert.

"Nothing would please us better," replied the lad.

"Then you shall haf it," said Mynheer, as he led the way up the stair and into the room. "Do you remember, Tayoga, how wild you wass when you came here to learn the good ways und bad ways uf the white people?"

"I do," replied Tayoga, "and the walls and the roof felt oppressive to me, although we have stout log houses of our own in our villages. But they were not our own walls and our own roof, and there was the great young warrior, Lennox, whom we now call Dagaeoga, who was to stay in the same room and even in the same bed with me. Do you wonder that I felt like climbing out of a window at night, and escaping into the woods?"

"You were eleven then," said Robert, "and I was just a shade younger. You were as strange to me as I was to you, and I thought, in truth, that you were going to run away into the wilderness. But you didn't, and you began to learn from books faster than I thought was possible for one whose mind before then had been turned in another direction."

"But you helped me, Dagaeoga. After our first and only battle in the garden, which I think was a draw, we became allies."

"Und you united against me," said Mynheer Huysman.

"And you helped me with the books," continued Tayoga. "Ah, those first months were hard, very hard!"

"And you taught me the use of the bow and arrow," continued Robert, "and new skill in both fishing and hunting."

"Und the two uf you together learned new tricks und new ways uf making my life miserable," grumbled Mynheer Huysman.

"But you must admit, Jacob," said Willet, "that they were not the worst boys in the world."

"Well, not the worst, perhaps, David, because I don't know all the boys uf all the countries in the world, but when you put an Onondaga lad und an American lad together in alliance it iss hard to find any one who can excel them, because they haf the mischief uf two nations."

"But you are tremendously glad to see them again, Jacob. Don't deny it. I read it over and over again in your eyes."

Willet's own eyes twinkled as he spoke, and he saw also that there was a light in those of the big Dutchman. But Huysman would admit nothing.

"Here iss your room," he said to Robert and Tayoga.

Robert saw that it was not changed. All the old, familiar objects were there, and they brought to him a rush of emotion, as inanimate things often do. On a heavy mahogany dresser lay two worn volumes that he touched affectionately. One was his Caesar and the other his algebra. Once he had hated both, but now he thought of them tenderly as links with, the peaceful boyhood that was slipping away. Hanging from a hook on the wall was an unstrung bow, the first weapon of the kind with which he had practiced under the teaching of Tayoga. He passed his hand over it gently and felt a thrill at the touch of the wood.

Tayoga, also was moving about the room. On a small shelf lay an English dictionary and several readers. They too were worn. He had spent many a grieving hour over them when he had come from the Iroquois forests to learn the white man's lore. He recalled how he had hated them for a time, and how he had looked out of his school windows at the freedom for which he had longed. But he was made of wrought steel, both mind and body, and always the white youth, Lennox, his comrade, was at his elbow in those days of his scholastic infancy to help him. It had been a great episode in the life of Tayoga, who had the intellect of a mighty chief, the mind of Pontiac or Thayendanegea, or Tecumseh, or Sequoia. He had forced himself to learn and in learning his books he had learned also to like the people of another race around him who were good to him and who helped him in the first hard days on the new road. So the young Onondaga felt an emotion much like that of Robert as he walked about the room and touched the old familiar things. Then he turned to Huysman.

"Mynheer Jacobus," he said, "you have a mighty body, and you have in it a great heart. If all the men at Albany were like you there would never be any trouble between them and the Hodenosaunee."

"Tayoga," said Huysman, "you haf borrowed Robert's tongue to cozen und flatter. I haf not a great heart at all. I haf a very bad heart. I could not get on in this world if I didn't."

Tayoga laughed musically, and Mynheer Jacobus gruffly bidding them not to destroy anything, while he was gone, departed to see that Caterina, the Dutch cook, fat like her master, should have ready a dinner, drawing upon every resource of his ample larder. It is but truth to say that the heart of Mynheer Jacobus was very full. A fat old bachelor, with no near kin, his heart yearned over the two lads who had spent so long a period in his home, and he knew them, too, for what they were, each a fine flower of his own racial stock.

They were to remain several days in Albany, and after dinner they visited Alexander McLean, the crusty teacher who had given them such a severe drilling in their books. Master McLean allowed himself a few brief expressions of pleasure when they came into his house, and then questioned them sharply:

"Do you remember any of your ancient history, Tayoga?" he asked. "Are the great deeds of the Greeks and Romans still in your mind?"

"At times they are, sir," replied the young Onondaga.

"Um-m. Is that so? What was the date of the battle of Zama?"

"It was fought 202 B.C., sir."

"You're correct, but it must have been only a lucky guess. I'll try you again. What was the date of the battle of Hastings?"

"It was fought 1066 A.D., sir."

"Very good. Since you have answered correctly twice it must be knowledge and not mere surmise on your part. Robert, whom do you esteem the greatest of the Greek dramatic poets?"

"Sophocles, sir."

"Why?"

"Because he combined the vigor and power of Aeschylus with the polish and refinement of Euripides."

"Correct. I see that you remember what I told you, as you have quoted almost my exact words. And now, lads, be seated, while I order refreshments for you."

"We thank you, sir," said Robert, "but 'tis less than an hour since we almost ate ourselves to death at the house of Mynheer Jacobus Huysman."

"A good man, Jacob, but too fat, and far too brusque in speech, especially to the young. I'll warrant me he has been addressing upbraiding words to you, finding fault, perhaps, with your manners and your parts of speech."

The two youths hid their smiles.

"Mynheer Jacobus was very good to us," said Robert. "Just as you are, Master McLean."

"I am not good to you, if you mean by it weakness and softness of heart. Never spoil the young. Speak sternly to them all the time. Use the strap and the rod freely upon them and you may make men of them."

Again Robert and Tayoga hid their smiles, but each knew that he had a soft place in the heart of the crusty teacher, and they spent a pleasant hour with him. That night they slept in their old room at Mynheer Huysman's and two days later they and Willet went on board a sloop for New York, where they intended to see Governor de Lancey. Before they left many more alarming reports about the French and Indians had come to Albany. They had made new ravages in the north and west, and their power was spreading continually.

France was already helping her colonists. When would England help hers?

But Robert forgot all alarm in the pleasure of the voyage. It was a good sloop, it had a stout Dutch captain, and with a favoring wind they sped fast southward. Pride in the splendid river swelled in Robert's soul and he and Tayoga, despite the cold, sat together on the deck, watching the lofty shores and the distant mountains.

But Willet, anxious of mind, paced back and forth. He had seen much at Albany that did not please him. The Indian Commissioners were doing little to cement the alliance with the Hodenosaunee. The Mohawks, alone of the great League, were giving aid against the French. The others remained in their villages, keeping a strict neutrality. That was well as far as it went, but the hunter had hoped that all the members of the Hodenosaunee would take the field for the English. He believed that Father Drouillard would soon be back among the Onondagas, seeking to sway his converts to France, and he dreaded, too, the activity and persistency of St. Luc.

But he kept his anxieties from Robert, knowing how eagerly the lad anticipated his arrival in New York, and not blaming him at all for it, since New York, although inferior in wealth, size and power to Philadelphia, and in leadership to Boston, was already, in the eye of the prophets, because of its situation, destined to become the first city of America. And Willet felt his own pulses beat a little faster at the thought of New York, a town that he knew well, and already a port famous throughout the world.

Tayoga, although he wore his Indian dress, attracted no particular attention from Captain Van Zouten and his crew. Indians could be seen daily at Albany, and along the river, and they had been for generations a part of American life. Captain Van Zouten, in truth, noticed the height and fine bearing of the Onondaga, but he was a close mouthed Dutchman, and if he felt like asking questions he put due Dutch restraint upon himself.

The wind held good all day long, and the sloop flew southward, leaving a long white trail in the blue water, but toward night it rose to a gale, with heavy clouds that promised snow. Captain Hendrick Van Zouten looked up with some anxiety at his sails, through which the wind was now whistling, and, after a consultation with his mate, decided to draw into a convenient cove and anchor for the night.

"I'm sorry," he said to Willet, "that our voyage to New York will be delayed, but there'll be nasty weather on the river, and I don't like to risk the sloop in it. But I didn't promise you that I'd get you to the city at any particular time."

"We don't blame wind, weather and water upon you, Captain Van Zouten," laughed Willet, "and although I'm no seaman if you'd have consulted me I too would have suggested shelter for the night."

Captain Van Zouten breathed his relief.

"If my passengers are satisfied," he said, "then so am I."

All the sails were furled, the sloop was anchored securely in a cove where she could not injure herself, no matter how fiercely the wind might beat, and Robert and Tayoga, wrapped in their fur cloaks, stood on her deck, watching the advance of the fierce winter storm, and remembering those other storms they had passed through on Lake Champlain, although there was no danger of Indians here.

It began to snow heavily, and a fierce wind whistled among the mountains behind them, lashing the river also into high waves, but the sloop was a tight, strong craft, and it rocked but little in its snug cove. Despite snow, wind and darkness Robert, Tayoga and the hunter remained a long, time on deck. The Onondaga's feather headdress had been replaced by a fur cap, similar to those now worn by Robert and Willet, and all three were wrapped in heavy cloaks of furs.

Robert was still thinking of New York, a town that he knew to some extent, and yet he was traveling toward it with a feeling akin to that with which he had approached Quebec. It was in a way and for its time a great port, in which many languages were spoken and to which many ships came. Despite its inferiority in size it was already the chief window through which the New World looked upon the Old. He expected to see life in the seething little city at the mouth of the Hudson and he expected also that a crisis in his fortunes would come there.

"Dave," he said to the hunter, "have you any plans for us in New York?"

"They've not taken very definite shape," replied Willet, "but you know you want to serve in the war, and so do I. A great expedition is coming out from England, and in conjunction with a Colonial force it will march against Fort Duquesne. The point to which that force advances is bound to be the chief scene of action."

"And that, Dave, is where we want to go."

"With proper commissions in the army. We must maintain our dignity and station, Robert."

"Of course, Dave. And you, Tayoga, are you willing to go with us?"

"It is far from the vale of Onondaga," replied the young Indian, "but I have already made the great journey to Quebec with my comrades, Dagaeoga and the Great Bear. I am willing to see more of the world of which I read in the books at Albany. If the fortunes of Dagaeoga take him on another long circle I am ready to go with him."

"Spoken like a warrior, Tayoga," said the hunter. "I have some influence, and if we join the army that is to march against Fort Duquesne I'll see that you receive a place befitting your Onondaga rank and your quality as a man."

"And so that is settled," said Robert. "We three stand together no matter what may come."

"Stand together it is, no matter what may come," said Willet.

"We are, perhaps, as well in one place as in another," said Tayoga philosophically, "because wherever we may be Manitou holds us in the hollow of his hand."

A great gust of wind came with a shriek down one of the gorges, and the snow was whipped into their faces, blinding them for a moment.

"It is good to be aboard a stout sloop in such a storm," said Robert, as he wiped his eyes clear. "It would be hard to live up there on those cliffs in all this driving white winter."

A deep rumbling sound came back from the mountains, and he felt a chill that was not of the cold creep into his bones.

"It is the wind in the deep gorges," said Tayoga, "but the winds themselves are spirits and the mountains too are spirits. On such a wild night as this they play together and the rumbling you hear is their voices joined in laughter."

Robert's vivid mind as usual responded at once to Tayoga's imagery, and his fancy went as far as that of the Onondaga, and perhaps farther. He filled the air with spirits. They lined the edge of the driving white storm. They flitted through every cleft and gorge, and above every ridge and peak. They were on the river, and they rode upon the waves that were pursuing one another over its surface. Then he laughed a little at himself.

"My fancy is seeing innumerable figures for me," he said, "where my eyes really see none. No human being is likely to be abroad on the river on such a night as this."

"And yet my own eyes tell me that I do see a human being," said Tayoga, "one that is living and breathing, with warm blood running in his veins."

"A living, breathing man! where, Tayoga?"

"Look at the sloping cliff above us, there where the trees grow close together. Notice the one with the boughs hanging low, and by the dark trunk you will see the figure. It is a tall man with his hat drawn low over his eyes, and a heavy cloak wrapped closely around his body."

"I see him now, Tayoga! What could a man want at such a place on such a night? It must be a farmer out late, or perhaps a wandering hunter!"

"Nay, Dagaeoga, it is not a farmer, nor yet a wandering hunter. The shoulders are set too squarely. The figure is too upright. And even without these differences we would be sure that it is not the farmer, nor yet the wandering hunter, because it is some one else whom we know."

"What do you mean, Tayoga?"

"Look! Look closely, Dagaeoga!"

"Now the wind drives aside the white veil of snow and I see him better. His figure is surely familiar!"

"Aye, Dagaeoga, it is! And do you not know him?"

"St. Luc! As sure as we live, Tayoga, it's St. Luc."

"Yes," said the hunter, who had not spoken hitherto. "It's St. Luc, and I could reach him from here with a rifle shot."

"But you must not! You must not fire upon him!" exclaimed Robert.

Willet laughed.

"I wasn't thinking of doing so," he said. "And now it's too late. St. Luc has gone."

The dark figure vanished from beside the trunk, and Robert saw only the lofty slope, and the whirling snow. He passed his hands before his eyes.

"Did we really see him?" he said.

"We beheld him alive and in the flesh," replied the hunter, "deep down in His Britannic Majesty's province of New York."

"What could have brought him here at such a time?"

"The cause of France, no doubt. He speaks English as well as you and I, and he is probably in civilian clothing, seeking information for his country. I know something of St. Luc. He has in him a spice of the daring and romantic. Luck and adventure would appeal to him. He probably knows already what forces we have at Albany and Kingston and what is their state of preparation. Valuable knowledge for Quebec, too."

"Do you think St. Luc will venture to New York?"

"Scarce likely, lad. He can obtain about all he wishes to know without going so far south."

"I'm glad of that, Dave. I shouldn't want him to be captured and hanged as a spy."

"Nor I, Robert. St. Luc is the kind of man who, if he falls at all in this war, should fall sword in hand on the battle field. He must know this region or he would not dare to come here, on such a terrible night. He has probably gone now to shelter. And, since there is nothing more to be seen we might do the same."

But Robert and Tayoga were not willing to withdraw yet. Well wrapped and warm, they found a pleasure in the fierce storm that raged among the mountains and over the river, and their own security on the deck of the stout sloop, fastened so safely in the little cove. They listened to the wind rumbling anew like thunder through the deep gorges and clefts, and they saw the snow swept in vast curtains of white over the wild river.

"I wonder what we shall find in New York, Tayoga," said Robert.

"We shall find many people, of many kinds, Dagaeoga, but what will happen to us there Manitou alone knows. But he has us in his keeping. Look how he watched over us in Quebec, and look how the sword of the Great Bear was stretched before you when your enemies planned to slay you."

"That's true, Tayoga. I don't look forward to New York with any apprehension, but I do wonder what fate has prepared for us there."

"We must await it with calm," said Tayoga philosophically.

The Onondaga himself was not a stranger to New York. He had gone there once with the chiefs of the Hodenosaunee for a grand council with the British and provincial authorities, and he had gone twice with Robert when they were schoolboys together in Albany. His enlightened mind, without losing any of its dignity and calm, took a deep interest in everything he saw at the port, through which the tide of nations already flowed. He had much of the quality shown later by the fiery Thayendanegea, who bore himself with the best in London and who was their equal in manners, though the Onondaga, while as brave and daring as the Mohawk, was gentler and more spiritual, being, in truth, what his mind and circumstances had made him, a singular blend of red and white culture.

Willet, also wrapped in a long fur cloak, came from the cabin of the sloop and looked at the two youths, each of whom had such a great place in his heart. Both were white with snow as they stood on the deck, but they did not seem to notice it.

"Come now," said the hunter with assumed brusqueness. "You needn't stand here all night, looking at the river, the cliffs and the storm. Off to your berths, both of you."

"Good advice, or rather command, Dave," said Robert, "and we'll obey it."

Their quarters were narrow, because sloops plying on the river in those days were not large, but the three who slept so often in the forest were not seekers after luxury. Robert undressed, crept into his bunk, which was not over two feet wide, and slept soundly until morning. After midnight the violence of the storm abated. It was still snowing, but Captain Van Zouten unfurled his sails, made for the middle of the river, and, when the sun came up over the eastern hills, the sloop was tearing along at a great rate for New York.

So when Robert awoke and heard the groaning of timbers and the creak of cordage he knew at once that they were under way and he was glad. The events of the night before passed rapidly through his mind, but they seemed vague and indistinct. At first he thought the vision of St. Luc on the cliff in the storm was but a dream, and he had to make an effort of the will to convince himself that it was reality. But everything came back presently, as vivid as it had been when it occurred, and rising he dressed and went on deck. Tayoga and Willet were already there.

"Sluggard," said the Onondaga. "The French warships would capture you while you are still in the land of dreams."

"We'll find no French warships in the Hudson," retorted Robert, "and as for sluggards, how long have you been on deck yourself, Tayoga?"

"Two minutes, but much may happen in two minutes. Look, Dagaeoga, we come now into a land of plenty. See, how many smokes rise on either shore, and the smoke is not of camps, but of houses."

"It comes from strong Dutch farmhouses, and from English manor houses, Tayoga. They nestle in the warm shelter of the hills or at the mouths of the creeks. Surely, the world cannot furnish a nobler scene."

All the earth was pure white from the fallen snow, but the river itself was a deep blue, reflected from the dazzling blue of the sky overhead. The air, thin and cold, was exhilarating, and as the sloop fled southward a panorama, increasing continually in magnificence, unfolded before them. Other vessels appeared upon the river, and Captain Van Zouten gave them friendly signals. Tiny villages showed and the shores were an obvious manifestation of comfort and opulence.

"I have heard that the French, if their success continues, mean to attack Albany," said Robert, "but we must stop them there, Dave. We can never let them invade such a region as this."

"They'll invade it, nevertheless," said the hunter, "unless stout arms and brave hearts stop them. We can drive both French and Indians back, if we ever unite. There lies the trouble. We must get some sort of concentrated action."

"And New York is the best place to see whether it will be done or not."

"So it is."

The wind remained favorable all that day, the next night there was a calm, but the following day they drew near to New York, Captain Van Zouten assuring them he would make a landing before sunset.

He was well ahead of his promise, because the sun was high in the heavens when the sloop began to pass the high, wooded hills that lie at the upper end of Manhattan Island, and they drew in to their anchorage near the Battery. They did not see the stone government buildings that had marked Quebec, nor the numerous signs of a fortress city, but they beheld more ships and more indications of a great industrial life.

"Every time I come here," said Willet, "it seems to me that the masts increase in number. Truly it is a good town, and an abundant life flows through it."

"Where shall we stop, Dave?" asked Robert. "Do you have a tavern in mind?"

"Not a tavern," replied the hunter. "My mind's on a private house, belonging to a friend of mine. You have not met him because he is at sea or in foreign parts most of the time. Yet we are assured of a welcome."

An hour later they said farewell to Captain Van Zouten, carried their own light baggage, and entered the streets of the port.

CHAPTER X
THE PORT

The three walked toward the Battery, and, while Tayoga attracted more attention in New York than in Quebec, it was not undue. The city was used to Indians, especially the Iroquois, and although comments were made upon Tayoga's height and noble appearance there was nothing annoying.

Meanwhile the two youths were using their excellent eyes to the full. Although the vivid imagination of Robert had foreseen a great future for New York he did not dream how vast it would be. Yet all things are relative, and the city even then looked large to him and full of life, both size and activity having increased visibly since his last visit. Some of the streets were paved, or at least in part, and the houses, usually of red brick, often several stories in height, were comfortable and strong. Many of them had lawns and gardens as at Albany, and the best were planted with rows of trees which would afford a fine shade in warm weather. Above the mercantile houses and dwellings rose the lofty spire of St. George's Chapel in Nassau Street, which had been completed less than three years before, and which secured Robert's admiration for its height and impressiveness.

The aspect of the whole town was a mixture of English and Dutch, but they saw many sailors who were of neither race. Some were brown men with rings in their ears, and they spoke languages that Robert did not understand. But he knew that they came from far southern seas and that they sailed among the tropic isles, looming large then in the world's fancy, bringing with them a whiff of romance and mystery.

The sidewalks in many places were covered with boxes and bales brought from all parts of the earth, and stalwart men were at work among them. The pulsing life and the air of prosperity pleased

Robert. His nature responded to the town, as it had responded to the woods, and his imagination, leaping ahead, saw a city many times greater than the one before his eyes, though it still stopped far short of the gigantic reality that was to come to pass.

"It's not far now to Master Hardy's," said Willet cheerfully. "It's many a day since I've seen trusty old Ben, and right glad I'll be to feel the clasp of his hand again."

On his way Willet bought from a small boy in the street a copy each of the *Weekly Post-Boy* and of the *Weekly Gazette* and *Mercury*, folding them carefully and putting them in an inside pocket of his coat.

"I am one to value the news sheets," he said. "They don't tell everything, but they tell something and 'tis better to know something than nothing. Just a bit farther, my lads, and we'll be at the steps of honest Master Hardy. There, you can see where fortunes are made and lost, though we're a bit too late to see the dealers!"

He pointed to the Royal Exchange, a building used by the merchants at the foot of Broad Street, a structure very unique in its plan. It consisted of an upper story resting upon arches, the lower part, therefore, being entirely open. Beneath these arches the merchants met and transacted business, and also in a room on the upper floor, where there were, too, a coffee house and a great room used for banquets, and the meetings of societies, the Royal Exchange being in truth the beginning of many exchanges that now mark the financial center of the New World.

"Perhaps we'll see the merchants there tomorrow," said Willet. "You'll note the difference between New York and Quebec. The French capital was all military. You saw soldiers everywhere, but this is a town of merchants. Now which, think you, will prevail, the soldiers or the merchants?"

"I think that in the end the merchants will win," replied Robert.

"And so do I. Now we have come to the home of Master Hardy. See you the big brick house with high stone steps? Well, that is his, and I repeat that he is a good friend of mine, a good friend of old and of today. I heard that in Albany, which tells me we will find him here in his own place."

But the big brick house looked to Robert and Tayoga like a fortress, with its massive door and iron-barred windows, although friendly smoke rose from a high chimney and made a warm line against the frosty blue air.

Willet walked briskly up the high stone steps and thundered on the door with a heavy brass knocker. The summons was quickly answered and the door swung back, revealing a tall, thin, elderly man, neatly dressed in the fashion of the time. He had the manner of one who served, although he did not seem to be a servant. Robert judged at once that he was an upper clerk who lived in the house, after the custom of the day.

"Is Master Benjamin within, Jonathan?" asked Willet.

The tall man blinked and then stared at the hunter in astonishment.

"Is it in very truth you, Master Willet?" he exclaimed.

"None other. Come, Jonathan, you know my voice and my face and my figure very well. You could not fail to recognize me anywhere. So cease your doubting. My young friends here are Robert Lennox, of whom you know, and Tayoga, a coming chief of the Clan of the Bear, of the nation Onondaga, of the great League of the Hodenosaunee, known to you as the Six Nations. He's impatient of disposition and unless you answer my question speedily I'll have him tomahawk you. Come now, is Master Benjamin within?"

"He is, Mr. Willet. I had no intent to delay my answer, but you must allow something to surprise."

"I grant you pardon," said the hunter whimsically. "Robert and Tayoga, this is Master Jonathan Pillsbury, chief clerk and man of affairs for Master Benjamin Hardy. They are two old bachelors who live in the same house, and who get along well together, because they're so unlike. As for Master Jonathan, his heart is not as sour as his face, and you could come to a worse place than the shop of Benjamin and Jonathan. Master Jonathan, you will take particular notice of Mr. Lennox. He is well grown and he appears intelligent, does he not?"

The old clerk blinked again, and then his appraising eyes swept over Robert.

"'Twould be hard to find a nobler youth," he said.

"I thought you would say so, and now lead us, without further delay, to Master Hardy."

"Who is it who demands to be led to me?" thundered a voice from the rear of the house. "I seem to know that voice! Ah, it's Willet! Good old Willet! Honest Dave, who wields the sharpest sword in North America!"

A tall, heavy man lunged forward. "Lunged" was the word that described it to Robert, and his impetuous motion was due to the sight of Willet, whom he grasped by both hands, shaking them with a vigor that would have caused pain in one less powerful than the hunter, and as he shook them he uttered exclamations, many of them bordering upon oaths and all of them pertaining to the sea.

Robert's eyes had grown used to the half light of the hall, and he took particular notice of Master Benjamin Hardy who was destined to become an important figure in his life, although he did not then dream of it. He saw a tall man of middle age, built very powerfully, his face burnt almost the color of an Indian's by the winds and suns of many seas. But his hair was thick and long and the eyes shining in the face, made dark by the weather, were an intensely bright blue. Robert, upon whom impressions were so swift and vivid, reckoned that here was one capable of great and fierce actions, and also with a heart that contained a large measure of kindness and generosity.

"Dave," said the tall man, who carried with him the atmosphere of the sea, "I feared that you might be dead in those forests you love so well, killed and perhaps scalped by the Hurons or some other savage tribe. You've abundant hair, Dave, and you'd furnish an uncommonly fine scalp."

"And I feared, Benjamin, that you'd been caught in some smuggling cruise near the Spanish Main, and had been put out of the way by the Dons. You love gain too much, Ben, old friend, and you court risks too great for its sake."

Master Benjamin Hardy threw back his head and laughed deeply and heartily. The laugh seemed to Robert to roll up spontaneously from his throat. He felt anew that here was a man whom he liked.

"Perchance 'tis the danger that draws me on," said Master Hardy. "You and I are much alike, Dave. In the woods, if all that I hear be true, you dwell continually in the very shadow of danger, while I incur it only at times. Moreover, I am come to the age of fifty years, the head is still on my shoulders, the breath is still in my body, and

Master Jonathan, to whom figures are Biblical, says the balance on my books is excellent."

"You talk o'er much, Ben, old friend, but since it's the way of seafaring men and 'tis cheerful it does not vex my ears. You behold with me, Tayoga, a youth of the best blood of the Onondaga nation, one to whom you will be polite if you wish to please me, Benjamin, and Master Robert Lennox, grown perhaps beyond your expectations."

Master Benjamin turned to Robert, and, as Master Jonathan had done, measured him from head to foot with those intensely bright blue eyes of his that missed nothing.

"Grown greatly and grown well," he said, "but not beyond my expectations. In truth, one could predict a noble bough upon such a stem. But you and I, Dave, having many years, grow garrulous and forget the impatience of youth. Come, lads, we'll go into the drawing-room and, as supper was to have been served in half an hour, I'll have the portions doubled."

Robert smiled.

"In Albany and New York alike," he said, "they welcome us to the table."

"Which is the utmost test of hospitality," said Master Benjamin.

They went into a great drawing-room, the barred windows of which looked out upon a busy street, warehouses and counting houses and passing sailors. Robert was conscious all the while that the brilliant blue eyes were examining him minutely. His old wonder about his parentage, lost for a while in the press of war and exciting events, returned. He felt intuitively that Master Hardy, like Willet, knew who and what he was, and he also felt with the same force that neither would reply to any question of his on the subject. So he kept his peace and by and by his curiosity, as it always did, disappeared before immediate affairs.

The drawing-room was a noble apartment, with dark oaken beams, a polished oaken floor, upon which eastern rugs were spread, and heavy tables of foreign woods. A small model of a sloop rested upon one table and a model of a schooner on another. Here and there were great curving shells with interiors of pink and white, and upon the walls were curious long, crooked knives of the Malay Islands. Everything savored of the sea. Again Robert's imagination leaped up. The blazing hues of distant tropic lands were in his eyes, and the odors of strange fruits and flowers were in his nostrils.

"Sit down, Dave," said Master Benjamin, "and you, too, Robert and Tayoga. I suppose you did not come to New Amsterdam—how the name clings!—merely to see me."

"That was one purpose, Benjamin," replied Willet, "but we had others in mind too."

"To join the war, I surmise, and to get yourselves killed?"

"The first part of your reckoning is true, Benjamin, but not the second. We would go to the war, in which we have had some part already, but not in order that we may be killed."

"You suffer from the common weakness. One entering war always thinks that it's the other man and not he who will be killed. You're too old for that, David."

Willet laughed.

"No, Benjamin," he said, "I'm not too old for it, and I never will be. It's the belief that carries us all through danger."

"Which way did you think of going in these warlike operations?"

"We shall join the force that comes out from England."

"The one that will march against Fort Duquesne?"

"Undoubtedly."

"I hear that it's to be commanded by a general named Braddock, Edward
Braddock. What do you know of him?"

"Nothing."

"But you do know, David, that regular army officers fare ill in the woods as a rule. You've told me often that the savages are a tricky lot, and, fighting in the forest in their own way, are hard to beat."

"You speak truth, Benjamin, and I'll not deny it, but there are many of our men in the woods who know the ways of the Indians and of the French foresters. They should be the eyes and ears of General Braddock's army."

"Well, maybe! maybe! David, but enough of war for the present. One cannot talk about it forever. There are other things under the sun. You will let these lads see New Amsterdam, will you not? Even

Tayoga can find something worth his notice in the greatest port of the New World."

"Is any play being given here?" asked Robert.

"Aye, we're having plays almost nightly," replied Master Hardy, "and they're being presented by some very good actors, too. Lewis Hallam, who came several years ago from Goodman's Fields Theater in England, and his wife, known on the stage as Mrs. Douglas, are offering the best English plays in New York. Hallam is said to be extremely fine in Richard III, in which tragedy he first appeared here, and he gives it tomorrow night."

"Then we're going," said Robert eagerly. "I would not miss it for anything."

"I had some thought of going myself, and if Dave hasn't changed, he has a fine taste for the stage. I'll send for seats and we'll go together."

Willet's eyes sparkled.

"In truth I'll go, too, and right gladly," he said. "You and I, Benjamin, have seen the plays of Master Shakespeare together in London, and 'twill please me mightily to see one of them again with you in New York. Jonathan, here, will be of our company, too, will he not?"

Master Pillsbury pursed his lips and his expression became severe.

"'Tis a frivolous way of passing the time," he said, "but it would be well for one of serious mind to be present in order that he might impose a proper dignity upon those who lack it."

Benjamin Hardy burst into a roar of laughter. Robert had never known any one else to laugh so deeply and with such obvious spontaneity and enjoyment. His lips curled up at each end, his eyes rolled back and then fairly danced with mirth, and his cheeks shook. It was contagious. Not only did Master Benjamin laugh, but the others had to laugh, not excluding Master Jonathan, who emitted a dry cackle as became one of his habit and appearance.

"Do you know, Dave, old friend," said Hardy, "that our good Jonathan is really the most wicked of us all? I go upon the sea on these cruises, which you call smuggling, and what not, and of which he speaks censoriously, but if they do not show a large enough profit on his books he rates me most severely, and charges me with a lack of enterprise. And now he would fain go to the play to see that we observe the proper decorum there. My lads, you couldn't keep the sour-visaged old hypocrite from it."

Master Jonathan permitted himself a vinegary smile, but made no other reply, and, a Dutch serving girl announcing that supper was ready, Master Hardy led them into the dining-room, where a generous repast was spread. But the room itself continued and accentuated the likeness of a ship. The windows were great portholes, and two large swinging lamps furnished the light. Pictures of naval worthies and of sea actions lined the walls. Two or three of the battle scenes were quite spirited, and Robert regarded them with interest.

"Have you fought in any of those encounters, Mr. Hardy?" he asked.

Willet laid a reproving hand upon his shoulder.

"'Twas a natural question of yours, Robert," he said, "but 'tis the fashion here and 'tis courtesy, too, never to ask Benjamin about his past life. Then he has no embarrassing questions to answer."

Robert reddened and Hardy broke again into that deep, spontaneous laughter which, in time, compelled all the others to laugh too and with genuine enjoyment.

"Don't believe all that David tells you, Robert, my brave macaroni," he said. "I may not answer your questions, but faith they'll never prove embarrassing. Bear in mind, lad, that our trade being restricted by the mother country and English subjects in this land not having the same freedom as English subjects in England, we must resort to secrecy and stratagem to obtain what our fellow subjects on the other side of the ocean may obtain openly. And when you grow older, Master Robert, you will find that it's ever so in the world. Those to whom force bars the way will resort to wiles and stratagems to achieve their ends. The fox has the cunning that the bear lacks, because he hasn't the bear's strength. Lads, you two will sit together on this side of the table, Jonathan, you take the side next to the portholes, and David, you and I will preside at the ends. Benjamin, David and Jonathan, it has quite a Biblical sound, and at least the friendship among the three of us, despite the sourness of Master Pillsbury, with which I bear as best I can, is equal to that of

David and Jonathan. Now, lads, fall on and see which of you can keep pace with me, for I am a mighty trencherman."

"Meanwhile tell us what is passing here," said Willet.

In the course of the supper Hardy talked freely of events in New York, where a great division of councils still prevailed. Shirley, the warlike and energetic governor of Massachusetts, had urged De Lancy, the governor of New York, to join in an expedition against the French in Canada, but there had been no agreement. Later, a number of the royal governors expected to meet at Williamsburg in Virginia with Dinwiddie, the governor of that province.

"At present there are plans for four enterprises, every one of an aspiring nature," he said. "One expedition is to reduce Nova Scotia entirely, another, under Governor Shirley of Massachusetts, is to attack the French at Fort Niagara, Sir William Johnson with militia and Mohawks is to head a third against Crown Point. The fourth, which I take to be the most important, is to be led by General Braddock against Fort Duquesne, its object being the recovery of the Ohio country. I cannot vouch for it, but such plans, I hear, will be presented at the conference of the governors at Williamsburg."

"As we mean to go to Williamsburg ourselves," said Willet, "we'll see what fortune General Braddock may have. But now, for the sake of the good lads, we'll speak of lighter subjects. Where is the play of Richard III to be given, Benjamin?"

"Mr. Hallam has obtained a great room in a house that is the property of Rip Van Dam in Nassau Street. He has fitted it up in the fashion of a stage, and his plays are always attended by a great concourse of ladies and gentlemen. Boston and Philadelphia say New York is light and frivolous, but I suspect that something of jealousy lies at the core of the charge. We of New Amsterdam—again the name leaps to my lips—have a certain freedom in our outlook upon life, a freedom which I think produces strength and not weakness. Manners are not morals, but I grow heavy and it does not become a seafaring man to be didactic. What is it, Piet?"

The door of the dining-room opened, admitting a serving man who produced a letter.

"It comes by the Boston post," he said, handing it to Master Hardy.

"Then it must have an importance which will not admit delay in the reading," said Master Hardy. "Your pardon, friends, while I peruse it."

He read it carefully, read it again with the same care, and then his resonant laughter boomed forth with such volume and in such continuity that he was compelled to take a huge red handkerchief and wipe the tears from his eyes.

"What is it, Benjamin, that amuses you so vastly?" asked Willet.

"A brave epistle from one of my captains, James Dunbar, a valiant man and a great mariner. In command of the schooner, *Good Hope*, he was sailing from the Barbados with a cargo of rum and sugar for Boston, which furnishes a most excellent market for both, when he was overhauled by the French privateer, *Rocroi*."

"What do you find to laugh at in the loss of a good ship and a fine cargo?"

"Did I say they were lost? Nay, David, I said nothing of the kind. You don't know Dunbar, and you don't know the *Good Hope*, which carries a brass twelve-pounder and fifteen men as valiant as Dunbar himself. He returned the attack of the *Rocroi* with such amazing skill and fierceness that he was able to board her and take her, with only three of his men wounded and they not badly. Moreover, they found on board the privateer a large store of gold, which becomes our prize of war. And Dunbar and his men shall have a fair share of it, too. How surprised the Frenchies must have been when Dunbar and his sailors swarmed aboard."

"'Tis almost our only victory," said Willet, "and I'm right glad, Benjamin, it has fallen to the lot of one of your ships to win it."

The long supper which was in truth a dinner was finished at last. Hardy made good his boast, proving that he was a mighty trencherman. Pillsbury pressed him closest, and the others, although they did well, lingered at some distance in the rear. Afterward they walked in the town, observing its varied life, and at a late hour returned to Hardy's house which he called a mansion.

Robert and Tayoga were assigned to a room on the second floor, and young Lennox again noted the numerous evidences of opulence. The furniture was mostly of carved mahogany, and every room contained articles of value from distant lands.

"Tayoga," said Robert, "what do you think of it all?"

"I think that the man Hardy is shrewd, Dagaeoga, shrewd like one of our sachems, and that he has an interest in you, greater than he would let you see. Do you remember him, Lennox?"

"No, I can't recall him, Tayoga. I've heard Dave speak of him many times, but whenever we were in New York before he was away, and we did not even come to his house. But he and Dave are friends of many years. I think that long ago they must have been much together."

"Truly there is some mystery here, but it can wait. In its proper time the unknown becomes the known."

"So it does, Tayoga, and I shall not vex my mind about the matter. Just now, what I wish most of all is sleep."

"I wish it too, Lennox."

But Robert did not sleep well, his nerves being attuned more highly than he had realized. Some of the talk that had passed between Willet and Hardy related obviously to himself, and in the quiet of the room it came back to him. He had not slept more than an hour when he awoke, and, being unable to go to sleep again, sat up in bed. Tayoga was deep in slumber, and Robert finally left the bed and went to the window, the shutter of which was not closed. It was a curious, round window, like a huge porthole, but the glass was clear and he had a good view of the street. He saw one or two sailors swaying rather more than the customary motion of a ship, pass by, and then a watchman carrying a club in one hand and a lantern in the other, and blowing his frosty breath upon his thick brown beard, indicating that the night although bright was very cold.

He looked through the glass at least a half hour, and then turned back to the bed, but found himself less inclined than ever to sleep. Throwing his coat over his shoulders, he opened the unlocked door and went into the hall, intending to walk back and forth a little, believing that the easy exercise would induce desire for sleep.

He was surprised to find a thread of light in the dusk of the hall, at a time when he was quite sure everybody in the house except himself was buried in slumber, and when he traced it he found it came from another room farther down. It was, upon the instant, his belief that robbers had entered. In a port like New York, where all nations come, there must be reckless and desperate men who would hesitate at no risk or crime.

He moved cautiously along the hall, until he reached the door from which the light shone. It was open about six inches, not allowing a look into the room except at the imminent risk of discovery, but by placing his ear at the sill he would be able to hear the footsteps of men if they were moving within. The sound of voices instead came to him, and as he listened he was able to note that it was two men talking in low tones. Undoubtedly they were robbers, who were common in all great towns in those days, and this must be a chamber in which Master Hardy kept many valuables. Doubtless they were assured that everybody was deep in slumber, or they would be more cautious.

Driven by an intense curiosity, Robert edged his head a little farther forward, and was able to look into the room, where, to his intense amazement, he saw no robbers at all, but Willet and Master Hardy seated at a small table opposite each other, with a candle, account books and papers between. Hardy had been reading a paper, and stopping at intervals to talk about it with the hunter.

"As you see, David," he said, "the list of the ships is three larger than it was five years ago. One was lost to the Barbary corsairs, another was wrecked on the coast of the Brazils, but we have five new ones."

"You have done well, Benjamin, but I knew you would," said the hunter.

"With the help of Jonathan. Don't forget him, David. In name he is my head clerk, and he pretends to serve me, but at times I think he is my master. A shrewd Massachusetts man, David, uncommonly shrewd, and loyal too."

"And the lands, Benjamin?"

"They're in abeyance, and are likely to be for some years, their title depending upon the course of events which are now in train."

"And they're uncertain, Benjamin, as uncertain as the winds. But give me your honest opinion of the lad, Benjamin. Have I done well with him?"

"None could have done better. He's an eagle, David. I marked him well. Spirit, imagination, force; youth and honesty looking out of his eyes. But have you no fears, David, that you will get him killed in the wars?"

"I could not keep him from going to them if I would, Benjamin. There my power stops. You old sailors have superstitions or beliefs, and I, a landsman, have a conviction, too. The invisible prophets tell me that he will not be killed."

"I don't laugh at such things, David. The greatness and loneliness of the sea does breed superstition in mariners. I know there is no such thing as the supernatural, and yet I am swayed at times by the unknown."

"At least I will watch over him as best I can, and he has uncommon skill in taking care of himself."

Robert's will triumphed over a curiosity that was intense and burning, and he turned away. He knew they were speaking of him, and he seemed to be connected with great affairs. It was enough to stir the most apathetic youth, and he was just the opposite. It required the utmost exertion of a very strong mind to pull himself from the door and then to drag his unwilling feet along the hall. Matter was in complete rebellion and mind was compelled to win its triumph, unaided, but win it did and kept the victory.

He reached his own room and softly closed the door behind him. Tayoga was still sleeping soundly. Robert went again to the window. His eyes were turned toward the street, but he did not see anything there, because he was looking inward. The talk of Willet and Hardy came back to him. He could say it over, every word, and none could deny that it was charged with significance. But he knew intuitively that neither of them would answer a single one of his questions, and he must wait for time and circumstance to disclose the truth. Nor could he bear to tell them that he had been listening at the door, despite the fact that it had been brought about by accident, and that he had come away, when he might have heard more.

Having resigned himself to necessity, he went back to bed and now, youth triumphing over excitement, he soon slept. The next morning, directly after breakfast, the three elders and the two lads went to the Royal Exchange, where there was soon a great concourse of merchants, clerks and seafaring men. Master Hardy was received with great respect, and many congratulations were given to him, when he told the story of the *Good Hope* and Captain Dunbar. In one of the rooms above the pillars he met another captain of his who had arrived the day before at New York itself.

This captain, a New England man, Eliphalet Simmons, had brought his schooner from the Mediterranean, and he told in a manner as brief and dry as his own log how he had outsailed one Barbary corsair by day, and by changing his course had tricked another in the night. But the voyage had been most profitable, and Master Jonathan duly entered the amount of gain in an account book, with a reward of ten pounds to Captain Simmons, five pounds to the first mate, three pounds to the second mate, and one pound to every member of the crew for their bravery and seamanship.

Captain Simmons' thanks were as brief and dry as his report, but Robert saw his eyes glisten, and knew that he was not lacking in gratitude. After the business was settled and the rewards adjusted they adjourned to a coffee house near Hanover Square where very good Madeira was brought and served to the men, Robert and Tayoga declining. Then Benjamin, David and Jonathan drank to the health of Eliphalet, while the two lads, the white and the red, devoted their attention to the others in the coffee house, of whom there were at least a dozen.

One who sat at a table very near was already examining Tayoga with the greatest curiosity. He wore the uniform of an English second lieutenant, very trim, and very red, he had an exceeding ruddiness of countenance, he was tall and well built, and he was only a year or two older than Robert. His curiosity obviously had been aroused by the appearance of Tayoga in the full costume of an Iroquois. It was equally evident to Robert that he was an Englishman, a member of the royal forces then in New York. Americans still called themselves Englishmen and Robert instantly had a feeling of kinship for the young officer who had a frank and good face.

The English youth's hat was lying upon the table beside him, and a gust of wind blowing it upon the floor, rolled it toward Robert, who picked it up and tendered it to its owner.

"Thanks," said the officer. "'Twas careless of me."

"By no means," said Robert. "The wind blows when it pleases, and you were taken by surprise."

The Englishman smiled, showing very white and even teeth.

"I haven't been very long in New York," he said, "but I find it a polite and vastly interesting town. My name is Grosvenor, Alfred

Grosvenor, and I'm a second lieutenant in the regiment of Colonel Brandon, that arrived but recently from England."

Master Hardy looked up and passed an investigating eye over the young Englishman.

"You're related to one of the ducal families of England," he said, "but your own immediate branch of it has no overplus of wealth. Still, your blood is reckoned highly noble in England, and you have an excellent standing in your regiment, both as an officer and a man."

Young Grosvenor's ruddy face became ruddier.

"How do you happen to know so much about me?" he asked. But there was no offense in his tone.

Hardy smiled, and Pillsbury, pursing his thin lips, measured Grosvenor with his eyes.

"I make it my business," replied Hardy, "to discover who the people are who come to New York. I'm a seafaring man and a merchant and I find profit in it. It's true, in especial, since the war has begun, and New York begins to fill with the military. Many of these sprightly young officers will be wishing to borrow money from me before long, and it will be well for me to know their prospects of repayment."

The twinkle in his eye belied the irony of his words, and the lieutenant laughed.

"And since you're alone," continued the merchant, "we ask you to join us, and will be happy if you accept. This is Mr. Robert Lennox, of very good blood too, and this is Tayoga, of the Clan of the Bear, of the nation Onondaga, of the great League of the Hodenosaunee, who, among his own people has a rank corresponding to a prince of the blood among yours, and who, if you value such things, is entitled therefore to precedence over all of us, including yourself. Mr. David Willet, Mr. Jonathan Pillsbury and Mr. Benjamin Hardy, who is myself, complete the catalogue."

He spoke in a tone half whimsical, half earnest, but the young Englishman, who evidently had a friendly and inquiring mind, received it in the best spirit and gladly joined them. He was soon deep in the conversation, but his greatest interest was for Tayoga, from whom he could seldom take his eyes. It was evident to Robert that he had expected to find only a savage in an Indian, and the delicate manners and perfect English of the Onondaga filled him with surprise.

"I would fain confess," he said at length, "that America is not what I expected to find. I did not know that it contained princes who could put some of our own to shame."

He bowed to Tayoga, who smiled and replied:

"What small merit I may possess is due to the training of my people."

"Do you expect early service, Lieutenant Grosvenor?" Mr. Hardy asked.

"Not immediate—I think I may say so much," replied the Englishman, "but I understand that our regiment will be with the first force that takes the field, that of General Braddock. 'Tis well known that we intend to march against Fort Duquesne, an expedition that should be easy. A powerful army like General Braddock's can brush aside any number of forest rovers."

Robert and Willet exchanged glances, but the face of Tayoga remained a mask.

"It's not well to take the French and Indians too lightly," said Mr. Hardy with gravity.

"But wandering bands can't face cannon and the bayonet."

"They don't have to face 'em. They lie hid on your flank and cut you down, while your fire and steel waste themselves on the uncomplaining forest."

They were words which were destined to come back to Robert some day with extraordinary force, but for the present they were a mere generalization that did not stay long in his mind.

"Our leaders will take all the needful precautions," said young Grosvenor with confidence.

Mr. Hardy did not insist, but spoke of the play they expected to witness that evening, suggesting to Lieutenant Grosvenor if he had leave, that he go with them, an invitation that was accepted promptly and with warmth. The liking between him and Robert, while of sudden birth, was destined to be strong and permanent. There was much similarity of temperament. Grosvenor also was imaginative and curious. His mind invariably projected itself into the future, and he was eager to know. He had come to America, inquiring, without prejudices, wishing to find the good rather than the bad, and he esteemed it a great stroke of fortune that he should make so early the acquaintance of two such remarkable youths as Robert and Tayoga. The three men with them were scarcely less interesting, and he knew that in their company at the play they would talk to him of strange new things. He would be exploring a world hidden from him hitherto, and nothing could have appealed to him more.

"You landed a week ago," said Hardy.

"Truly, sir," laughed Grosvenor, "you seem to know not only who I am, but what I do."

"And then, as you've had a certain amount of military duty, although 'tis not excessive, you've had little chance to see this most important town of ours. Can you not join this company of mine at my house for supper, and then we'll all go together to the play? I'll obtain your seat for you."

"With great pleasure, sir," replied Grosvenor. "'Twill be easy for me to secure the needed leave, and I'll be at your house with promptness."

He departed presently for his quarters, and the three men also went away together on an errand of business, leaving Robert and Tayoga to go whithersoever they pleased and it pleased them to wander along the shores of the port. Young Lennox was impressed more than ever by the great quantity of shipping, and the extreme activity of the town. The war with France, so far from interfering with this activity, had but increased it.

Privateering was a great pursuit of the day, all nations deeming it legal and worthy in war, and bold and enterprising merchants like Mr. Hardy never failed to take advantage of it. The weekly news sheets that Willet had bought contained lists of vessels captured already, and Robert's hasty glances showed him that at least sixty or seventy had been taken by the privateers out of New York. Most of the prizes had been in the West India trade, although some had been captured far away near the coast of Africa, and nearly all had been loaded richly.

They saw several of the privateers in port, armed powerfully, and as they were usually built for speed, Robert admired their graceful lines. He felt anew the difference between military Quebec and commercial New York. Quebec was prepared to send forth forces for destruction, but, here, life-giving commerce flowed in and flowed out again through arteries continually increasing in number and power. Once again came to him the thought that the merchant more than the soldier was the builder of a great nation. The impression made upon him was all the more vivid because New York, even in the middle of the eighteenth century, when it was in its infancy, surprised even travelers from Europe with its manifold activities and intense energy.

After a day, long but of extraordinary interest, they returned to the house of Mr. Hardy, where Grosvenor joined them in half an hour, and then, after another abundant supper, they all went to the play.

CHAPTER XI
THE PLAY

They were all arrayed in their very best clothes, even Master Jonathan having powdered his hair, and tied it in an uncommonly neat queue, while his buckled shoes, stockings and small clothes, though of somewhat ancient fashion, were of fine quality. Mr. Hardy gazed at him admiringly.

"Jonathan," he said, "you are usually somewhat sour of visage, but upon occasion you can ruffle it with the best macaroni of them all."

Master Jonathan pursed his lips, and smiled with satisfaction. All of them, in truth, presented a most gallant appearance, but by far the most noticeable figure was that of Tayoga. Indians often appeared in New York, but such Indians as the young Onondaga were rare anywhere. He rose half a head above the ordinary man, and he wore the costume of a chief of the mighty League of the Hondenosaunee, the feathers in his lofty headdress blowing back defiantly with the wind. He attracted universal, and at the same time respectful, attention.

They were preceded by a stout link boy who bore aloft a blazing torch, and as they walked toward the building in Nassau Street, owned by Rip Van Dam, in which the play was to be given, they overtook others who were upon the same errand. A carriage drawn by two large white horses conveyed Governor de Lancey and his wife, and another very much like it bore his brother-in-law, the conspicuous John Watts, and Mrs. Watts. All of them saw Mr. Hardy and his party and bowed to them with great politeness. Robert already understood enough of the world to know that it denoted much importance on the part of the merchant.

"A man of influence in our community," said Master Benjamin, speaking of Mr. Watts. "An uncommonly clear mind and much firmness and decision. He will leave a great name in New York."

As he spoke they overtook a tall youth about twenty-three years old, walking alone, and dressed in the very latest fashion out of England. Mr. Hardy hailed him with great satisfaction and asked him to join them.

"Master Edward Charteris,[A] who is soon to become a member of the Royal Americans," he said to the others. "He is a native of this town and belongs to one of our best families here. When he does become a Royal American he will probably have the finest uniform in his regiment, because Edward sets the styles in raiment for young men of his age here."

[Footnote A: The story of Edward Charteris, and his adventures at Ticonderoga and Quebec are told in the author's novel, "A Soldier of Manhattan."]

Charteris smiled. It was evident that he and the older man were on the most friendly footing. But he held himself with dignity and had pride, qualities which Robert liked in him. His manner was most excellent too, when Mr. Hardy introduced all of his party in turn, and he readily joined them, speaking of his pleasure in doing so.

"I shall be able to exchange my seat and obtain one with you," he said. "We shall be early, but I am glad of it. Mr. Hallam and his fine company have been performing in Philadelphia, and as we now welcome them back to New York, nearly all the notable people of our city will be present. Unless Mr. Hardy wishes to do so, it will give me pleasure to point them out to you."

"No, no!" exclaimed Master Benjamin. "The task is yours, Edward, my lad. You can put more savor and unction into it than I can."

"Then let it be understood that I'm the guide and expounder," laughed
Charteris.

"He has a great pride in his city, and it won't suffer from his telling," said Master Benjamin.

They were now in Nassau Street near the improvised theater, and many other link boys, holding aloft their torches, were preceding their masters and mistresses. Heavy coaches were rolling up, and men and women in gorgeous costumes were emerging from them. The display of wealth was amazing for a town in the New World, but Mr. Hardy and his company quickly went inside and obtained their seats, from which they watched the fashion of New York enter. Charteris knew them all, and to many of them he was related.

The number of De Lanceys was surprising and there was also a profusion of Livingstons, the two families between them seeming to dominate the city, although they lived in bitter rivalry, as Charteris whispered to Robert. There were also Wattses and Morrises and Crugers and Waltons and Van Rensselaers, Van Cortlandts and Kennedys and Barclays and Nicolls and Alexanders, and numerous others that endured for generations in New York. The diverse origin of these names, English, Scotch, Dutch and Huguenot French, showed even at such an early date the cosmopolitan nature of New York that it was destined to maintain.

Robert was intensely interested. Charteris' fund of information was wonderful, and he flavored it with a salt of his own. He not only knew the people, but he knew all about them, their personal idiosyncrasies, their rivalries and jealousies. Robert soon gathered that New York was not only a seething city commercially, but socially as well. Family was of extreme importance, and the great landed proprietors who had received extensive grants along the Hudson in the earlier days from the Dutch Government, still had and exercised feudal rights, and were as full of pride and haughtiness as ducal families in Europe. Class distinctions were preserved to the utmost possible extent, and, while the original basis of the town had been Dutch, the fashion was now distinctly English. London set the style for everything.

When they were all seated, the display of fine dress and jewels was extraordinary, just as the wealth and splendor shown in some of the New York houses had already attracted the astonished attention of many of the British officers, to whom the finest places in their own country were familiar.

And while Robert was looking so eagerly, the party to which he belonged did not pass unnoticed by any means. Master Benjamin Hardy was well known. He was bold and successful and he was a man of great substance. He had qualities that commanded respect in colonial New York, and people were not averse to being seen receiving his friendly nod. And those who surrounded him and who were evidently his guests were worthy of notice too. There was Edward Charteris, as well born as any in the hall, and a pattern in manners and dress for the young men of New York, and there was the tall youth with the tanned face, and the wonderful, vivid eyes, who must surely, by his appearance, be the representative of some noble family, there was the young Indian chief, uncommon in height and with the dignity and majesty of the forest, an Indian whose like had never been seen in New York before, and there was the gigantic Willet, whose massive head and calm face were so redolent of strength. Beyond all question it was a most unusual and striking company that Master Benjamin Hardy had brought with him, and old and young whispered together as they looked at them, especially at Robert and Tayoga.

Mr. Hardy was conscious of the stir he had made, and he liked it, not for himself alone, but also for another. He glanced at Robert and saw how finely and clearly his features were cut, how clear was the blue of his eyes and the great width between them, and he drew a long breath of satisfaction.

"'Tis a good youth. Nature, lineage and Willet have done well," he said to himself.

More of the fashion of New York came in and then a group of British officers, several of whom nodded to Grosvenor.

"The tall man with the gray hair at the temples is my colonel, Brandon," he said. "Very strict, but just to his men, and we like him. He spent some years in the service of the East India Company, in one of the hottest parts of the peninsula. That's why he's so brown, and it made his blood thin, too. He can't endure cold. The officer with him is one of our majors, Apthorpe. He has had less experience than the colonel, but thinks he knows more. His opinion of the French is very poor. Believes we ought to brush 'em aside with ease."

"I hope you don't think that way, Grosvenor," said Robert. "We in this country know that the French is one of the most valiant races the world has produced."

"And so do most thinking Englishmen. The only victories we boast much about are those we have won over the French, which shows that we consider them foes worthy of anybody's steel. But the play is going to begin, I believe. The hall is well filled now, and I'm not trying to make an appeal to your local pride, Lennox, when I tell you 'tis an audience that will compare well with one at Drury Lane or Covent Garden for splendor, and for variety 'twill excel it."

Robert was pleased secretly. Although more identified with Albany than New York, he considered himself nevertheless one of the people who belonged to the city at the mouth of the Hudson, and he felt already its coming greatness.

"We call ourselves Englishmen," he said modestly, "and we hope to achieve as much as the older Englishmen, our brethren across the seas."

"Have you seen many plays, Lennox?"

"But few, and none by great actors like Mr. Hallam and Mrs. Douglas. I suppose, Grosvenor, you've seen so many that they're no novelty to you."

"I can scarcely lay claim to being such a man about town as that. I have seen plays, of course, and some by the great Master Will, and I do confess that the mock life I behold beyond the footlights often thrills me more than the real life I see this side of them. Once, I witnessed this play 'Richard III,' which we are now about to see, and it stirred me so I could scarce contain myself, though some do say that our Shakespeare has made the hunchback king blacker than he really was."

Presently a little bell rang, the curtain rolled up, and Robert passed into an enchanted land. To vivid and imaginative youth the great style and action of Shakespeare make an irresistible appeal. Robert had never seen one of the mighty bard's plays before, and now he was in another world of romance and tragedy, suffused with poetry and he was held completely by the spell. Shakespeare may have blackened the character of the hunchback, but Robert believed him absolutely. To him Richard was exactly what the play made him.

Although the stage was but a temporary one, built in the hall of Rip Van Dam, it was large, the seating capacity was great and Hallam and his wife were among the best actors of their day, destined to a long career as stars in the colonies, and also afterward, when they ceased to be colonies. They and an able support soon took the whole audience captive, and all, fashionable and unfashionable alike, hung with breathless attention upon the play. Robert forgot absolutely everything around him, Willet was carried back to days of his youth, and Master Benjamin Hardy, who at heart was a lover of adventure and romance, responded to the great speeches the author has written for his characters. Tayoga did not stir, his face of bronze was unmoved, but now and then his dark eyes gleamed.

In reality the influence of the tragedy upon Tayoga was as great as it was upon Robert. The Onondaga had an unusual mind and being sent at an early age to school at Albany he had learned that the difference between white man and red was due chiefly to environment. Their hopes and fears, their rivalries and ambitions were, in truth, about the same. He had seen in some chief a soul much like that of humpbacked Richard, but, as he looked and listened, he also had a certain feeling of superiority. As he saw it, the great League, the Hodenosaunee, was governed better than England when York and Lancaster were tearing it to pieces. The fifty old sachems in the vale of Onondaga would decide more wisely and more justly than the English nobles. Tayoga, in that moment, was prouder than ever that he was born a member of the Clan of the Bear, of the nation Onondaga, and doubtless his patron saint, Tododaho, in his home on the great, shining star, agreed with him.

The first act closed amid great applause, several recalls of smiling and bowing actors followed, and then, during the wait, came a great buzz of talk. Robert shook himself and returned to the world.

"What do you like best about it, Lennox?" asked Grosvenor.

"The poetry. The things the people say. Things I've thought often myself, but which I haven't been able to put in a way that makes them strike upon you like a lightning flash."

"I think that describes Master Will. In truth, you've given me a description for my own feelings. Once more I repeat to you, Lennox, that 'tis a fine audience. I see here much British and Dutch wealth, and people whose lives have been a continuous drama."

"Truly it's so," said Robert, and, as his examining eye swept the crowd, he almost rose in his seat with astonishment, with difficulty suppressing a cry. Then he charged himself with being a fool. It could not be so! The thing was incredible! The man might look like him, but surely he would not be so reckless as to come to such a place.

Then he looked again, and he could no longer doubt. The stranger sat near the door and his dress was much like that of a prosperous seafaring man of the Dutch race. But Robert knew the blue eyes, lofty and questing like those of the eagle, and he was sure that the reddish beard had grown on a face other than the one it now adorned. It was St. Luc, whom he knew to be romantic, adventurous, and ready for any risk.

Robert moved his body forward a little, in order that it might be directly between Tayoga and the Frenchman, it being his first impulse to shelter St. Luc from the next person who was likely to recognize him. But the Onondaga was not looking in that direction. The young English officer, moved by his intense interest, had engaged him in conversation continually, surprised that Tayoga should know so much about the white race and history.

Robert looked so long at St. Luc, and with such a fixed and powerful gaze, that at last the chevalier turned and their eyes met. Robert's said:

"Why are you here? Your life is in danger every moment. If caught you will be executed as a spy."

"I'm not afraid," replied the eyes of St. Luc. "You alone have seen me as I am."

"But others will see you."

"I think not."

"How do you know that I will not proclaim at once who you are?"

"You will not because you do not wish to see me hanged or shot."

Then the eyes of St. Luc left Robert and wandered over the audience, which was now deeply engrossed in talk, although the Livingstons and the De Lanceys kept zealously away from one another, and the families who were closely allied with them by blood, politics or business also, stayed near their chiefs. Robert began to fancy that he might have been mistaken, it was not really St. Luc, he had allowed an imaginary resemblance to impose upon him, but reflection told him that it was no error. He would have known the intense gaze of those burning blue eyes anywhere. He was still careful to keep his own body between Tayoga and the Frenchman.

The curtain rose and once more Robert fell under the great writer's spell. Vivid action and poetic speech claimed him anew, and for the moment he forgot St. Luc. When the second act was finished, and while the applause was still filling the hall, he cast a fearful glance toward the place where he had seen the chevalier. Then, in truth, he rubbed his eyes. No St. Luc was there. The chair in which he had sat was not empty, but was occupied by a stolid, stout Dutchman, who seemed not to have moved for hours.

It had been a vision, a figment of the fancy, after all! But it was merely an attempt of the will to persuade himself that it was so. He could not doubt that he had seen St. Luc, who, probably listening to some counsel of providence, had left the hall. Robert felt an immense relief, and now he was able to assume his best manner when Mr. Hardy began to present him and Tayoga to many of the notables. He met the governor, Mr. Watts, and more De Lanceys, Wilsons and Crugers than he could remember, and he received invitations to great houses, and made engagements which he intended to keep, if it were humanly possible. Willet and Hardy exchanged glances when they noticed how easily he adapted himself to the great world of his day. He responded here as he had responded in Quebec, although Quebec and New York, each a center in its own way, were totally unlike.

The play went on, and Robert was still absorbed in the majestic lines. At the next intermission there was much movement in the audience. People walked about, old acquaintances spoke and strangers were introduced to one another. Robert looked sharply for St. Luc, but there was no trace of him. Presently Mr. Hardy was introducing him to a heavy man, dressed very richly, and obviously full of pride.

"Mynheer Van Zoon," he said, "this is young Robert Lennox. He has been for years in the care of David Willet, whom you have met in other and different times. Robert, Mynheer Van Zoon is one of our greatest merchants, and one of my most active rivals."

Robert was about to extend his hand, but noticing that Mynheer Van Zoon did not offer his he withheld his own. The merchant's face, in truth, had turned to deeper red than usual, and his eyes lowered. He was a few years older than Hardy, somewhat stouter, and his heavy strong features showed a tinge of cruelty. The impression that he made upon Robert was distinctly unfavorable.

"Yes, I have met Mr. Willet before," said Van Zoon, "but so many years have passed that I did not know whether he was still living. I can say the same about young Mr. Lennox."

"Oh, they live hazardous lives, but when one is skilled in meeting peril life is not snuffed out so easily," rejoined Mr. Hardy who seemed to be speaking from some hidden motive. "They've returned to civilization, and I think and trust, Adrian, that we'll hear more of them than for some years past. They're especial friends of mine, and I shall do the best I can for them, even though my mercantile rivalry with you absorbs, of necessity, so much of my energy."

Van Zoon smiled sourly, and then Robert liked him less than ever.

"The times are full of danger," he said, "and one must watch to keep his own."

He bowed, and turned to other acquaintances, evidently relieved at parting with them.

"He does not improve with age," said Willet thoughtfully.

Robert was about to ask questions concerning this Adrian Van Zoon, who seemed uneasy in their presence, but once more he restrained himself, his intuition telling him as before that neither Willet nor Master Hardy would answer them.

The play moved on towards its dramatic close and Robert was back in the world of passion and tragedy, of fancy and poetry. Van Zoon was forgotten, St. Luc faded quite away, and he was not conscious of the presence of Tayoga, or of Grosvenor, or of any of his friends. Shakespeare's *Richard* was wholly the humpbacked villain to him, and when he met his fate on Bosworth Field he rejoiced greatly. As the curtain went down for the last time he saw that Tayoga, too, was moved.

"The English king was a wicked man," he said, "but he died like a great chief."

They all passed out now, the street was filled with carriages and the torches of the link boys and there was a great hum of conversation. St. Luc returned to Robert's mind, but he kept to himself the fact that he had been in the theater. It might be his duty to state to the military that he had seen in the city an important Frenchman who must have come as a spy, but he could not do so. Nor did he feel any pricklings of the conscience about it, because he believed, even if he gave warning of St. Luc's presence, the wary chevalier would escape.

They stood at the edge of the sidewalk, watching the carriages, great high-bodied vehicles, roll away. Mr. Hardy had a carriage of his own, but the distance between his house and the theater was so short that he had not thought it necessary to use it. The night was clear, very cold and the illusion of the play was still upon the younger members of his group.

"You liked it?" said Mr. Hardy, looking keenly at Robert.

"It was another and wonderful world to me," replied the youth.

"I thought it would make a great appeal to you," said Master Benjamin. "Your type of mind always responds quickly to the poetic drama. Ah, there goes Mynheer Adrian Van Zoon. He has entered his carriage without looking once in our direction."

He and Willet and Master Jonathan laughed together, softly but with evident zest. Whatever the feeling between them and whatever the cause might be, Robert felt that they had the advantage of Mynheer Van Zoon that night and were pushing it. They watched the crowd leave and the lights fade in the darkness, and then they walked back together to the solid red brick house of Mr. Hardy, where Grosvenor took leave of them, all promising that the acquaintance should be continued.

"A fine young man," said Mr. Hardy, thoughtfully. "I wish that more of his kind would come over. We can find great use for them in this country."

Charteris also said farewell to them, telling them that his own house was not far away, and offering them his services in any way they wished as long as they remained in the city.

"Another fine young man," said Master Benjamin, as the tall figure of Charteris melted away in the darkness. "A good representative of our city's best blood and manners, and yes, of morals, too."

Robert went alone the next morning to the new public library, founded the year before and known as the New York Society Library, a novelty then and a great evidence of municipal progress. The most eminent men of the city, appointed by Governor de Lancey, were its trustees, and, the collection already being large, Robert spent a happy hour or two glancing through the books. History and fiction appealed most to him, but he merely looked a little here and there, opening many volumes. He was proud that the intelligence and enterprise of New York had founded so noble an institution and he promised himself that if, in the time to come, he should be a permanent resident of the city, his visits there would be frequent.

When he left the library it was about noon, the day being cloudy and dark with flurries of snow, those who were in the streets shivering with the raw cold. Robert drew his own heavy cloak closely about him, and, bending his head a little, strolled toward the Battery, in order to look again at the ships that came from so many parts of the earth. A stranger, walking in slouching fashion, and with the collar of his coat pulled well up about his face, shambled directly in his way. When Robert turned the man turned also and said in a low tone:

"Mr. Lennox!"

"St. Luc!" exclaimed Robert. "Are you quite mad? Don't you know that your life is in danger every instant?"

"I am not mad, nor is the risk as great as you think. Walk on by my side, as if you knew me."

"I did not think, chevalier, that your favorite role was that of a spy."

"Nor is it. This New York of yours is a busy city, and a man, even a Frenchman, may come here for other reasons than to learn military secrets."

Robert stared at him, but St. Luc admonished him again to look in front of him, and walk on as if they were old acquaintances on some business errand.

"I don't think you want to betray me to the English," he said.

"No, I don't," said Robert, "though my duty, perhaps, should make me do so."

"But you won't. I felt assured of it, else I should not have spoken to you."

"What duty, other than that of a spy, can have brought you to New York?"

"Why make it a duty? It is true the times are troubled, and full of wars, but one, on occasion, may seek his pleasure, nevertheless. Let us say that I came to New York to see the play which both of us witnessed last night. 'Twas excellently done. I have seen plays presented in worse style at much more pretentious theaters in Paris.

Moreover I, a Frenchman, love Shakespeare. I consider him the equal of our magnificent Molière."

"Which means that if you were not a Frenchman you would think him better."

"A pleasant wit, Mr. Lennox. I am glad to see it in you. But you will admit that I have come a long distance and incurred a great risk to attend a play by a British author given in a British town, though it must be admitted that the British town has strong Dutch lineaments. Furthermore, I do bear witness that I enjoyed the play greatly. 'Twas worth the trouble and the danger."

"Since you insist, chevalier, that you came so great a distance and incurred so great a risk merely to worship at the shrine of our Shakespeare, as one gentleman to another I cannot say that I doubt your word. But when we sailed down the Hudson on a sloop, and were compelled to tie up in a cove to escape the wrath of a storm, I saw you on the slope above me."

"I saw you, too, then, Mr. Lennox, and I envied you your snug place on the sloop. That storm was one of the most unpleasant incidents in my long journey to New York to see Shakespeare's 'Richard III.' Still, when one wishes a thing very badly one must be willing to pay a high price for it. It was a good play by a good writer, the actors were most excellent, and I have had sufficient reward for my trouble and danger."

The collar of his cloak was drawn so high now that it formed almost a hood around his head and face, but he turned a little, and Robert saw the blue eyes, as blue as his own, twinkling with a humorous light. It was borne upon him with renewed force that here was a champion of romance and high adventure. St. Luc was a survival. He was one of those knights of the Middle Ages who rode forth with lance and sword to do battle, perhaps for a lady's favor, and perhaps to crush the infidel. His own spirit, which had in it a lightness, a gayety and a humor akin to St. Luc's, responded at once.

"Since you found the play most excellent, and I had the same delight, I presume that you will stay for all the others. Mr. Hallam and his fine company are in New York for two weeks, if not longer. Having come so far and at such uncommon risks, you will not content yourself with a single performance?"

"Alas! that is the poison in my cup. The leave of absence given me by the Governor General of Canada is but brief, and I can remain in this city and stronghold of my enemy but a single night."

They passed several men, but none took any notice of them. The day had increased in gloominess. Heavy clouds were coming up from the sea, enveloping the solid town in a thick and somber atmosphere. Snow began to fall and a sharp wind drove the flakes before it. Pedestrians bent forward, and drew their cloaks or coats about their faces to protect themselves from the storm.

"The weather favors us," said St. Luc. "The people of New York defending themselves from the wind and the flakes will have no time to be looking for an enemy among them."

"Where are we going, chevalier?"

"That I know not, but being young, healthy and strong, perhaps we walk in a circle for the sake of exercise."

"For which also you have come to New York—in order that you may walk about our Battery and Bowling Green."

"True! Quite true! You have a most penetrating mind, Mr. Lennox, and since we speak of the objects of my errand here I recall a third, but of course, a minor motive."

"I am interested in that third and minor motive, Chevalier de St. Luc."

"I noticed last night at the play that you were speaking to a merchant, one Adrian Van Zoon."

"'Tis true, but how do you know Van Zoon?"

"Let it suffice, lad, that I know him and know him well. I wish you to beware of him."

He spoke with a sudden softness of tone that touched Robert, and there could be no doubt that his meaning was good. They were still walking in the most casual manner, their faces bent to the driving snow, and almost hidden by the collars of their cloaks.

"What can Adrian Van Zoon and I have in common?" asked Robert.

"Lad, I bid thee again to beware of him! Look to it that you do not fall into his treacherous hands!"

His sudden use of the pronoun "thee," and his intense earnestness, stirred Robert deeply.

"Friends seem to rise around me, due to no merit of mine," he said. "Willet has always watched over me. Tayoga is my brother. Jacobus Huysman has treated me almost as his own son, and Master Benjamin Hardy has received me with great warmth of heart. And now you deliver to me a warning that I cannot but believe is given with the best intent. But again I ask you, why should I fear Adrian Van Zoon?"

"That, lad, I will not tell you, but once more I bid you beware of him. Think you, I'd have taken such a risk to prepare you for a danger, if it were not real?"

"I do not. I feel, Chevalier de St. Luc, that you are a friend in truth. Shall I speak of this to Mr. Willet? He will not blame me for hiding the knowledge of your presence here."

"No. Keep it to yourself, but once more I tell you beware of Adrian Van Zoon. Now you will not see me again for a long time, and perhaps it will be on the field of battle. Have no fears for my safety. I can leave this solid town of yours as easily as I entered it. Farewell!"

"Farewell!" said Robert, with a real wrench at the heart. St. Luc left him and walked swiftly in the direction of St. George's Chapel. The snow increased so much and was driving so hard that in forty or fifty paces he disappeared entirely and Robert, wishing shelter, went back to the house of Benjamin Hardy, moved by many and varied emotions.

He could not doubt that St. Luc's warning was earnest and important, but why should he have incurred such great risks to give it? What was he to Adrian Van Zoon? and what was Adrian Van Zoon to him? And what did the talk at night between Willet and Hardy mean? He, seemed to be the center of a singular circle of complications, of which other people might know much, but of which he knew nothing.

Mr. Hardy's house was very solid, very warm and very comfortable. He was still at the Royal Exchange, but Mr. Pillsbury had come home, and was standing with his back to a great fire, his coattails drawn under either arm in front of him. A gleam of warmth appeared in his solemn eyes at the sight of Robert.

"A fierce day, Master Robert," he said. "'Tis good at such a time to stand before a red fire like this, and have stout walls between one and the storm."

"Spoken truly, Master Jonathan," said Robert, as he joined him before the fire, and imitated his position.

"You have been to our new city library? We are quite proud of it."

"Yes, I was there, but I have also been thinking a little."

"Thought never hurts one. We should all be better if we took more thought upon ourselves."

"I was thinking of a man whom we saw at the play last night, the merchant, Adrian Van Zoon."

Master Jonathan let his coattails fall from under his arms, and then he deliberately gathered them up again.

"A wealthy and powerful merchant. He has ships on many seas."

"I have inferred that Mr. Hardy does not like him."

"Considering my words carefully, I should say that Mr. Hardy does not like Mr. Van Zoon and that Mr. Van Zoon does not like Mr. Hardy."

"I'm not seeking to be intrusive, but is it just business rivalry?"

"You are not intrusive, Master Robert. But my knowledge seldom extends beyond matters of business."

"Which means that you might be able to tell me, but you deem it wiser not to do so."

"The storm increases, Master Robert. The snow is almost blinding. I repeat that it is a most excellent fire before which we are standing. Mr. Hardy and your friends will be here presently and we shall have food."

"It seems to me, Master Jonathan, that the people of New York eat much and often."

"It sustains life and confers a harmless pleasure."

"To return a moment to Adrian Van Zoon. You say that his ships are upon every sea. In what trade are they engaged, mostly?"

"In almost everything, Master Robert. They say he does much smuggling—but I don't object to a decent bit of smuggling—and I fear that certain very fast vessels of his know more than a little about the slave trade."

"I trust that Mr. Hardy has never engaged in such a traffic."

"You may put your mind at rest upon that point, Master Robert. No amount of profit could induce Mr. Hardy to engage in such commerce."

Mr. Hardy, Tayoga and Willet came in presently, and the merchant remained a while after his dinner. The older men smoked pipes and talked together and Robert and Tayoga looked out at the driving snow. Tayoga had received a letter from Colonel William Johnson that morning, informing him that all was well at the vale of Onondaga, and the young Onondaga was pleased. They were speaking of their expected departure to join Braddock's army, but they had heard from Willet that they were to remain longer than they had intended in New York, as the call to march demanded no hurry.

CHAPTER XII
THE SLAVER

Robert spent more days in New York, and they were all pleasant. His own handsome face and winning manner would have made his way anywhere, but it became known universally that a great interest was taken in him by Mr. Benjamin Hardy, who was a great figure in the city, a man not to be turned lightly into an enemy. It also seemed that some mystery enveloped him—mystery always attracts—and the lofty and noble figure of the young Onondaga, who was nearly always by his side, heightened the romantic charm he had for all those with whom he came in contact. Both Hardy and Willet urged him to go wherever he was asked by the great, and clothes fitted to such occasions were provided promptly.

"I am not able to pay for these," said Robert to Willet when he was being measured for the first of his fine raiment.

"Don't trouble yourself about it," said the hunter, smiling, "I have sufficient to meet the bills, and I shall see that all your tailors are reimbursed duly. Some one must always look after a man of fashion."

"I wish I knew more than I do," said Robert in troubled tones, "because I've a notion that the money with which you will pay my tailor comes from the till of Master Benjamin Hardy. It's uncommon strange that he does so much for me. I'm very grateful, but surely there must be some motive behind it."

He glanced at Willet to see how he took his words, but the hunter merely smiled, and Robert knew that the smile was a mask through which he could not penetrate.

"Take the goods the gods provide thee," said the hunter.

"I will," said Robert, cheerfully, "since it seems I can't do anything else."

And he did. His response to New York continued to be as vigorous as it had been to Quebec, and while New York lacked some of the brilliancy, some of the ultimate finish that, to his mind, had distinguished Quebec, it was more solid, there was more of an atmosphere of resource, and it was all vastly interesting. Charteris proved himself a right true friend, and he opened for him whatever doors he cared to enter that Mr. Hardy may have left unlocked. He was also thrown much with Grosvenor, and the instinctive friendship between the two ripened fast.

On the fifth day of his stay in New York a letter came out of the wilderness from Wilton at Fort Refuge. It had been brought by an Oneida runner to Albany, and was sent thence by post to New York.

Wilton wrote that time would pass rather heavily with them in the little fortress, if the hostile Indians allowed it. Small bands now infested that region, and the soldiers were continually making marches against them. The strange man, whom they called Black Rifle, was of vast help, guiding them and saving them from ambush.

Wilton wrote that he missed Philadelphia, which was certainly the finest city outside of Europe, but he hoped to go back to it, seasoned and improved by life in the woods. New York, where he supposed Robert now to be, was an attractive town, in truth, a great port, but it had not the wealth and cultivation of Philadelphia, as he hoped to show Robert some day. Meanwhile he wished him well.

Robert smiled. He had pleasant memories of Wilton, Colden, Carson and the others, and while he was making new friends he did not commit the crime of forgetting old ones. It was his hope that he should meet them all again, not merely after the war, but long before.

In his comings and goings among the great of their day Robert kept a keen eye for the vision of St. Luc. He half hoped, half feared that some time in the twilight or the full dusk of the night he would see in some narrow street the tall figure wrapped in its great cloak. But the chevalier did not appear, and Robert felt that he had not really come as a spy upon the English army and its preparations. He must have gone, days since.

He met Adrian Van Zoon three times, that is, he was in the same room with him, although they spoke together only once. The merchant had in his presence an air of detachment. He seemed to be one who continually carried a burden, and a stripling just from the woods could not long have a place, either favorable or unfavorable, in his memory. Robert began to wonder if St. Luc had net been mistaken. What could a man born and bred in France, and only in recent years an inhabitant of Canada, know of Adrian Van Zoon of New York? What, above all, could he know that would cause him to warn Robert against him? But this, like all his other questions, disappeared in the enjoyments of the moment. Nature, which had been so kind in giving to him a vivid imagination, had also given with it an intense appreciation. He liked nearly everything, and nearly everybody, he could see a rosy mist where the ordinary man saw only a cloud, and just now New York was so kind to him that he loved it all.

A week in the city and he attended a brilliant ball given by William Walton in the Walton mansion, in Franklin Square, then the most elaborate and costly home in North America. It was like a great English country house, with massive brick walls and woodwork, all imported and beautifully carved. The staircase in particular made of dark ebony was the wonder of its day, and, in truth, the whole interior was like that of a palace, instead of a private residence, at that time, in America.

Robert enjoyed himself hugely. He realized anew how close was the blood relationship among all those important families, and he was already familiar with their names. The powerful sponsorship of Mr. Hardy had caused them to take him in as one of their number, and for that reason he liked them all the more. He was worldly wise enough already to know that we are more apt to call a social circle snobbish when we do not belong to it. Now, he was a welcome visitor at the best houses in New York, and all was rose to him.

Adrian Van Zoon, who had not only wealth but strong connections, was there, but, as on recent occasions he took no notice of Robert, until late in the evening when the guests were dancing the latest Paris and London dances in the great drawing-room. Robert was resting for a little space and as he leaned against the wall the merchant drew near him and addressed him with much courtesy.

"I fear, Mr. Lennox," he said, "that I have spoken to you rather brusquely, for which I offer many apologies. It was due, perhaps, to the commercial rivalries of myself and Mr. Hardy, in whose house you are staying. It was but natural for me to associate you with him."

"I wish to be linked with him," said Robert, coldly. "I have a great liking and respect for Mr. Hardy."

Mynheer Van Zoon laughed and seemed not at all offended.

"The answer of a lad, and a proper one for a lad," he said. "'Tis well to be loyal to one's friends, and I must admit, too, that Mr. Hardy is a man of many high qualities, a fact that a rivalry in business extending over many years, has proved to me. He and I cannot become friends, but I do respect him."

He had imparted some warmth to his tone, and his manner bore the appearance of geniality. Robert, so susceptible to courtesy in others, began to find him less repellent. He rejoined in the same polite manner, and Mynheer Van Zoon talked to him a little while as a busy man of middle age would speak to a youth. He asked him of his experiences at Quebec, of which he had heard some rumor, and Robert, out of the fullness of his mind, spoke freely on that subject.

"Is it true," asked Mynheer Van Zoon, "that David Willet in a duel with swords slew a famous bravo?"

"It's quite true," replied Robert. "I was there, and saw it with my own eyes. Pierre Boucher was the man's name, and never was a death more deserved."

"Willet is a marvel with the sword."

"You knew him in his youth, Mynheer Van Zoon?"

"I did not say that. It is possible that I was thinking of some one who had talked to me about him. But, whatever thought may have been in my mind, David Willet and I are not likely to tread the same path. I repeat, Master Lennox, that although my manner may have seemed to you somewhat brusque in the past, I wish you well. Do you remain much longer in New York?"

"Only a few days, I think."

"And you still find much of interest to see?"

"Enough to occupy the remainder of my time. I wish to see a bit of Long Island, but tomorrow I go to Paulus Hook to find one Nicholas Suydam and to carry him a message from Colonel William Johnson, which has but lately come to me in the post. I suppose it will be easy to get passage across the Hudson."

"Plenty of watermen will take you for a fare, but if you are familiar with the oars yourself it would be fine exercise for a strong youth like you to row over and then back again."

"It's a good suggestion, as I do row, and I think I'll adopt it."

Mynheer Van Zoon passed on a moment or two later, and Robert, with his extraordinary susceptibility to a friendly manner, felt a pleasant impression. Surely St. Luc, who at least was an official enemy, did not know the truth about Van Zoon! And if the Frenchman did happen to be right, what did he have to fear in New York, surrounded by friends?

The evening progressed, but Mynheer Van Zoon left early, and then in the pleasures of the hour, surrounded by youth and brightness, Robert forgot him, too. A banquet was served late, and there was such a display of silver and gold plate that the British officers themselves opened their eyes and later wrote letters to England, telling of the amazing prosperity and wealth of New York, as proven by what they had seen in the Walton and other houses.

Robert did not go back to the home of Mr. Hardy, until a very late hour, and he slept late the next day. When he rose he found that all except himself had gone forth for one purpose or another, but it suited his own plan well, as he could now take the letter of Colonel William Johnson to his friend, Master Nicholas Suydam, in Paulus Hook. It was another dark, gloomy day, but clouds and cold had little effect on his spirits, and when he walked along the shore of the North River, looking for a boat, he met the chaff of the watermen with humorous remarks of his own. They discouraged his plan to row himself across, but being proud of his skill he clung to it, and, having deposited two golden guineas as security for its return, he selected a small but strong boat and rowed into the stream.

A sharp wind was blowing in from the sea, but he was able to manage his little craft with ease, and, being used to rough water, he enjoyed the rise and dip of the waves. A third of the way out and he paused and looked back at New York, the steeple of St. George's showing above the line of houses. He could distinguish from the mass other buildings that he knew, and his heart suddenly swelled with affection for this town, in which he had received such a warm welcome. He would certainly live here, when the wars were over, and he could settle down to his career.

Then he turned his eyes to the inner bay, where he saw the usual amount of shipping, sloops, schooners, brigs and every other kind of vessel known to the times. Behind them rose the high wooded shores of Staten Island, and through the channel between it and Long Island Robert saw other ships coming in. Truly, it was a noble bay, apparently made for the creation of a great port, and already busy man was putting it to its appointed use. Then he looked up the Hudson at the lofty Palisades, the precipitous shores facing them, and his eyes came back to the stream. Several vessels under full sail were steering for the mouth of the Hudson, but he looked longest at a schooner, painted a dark color, and very trim in her lines. He saw two men standing on her decks, and two or three others visible in her rigging.

Evidently she was a neat and speedy craft, but he was not there to waste his time looking at schooners. The letter of Colonel William Johnson to Master Nicholas Suydam in Paulus Hook must be delivered, and, taking up his oars, he rowed vigorously toward the hamlet on the Jersey shore.

When he was about two-thirds of the way across he paused to look back again, but the air was so heavy with wintry mists that New York did not show at all. He was about to resume the oars once more when the sound of creaking cordage caused him to look northward. Then he shouted in alarm. The dark schooner was bearing down directly upon him, and was coming very swiftly. A man on the deck whom he took to be the captain shouted at him, but when Robert, pulling hard, shot his boat ahead, it seemed to him that the schooner changed her course also.

It was the last impression he had of the incident, as the prow of the schooner struck his boat and clove it in twain. He jumped instinctively, but his head received a glancing blow, and he did not remember anything more until he awoke in a very dark and close place. His head ached abominably, and when he strove to raise a hand to it he found that he could not do so. He thought at first that it was due to weakness, a sort of temporary paralysis, coming from the blow that he dimly remembered, but he realized presently that his hands were bound, tied tightly to his sides.

He moved his body a little, and it struck against wood on either side. His feet also were bound, and he became conscious of a swaying motion. He was in a ship's bunk and he was a prisoner of somebody.

He was filled with a fierce and consuming rage. He had no doubt that he was on the schooner that had run him down, nor did he doubt either that he had been run down purposely. Then he lay still and by long staring was able to make out a low swaying roof above him and very narrow walls. It was a strait, confined place, and it was certainly deep down in the schooner's hold. A feeling of horrible despair seized him. The darkness, his aching head, and his bound hands and feet filled him with the worst forebodings. Nor did he have any way of estimating time. He might have been lying in the bunk at least a week, and he might now be far out at sea.

In misfortune, the intelligent and imaginative suffer most because they see and feel everything, and also foresee further misfortunes to come. Robert's present position brought to him in a glittering train all that he had lost. Having a keen social sense his life in New York had been one of continuing charm. Now the balls and receptions that he had attended at great houses came back to him, even more brilliant and vivid than their original colors had been. He remembered the many beautiful women he had seen, in their dresses of silk or satin, with their rosy faces and powdered hair, and the great merchants and feudal landowners, and the British and American officers in their bright new uniforms, talking proudly of the honors they expected to win.

Then that splendid dream was gone, vanishing like a mist before a wind, and he was back in the swaying darkness of the bunk, hands and feet bound, and head aching. All things are relative. He felt now if only the cruel cords were taken off his wrists and ankles he could be happy. Then he would be able to sit up, move his limbs, and his head would stop aching. He called all the powers of his will to his aid. Since he could not move he would not cause himself any increase of pain by striving to do so. He commanded his body to lie still and compose itself and it obeyed. In a little while his head ceased to ache so fiercely, and the cords did not bite so deep.

Then he took thought. He was still sure that he was on board the schooner that had run him down. He remembered the warning of St. Luc against Adrian Van Zoon, and Adrian Van Zoon's suggestion that he row his own boat across to Paulus Hook. But it seemed incredible. A merchant, a rich man of high standing in New York, could not plan his murder. Where was the motive? And, if such a motive did exist, a man of Van Zoon's standing could not afford to take so great a risk. In spite of St. Luc and his faith in him he dismissed it as an impossibility. If Van Zoon had wished his death he would not have been taken out of the river. He must seek elsewhere the reason of his present state.

He listened attentively, and it seemed to him that the creaking and groaning of the cordage increased. Once or twice he thought he heard footsteps over his head, but he concluded that it was merely the imagination. Then, after an interminable period of waiting, the door to the room opened and a man carrying a ship's lantern entered, followed closely by another. Robert was able to turn on his side and stare at them.

The one who carried the lantern was short, very dark, and had gold rings in his ears. Robert judged him to be a Portuguese. But his attention quickly passed to the man behind him, who was much taller, rather spare, his face clean shaven, his hard blue eyes set close together. Robert knew instinctively that he was master of the ship.

"Hold up the lantern, Miguel," the tall man said, "and let's have a look at him."

The Portuguese obeyed.

Then Robert felt the hard blue eyes fastened upon him, but he raised himself as much as he could and gave back the gaze fearlessly.

"Well, how's our sailorman?" said the captain, laughing, and his laughter was hideous to the prisoner.

"I don't understand you," said Robert.

"My meaning is plain enough, I take it."

"I demand that you set me free at once and restore me to my friends in New York."

The tall man laughed until he held his sides, and the short man laughed with him, laugh for laugh. Their laughter so filled Robert with loathing and hate that he would have attacked them both had he been unbound.

"Come now, Peter," said the captain at last. "Enough of your grand manner. You carry it well for a common sailor, and old Nick himself knows where you got your fine clothes, but here you are back among your old comrades, and you ought to be glad to see 'em."

"What do you mean?" asked the astonished Robert.

"Now, don't look so surprised. You can keep up a play too long. You know as well as we do that you're plain Peter Smith, an able young sailorman, when you're willing, who deserted us in Baltimore three months ago, and you with a year yet to serve. And here's your particular comrade, Miguel, so glad to see you. When we ran your boat down, all your own fault, too, Miguel jumped overboard, and he didn't dream that the lad he was risking his life to save was his old chum. Oh, 'twas a pretty reunion! And now, Peter, thank Miguel for bringing you back to life and to us."

A singular spirit seized Robert. He saw that he was at the mercy of these men, who utterly without scruple wished for some reason to hold him. He could be a player too, and perhaps more was to be won by being a player.

"I'm sorry," he said, "but I was tempted by the follies of the land, and I've had enough of 'em. If you'll overlook it and let the past be buried, captain, you'll have no better seaman than Peter Smith. You've always been a just but kind man, and so I throw myself on your mercy."

The captain and Miguel exchanged astonished glances.

"I know you'll do it, captain," Robert went on in his most winning tones, "because, as I've just said, you've always been a kind man, especially kind to me. I suppose when I first signed with you that I was as ignorant and awkward a land lubber as you ever saw. But your patient teaching has made me a real sailor. Release me now, and I think that in a few hours I will be fit to go to work again."

"Cut the lashings, Miguel," said the captain.

Miguel's sharp knife quickly severed them, and Robert sat up in the bunk. When the blood began to flow freely in the veins, cut off hitherto, he felt stinging pains at first, but presently heavenly relief came. The captain and Miguel stood looking at him.

"Peter," said the captain, "you were always a lad of spirit, and I'm glad to get you back, particularly as we have such a long voyage ahead of us. One doesn't go to the coast of Africa, gather a cargo of slaves and get back in a day."

In spite of himself Robert could not repress a shudder of horror. A slaver and he a prisoner on board her! He might be gone a year or more. Never was a lad in worse case, but somewhere in him was a spark of hope that refused to be extinguished. He gave a more imperious summons than ever to his will, and it returned to his aid.

"You've been kind to Peter Smith. Few captains would forgive what I've done, but I'll try to make it up to you. How long are we out from New York?" he said.

"It might be an hour or it might be a day or what's more likely it might be two days. You see, Peter, a lad who gets a crack on the head like yours lies still and asleep for a long time. Besides, it don't make any difference to you how long we've been out. So, just you stay in your bunk a little while longer, and Miguel will bring you something to eat and drink."

"Thank you, captain. You're almost a father to me."

"That's a good lad, Peter. I am your father, I'm the father of all my crew, and don't forget that a father sometimes has to punish his children, so just you stay in your bunk till you're bid to come out of it."

"Thank you, captain. I wouldn't think of disobeying you. Besides, I'm too weak to move yet."

The captain and Miguel went out, and Robert heard them fastening the door on the outside. Then the darkness shut him in again, and he lay back in his bunk. The spark of hope somewhere in his mind had grown a little larger. His head had ceased to ache and his limbs were free. The physical difference made a mental difference yet greater. Although there seemed to be absolutely no way out, he would find one.

The door was opened again, and Miguel, bearing the ship's lantern in one hand and a plate of food in the other, came in. It was rough food such as was served on rough ships, but Robert sat up and looked at it hungrily. Miguel grinned, and laughed until the gold hoops in his ears shook.

"You, Peter Smith," he said. "Me terrible glad to see you again. Miss my old comrade. Mourn for him, and then when find him jump into the cold river to save him."

"It's true," said Robert, "it was a long and painful parting, but here we are, shipmates again. It was good of you, Miguel, to risk your life to save me, and now that we've had so many polite interchanges, suppose you save me from starving to death and pass that plate of food."

"With ver' good will, Peter. Eat, eat with the great heartiness, because we have ver', ver' hard work before us and for a long time. The captain will want you to do as much work in t'ree mont' as t'ree men do, so you can make up the t'ree mont' you have lost."

"Tell him I'm ready. I've already confessed all my sins to him."

"He won't let you work as sailor at first. He make you help me in the cook's galley."

"I'm willing to do that too. You know I can cook. You'll remember, Miguel, how I helped you in the Mediterranean, and how I did almost all your work that time you were sick, when we were cruising down to the Brazils?"

Miguel grinned.

"You have the great courage, you Peter," he said. "You always have. Feel better now?"

"A lot, Miguel. The bread was hard, I suppose, and better potatoes have been grown, but I didn't notice the difference. That was good water, too. I've always thought that water was a fine drink. And now, Miguel, hunger and thirst being satisfied, I'll get up and stretch my limbs a while. Then I'll be ready to go to work."

"I tell you when the captain wants you. Maybe an hour from now, maybe two hours."

He took his lantern and the empty plate and withdrew, but Robert heard him fastening the door on the outside again. Evidently they did not yet wholly trust the good intentions of Peter Smith, the deserter, whom they had recaptured in the Hudson. But the spark of hope lodged somewhere in the mind of Peter Smith was still growing and glowing. The removal of the bonds from his wrist and ankles had brought back a full and free circulation, and the food and water had already restored strength to one so young and strong. He stood up, flexed his muscles and took deep breaths.

He had no familiarity with the sea, but he was used to navigation in canoes and boats on large and small lakes in the roughest kind of weather, and the rocking of the schooner, which continued, did not make him seasick, despite the close foul air of the little room in which he was locked. He still heard the creaking of cordage and now he heard the tumbling of waves too, indicating that the weather was rough. He tried to judge by these sounds how fast the schooner was moving, but he could make nothing of it. Then he strained his memory to see if he could discover in any manner how long he had been on the vessel, but the period of his unconsciousness remained a mystery, which he could not unveil by a single second.

Long stay in the room enabled him to penetrate its dusk a little, and he saw that its light and air came in normal times from a single small porthole, closed now. Nevertheless a few wisps of mist entered the tiny crevices, and he inferred the vessel was in a heavy fog. He was glad of it, because he believed the schooner would move slowly at such a time, and anything that impeded the long African journey was to his advantage.

A period which seemed to be six hours but which he afterward knew to be only one, passed, and his door swung back for the third time. The face of Miguel appeared in the opening and again he grinned, until his mouth formed a mighty slash across his face.

"You come on deck now, you Peter," he said, "captain wants you."

Robert's heart gave a mighty beat. Only those who have been shut up in the dark know what it is to come out into the light. That alone was sufficient to give him a fresh store of courage and hope. So he followed Miguel up a narrow ladder and emerged upon the deck. As he had inferred, the schooner was in a heavy fog, with scarcely any wind and the sails hanging dead.

The captain stood near the mast, gazing into the fog. He looked taller and more evil than ever, and Robert saw the outline of a pistol beneath his heavy pea jacket. Several other men of various nationalities stood about the deck, and they gave Robert malicious smiles. Forward he saw a twelve pound brass cannon, a deadly and dangerous looking piece. It was extremely cold on deck, too, the raw fog seeming to be so much liquid ice, but, though Robert shivered, he liked it. Any kind of fresh air was heaven after that stuffy little cabin.

"How are you feeling, Peter?" asked the captain, although there was no note of sympathy in his voice.

"Very well, sir, thank you," replied Robert, "and again I wish to make my apologies for deserting, but the temptations of New York are very strong, sir. The city went to my head."

"So it seems. We missed you on the voyage to Boston and back, but we have you now. Doubtless Miguel has told you that you are to help him a couple of days in his galley, and you'll stay there close. If you come out before I give the word it's a belaying pin for you. But when I do give the word you'll go back to your work as one of the cleverest sailormen I ever had. You'll remember how you used to go out on the spars in the iciest and slipperiest weather. None so clever at it as you, Peter, and I'll soon see that you have the chance to show again to all the men that you're the best sailor aboard ship."

Robert shivered mentally. He divined the plan of this villain, who would send him in the icy rigging to sure death. He, an untrained sailor, could not keep his footing there in a storm, and it could be said that it was an accident, as it would be in the fulfilment though not in the intent. But he divined something else that stopped the mental shudder and that gave him renewed hope. Why should the captain threaten him with a belaying pin if he did not stay in the cook's galley for two days? To Robert's mind but one reason appeared, and it was the fear that he should be seen on deck. And that fear existed because they were yet close to land. It was all so clear to him that he never doubted and again his heart leaped. He was bareheaded, but he touched the place where his cap brim should have been and replied:

"I'll remember, captain."

"See that you do," said the man in level tones, instinct nevertheless with hardness and cruelty.

Robert touched his forehead again and turned away with Miguel, descending to the cook's galley, resolved upon some daring trial, he did not yet know what. Here the Portuguese set him to work at once, scouring pots and kettles and pans, and he toiled without complaint until his arms ached. Miguel at last began to talk. He seemed to suffer from the lack of companionship, and Robert divined that he was the only Portuguese on board.

"Good helper, you Peter," he said. "It no light job to cook for twenty men, and all of them hungry all the time."

"Have we our full crew on board, Miguel?"

"Yes, twenty men and four more, and plenty guns, plenty powder and ball. Fine cannon, too."

Robert judged that the slaver would be well armed and well manned, but he decided to ask no more questions at present, fearing to arouse the suspicions of Miguel, and he worked on with shut lips. The Portuguese himself talked—it seemed that he had to do so, as the longing for companionship overcame him—but he did not tell the name of the schooner or its captain. He merely chattered of former voyages and of the ports he had been in, invariably addressing his helper as Peter, and speaking of him as if he had been his comrade.

Robert, while apparently absorbed in his tasks, listened attentively to all that he might hear from above He knew that the fog was as thick as ever, and that the ship was merely moving up and down with the swells. She might be anchored in comparatively shallow water. Now he was absolutely sure that they were somewhere near the coast, and the coast meant hope and a chance.

Dinner, rude but plentiful, was served for the sailors and food somewhat more delicate for the captain in his cabin.

Robert himself attended to the captain, and he could see enough now to know that the dark had come. He inferred there would be no objection to his going upon deck in the night, but he made no such suggestion. Instead he waited upon the tall man with a care and deftness that made that somber master grin.

"I believe absence has really improved you, Peter," he said. "I haven't been waited on so well in a long time."

"Thank you, sir," said Robert.

Secretly he was burning with humiliation. It hurt his pride terribly to serve a rough sea captain in such a manner, but he had no choice and he resolved that if the chance came he would pay the debt. When the dinner or supper, whichever it might be called, was over, he went back to the galley and cheerfully began to clear away, and to wash and wipe dishes. Miguel gave him a compliment, saying that he had improved since their latest voyage and Robert thanked him duly.

When all the work was done he crawled into a bunk just over the cook's and in any other situation would have fallen asleep at once. But his nerves were on edge, and he was not sleepy in the least. Miguel, without taking off his clothes, lay down in the bunk beneath him, and Robert soon heard him snoring. He also heard new sounds from above, a whistle and a shriek and a roar combined that he did not recognize at first, but which a little thought told him to be a growing wind and the crash of the waves. The schooner began to dip and rise violently. He was dizzy for a little while, but he soon recovered. A storm! The knowledge gave him pleasure. He did not know why, but he felt that it, too, contributed hope and a chance.

The roar of the storm increased, but Miguel, who had probably spent nearly all his life at sea, continued to sleep soundly. Robert was never in his life more thoroughly awake.

He sat up in his bunk, and now and then he heard the sound of voices and of footsteps overhead, but soon they were lost entirely in the incessant shrieking of the wind and the continuous thunder of the great waves against the side of the schooner. In truth, it was a storm, one of great fury. He knew that the ship although stripped to the utmost, must be driving fast, but in what direction he had no idea. He would have given much to know.

The tumult grew and by and by he heard orders shouted through a trumpet. He could stand it no longer, and, leaping down, he seized the Portuguese by the shoulder and shook him.

"Up, Miguel," he cried. "A great storm is upon us!"

The cook opened his eyes sleepily, and then sprang up, a look of alarm on his face. While the eyes of the Portuguese were filled with fear, he also seemed to be in a daze. It was apparent to Robert that he was a heavy sleeper, and his long black hair falling about his forehead he stared wildly. His aspect made an appeal to Robert's sense of humor, even in those tense moments.

"My judgment tells me, Miguel," he shouted—he was compelled to raise his voice to a high pitch owing to the tremendous clatter overhead—"that there is a great storm, and the schooner is in danger! And you know, too, that your old comrade, Peter Smith, who has sailed the seas with you so long, is likely to be right in his opinions!"

The gaze of Miguel became less wild, but he looked at Robert with awe and then with superstition.

"You have brought us bad luck," he exclaimed. "An evil day for us when you came aboard."

Robert laughed. A fanciful humor seized him.

"But this is my place," he said. "I, Peter Smith, belong on board this schooner and you know, Miguel, that you and the captain insisted on my coming back."

"We go on deck!" cried the cook, now thoroughly alarmed by the uproar, which always increased. He rushed up the ladder and Robert followed him, to be blown completely off his feet when he reached the deck. But he snatched at the woodwork, held fast, and regained an upright position. The captain stood not far away, holding to a rope, but he was so deeply engrossed in directing his men that he paid no attention to Robert.

The youth cleared the mist and spray from his eyes and took a comprehensive look. The aspect of sea and sky was enough to strike almost any one with terror, but upon this occasion he was an exception. He had never looked upon a wilder world, but in its very wildness lay his hope. The icy spars from which he would slip to plunge to his death in the chilling sea were gone, and so was far Africa, and the slaver's hunt. He was not a seaman, his experience had been with lakes, but one could reason from lakes to the universal ocean, and he knew that the schooner was in a fight for life. And involved in it was his fight for freedom.

The wind, cold as death, and sharp as a sword, blew out of the northeast, and the schooner, heeled far over, was driving fast before it, in spite of every effort of a capable captain and crew. The ship rose and fell violently with the huge swells, and water that stung like an icy sleet swept over her continually. Looking to the westward Robert saw something that caused his heart to throb violently. It was a dim low line, but he knew it to be land.

What land it was he had no idea, nor did he at the moment care, but there lay freedom. Rows of breakers opening their strong teeth for the ship might stretch between, but better the breakers than the slaver's deck and the man hunt in the slimy African lagoons. For him the icy wind was the breath of life, and he soon ceased to shiver. But he became conscious of chattering teeth near him and he saw Miguel, his face a reproduction of terror in all its aspects.

"We go!" shouted the Portuguese. "The storm drive the ship on the breakers and she break to pieces, and all of us lost!"

Robert's fantastic spirit was again strong upon him.

"Then let us go!" he shouted back. "Better this clean, cold coast than the fever swamps of Africa! Hold fast, Miguel, and we'll ride in together!"

The superstitious awe of the Portuguese deepened, and he drew away from Robert. In the moment of terrible storm and approaching death this could be no mortal youth who showed not fear, but instead a joy that was near to exaltation. Then and there he was convinced that when they had seized him and brought him aboard they had made their own doom certain.

"In twenty minutes, we strike!" cried Miguel. "Ah, how the wind rise! Many a year since I see such a storm!"

Spars snapped and were carried away in the foaming sea. Then the mast went, and the crew began to launch the boats. Robert rushed to the captain's cabin. When he served the man there he had not failed to observe what the room contained, and now he snatched from the wall a huge greatcoat, a belt containing a brace of pistols in a holster with ammunition, and a small sword. He did not know why he took the sword, but it was probably some trick of the fancy and he buckled it on with the rest. Then he returned to the deck, where he could barely hold his footing, the schooner had heeled so far over, and so powerful was the wind and the driving of the spray. One of the boats had been launched under the command of the second mate, but she was overturned almost instantly, and all on board her were lost. Robert was just in time to see a head bob once or twice on the surface of the sea, and then disappear.

A second boat commanded by the first mate was lowered and seven or eight men managed to get into it, rowing with all their might toward an opening that appeared in the white line of foam. A third which could take the remainder of the crew was made ready and the captain himself would be in charge of it.

It was launched successfully and the men dropped into it, one by one, but very fast. Miguel swung down and into a place. Robert advanced for the same purpose, but the captain, who was still poised on the rail of the ship, took notice of him for the first time.

"No! No, Peter!" he shouted, and even in the roar of the wind Robert observed the grim humor in his voice. "You've been a good and faithful sailorman, and we leave you in charge of the ship! It's a great promotion and honor for you, Peter, but you deserve it! Handle her well because she's a good schooner and answers kindly to a kind hand! Now, farewell, Peter, and a long and happy voyage to you!"

A leveled pistol enforced his command to stop, and the next moment he slid down a rope and into the boat. A sailor cut the rope and they pulled quickly away, leaving Robert alone on the schooner. His exultation turned to despair for a moment, and then his courage came back. Tayoga in his place would not give up. He would pray to his Manitou, who was Robert's God, and put complete faith in His wisdom and mercy. Moreover, he was quit of all that hateful crew. The ship of the slavers was beneath his feet, but the slavers themselves were gone.

As he looked, he saw the second boat overturn, and he thought he heard the wild cry of those about to be lost, but he felt neither pity nor sympathy. A stern God, stern to such as they, had called them to account. The captain's boat had disappeared in the mist and spray.

Robert, with the huge greatcoat wrapped about him clung to the stump of the mast, which long since had been blown overboard, and watched the white line of the breakers rapidly coming nearer, as they reached out their teeth for the schooner. He knew that he could do nothing more for himself until the ship struck. Then, with some happy chance aiding him, he would drop into the sea and make a desperate try for the land. He would throw off the greatcoat when he leaped, but meanwhile he kept it on, because one would freeze without it in the icy wind.

He heard presently the roaring of the breakers mingled with the roaring of the wind, and, shutting his eyes, he prayed for a miracle.

He felt the foam beating upon his face, and believing it must come from the rocks, he clung with all his might to the stump of the mast, because the shock must occur within a few moments. He felt the schooner shivering under him, and rising and falling heavily, and then he opened his eyes to see where best to leap when the shock did come.

He beheld the thick white foam to right and left, but he had not prayed in vain. The miracle had happened. Here was a narrow opening in the breakers, and, with but one chance in a hundred to guide it, the schooner had driven directly through, ceasing almost at once to rock so violently. But there was enough power left in the waves even behind the rocks to send the schooner upon a sandy beach, where she must soon break up.

But Robert was saved. He knew it and he murmured devout thanks. When the schooner struck in the sand he was thrown roughly forward, but he managed to regain his feet for an instant, and he leaped outward as far as he could, forgetting to take off his greatcoat. A returning wave threw him down and passed over his head, but exerting all his will, and all his strength he rose when it had passed, and ran for the land as hard as he could. The wave returned, picked him up, and hurried him on his way. When it started back again its force was too much spent and the water was too shallow to have much effect on Robert. He continued running through the yielding sand, and, when the wave came in again and snatched at him, it was not able to touch his feet.

He reached weeds, then bushes, and clutched them with both hands, lest some wave higher and more daring than all the rest should yet come for him and seize him. But, in a moment, he let them go, knowing that he was safe, and laughing rather giddily, sank down in a faint.

CHAPTER XIII
THE MEETING

When Robert revived the wind was still blowing hard, although there had been some decrease in its violence, and it was yet night. He was wet and very cold, and, as he arose, he shivered in a chill. The greatcoat was still wrapped about his body, and although it was soaked he always believed, nevertheless, that in some measure it had protected him while he slept. The pistols, the ammunition and the sword were in his belt, and he believed that the ammunition, fastened securely in a pouch, was dry, though he would look into that later.

He was quite sure that he had not been unconscious long, as the appearance of the sky was unchanged. The bushes among which he had lain were short but tough, and had run their roots down deeply into the sand. They were friendly bushes. He remembered how glad he had been to grasp them when he made that run from the surf, and to some extent they had protected him from the cold wind when he lay among them like one dead.

The big rollers, white at the top, were still thundering on the beach, and directly in front of him he saw a lowering hulk, that of the schooner. The slaver's wicked days were done, as every wave drove it deeper into the sand, and before long it must break up. Robert felt that it had been overtaken by retributive justice, and, despite the chill that was shaking him, he was shaken also by a great thrill of joy. Wet and cold and on a desolate shore, he was, nevertheless, free.

He began to run back and forth with great vigor, until he felt the blood flowing in a warm, strong current through his veins again, and he believed that in time his clothes would dry upon him. He took off the greatcoat, and hung it upon the bushes where the wind would have a fair chance at it, and he believed that in the morning it would be dry, too. Then, finding his powder untouched by the water, he withdrew the wet charges from the pistols and reloaded them.

If he had not been seasoned by a life in the wilderness and countless hardships he probably would have perished from exhaustion and cold, but his strong, enduring frame threw off the chill, and he did not pause for three full hours until he had made a successful fight for his life. Then very tired but fairly warm he stopped for a while, and became conscious that the wind had died to a great extent. The rollers were not half so high and the hulk of the ship showed larger and clearer than ever. He believed that when the storm ceased he could board her and find food, if he did not find it elsewhere. Meanwhile he would explore.

Buckling on his pistols and sword, but leaving the greatcoat to continue its process of drying, he walked inland, finding only a desolate region of sand, bushes and salt marshes, without any sign of human habitation. He believed it was the Jersey coast, and that he could not be any vast distance from New York. But it seemed hopeless to continue in that direction and being worn to the bone he returned to his greatcoat, which had become almost dry in the wind.

Now he felt that he must address himself to the need of the moment, which was sleep, and he hunted a long time for a suitable lair. A high bank of sand was covered with bushes larger and thicker than the others, and at the back of the bank grew a tree of considerable size with two spreading roots partly above ground. The sand was quite dry, and he heaped it much higher along the roots. Then he lay down between them, being amply protected on three sides, while the bushes waved over his head. He was not only sheltered, he was hidden also, and feeling safe, with the greatcoat, now wholly dry, wrapped around him, and the pistols and sword beside him, he closed his eyes and fell asleep.

The kindly fortune that had taken the lad out of such desperate circumstances remained benevolent. The wind ceased entirely and the air turned much warmer. Day soon came, and with it a bright cheerful sun, that gilded the great expanse of low and desolate shore. The boy slept peacefully while the morning passed and the high sun marked the coming of the afternoon.

He had been asleep about ten hours when he awoke, turned once or twice in his lair and then stood up. It was a beautiful day, in striking contrast with the black night of storm, and he knew by the position of the sun that it was within about three hours of its setting. He tested his body, but there was no soreness. He was not conscious of anything but a ravening hunger, and he believed that he knew where he could satisfy it.

There was no wind and the sea was calm, save for a slight swell. The schooner, its prow out of the water, was in plain view. It was so deeply imbedded in the sand that Robert considered it a firm house of shelter, until it should be broken to pieces by successive storms. But at present he looked upon it as a storehouse of provisions, and he hurried down the beach.

His foot struck against something, and he stopped, shuddering. It was the body of one of the slavers and presently he passed another. The sea was giving up its dead. He reached the schooner, glad to leave these ghastly objects behind him, and, with some difficulty, climbed aboard. The vessel had shipped much water, but she was not as great a wreck as he had expected, and he instantly descended to the cook's galley, where he had given his brief service. In the lockers he found an abundance of food of all kinds, as the ship had been equipped for a long voyage, and he ate hungrily, though sparingly at first. Then he went into the captain's cabin, lay down on a couch, and took a long and luxurious rest.

Robert was happy. He felt that he had won, or rather that Providence had won for him, a most wonderful victory over adverse fate. His brilliant imagination at once leaped up and painted all things in vivid colors. Tayoga, Willet and the others must be terribly alarmed about him as they had full right to be, but he would soon be back in New York, telling them of his marvelous risk and adventure.

Then he deliberated about taking a supply of provisions to his den in the bushes, but when he went on deck the sun was already setting, and it was becoming so cold again that he decided to remain on the schooner. Why not? It seemed strange to him that he had not thought of it at first. The skies were perfectly clear, and he did not think there was any danger of a storm.

He rummaged about, discovered plenty of blankets and made a bed for himself in the captain's cabin, finding a grim humor in the fact that he should take that sinister man's place. But as it was only three or four hours since he had awakened he was not at all sleepy and he returned to the deck, where he wrapped his treasure, the huge greatcoat, about his body and sat and watched. He saw the big red sun set and the darkness come down again, the air still and very cold.

But he was snug and warm, and bethought himself of what he must undertake on the morrow. If he continued inland long enough he would surely come to somebody, and at dawn, taking an ample supply of provisions, he would start. That purpose settled, he let his mind rest, and remained in a luxurious position on the deck. The rebound from the hopeless case in which he had seemed to be was so great that he was not lonely. He had instead a wholly pervading sense of ease and security. His imagination was able to find beauty in the sand and the bushes and the salt marshes, and he did not need imagination at all to discover it in the great, mysterious ocean, which the moon was now tinting with silver. It was a fine full moon, shedding its largest supply of beams, and swarms of bright stars sparkled in the cold, blue skies. A fine night, thought Robert, suited to his fine future.

It was very late, when he went down to the captain's cabin, ate a little more food and turned in. He soon slept, but not needing sleep much now, he awoke at dawn. His awakening may have been hastened by the footsteps and voices he heard, but in any event he rose softly and buckled on his sword and pistols. One of the voices, high and sharp, he recognized, and he believed that once more he was the child of good fortune, because he had been awakened in time.

He sat on the couch, facing the door, put the sword by his side and held one of the pistols, cocked and resting on his knee. The footsteps and voices came nearer, and then the keen, cruel face appeared at the door.

"Good morning, captain," said Robert, equably. "You left me in command of the ship and I did my best with her. I couldn't keep her afloat, and so I ran her up here on the beach, where, as you see, she is still habitable."

"You're a good seaman, Peter," said the captain, hiding any surprise that he may have felt, "but you haven't obeyed my orders in full. I expected you to keep the ship afloat, and you haven't done so."

"That was too much to expect. I see that you have two men with you. Tell them to step forward where I can cover them as well as you with the muzzle of this pistol. That's right. Now, I'm going to confide in you."

"Go ahead, Peter."

"I haven't liked your manner for a long time, captain. I'm only Peter Smith, a humble seaman, but since you left me in command of the ship last night I mean to keep the place, with all the responsibilities, duties and honors appertaining to it. Take your hands away from your belt. This is a lone coast, and I'm the law, the judge and the executioner. Now, you and the two men back away from the door, and as sure as there's a God in Heaven, if any one of you tries to draw a weapon I'll shoot him. You'll observe that I've two pistols and also a sword. A sailor engaged in a hazardous trade like ours, catching and selling slaves, usually learns how to use firearms, but I'm pretty good with the sword, too, captain, though I've hid the knowledge from you before. Now, just kindly back into the cook's galley there, and you and your comrades make up a good big bag of food for me. I'll tell you what to choose. I warn you a second time to keep your hands away from your belt. I'll really have to shoot off a finger or two as a warning, if you don't restrain your murderous instincts. Murder is always a bad trade, captain. Put in some of those hard biscuits, and some of the cured meats. No, none of the liquors, I have no use for them. By the way, what became of Miguel, with whom I worked so often?"

"He's drowned," replied the captain.

"I'm sorry," said Robert, and he meant it. Miguel was the only one on board the slaver who had shown a ray of human sympathy.

"What do you mean to do?" asked the captain, his face contorted with rage and chagrin.

"First, I'll see that you finish filling that bag as I direct. Put in the packages yourself. I like to watch you work, captain, it's good for you, and after you fill the bag and pass it to me I'm going to hand the ship back to you. I've never really liked her, and I mean to resign the command. I think Peter Smith is fit for better things."

"So, you intend to leave the schooner?"

"Yes, but you won't see me do it. Pass me the bag now. Be careful with your hands. In truth, I think you'd better raise them above your head, and your comrades can do the same. Quick, up with them, or I shoot! That's right. Now, I'll back away. I'm going up the ladder backward, and when I go out I intend to shove in place the grating that covers the entrance to the deck there. You can escape in five minutes, of course, but by that time I'll be off the ship and among the bushes out of your reach. Oh, I know it's humiliating, captain, but you've had your way a long time, and the slaver's trade is not a nice one. The ghosts of the blacks whom you have caused to die must haunt you some time, captain, and since your schooner is lost you'll now have a chance to turn to a better business. For the last time I tell you to be careful with your hands. A sailor man would miss his fingers."

He backed cautiously until his heels touched the ladder, meanwhile watching the eyes of the man. He knew that the captain was consumed with rage, but angry and reckless as he was he would not dare to reach for a weapon of his own, while the pistol confronting him was held with such a steady hand. He also listened for sounds made by other men on the ship, but heard none. Then he began to back slowly up the stairway, continuing his running address.

"I know that your arms must be growing weary, captain," he said, and he enjoyed it as he said it, "but you won't have to keep 'em up much longer. Two more steps will take me out upon the deck, and then you'll be free to do as you please."

It was the last two steps that troubled him most. In order to keep the men covered with the pistol he had to bend far down, and he knew that when he could no longer bend far enough the danger would come. But he solved it by straightening up suddenly and taking two steps at a leap. He heard shouts and oaths, and the report of a pistol, but the bullet was as futile as the cries. He slammed down the grating, fastened it in an instant, ran to the low rail and swiftly lowered himself and his pack over it and into the sand. Then he ran for the bushes.

Robert did not waste his breath. Having managed the affair of the grating, he knew that he was safe for the present. So, when he reached the higher bushes, he stopped, well hidden by them, and looked back. In two or three minutes the captain and the two men appeared on the deck, and he laughed quietly to himself. He could see that their faces were contorted by rage. They could follow his trail some distance at least in the sand, but he knew that they would be cautious. He had shown them his quality and they would fear an ambush.

He was justified in his opinion, as they remained on the deck, evidently searching for a glimpse of him among the bushes, and, after watching them a little while, he set out inland, bearing his burden of weapons and food, and laughing to himself at the manner in which he had made the captain serve him. He felt now that the score between them was even, and he was willing to part company forever.

Youth and success had an enormous effect upon him. When one triumph was achieved his vivid temperament always foresaw others. Willet had often called him the child of hope, and hope is a powerful factor in victory. Now it seemed to him for a little while that his own rescue, achieved by himself, was complete. He had nothing to do but to return to New York and his friends, and that was just detail.

He swung along through the bushes, forgetting the burden of his weapons and his pack of food. In truth, he swaggered a bit, but it was a gay and gallant swagger, and it became him. He walked for some distance, feeling that he had been changed from a seaman into a warrior, and then from a warrior into an explorer, which was his present character. But he did not see at present the variety and majesty that all explorers wish to find. The country continued low, the same alternation of sand and salt marsh, although the bushes were increasing in size, and they were interspersed here and there with trees of some height.

Reaching the crest of a low hill he took his last look backward, and was barely able to see the upper works of the stranded schooner. Then he thought of the captain and his exuberant spirits compelled him to laugh aloud. With the chances a hundred to one against him he had evened the score. While he had been compelled to serve the captain, the captain in turn had been forced to serve him. It was enough to make a sick man well, and to turn despair into confidence. He was in very truth and essence the child of hope.

Another low hill and from its summit he saw nothing but the bushy wilderness, with a strip of forest appearing on the sunken horizon. He searched the sky for a wisp of smoke that might tell of a human habitation, below, but saw none. Yet people might live beyond the strip of forest, where the land would be less sandy and more fertile, and, after a brief rest, he pushed on with the same vigor of the body and elation of the spirit, coming soon to firmer ground, of which he was glad, as he now left no trail, at least none that an ordinary white man could follow.

He trudged bravely on for hours through a wilderness that seemed to be complete so far as man was concerned, although its character steadily changed, merging into a region of forest and good soil. When he came into a real wood, of trees large and many, it was about noon, and finding a comfortable place with his back to a tree he ate from the precious pack.

The day was still brilliant but cold and he wisely kept himself thoroughly wrapped in the greatcoat. As he ate he saw a large black bear walk leisurely through the forest, look at him a moment or two, and then waddle on in the same grave, unalarmed manner. The incident troubled Robert, and his high spirits came down a notch or two.

If a black bear cared so little for the presence of an armed human being then he could not be as near to New York as he had thought. Perhaps he had been unconscious on the schooner a long time. He felt of the lump which was not yet wholly gone from his head, and tried his best to tell how old it was, but he could not do it.

The little cloud in his golden sky disappeared when he rose and started again through a fine forest. His spirits became as high as ever. Looking westward he saw the dim blue line of distant hills, and he turned northward, inferring that New York must lie in that direction. In two hours his progress was barred by a river running swiftly between high banks, and with ice at the edges. He could have waded it as the water would not rise past his waist, but he did not like the look of the chill current, and he did not want another wetting on a winter day.

He followed the stream a long distance, until he came to shallows, where he was able to cross it on stones. His search for a dry ford had caused much delay, but he drew comfort from his observation that the stones making his pathway through the water were large and almost round. He had seen many such about New York, and he had often marveled at their smoothness and roundness, although he did not yet know the geological reason. But the stones in the river seemed to him to be close kin to the stones about New York, and he inferred, or at least he hoped, that it indicated the proximity of the city.

But he believed that he would have to spend another night in the wilderness. Search the sky as he would, and he often did, there was no trace of smoke, and, as the sun went down the zenith and the cold began to increase, his spirits fell a little. But he reasoned with himself. Why should one inured as he was to the forest and winter, armed, provisioned and equipped with the greatcoat, be troubled? The answer to his question was a return of confidence in full tide, and resolving to be leisurely he looked about in the woods for his new camp. What he wanted was an abundance of dead leaves out of which to make a nest. Dead leaves were cold to the touch, but they would serve as a couch and a wall, shutting out further cold from the earth and from the outside air, and with the greatcoat between, he would be warm enough. He would have nothing to fear except snow, and the skies gave no promise of that danger.

He found the leaves in a suitable hollow, and disposed them according to his plan, the whole making a comfortable place for a seasoned forester, and, while he ate his supper, he watched the sun set over the wilderness. Long after it was gone he saw the stars come out and then he looked at the particular one on which Tododaho, Tayoga's patron saint, had been living more than four hundred years. It was glittering in uncommon splendor, save for a slight mist across its face, which must be the snakes in the hair of the great Onondaga chieftain who he felt was watching over him, because he was the friend of Tayoga.

Then he fell asleep, sleeping soundly, all through the night, and although he was a little stiff in the morning a few minutes of exercise relieved him of it and he ate his breakfast. His journey toward the north was resumed, and in an hour he emerged into a little valley, to come almost face to face with the captain and the two sailors. They were sitting on a log, apparently weary and at a loss, but they rose quickly at his coming and the captain's hand slid down to his pistol. Robert's slid to his, making about the same speed. Although his heart pounded a moment or two at first he was surprised to find how soon he became calm. It was perhaps because he had been through so many dangers that one more did not count for much.

"You see, captain," he said, "that neither has the advantage of the other. I did not expect to meet you here, or in truth, anywhere else. I left you in command of the schooner, and you have deserted your post. When I held that position I remained true to my duty."

The captain, who was heavily armed, carrying a cutlass as well as pistols, smiled sourly.

"You're a lad of spirit, Peter," he said. "I've always given you credit for that. In my way I like you, and I think I'll have you to go along with us again."

"I couldn't think of it. We must part company forever. We did it once, but perhaps the second time will count."

"No, my crew is now reduced to two—the ocean has all the others—and I need your help. It would be better anyway for you to come along with us. This Acadia is a desolate coast."

There was a log opposite the one upon which they had been sitting and Robert took his place upon it easily, not to say confidently. He felt sure that they would not fire upon him now, having perhaps nothing to gain by it, but he kept a calculating eye upon them nevertheless.

"And so this is Acadia," he said. "I've been wondering what land it might be. I did not know that we had come so far. Acadia is a long way from New York."

"A long, long way, Peter."

"But you know the coast well, of course, captain?"

"Of course. I've made several voyages in the neighboring waters. There's only one settlement within fifty miles of us, and you'd never find it, it's so small and the wilderness is such a maze."

"The country does look like much of a puzzle, but I've concluded, captain, that I won't go with you."

"Why not?"

"I'm persuaded that you're the very prince of liars, and in your company my morals might be contaminated."

The man's face was too tanned to flush, but his eyes sparkled.

"You're over loose with words, lad," he said, "and it's an expensive habit."

"I can afford it. I know as surely as we're sitting here facing each other that this is not the coast of Acadia."

"Then what coast is it?"

"That I know not, but taking the time, I mean to have, I shall find out. Then I'll tell you if you wish to know. Where shall I deliver my message?"

"I think you're insolent. I say again that it's the coast of Acadia, and you're going with us. We're three to your one, and you'll have to do as I say."

Robert turned his gaze from the captain to his two men. While their faces were far from good they showed no decision of character. He knew at once that they belonged to the large class of men who are always led. Both carried pistols, but he did not think it likely that they would attempt to use them, unless the captain did so first. His gaze came back to the tall man, and, observing again the heavy cutlass he carried, a thought leaped up in his mind.

"You wish me to go with you," he said, "and I don't wish to go, which leaves it an open question. It's best to decide it in clean and decisive fashion, and I suggest that we leave it to your cutlass and my sword."

The close-set eyes of the captain gleamed.

"I don't want to kill you, but to take you back alive," he said. "You were always a strong and handy lad, Peter, and I need your help."

"You won't kill me. That I promise you."

"You haven't a chance on earth."

"You pledge your word that your men will not interfere while the combat is in progress, nor will they do so afterward, if I win."

"They will not stir. Remain where you are, lads."

The two sailors settled themselves back comfortably, clasping their knees with their hands, and Robert knew that he had nothing to fear from them. Their confidence in the captain's prowess and easy victory was sufficient assurance. They were not to be blamed for the belief, as their leader's cutlass was heavy and his opponent was only a youth. The captain was of the same opinion and his mood became light and gay.

"I don't intend to kill you, Peter," he said, "but a goodly cut or two will let out some of your impertinent blood."

"Thanks, captain, for so much saving grace, because I like to live. I make you the same promise. I don't want your death on my hands, but there is poison in the veins of a man who is willing to be a slaver. I will let it out, in order that its place may be taken by pure and wholesome blood."

The captain frowned, and made a few swings with his cutlass. Then he ran a finger along its keen edge, and he felt satisfied with himself. A vast amount of rage and mortification was confined in his system, and not charging any of it to the storm, the full volume of his anger was directed against his cook's former assistant, Peter Smith, who was entirely too jaunty and independent in his manner. He could not understand Robert's presumption in challenging him to a combat with swords, but he would punish him cruelly, while the two sailors looked on and saw it well done.

Robert put his pack, his greatcoat, his coat, and his belt with the pistols and ammunition in a heap, and looked carefully to the sword that he had taken from the captain's cabin. It was a fine weapon, though much lighter than the cutlass. He bent the blade a little, and then made it whistle in curves about his head. He had a purpose in doing so, and it was attained at once. The captain looked at him with rising curiosity.

"Peter," he said, "you don't seem to be wholly unfamiliar with the sword, and you nothing but a cook's helper."

"It's true, captain. The hilt fits lovingly into my hand. In my spare moments and when nobody was looking I've often stolen this sword of yours from the cabin and practiced with it. I mean now to make you feel the result of that practice."

The captain gazed at him doubtfully, but in a moment or two the confident smile returned to his eyes. It was not possible that a mere stripling could stand before him and his cutlass. But he took off his own coat which he had believed hitherto was a useless precaution.

There was a level space about thirty feet across, and Robert, sword in hand, advanced toward the center of it. He had already chosen his course, which would be psychological as well as physical. He intended that the battle should play upon the slaver's mind as well as upon his body.

"I'm ready, captain," he said. "Don't keep us waiting. It's winter as you well know, and we'll both grow cold standing here. In weather like this we need work quick and warm."

The angry blood surged into the captain's face, although it did not show through his tan. But he made an impatient movement, and stepped forward hastily.

"It can't be told of me that I kept a lad waiting," he said. "I'll warrant you you'll soon be warm enough."

"Then we're both well suited, captain, and it should be a fine passage at arms."

The two sailors, sitting on the log, looked at each other and chuckled. It was evident to Robert that they had supreme confidence in the captain and expected to see Peter Smith receive a lesson that would put him permanently in his place. The mutual look and the mutual chuckle aroused some anger in Robert, but did not impair his certainty of victory. Nevertheless he neglected no precaution.

The captain advanced, holding the heavy cutlass with ease and lightness. He was a tall and very strong man, and Robert noted the look of cruelty in the close-set eyes. He knew what he must expect in case of defeat, and again telling himself to be careful he recalled all the cunning that Willet had taught him.

"Are you ready?" he asked quietly.

"Aye, Peter, and your bad quarter of an hour is upon you."

Again the two sailors on the log looked at each other and chuckled.

"I don't think so, captain," said Robert. "Perhaps the bad quarter of an hour is yours."

He stared straight into the close-set cruel eyes so fixedly and so long that the captain lowered his gaze, proving that the superior strength of will lay with his younger opponent. Then he shook himself angrily, his temper stirred, because his eyes had given way.

"Begin!" said Robert.

The captain slashed with the heavy cutlass, and Robert easily turned aside the blow with his lighter weapon. He saw then that the captain was no swordsman in the true sense, and he believed he had nothing to fear. He waited until the man attacked again, and again he deftly turned aside the blow.

The two sailors sitting on the log looked at each other once more, but they did not chuckle.

Robert, still watching the close-set cruel eyes, saw a look of doubt appear there.

"My bad quarter of an hour seems to be delayed, captain," he said with irony.

The man, stung beyond endurance, attacked with fury, the heavy cutlass singing and whistling as he slashed and thrust. Robert contented himself with the defense, giving ground slowly and moving about in a circle. The captain's eye at first glittered with a triumphant light as he saw his foe retreat, and the two sailors sitting on the log and exchanging looks found cause to chuckle once more.

But the light sank as they completed the circle, leaving Robert untouched, and breathing as easily as ever, while the captain was panting. Now he decided that his own time had come and knowing that the combat was mental as well as physical he taunted his opponent.

"In truth, captain," he said, "my bad quarter of an hour did not arrive, but yours, I think, is coming. Look! Look! See the red spot on your waistcoat!"

Despite himself the captain looked down. The sword flickered in like lightning, and then flashed away again, but when it was gone the red spot on the waistcoat was there. His flesh stung with a slight wound, but the wound to his spirit was deeper. He rushed in and slashed recklessly.

"Have a care, captain!" cried Robert. "You are fencing very wildly! I tell you again that your play with the cutlass is bad. You can't see it, but there is now a red spot on your cheek to match the one on your waistcoat."

His sword darted by the other's guard, and when it came away it's point was red with blood. A deep and dripping gash in the captain's left cheek showed where it had passed. The two sailors sitting on the log exchanged looks once more, but there was no sign of a chuckle.

"That's for being a slaver, captain," said Robert. "It's a bad occupation, and you ought to quit it. But your wound will leave a scar, and you will not like to say that it was made by one whom you kidnapped, and undertook to carry away to his death."

The captain in a long career of crime and cruelty had met with but few checks, and to experience one now from the hands of a lad was bitter beyond endurance. The sting was all the greater because of his knowledge that the two sailors who still exchanged looks but no chuckles, were witnesses of it. The blood falling from his left cheek stained his left shoulder and he was a gruesome sight. He rushed in again, mad with anger.

"Worse and worse, captain," said his young opponent. "You're not showing a single quality of a swordsman. You've nothing but strength. I bade you have a care! Now your right cheek is a match for your left!"

The captain uttered a cry, drawn as much by anger as by pain. The deep point of his opponent's sword had passed across his right cheek and the red drops fell on both shoulders. The two sailors looked at each other in dismay. The man paused for breath and he was a ghastly sight.

"I told you more than once to beware, captain," said Robert, "but you would not heed me. Your temper has been spoiled by success, but in time nearly every slaver meets his punishment. I'm grateful that it's been permitted to me to inflict upon you a little of all that's owing to you. Wounds in the face are very painful and they leave scars, as you'll learn."

He had already decided upon his finishing stroke, and his taunts were meant to push the captain into further reckless action. They were wholly successful as the man sprang forward, and slashed almost at random. Now, Robert, light of foot and agile, danced before him like a fencing master. The captain cut and thrust at the flitting form but always it danced away, and the heavy slashes of his cutlass cut the empty air, his dripping wounds and his vain anger making him weaker and weaker. But he would not stop. Losing all control of his temper he rushed continually at his opponent.

The two sailors looked once more at each other, half rose to their feet, but sat down again, and were silent.

Now the captain saw a flash of light before him, and he felt a darting pain across his brow, as the keen point of the sword passed there. The blood ran down into his eyes, blinding him for the time. He could not see the figure before him, but he knew that it was tense and waiting. He groped with his cutlass, but touching only thin air he threw it away, and clapped his hands to his eyes to keep away the trickling blood.

"You'll have three scars, captain," came the maddening voice, "one on each cheek and one on the forehead. It's not enough punishment for a slaver, but, in truth, it's something. And now I'm going. You can't see to follow me, or even to take care of yourself but I leave you in the hands of your two sailors."

Robert put on his coat and greatcoat, resumed all his weapons and his pack and turned away. The sailors were still sitting on the log, gazing at each other in amazement and awe. Neither had spoken throughout the duel, nor did they speak now. The victor did not look back, but walked swiftly toward the north, glad that he had been the instrument in the hands of fate to give to the slaver at least a part of the punishment due him.

He kept steadily on several hours, until he saw a smoke on the western sky, when he changed his course and came in another half hour to a small log house, from which the smoke arose. A man standing on the wooden step looked at him with all the curiosity to which he had a right.

"Friend," said Robert, "how far is it to New York?"

"About ten miles."

"And this is not the coast of Acadia."

"Acadia! What country is that? I never heard of it."

"It exists, but never mind. And New York is so near? Tell me that distance again. I like to hear it."

"Ten miles, stranger. When you reach the top of the hill there you can see the houses of Paulus Hook."

Robert felt a great sense of elation, and then of thankfulness. While fortune had been cruel in putting him into the hands of the slaver, it had relented and had taken him out of them, when the chance of escape seemed none.

"Stranger," said the man, "you look grateful about something."

"I am. I have cause to be grateful. I'm grateful that I have my life, I'm grateful that I have no wounds and I'm grateful that from the top of the hill there I shall be able to see the houses of Paulus

Hook. And I say also that yours is the kindliest and most welcome face I've looked upon in many a day. Farewell."

"Farewell," said the man, staring after him.

Two hours later Robert was being rowed across the Hudson by a stalwart waterman. As he passed by the spot where his boat had been cut down by the schooner he took off his hat.

"Why do you do that?" asked the waterman.

"Because at this spot my life was in great peril a few days ago, or rather, here started the peril from which I have been delivered most mercifully."

An hour later he stood on the solid stone doorstep of Master Benjamin Hardy, important ship owner, merchant and financier. The whimsical fancy that so often turned his troubles and hardships into little things seized Robert again. He adjusted carefully his somewhat bedraggled clothing, set the sword and pistols in his belt at a rakish slant, put the pack on the step beside him, and, lifting the heavy brass knocker, struck loudly. He heard presently the sound of footsteps inside, and Master Jonathan Pillsbury, looking thinner and sadder than ever, threw open the door. When he saw who was standing before him he stared and stared.

"Body o' me!" he cried at last, throwing up his hands. "Is it Mr. Lennox or his ghost?"

"It's Mr. Lennox and no ghost," said Robert briskly. "Let me in, Mr. Pillsbury. I've grown cold standing here on the steps."

"Are you sure you're no ghost?"

"Quite sure. Here pinch me on the arm and see that I'm substantial flesh. Not quite so hard! You needn't take out a piece. Are you satisfied now?"

"More than satisfied, Mr. Lennox! I'm delighted, Overjoyed! We feared that you were dead! Where have you been?"

"I've been serving on board a slaver on the Guinea coast. That's a long distance from here, and it was an exciting life, but I'm back again safe and sound, Master Jonathan."

"I don't understand you. You jest, Mr. Lennox."

"And so I do, but I tell you, Master Jonathan, I'm glad to be back again, you don't know how glad. Do you hear me, Master Jonathan? The sight of you is as welcome as that of an angel!"

The air grew black before him, and he reeled and would have fallen, but the strong arm of Jonathan Pillsbury caught him. In a moment or two his eyes cleared and he became steady.

"It was not altogether a pleasure voyage of yours," said Master Jonathan, dryly.

"No, Mr. Pillsbury, it wasn't. But I came near fainting then, because I was so glad to see you. Is Mr. Hardy here?"

"No, he has gone to the Royal Exchange. He has been nigh prostrated with grief, but I persuaded him that business might lighten it a little, and he went out today for the first time. Oh, young sir, he will be truly delighted to find that you have come back safely, because, although you may know it not, he has a strong affection for you!"

"And I have a high regard for him, Master Jonathan. He has been most kind to me."

"Come in, Mr. Lennox. Sit down in the drawingroom and rest yourself, while I hurry forth with the welcome news."

Robert saw that his prim and elderly heart was in truth rejoiced, and his own heart warmed in turn. Obscure and of unknown origin though he might be, friends were continually appearing for him everywhere. A servant took his weapons and what was left of his pack, Master Jonathan insisted upon his drinking a small glass of wine to refresh himself, and then he was left alone in the imposing drawing-room of Mr. Hardy.

He sank back in a deep chair of Spanish leather, and shutting his eyes took several long breaths of relief. He had come back safely and his escape seemed marvelous even to himself. As he opened his eyes a mild voice said:

"And so Dagaeoga who went, no one knows where, has returned no one knows how."

Tayoga, smiling but grave, and looking taller and more majestic than ever, stood before him.

"Aye, I'm back, and right glad I am to be here!" exclaimed Robert, springing to his feet and seizing Tayoga's hand. "Oh, I've been on a long voyage, Tayoga! I've been to the coast of Africa on a slaver, though we caught no slaves, and I was wrecked on the coast of Acadia, and I fought and walked my way back to New York! But it's a long tale, and I'll not tell it till all of you are together. I hope you were not too much alarmed about me, Tayoga."

"I know that Dagaeoga is in the keeping of Manitou. I have seen too many proofs of it to doubt. I was sure that at the right time he would return."

Mr. Hardy came presently and then Willet. They made no display of emotion, but their joy was deep. Then Robert told his story to them all.

"Did you see any name on the wrecked schooner?" asked Mr. Hardy.

"None at all," replied Robert. "If she had borne a name at any time I'm sure it was painted out."

"Nor did you hear the captain called by name, either?"

"No, sir. It was always just 'captain' when the men addressed him."

"That complicates our problem. There's no doubt in my mind that you were the intended victim of a conspiracy, from which you were saved by the storm. I can send a trusty man down the North Jersey coast to examine the wreck of the schooner, but I doubt whether he could learn anything from it."

He drew Willet aside and the two talked together a while in a low voice, but with great earnestness.

"We have our beliefs," said Willet at length, "but we shall not be able to prove anything, no, not a thing, and, having nothing upon which to base an accusation against anybody, we shall accuse nobody."

"'Tis the prudent way," Hardy concurred, "though there is no doubt in my mind about the identity of the man who set this most wicked pot to brewing."

Robert had his own beliefs, too, but he remained silent.

"We'll keep the story of your absence to ourselves," said Mr. Hardy. "We did not raise any alarm, believing that you would return, a belief due in large measure to the faith of Tayoga, and we'll explain that you were called away suddenly on a mission of a somewhat secret nature to the numerous friends who have been asking about you."

Willet concurred, and he also said it was desirable that they should depart at once for Virginia, where the provincial governors were to meet in council, and from which province Braddock's force, or a considerable portion of it, would march. Then Robert, after a substantial supper, went to his room and slept. The next morning, both Charteris and Grosvenor came to see him and expressed their delight at his return. A few days later they were at sea with Grosvenor and other young English officers, bound for the mouth of the James and the great expedition against Fort Duquesne.

CHAPTER XIV
THE VIRGINIA CAPITAL

They were on a large schooner, and while Robert looked forward with eagerness to the campaign, he also looked back with regret at the roofs of New York, as they sank behind the sea. The city suited him. It had seemed to him while he was there that he belonged in it, and now that he was going away the feeling was stronger upon him than ever. He resolved once more that it should be his home when the war was over.

Their voyage down the coast was stormy and long. Baffling winds continually beat them back, and, then they lay for long periods in dead calms, but at last they reached the mouth of the James, going presently the short distance overland to Williamsburg, the town that had succeeded Jamestown as the capital of the great province of Virginia.

Spring was already coming here in the south and in the lowlands by the sea, and the tinge of green in the foliage and the warm winds were grateful after the winter of the cold north. Robert, eager as always for new scenes, and fresh knowledge, anticipated with curiosity his first sight of Williamsburg, one of the oldest British towns in North America. He knew that it was not large, but he found it even smaller than he had expected.

He and his comrades reached it on horseback, and they found that it contained only a thousand inhabitants, and one street, straight and very wide. On this street stood the brick buildings of William and Mary, the oldest college in the country, a new capitol erected in the place of one burned, not long before, and a large building called the Governor's Palace. It looked very small, very quiet, and very content.

Robert was conscious of a change in atmosphere that was not a mere matter of temperature. Keen, commercial New York was gone.

Here, people talked of politics and the land. The men who came into Williamsburg on horseback or in their high coaches were owners of great plantations, where they lived as patriarchs, and feudal lords. The human stock was purely British and the personal customs and modes of thought of the British gentry had been transplanted.

"I like it," said Grosvenor. "I feel that I've found England again."

"There appears to be very little town life," said Robert. "It seems strange that Williamsburg is so small, when Virginia has many more people than New York or Pennsylvania or Massachusetts."

"They're spread upon the land," said Willet. "I've been in Virginia before. They don't care much about commerce, but you'll find that a lot of the men who own the great plantations are hard and good thinkers."

Robert soon discovered that in Virginia a town was rather a meeting place for the landed aristocracy than a commercial center. The arrival of the British troops and of Americans from other colonies brought much life into the little capital. The people began to pour in from the country houses, and the single street was thronged with the best horses and the best carriages Virginia could show, their owners, attended by swarms of black men and black women whose mouths were invariably stretched in happy grins, their splendid white teeth glittering.

There was much splendor, a great mingling of the fine and the tawdry, as was inevitable in a society that maintained slavery on a large scale. Nearly all the carriages had been brought from London, and they were of the best. When their owners drove forth in the streets or the country roundabout they were escorted by black coachmen and footmen in livery. The younger men were invariably on horseback, dressed like English country gentlemen, and they rode with a skill and grace that Robert had never before seen equaled. The parsons, as in England, rode with the best, and often drank with them too.

It was a proud little society, exclusive perhaps, and a little bit provincial too, possibly, but it was soon to show to the world a group of men whose abilities and reputation and service to the state have been unequaled, perhaps, since ancient Athens. One warm afternoon as Robert walked down the single street with Tayoga and Grosvenor, he saw a very young man, only three or four years older than himself, riding a large, white horse.

The rider's lofty stature, apparent even on horseback, attracted Robert's notice. He was large of bone, too, with hands and feet of great size, and a very powerful figure. His color was ruddy and high, showing one who lived out of doors almost all the time.

The man, Robert soon learned, was the young officer, George Washington, who had commanded the Virginians in the first skirmish with the French and Indians in the Ohio country.

"One of most grave and sober mien," said Grosvenor. "I take him to be of fine quality."

"There can scarce be a doubt of it," said Robert.

But he did not dream then that succeeding generations would reckon the horseman the first man of all time.

Robert, Willet and Tayoga saw the governor, Dinwiddie, a thrifty Scotchman, and offered to him their services, saying that they wished to go with the Braddock expedition as scouts.

"But I should think, young sir," said Dinwiddie to Robert, "that you, at least, would want a commission. 'Twill be easy to obtain it in the Virginia troops."

"I thank you, sir, for the offer, which is very kind," said Robert, "but I have spent a large part of my life in the woods with Mr. Willet, and I feel that I can be of more use as a scout and skirmisher. You know that they will be needed badly in the forest. Moreover, Mr. Willet would not be separated from Tayoga, who in the land of the Six Nations, known to themselves as the Hodenosaunee, is a great figure."

Governor Dinwiddie regarded the Onondaga, who gave back his gaze steadily. The shrewd Scotchman knew that here stood a man, and he treated him as one.

"Have your way," he said. "Perhaps you are right. Many think that General Braddock has little to fear from ambush, they say that his powerful army of regulars and colonials can brush aside any force the French and Indians may gather, but I've been long enough in this country to know that the wilderness always has its dangers. Such eyes as the eyes of you three will have their value. You shall have the commissions you wish."

Willet was highly pleased. He had been even more insistent than Robert on the point, saying they must not sacrifice their freedom and independence of movement, but Grosvenor was much surprised.

"An army rank will help you," he said.

"It's help that we don't need," said Robert smiling.

The governor showed them great courtesy. He liked them and his penetrating Scotch mind told him that they had quality. Despite his hunter's dress, which he had resumed, Willet's manners were those of the great world, and Dinwiddie often looked at him with curiosity. Robert seemed to him to be wrapped in the same veil of mystery, and he judged that the lad, whose manners were not inferior to those of Willet, had in him the making of a personage. As for Tayoga, Dinwiddie had been too long in America and he knew too much of the Hodenosaunee not to appreciate his great position. An insult or a slight in Virginia to the coming young chief of the Clan of the Bear, of the nation Onondaga would soon be known in the far land of the Six Nations, and its cost would be so great that none might count it. Just as tall oaks from little acorns grow, so a personal affront may sow the seed of a great war or break a great alliance, and Dinwiddie knew it.

The governor, assisted by his wife and two daughters, entertained at his house, and Robert, Tayoga, Willet, and Grosvenor, arrayed in their best, attended, forming conspicuous figures in a great crowd, as the Virginia gentry, also clad in their finest, attended. Robert, with his adaptable and imaginative mind, was at home at once among them. He liked the soft southern speech, the grace of manner and the good feeling that obtained. They were even more closely related than the great families of New York, and it was obvious that they formed a cultivated society, in close touch with the mother country, intensely British in manner and mode of thought, and devoted in both theory and practice to personal independence.

As the spring was now well advanced the night was warm and the windows and doors of the Governor's Palace were left open. Negroes in livery played violins and harps while all the guests who wished danced. Others played cards in smaller rooms, but there was no such betting as Robert had seen at Bigot's ball in Quebec. There was some drinking of claret and punch, but no intoxication. The general note was of great gayety, but with proper restraints.

Robert noticed that the men, spending their lives in the open air and having abundant and wholesome food, were invariably tall and big of bone. The women looked strong and their complexions were rosy. The same facility of mind that had made him like New York and Quebec, such contrasting places, made him like Williamsburg too, which was different from either.

Quickly at home, in this society as elsewhere, the hours were all too short for him. Both he and Grosvenor, who was also adaptable, seeing good in everything, plunged deep into the festivities. He danced with young women and with old, and Willet more than once gave him an approving glance. It seemed that the hunter always wished him to fit himself into any group with which he might be cast, and to make himself popular, and to do so Robert's temperament needed little encouragement.

The music and the dancing never ceased. When the black musicians grew tired their places were taken by others as black and as zealous, and on they went in a ceaseless alternation. Robert learned that the guests would dance all night and far into the next day, and that frequently at the great houses a ball continued two days and two nights.

About three o'clock in the morning, after a long dance that left him somewhat weary, he went upon one of the wide piazzas to rest and take the fresh air. There, his attention was specially attracted by two young men who were waging a controversy with energy, but without acrimony.

"I tell you, James," said one, who was noticeable for his great shock of fair hair and his blazing red face, "that at two miles Blenheim is unbeatable."

"Unbeatable he may be, Walter," said the other, "but there is no horse so good that there isn't a better. Blenheim, I grant you, is a splendid three year old, but my Cressy is just about twenty yards swifter in two miles. There is not another such colt in all Virginia, and it gives me great pride to be his owner."

The other laughed, a soft drawling laugh, but it was touched with incredulity.

"You're a vain man, James," he said, "not vain for yourself, but vain for your sorrel colt."

"I admit my vanity, Walter, but it rests upon a just basis. Cressy, I repeat, is the best three year old in Virginia, which of course means the best in all the colonies, and I have a thousand weight of prime tobacco to prove it."

"My plantation grows good tobacco too, James, and I also have a thousand weight of prime leaf which talks back to your thousand weight, and tells it that Cressy is the second best three year old in Virginia, not the best."

"Done. Nothing is left but to arrange the time."

Both at this moment noticed Robert, who was sitting not far away, and they hailed him with glad voices. He remembered meeting them earlier in the evening. They were young men, Walter Stuart and James Cabell, who had inherited great estates on the James and they shipped their tobacco in their own vessels to London, and detecting in Robert a somewhat kindred spirit they had received him with great friendliness. Already they were old acquaintances in feeling, if not in time.

"Lennox, listen to this vain boaster!" exclaimed Cabell. "He has a good horse, I admit, but his spirit has become unduly inflated about it. You know, don't you, Lennox, that my colt, Cressy, has all Virginia beaten in speed?"

"You know nothing of the kind, Lennox!" exclaimed Stuart, "but you do know that my three year old Blenheim is the swiftest horse ever bred in the colony. Now, don't you?"

"I can't give an affirmative to either of you," laughed Robert, "as I've never seen your horses, but this I do say, I shall be very glad to see the test and let the colts decide it for themselves."

"A just decision, O Judge!" said Stuart. "You shall have an honored place as a guest when the match is run. What say you to tomorrow morning at ten, James?"

"A fit hour, Walter. You ride Blenheim yourself, of course?"

"Truly, and you take the mount on Cressy?"

"None other shall ride him. I've black boys cunning with horses, but since it's horse against horse it should also be master against master."

"A match well made, and 'twill be a glorious contest. Come, Lennox, you shall be a judge, and so shall be your friend Willet, and so shall that splendid Indian, Tayoga."

Robert was delighted. He had thrown himself with his whole soul into the Virginia life, and he was eager to see the race run. So were all the others, and even the grave eyes of Tayoga sparkled when he heard of it.

It was broad daylight when he went to bed, but he was up at noon, and in the afternoon he went to the House of Burgesses to hear the governor make a speech to the members on the war and its emergencies. Dinwiddie, like Shirley, the governor of Massachusetts, appreciated the extreme gravity of the crisis, and his address was solemn and weighty.

He told them that the shadow in the north was black and menacing. The French were an ambitious people, brave, tenacious and skillful. They had won the friendship of the savages and now they dominated the wilderness. They would strike heavy blows, but their movements were enveloped in mystery, and none knew where or when the sword would fall. The spirit animating them flowed from the haughty and powerful court at Versailles that aimed at universal dominion. It became the Virginians, as it became the people of all the colonies, to gather their full force against them.

The members listened with serious faces, and Robert knew that the governor was right. He had been to Quebec, and he had already met Frenchmen in battle. None understood better than he their skill, courage and perseverance, and the shadow in the north was very heavy and menacing to him too.

But his depression quickly disappeared when he returned to the bright sunshine, and met his young friends again. The Virginians were a singular compound of gayety and gravity. Away from the House of Burgesses the coming horse race displaced the war for a brief space. It was the great topic in Williamsburg and the historic names, Blenheim and Cressy, were in the mouths of everybody.

Robert soon discovered that the horses were well known, and each had its numerous group of partisans. Their qualities were discussed by the women and girls as well as the men and with intelligence. Robert, filled with the spirit of it, laid a small wager on Blenheim, and then, in order to show no partiality, laid another in another quarter, but of exactly the same amount on Cressy.

The evening witnessed more arrivals in Williamsburg, drawn by the news of the race, and young men galloped up and down the wide street in the moonlight, testing their own horses, and riding improvised matches. The rivalry was always friendly, the gentlemen's code that there should be no ill feeling prevailed, and more than ever the entire gathering seemed to Robert one vast family. Grosvenor was intensely interested in the race, and also in the new sights he was seeing.

"Still," he said, "if it were not for the colored people I could imagine with ease that I was back at a country meeting at home. Do you know anything, Lennox, about these horses, Blenheim and Cressy—patriotic fellows their owners must be—and could you give a chap advice about laying a small wager?"

"I know nothing about them except what Stuart and Cabell say."

"What do they say?"

"Stuart knows that Blenheim is the fastest horse in Virginia, and Cabell knows that Cressy is, and so there the matter stands until the race is run."

"I think I'll put a pound on Blenheim, nevertheless. Blenheim has a much more modern sound than Cressy, and I'm all for modernity."

There was an excellent race track, the sport already being highly developed in Virginia, and, the next day being beautiful, the seats were filled very early in the morning. The governor with his wife and daughters was present, and so were many other notables. Robert, Tayoga and Grosvenor were in a group of nearly fifty young Virginians. All about were women and girls in their best spring dresses, many imported from London, and there were several men whom Robert knew by their garb to be clergymen. Colored women, their heads wrapped in great bandanna handkerchiefs, were selling fruits or refreshing liquids.

The whole was exhilarating to the last degree, and all the youth and imagination in Robert responded. Dangers befell him, but delights offered themselves also, and he took both as they came. Several preliminary races, improvised the day before, were run, and they served to keep the crowd amused, while they waited for the great match.

Robert and Tayoga then moved to advanced seats near the Governor, where Willet was already placed, in order that they might fulfill their honorable functions as judges, and the people began to stir with a great breath of expectation. They were packed in a close group for a long distance, and Robert's eye roved over them, noting that their faces, ruddy or brown, were those of an open air race, like the English. Almost unconsciously his mind traveled back to a night in New York, when he had seen another crowd gather in a theater, and then with a thrill he recalled the face that he had beheld there. He could never account for it, although some connection of circumstances was back of it, but he had a sudden instinctive belief that in this new crowd he would see the same face once more.

It obsessed him like a superstition, and, for the moment, he forgot the horses, the race, and all that had brought him there. His eye roved on, and then, down, near the front of the seats he found him, shaved cleanly and dressed neatly, like a gentleman, but like one in poor circumstances. Robert saw at first only the side of his face, the massive jaw, the strong, curving chin, and the fair hair crisping slightly at the temples, but he would have known him anywhere and in any company.

St. Luc sat very still, apparently absorbed in the great race which would soon be run. In an ordinary time any stranger in Williamsburg would have been noticed, but this was far from being an ordinary time. The little town overflowed with British troops, and American visitors known and unknown. Tayoga or Willet, if they saw him, might recognize him, although Robert was not sure, but they, too, might keep silent.

For a little while, he wondered why St. Luc had come to the Virginia capital, a journey so full of danger for him. Was he following him? Was it because of some tie between them? Or was it because St. Luc was now spying upon the Anglo-American preparations? He understood to the full the romantic and adventurous nature of the Frenchman, and knew that he would dare anything. Then he had a consuming desire for the eyes of St. Luc to meet his, and he bent upon him a gaze so long, and of such concentration, that at last the chevalier looked up.

St. Luc showed recognition, but in a moment or two he looked away. Robert also turned his eyes in another direction, lest Tayoga or

Willet should follow his gaze, and when he glanced back again in a minute or two St. Luc was gone. His roving eyes, traveling over the crowd once more, could not find him, and he was glad. He believed now that St. Luc had come to Williamsburg to discover the size and preparations of the American force and its plan, and Robert felt that he must have him seized if he could. He would be wanting in his patriotism and duty if he failed to do so. He must sink all his liking for St. Luc, and make every effort to secure his capture.

But there was a sudden murmur that grew into a deep hum of expectation, punctuated now and then by shouts: "Blenheim!" "Cressy!" "Cabell!" "Stuart!" Horses and horsemen alike seemed to have their partisans in about equal numbers. Ladies rose to their feet, and waved bright fans, and men gave suggestions to those on whom they had laid their money.

The race, for a space, crowded St. Luc wholly out of Robert's mind. Stuart and Cabell, each dressed very neatly in jockey attire, came out and mounted their horses, which the grooms had been leading back and forth. The three year olds, excited by the noise and multitude of faces, leaped and strained at their bits. Robert did not know much of races, but it seemed to him that there was little to choose between either horses or riders.

The circular track was a mile in length, and they would round it twice, start and finish alike being made directly in front of the judges' stand. The starter, a tall Virginian, finally brought the horses to the line, neck and neck, and they were away. The whole crowd rose to its feet and shouted approval as they flashed past. Blenheim was a bay and Cressy was a sorrel, and when they began to turn the curve in the distance Robert saw that bay and sorrel were still neck and neck. Then he saw them far across the field, and neither yet had the advantage.

Now, Robert understood why the Virginians loved the sport. The test of a horse's strength and endurance and of a horseman's skill and judgment was thrilling. Presently he found that he was shouting with the shouting multitude, and sometimes he shouted Cressy and sometimes he shouted Blenheim.

They came around the curve, the finish of the first mile being near, and Robert saw the nose of the sorrel creeping past the nose of the bay. A shout of triumph came from the followers of Cressy and

Cabell, but the partisans of Blenheim and Stuart replied that the race was not yet half run. Cressy, though it was only in inches, was still gaining. The sorrel nose crept forward farther and yet a little farther. When they passed the judges' stand Cressy led by a head and a neck.

Robert, having no favorite before, now felt a sudden sympathy for Blenheim and Stuart, because they were behind, and he began to shout for them continuously, until sorrel and bay were well around the curve on the second mile, when the entire crowd became silent. Then a sharp shout came from the believers in Blenheim and Stuart. The bay was beginning to win back his loss. The Cressy men were silent and gloomy, as Blenheim, drawing upon the stores of strength that had been conserved, continued to gain, until now the bay nose was creeping past the sorrel. Then the bay was a full length ahead and that sharp shout of triumph burst now from the Blenheim people. Robert found his feelings changing suddenly, and he was all for Cressy and Cabell.

The joy of the Blenheim people did not last long. The sorrel came back to the side of the bay, the second mile was half done, and a blanket would have covered the two. It was yet impossible to detect any sign indicating the winner. The eyes of Tayoga, sitting beside Robert, sparkled. The Indians from time unknown had loved ball games and had played them with extraordinary zest and fire. As soon as they came to know the horse of the white man they loved racing in the same way. Their sporting instincts were as genuine as those of any country gentleman.

"It is a great race," said Tayoga. "The horses run well and the men ride well. Tododaho himself, sitting on his great and shining star, does not know which will win."

"The kind of race I like to see," said Robert. "Stuart and Cabell were justified in their faith in their horses. A magnificent pair, Blenheim and Cressy!"

"It has been said, Dagaeoga, that there is always one horse that can run faster than another, but it seems that neither of these two can run faster than the other. Now, Blenheim thrusts his nose ahead, and now Cressy regains the lead by a few inches. Now they are so nearly even that they seem to be but one horse and one rider."

"A truly great race, Tayoga, and a prettily matched pair! Ah, the bay leads! No, 'tis the sorrel! Now, they are even again, and the finish is not far away!"

The great crowd, which had been shouting, each side for its favorite, became silent as Blenheim and Cressy swept into the stretch. Stuart and Cabell, leaning far over the straining necks, begged and prayed their brave horses to go a little faster, and Blenheim and Cressy, hearing the voices that they knew so well, responded but in the same measure. The heads were even, as if they had been locked fast, and there was still no sign to indicate the winner. Faster and faster they came, their riders leaning yet farther forward, continually urging them, and they thundered past the stand, matched so evenly that not a hair's breadth seemed to separate the noses of the sorrel and the bay.

"It's a dead heat!" exclaimed Robert, as the people, unable to restrain their enthusiasm, swarmed over the track, and such was the unanimous opinion of the judges. Yet it was the belief of all that a finer race was never run in Virginia, and while the horses, covered with blankets, were walked back and forth to cool, men followed them and uttered their admiration.

Stuart and Cabell were eager to run the heat over, after the horses had rested, but the judges would not allow it.

"No! No, lads!" said the Governor. "Be content! You have two splendid horses, the best in Virginia, and matched evenly. Moreover, you rode them superbly. Now, let them rest with the ample share of honor that belongs to each."

Stuart and Cabell, after the heat of rivalry was over, thought it a good plan, shook hands with great warmth three or four times, each swearing that the other was the best fellow in the world, and then with a great group of friends they adjourned to the tavern where huge beakers of punch were drunk.

"And mighty Todadaho himself, although he looks into the future, does not yet know which is the better horse," said Tayoga. "It is well. Some things should remain to be discovered, else the salt would go out of life."

"That's sound philosophy," said Willet. "It's the mystery of things that attracts us, and that race ended in the happiest manner possible. Neither owner can be jealous or envious of the other; instead they are feeling like brothers."

Then Robert's mind with a sudden rush, went back to St. Luc, and his sense of duty tempted him to speak of his presence to Willet, but he concluded to wait a little. He looked around for him again, but he did not see him, and he thought it possible that he had now left the dangerous neighborhood of Williamsburg.

As they walked back to their quarters at a tavern Willet informed them that there was to be, two days later, a grand council of provincial governors and high officers at Alexandria on the Potomac, where General Braddock with his army already lay in camp, and he suggested that they go too. As they were free lances with their authority issuing from Governor Dinwiddie alone, they could do practically as they pleased. Both Robert and Tayoga were all for it, but in the afternoon they, as well as Willet, were invited to a race dinner to be given at the tavern that evening by Stuart and Cabell in honor of the great contest, in which neither had lost, but in which both had won.

"I suppose," said Willet, "that while here we might take our full share of Virginia hospitality, which is equal to any on earth, because, as I see it, before very long we will be in the woods where so much to eat and drink will not be offered to us. March and battle will train us down."

The dinner to thirty guests was spread in the great room of the tavern and the black servants of Stuart and Cabell, well trained, dextrous and clad in livery, helped those of the landlord to serve. The abundance and quality of the food were amazing. Besides the resources of civilization, air, wood and water were drawn upon for game. Virginia, already renowned for hospitality, was resolved that through her young sons, Stuart and Cabell, she should do her best that night.

A dozen young British officers were present, and there was much toasting and conviviality. The tie of kinship between the old country and the new seemed stronger here than in New England, where the England of Cromwell still prevailed, or in New York, where the Dutch and other influences not English were so powerful. They had begun with the best of feeling, and it was heightened by the warmth that food and drink bring. They talked with animation of the great adventure, on which they would soon start, as Stuart and Cabell and most of the Virginians were going with Braddock. They drank a speedy capture of Fort Duquesne, and confusion to the French and their red allies.

Robert, imitating the example of Tayoga, ate sparingly and scarcely tasted the punch. About eleven o'clock, the night being warm, unusually warm for that early period of spring, and nearly all the guests having joined in the singing, more or less well, of patriotic songs, Robert, thinking that his absence would not be noticed, walked outside in search of coolness and air.

It was but a step from the lights and brilliancy of the tavern to the darkness of Williamsburg's single avenue. There were no street lanterns, and only a moon by which to see. He could discern the dim bulk of William and Mary College and of the Governor's Palace, but except near at hand the smaller buildings were lost in the dusk. A breeze touched with salt, as if from the sea, was blowing, and its touch was so grateful on Robert's face that he walked on, hat in hand, while the wind played on his cheeks and forehead and lifted his hair. Then a darker shadow appeared in the darkness, and St. Luc stood before him.

"Why do you come here! Why do you incur such danger? Don't you know that I must give warning of your presence?" exclaimed Robert passionately.

The Frenchman laughed lightly. He seemed very well pleased with himself, and then he hummed:

"Hier sur le pont d'Avignon
J'ai oui chanter la belle
Lon, la."

"Your danger is great!" repeated Robert.

"Not as great as you think," said St. Luc. "You will not protect me. You will warn the British officers that a French spy is here. I read it in your face at the race today, and moreover, I know you better than you know yourself. I know, too, more about you than you know about yourself. Did I not warn you in New York to beware of Mynheer Adrian Van Zoon?"

"You did, and I know that you meant me well."

"And what happened?"

"I was kidnapped by a slaver, and I was to have been taken to the coast of Africa, but a storm intervened and saved me. Perhaps the slaver was acting for Mynheer Van Zoon, but I talked it over with Mr. Hardy and we haven't a shred of proof."

"Perhaps a storm will not intervene next time. You must look to yourself, Robert Lennox."

"And you to yourself, Chevalier de St. Luc. I'm grateful to you for the warning you gave me, and other acts of friendship, but whatever your mission may have been in New York I'm sure that one of your errands, perhaps the main one, in Williamsburg, is to gather information for France, and, sir, I should be little of a patriot did I not give the alarm, much as it hurts me to do so."

Robert saw very clearly by the moonlight that the blue eyes of St. Luc were twinkling. His situation might be dangerous, but obviously he took no alarm from it.

"You'll bear in mind, Mr. Lennox," he said, "that I'm not asking you to shield me. Consider me a French spy, if you wish—and you'll not be wholly wrong—and then act as you think becomes a man with a commission as army scout from Governor Dinwiddie of Virginia."

There was a little touch of irony in his voice. His adventures and romantic spirit was in the ascendant, and it seemed to Robert that he was giving him a dare. That he would have endured because of his admiration for St. Luc, and also because of his gratitude, but the allusion to his commission from the governor of Virginia recalled him to his sense of duty.

"I can do nothing else!" he exclaimed. "'Tis a poor return for the services you have done me, and I tender my apologies for the action I'm about to take. But guard yourself, St. Luc!"

"And you, Lennox, look well to yourself when Braddock marches! Every twig and leaf will spout danger!"

His light manner was wholly gone for the moment, and his words were full of menace. Up the street, a sentinel walked back and forth, and Robert could hear the faint fall of his feet on the sand.

"Once more I bid you beware, St. Luc!" he exclaimed, and raising his voice he shouted: "A spy! A spy!"

He heard the sentinel drop the butt of his musket heavily against the earth, utter an exclamation and then run toward them. His shout had also been heard at the tavern, and the guests, bareheaded, began to pour out, and look about confusedly to see whence the alarm had come.

Robert looked at the sentinel who was approaching rapidly, and then he turned to see what St Luc would do. But the Frenchman was gone. Near them was a mass of shrubbery and he believed that he had flitted into it, as silently as the passing of a shadow. But the sentinel had caught a glimpse of the dusky figure, and he cried:

"Who was he? What is it?"

"A spy!" replied Robert hastily. "A Frenchman whom I have seen in Canada! I think he sprang into those bushes and flowers!"

The sentinel and Robert rushed into the shrubbery but nothing was there. As they looked about in the dusk, Robert heard a refrain, distant, faint and taunting:

"Hier sur le pont d'Avignon
J'ai oui chanter la belle
Lon, la."

It was only for an instant, then it died like a summer echo, and he knew that St. Luc was gone. An immense weight rolled from him. He had done what he should have done, but the result that he feared had not followed.

"I can find nothing, sir," said the sentinel, who recognized in Robert one of superior rank.

"Nor I, but you saw the figure, did you not?"

"I did, sir. 'Twas more like a shadow, but 'twas a man, I'll swear."

Robert was glad to have the sentinel's testimony, because in another moment the revelers were upon him, making sport of him for his false alarm, and asserting that not his eyes but the punch he had drunk had seen a French spy.

"I scarce tasted the punch," said Robert, "and the soldier here is witness that I spoke true."

A farther and longer search was organized, but the Frenchman had vanished into the thinnest of thin air. As Robert walked with Willet and Tayoga back to the tavern, the hunter said:

"I suppose it was St. Luc?"

"Yes, but why did you think it was he?"

"Because it was just the sort of deed he would do. Did you speak with him?"

"Yes, and I told him I must give the alarm. He disappeared with amazing speed and silence."

Robert made a brief report the next day to Governor Dinwiddie, not telling that St. Luc and he had spoken together, stating merely that he had seen him, giving his name, and describing him as one of the most formidable of the French forest leaders.

"I thank you, Mr. Lennox," said the Governor. "Your information shall be conveyed to General Braddock. Yet I think our force will be too great for the wilderness bands."

On the following day they were at Alexandria on the Potomac, where the great council was to be held. Here Braddock's camp was spread, and in a large tent he met Governor Dinwiddie of Virginia, Governor de Lancey of New York, Governor Sharpe of Maryland, Governor Dobbs of North Carolina and Governor Shirley of Massachusetts, an elderly lawyer, but the ablest and most energetic of all the governors.

It was the most momentous council yet held in North America, and all the young officers waited with the most intense eagerness the news from the tent. Robert saw Braddock as he went in, a middle-aged man of high color and an obstinate chin. Grosvenor gave him some of the gossip about the general.

"London has many stories of him," he said. "He has spent most of his life in the army. He is a gambler, but brave, rough but generous, irritable, but often very kind. Opposition inflames him, but he likes zeal and good service. He is very fond of your young Mr. Washington, who, I hear is much of a man."

The council in the great tent was long and weighty, and well it might have been, even far beyond the wildest thoughts of any of the participants. These were the beginnings of events that shook not only America but Europe for sixty years. In the tent they agreed upon a great and comprehensive scheme of campaign that had been proposed some time before. Braddock would proceed with his attack upon Fort

Duquesne, Shirley would see that the forces of New England seized Beauséjour and De Lancey would have Colonel William Johnson to move upon Crown Point and then Niagara. Acadia also would be taken. Dinwiddie after Shirley was the most vigorous of the governors, and he promised that the full force of Virginia should be behind Braddock. But to Shirley was given the great vision. He foresaw the complete disappearance of French power from North America, and, to achieve a result that he desired so much, it was only necessary for the colonists to act together and with vigor. While he recognized in Braddock infirmities of temper and insufficient knowledge of his battlefield, he knew him to be energetic and courageous and he believed that the first blow, the one that he was to strike at Fort Duquesne, would inflict a mortal blow upon France in the New World. In every vigorous measure that he proposed Dinwiddie backed him, and the other governors, overborne by their will, gave their consent.

While Robert sat with his friends in the shade of a grove, awaiting the result of the deliberations in the tent, his attention was attracted by a strong, thick-set figure in a British uniform.

"Colonel Johnson!" he cried, and running forward he shook hands eagerly with Colonel William Johnson.

"Why, Colonel!" he exclaimed, "I didn't dream that you were here, but
I'm most happy to see you."

"And I to see you, Mr. Lennox, or Robert, as I shall call you," said Colonel Johnson. "Alexandria is a long journey from Mount Johnson, but you see I'm here, awaiting the results of this council, which I tell you may have vast significance for North America."

"But why are you not in the tent with the others, you who know so much more about conditions on the border than any man who is in there?"

"I am not one of the governors, Robert, my lad, nor am I General Braddock. Hence I'm not eligible, but I'm not to be neglected. I may as well tell you that we are planning several expeditions, and that I'm to lead one in the north."

"And Madam Johnson, and everybody at your home? Are they well?"

"As well of body as human beings can be when I left. Molly told me that if I saw you to give you her special love. Ah, you young blade, if you were older I should be jealous, and then, again, perhaps I shouldn't!"

"And Joseph?"

"Young Thayendanegea? Fierce and warlike as becomes his lineage. He demands if I lead an army to the war that he go with me, and he scarce twelve. What is more, he will demand and insist, until I have to take him. 'Tis a true eagle that young Joseph. But here is Willet! It soothes my eyes to see you again, brave hunter, and Tayoga, too, who is fully as welcome."

He shook hands with them both and the Onondaga gravely asked:

"What news of my people, Waraiyageh?"

Colonel Johnson's face clouded.

"Things do not go well between us and the vale of Onondaga," he replied. "The Hodenosaunee complain of the Indian commissioners at Albany, and with justice. Moreover, the French advance and the superior French vigor create a fear that the British and Americans may lose. Then the Hodenosaunee will be left alone to fight the French and all the hostile tribes. Father Drouillard has come back and is working with his converts."

"The nations of the Hodenosaunee will never go with the French," declared Tayoga with emphasis. "Although the times seem dark, and men's minds may waver for a while, they will remain loyal to their ancient allies. Their doubts will cease, Waraiyageh, when the king across the sea takes away the power of dealing with us from the Dutch commissioners at Albany, and gives it to you, you who know us so well and who have always been our friend."

Colonel Johnson's face flushed with pleasure.

"Your opinion of me is too high, Tayoga," he said, "but I'll not deny that it gratifies me to hear it."

"Have you heard anything from Fort Refuge, and Colden and Wilton and the others?" asked Robert.

"An Oneida runner brought a letter just before I left Mount Johnson. The brave Philadelphia lads still hold the little fortress, and have occasional skirmishes with wandering bands. Theirs has been a good work, well done."

But while Colonel Johnson was not a member of the council and could not sit with it, he had a great reputation with all the governors, and the next day he was asked to appear before them and General Braddock, where he was treated with the consideration due to a man of his achievements, and where the council, without waiting for the authority of the English king, gave him full and complete powers to treat with the Hodenosaunee, and to heal the wounds inflicted upon the pride of the nations by the commissioners at Albany. He was thus made superintendent of Indian affairs in North America, and he was also as he had said to lead the expedition against Crown Point. He came forth from the council exultant, his eyes glowing.

"'Tis even more than I had hoped," he said to Willet, "and now I must say farewell to you and the brave lads with you. We have come to the edge of great things, and there is no time to waste."

He hastened northward, the council broke up the next day, and the visiting governors hurried back to their respective provinces to prepare for the campaigns, leaving Braddock to strike the first blow.

CHAPTER XV
THE FOREST FIGHT

Robert thought they would march at once, but annoying delays occurred. He had noticed that Hamilton, the governor of the great neighboring province of Pennsylvania, was not present at the council, but he did not know the cause of it until Stuart, the young Virginian, told him.

"Pennsylvania is in a huff," he said, "because General Braddock's army has been landed at Alexandria instead of Philadelphia. Truth to tell, for an expedition against Fort Duquesne, Philadelphia would have been a nearer and better place, but I hear that one John Hanbury, a powerful merchant who trades much in Virginia, wanted the troops to come this way that he might sell them supplies, and he persuaded the Duke of Newcastle to choose Alexandria. 'Tis a bad state of affairs, Lennox, but you and I can't remedy it. The chief trouble is between the general and the Pennsylvanians, many of whom are Quakers and Germans, as obstinate people as this world has ever produced."

The differences and difficulties were soon patent to all. A month of spring was passing, and the army was far from having the necessary supplies. Neither Virginia nor Pennsylvania responded properly. In Pennsylvania there was a bitter quarrel between the people and the proprietary government that hampered action. Many of the contractors who were to furnish equipment thought much more of profit than of patriotism. Braddock, brave and honest, but tactless and wholly ignorant of the conditions predominant in any new country, raged and stormed. He denounced the Virginia troops that came to his standard, calling shameful their lack of uniforms and what he considered their lack of discipline.

Robert heard that in these turbulent days young Washington, whom Braddock had taken on his staff as a colonel and for whom he had a warm personal regard, was the best mediator between the testy general and the stubborn population. In his difficult position, and while yet scarcely more than a boy, he was showing all the great qualities of character that he was to display so grandly in the long war twenty years later.

"Tis related," said Willet, "that General Braddock will listen to anything from him, that he has the most absolute confidence in his honesty and good judgment, and, judging from what I hear, General Braddock is right."

But to Robert, despite the anxieties, the days were happy. As he had affiliated readily with the young Virginians he was also quickly a friend of the young British officers, who were anxious to learn about the new conditions into which they had been cast with so little preparation. There was Captain Robert Orme, Braddock's aide-de-camp, a fine manly fellow, for whom he soon formed a reciprocal liking, and the son of Sir Peter Halket, a lieutenant, and Morris, an American, another aide-de-camp, and young William Shirley, the son of the governor of Massachusetts, who had become Braddock's secretary. He also became well acquainted with older officers, Gladwin who was to defend Detroit so gallantly against Pontiac and his allied tribes, Gates, Gage, Barton and others, many of whom were destined to serve again on one side or other in the great Revolution.

Grosvenor knew all the Englishmen, and often in the evenings, since May had now come they sat about the camp fires, and Robert listened with eagerness as they told stories of gay life in London, tales of the theater, of the heavy betting at the clubs and the races, and now and then in low tones some gossip of royalty. Tayoga was more than welcome in this group, as the great Thayendanegea was destined to be years later. His height, his splendid appearance, his dignity and his manners were respected and admired. Willet sometimes sat with them, but said little. Robert knew that he approved of his new friendships.

Willet was undoubtedly anxious. The delays which were still numerous weighed heavily upon him, and he confided to Robert that every day lost would increase the danger of the march.

"The French and Indians of course know our troubles," he said. "St. Luc has gone like an arrow into the wilderness with all the news about us, and he's not the only one. If we could adjust this trouble with the Pennsylvanians we might start at once."

An hour or two after he uttered his complaint, Robert saw a middle aged man, not remarkable of appearance, talking with Braddock. His dress was homespun and careless, but his large head was beautifully shaped, and his features, though they might have been called homely, shone with the light of an extraordinary intelligence. His manner as he talked to Braddock, without showing any tinge of deference, was soothing. Robert saw at once, despite his homespun dress, that here was a man of the great world and of great affairs.

"Who is he?" he said to Willet.

"It's Benjamin Franklin, of Pennsylvania," replied the hunter. "I hear he's one of the shrewdest men in all the colonies, and I don't doubt the report."

It was Robert's first sight of Franklin, certainly not the least in that amazing group of men who founded the American Union.

"They say," continued Willet, "that he's already achieved the impossible, that he's drawing General Braddock and the Pennsylvanians together, and that we'll soon get weapons, horses and all the other supplies we need."

It was no false news. Franklin had done what he alone could do. One of the greatest masters of diplomacy the world has ever known, he brought Braddock and Pennsylvania together, and smoothed out the difficulties. All the needed supplies began to flow in, and on the tenth of an eventful May the whole army started from Wills Creek to which point it had advanced, while Franklin was removing the difficulties. A new fort named Cumberland had been established there, and stalwart Virginians had been cutting a road ahead through the wilderness.

The place was on the edge of the unending forest. The narrow fringe of settlements on the Atlantic coast was left behind, and henceforth they must march through regions known only to the Indians and the woods rangers. But it was a fine army, two British regiments under Halket and Dunbar, their numbers reinforced by Virginia volunteers, and five hundred other Virginians, divided into nine companies. There was a company of British sailors, too, and artillery, and hundreds of wagons and baggage horses. Among the teamsters was a strong lad named Daniel Boone destined to immortality as the most famous of all pioneers.

Robert, Willet and Tayoga could have had horses to ride, but against the protests of Grosvenor and their other new English friends they declined them. They knew that they could scout along the flanks of an army far better on foot.

"In one way," said Willet, to Grosvenor, "we three, Robert, Tayoga and I, are going back home. The lads, at least have spent the greater part of their lives in the forest, and to me it has given a kindly welcome for these many years. It may look inhospitable to you who come from a country of roads and open fields, but it's not so to us. We know its ways. We can find shelter where you would see none, and it offers food to us, where you would starve, and you're a young man of intelligence too."

"At least I can see its beauty," laughed Grosvenor, as he looked upon the great green wilderness, stretching away and away to the far blue hills. "In truth 'tis a great and romantic adventure to go with a force like ours into an unknown country of such majestic quality."

He looked with a kindling eye from the wilderness back to the army, the greatest that had yet been gathered in the forest, the red coats of the soldiers gleaming now in the spring sunshine, and the air resounding with whips as the teamsters started their trains.

"A great force! A grand force!" said Robert, catching his enthusiasm. "The French and Indians can't stand before it!"

"How far is Fort Duquesne?" asked Grosvenor.

"In the extreme western part of the province of Pennsylvania, many days' march from here. At least, we claim that it's in Pennsylvania province, although the French assert it's on their soil, and they have possession. But it's in the Ohio country, because the waters there flow westward, the Alleghany and Monongahela joining at the fort and forming the great Ohio."

"And so we shall see much of the wilderness. Well, I'm not sorry, Lennox. 'Twill be something to talk about in England. I don't think they realize there the vastness and magnificence of the colonies."

That day a trader named Croghan brought about fifty Indian warriors to the camp, among them a few belonging to the Hodenosaunee, and offered their services as scouts and skirmishers.

Braddock, who loved regularity and outward discipline, gazed at them in astonishment.

"Savages!" he said. "We will have none of them!"

The Indians, uttering no complaint, disappeared in the green forest, with Willet and Tayoga gazing somberly after them.

"'Twas a mistake," said the hunter. "They would have been our eyes and ears, where we needed eyes and ears most."

"A warrior of my kin was among them," said Tayoga. "Word will fly north that an insult has been offered to the Hodenosaunee."

"But," said Willet, "Colonel William Johnson will take a word of another kind. As you know, Tayoga, as I know, and, as all the nations of the Hodenosaunee know, Waraiyageh is their friend. He will speak to them no word that is not true. He will brush away all that web of craft, and cunning and cheating, spun by the Indian commissioners at Albany, and he will see that there is no infringement upon the rights of the great League."

"Waraiyageh will do all that, if he can reach Mount Johnson in time," said Tayoga, "but Onontio rises before the dawn, and he does not sleep until after midnight. He sings beautiful songs in the ears of the warriors, and the songs he sings seem to be true. Already the French and their allies have been victorious everywhere save at Fort Refuge, and they carry the trophies of triumph into Canada."

"But the time for us to strike a great blow is at hand, Tayoga," said Robert, who, with Grosvenor had been listening. "Behold this splendid army! No such force was ever before sent into the American wilderness. When we take Fort Duquesne we shall hold the key to the whole Ohio country, and we shall turn it in the lock and fasten it against the Governor General of Canada and all his allies."

"But the wilderness is mighty," said Tayoga. "Even the army of the great English king is small when it enters its depths."

"On the other hand so is that of the enemy, much smaller than ours," said Grosvenor.

Soon after Croghan and his Indians left the camp a figure tall, dark and somber, followed by a dozen men wild of appearance and clad in hunter's garb, emerged from the forest and walked in silence toward General Braddock's tent. The regular soldiers stared at them in astonishment, but their dark leader took no notice. Robert uttered an exclamation of surprise and pleasure.

"Black Rifle!" he said.

"And who is Black Rifle?" asked Grosvenor.

"A great hunter and scout and a friend of mine. I'm glad he's here. The general can find many uses for Black Rifle and his men."

He ran forward and greeted Black Rifle, who smiled one of his rare smiles at sight of the youth. Willet and Tayoga gave him the same warm welcome.

"What news, Black Rifle?" asked Robert.

"The French and Indians gather at Fort Duquesne to meet you. They are not in great force, but the wilderness will help them and the best of the French leaders are there."

"Have you heard anything of St. Luc?" asked Robert.

"We met a Seneca runner who had seen him. The Senecas are not at war with the French, and the man talked with him a little, but the Frenchman didn't tell him anything. We think he was on the way to Fort Duquesne to join the other French leaders there."

"Have you heard the names of any of these Frenchmen?"

"Besides St. Luc there's Beaujeu, Dumas, Ligneris and Contrecoeur who commands. French regulars and Canadian troops are in the fort, and the heathen are pouring in from the west and north."

"Those are brave and skillful men," said Willet, as he listened to the names of the French leaders who would oppose them. "But 'twas good of you, Black Rifle, to come with these lads of yours to help us."

After the men had enjoyed food and a little rest, they were taken into the great tent, where the general sat, Willet having procured the interview, and accompanying them. Robert waited near with Grosvenor and Tayoga, knowing how useful Black Rifle and his men could be to a wilderness expedition, and hoping that they would be thrown together in future service.

A quarter of an hour passed, and then Black Rifle strode from the tent, his face dark as night. His men followed him, and, almost without a word, they left the camp, plunged into the forest and disappeared. Willet also came from the tent, crestfallen.

"What has happened, Dave?" asked Robert in astonishment.

"The worst. I suppose that when unlike meets unlike only trouble can come. I introduced Black Rifle and his men to General Braddock. They did not salute. They did not take off their caps in his presence, — not knowing, of course, that such things were done in armies. General Braddock rebuked them. I smoothed it all over as much as I could. Then he demanded what they wanted there, as a haughty giver of gifts would speak to a suppliant. Black Rifle said he and his men came to watch on the front and flanks of the army against Indian ambush, knowing how much it was needed. Braddock laughed and sneered. He said that an army such as his did not need to fear a few wandering Indians, and, in any event, it had eyes of its own to watch for itself. Black Rifle said he doubted it, that soldiers in the woods could seldom see anything but themselves. There was blame on both sides, but men like General Braddock and Black Rifle can't understand each other, they'll never understand each other, and, hot with wrath Black Rifle has taken his band and gone into the woods. Nor will he come back, and we need him! I tell you, Robert, we need him! We need him!"

"It is bad," said Tayoga. "An army can never have too many eyes."

Robert was deeply disappointed. He regretted not only the loss of Black Rifle and his men, but the further evidence of an unyielding temperament on the part of their commander. His own mind however so ready to comprehend the mind of others, could understand Braddock's point of view. To the general Black Rifle and his men were mere woods rovers, savages themselves in everything except race, and the army that he led was invincible.

"We'll have to make the best of it," he said.

"They've gone and they're a great loss, but the rest of us will try to do the work they would have done."

"That is so," said Tayoga, gravely.

At last the army moved proudly away into the wilderness. Hundreds of axmen, going ahead, cut a road twelve feet wide, along which cavalry, infantry, artillery and wagons and pack horses stretched for miles. The weather was beautiful, the forest was both beautiful and grand, and to most of the Englishmen and Virginians the march appealed as a great and romantic adventure. The trees were in the tender green leafage of early May, and their solid expanse stretched away hundreds and thousands of miles into the unknown west. Early wild flowers, a shy pink or a modest blue, bloomed in the grass. Deer started from their coverts, crashed through the thickets, and the sky darkened with the swarms of wild fowl flying north. Birds of brilliant plumage flashed among the leaves and often chattered overhead, heedless of the passing army. Now and then the soldiers sang, and the song passed from the head of the column along its rippling red, yellow and brown length of four miles.

It was a cheerful army, more it was a gay army, enjoying the wilderness which it was seeing at one of the finest periods of the year, wondering at the magnificence of the forest, and the great number of streams that came rushing down from the mountains.

"It's a noble country," said Grosvenor to Robert. "I'll admit all that you claim for it."

"And there's so much of it, Grosvenor, even allowing for the portion, the very big portion, the French claim."

"But from which we are going to drive them very soon, Robert, my lad."

"I think so, too, Grosvenor."

Often Robert, Willet and Tayoga went far ahead on swift foot, searching the forest for ambush, and finding none, they would come back and watch the axmen, three hundred in number, who were cutting the road for the army. They were stalwart fellows, skilled in their business, and their axes rang through the woods. Robert felt regret when he saw the splendid trees fall and be dragged to one side, there to rot, despite the fact that the unbroken forest covered millions of square miles.

The camps at night were scenes of good humor. Scouts and flankers were thrown out in the forest, and huge fires were built of the fallen wood which was abundant everywhere. The flames, roaring and leaping, threw a ruddy light over the soldiers, and gave them pleasant warmth, as often in the hills the dusk came on heavy with chill.

Despite the favorable nature of the season some of the soldiers unused to hardships fell ill, and, more than a week later, when they reached a place known as the Little Meadows, Braddock left there the sick and the heavy baggage with a rear guard under Colonel Dunbar. A scout had brought word that a formidable force of French regulars was expected to reinforce the garrison at Fort Duquesne, and the general was anxious to forestall them. Young Washington, in whom he had great confidence, also advised him to push on, and now the army of chosen troops increased its speed.

Robert came into contact with Braddock only once or twice, and then he was noticed with a nod, but on the whole he was glad to escape so easily. The general brave and honest, but irritable, had a closed mind. He thought all things should be done in the way to which he was used, and he had little use for the Americans, save for young Washington, and young Morris, who were on his staff, and young Shirley who was his secretary. To them he was invariably kind and considerate.

The regular officers made no attempt to interfere with Robert, Tayoga and Willet, who, having their commissions as scouts, roamed as they pleased, and, even on foot, their pace being so much greater than that of the army, they often went far ahead in the night seeking traces of the enemy. Now, although the march was not resisted, they saw unmistakable signs that it was watched. They found trails of small Indian bands and several soldiers who straggled into the forest were killed and scalped. Braddock was enraged but not alarmed. The army would brush away these flies and proceed to the achievement of its object, the capture of Fort Duquesne. The soldiers from England shuddered at the sight of their scalped comrades. It was a new form of war to them, and very ghastly.

Robert, Tayoga and Willet were the best scouts and the regular officers soon learned to rely on them. Grosvenor often begged to go with them, but they laughingly refused.

"We don't claim to be of special excellence ourselves, Grosvenor," said Robert, "but such work needs a very long training. One, so to speak, must be born to it, and to be born to it you have to be born in this country, and not in England."

It was about the close of June and they had been nearly three weeks on the way when the three, scouting on a moonlight night, struck a trail larger than usual. Tayoga reckoned that it had been made by at least a dozen warriors, and Willet agreed with him.

"And behold the trace of the big moccasin, Great Bear," said the Onondaga, pointing to a faint impression among the leaves. "It is very large, and it turns in much. We do not see it for the first time."

"Tandakora," said Willet.

"It can be none other."

"We shouldn't be surprised at seeing it. The Ojibway, like a wolf, will rush to the place of killing."

"I am not surprised, Great Bear. It is strange, perhaps, that we have not seen his footsteps before. No doubt he has looked many times upon the marching army."

"Since Tandakora is here, probably leading the Indian scouts, we'll have to take every precaution ourselves. I like my scalp, and I like for it to remain where it has grown, on the top of my head."

They moved now with the most extreme care, always keeping under cover of bushes, and never making any sound as they walked, but the army kept on steadily in the road cut for it by the axmen. Encounters between the flankers and small bands still occurred, but there was yet no sign of serious resistance, and the fort was drawing nearer and nearer.

"I've no doubt the French commander will abandon it," said Grosvenor to Robert. "He'll conclude that our army is too powerful for him."

"I scarce think so," replied Robert doubtfully. "'Tis not the French way, at least, not on this continent. Like as not they will depend on the savages, whom they have with them."

They had been on the march nearly a month when they came to Turtle Creek, which flows into the Monongahela only eight miles from Fort Duquesne a strong fortress of logs with bastions, ravelins, ditch, glacis and covered ways, standing at the junction of the twin streams, the Monongahela and the Alleghany, that form the great Ohio. Here they made a little halt and the scouts who had been sent into the woods reported silence and desolation.

The army rejoiced. It had been a long march, and the wilderness is hard for those not used to it, even in the best of times. Victory was now almost in sight. The next day, perhaps, they would march into Fort Duquesne and take possession, and doubtless a strong detachment would be sent in pursuit of the flying French and Indians.

Full warrant had they for their expectations, as nothing seemed more peaceful than the wilderness. The flames from the cooking fires threw their ruddy light over bough and bush, and disclosed no enemy, and, as the glow of the coals died down, the peaceful tails of the night birds showed that the forest was undisturbed.

Far in the night, Robert, Tayoga and Willet crept through the woods to Fort Duquesne. They found many small trails of both white men and red men, but none indicating a large force. At last they saw a light under the western horizon, which they believed to come from Duquesne itself.

"Perhaps they've burned the fort and are abandoning it," said Robert.

Willet shook his head.

"Not likely," he said. "It's more probable that the light comes from great fires, around which the savages are dancing the war dance."

"What do you think, Tayoga?"

"That the Great Bear is right."

"But surely," said Robert, "they can't hope to withstand an army like ours."

"Robert," said Willet, "you've lived long enough in it to know that anything is possible in the wilderness. Contrecoeur, the French commander at Duquesne, is a brave and capable man. Beaujeu, who stands next to him, has, they say, a soul of fire. You know what St. Luc is, the bravest of the brave, and as wise as a fox, and Dumas and Ligneris are great partisan leaders. Do you think these men will run away without a fight?"

"But they must depend chiefly on the Indians!"

"Even so. They won't let the Indians run away either. We're bound to have some kind of a battle somewhere, though we ought to win."

"Do you know the general's plans for tomorrow?"

"We're to start at dawn. We'll cross the Monongahela for the second time about noon, or a little later, and then, if the French and Indians have run away, as you seemed a little while ago to believe they would, we'll proceed, colors flying into the fort."

"If the enemy makes a stand I should think it would be at the ford."

"Seems likely."

"Come! Come, Dave! Be cheerful. If they meet us at the ford or anywhere else we'll brush 'em aside. That big body of French regulars from Canada hasn't come—we know that—and there isn't force enough in Duquesne to withstand us."

Willet did not say anything more, but his steps were not at all buoyant as they walked back toward the camp. Robert, lying on a blanket, slept soundly before one of the fires, but awoke at dawn, and took breakfast with Willet, Tayoga, Grosvenor and the two young Virginians, Stuart and Cabell.

"We'll be in Duquesne tonight," said the sanguine Stuart.

"In very truth we will," said the equally confident Grosvenor.

The dawn came clear and brilliant, and the army advanced, to the music of a fine band. The light cavalry led the way, then came a detachment of sailors who had been loaned by Admiral Keppel, followed by the English regulars in red and the Virginians in blue. Behind them came the cannon, the packhorses, and all the elements that make up the train of an army.

It was a gay and inspiriting sight, especially so to youth, and Robert's heart thrilled as he looked. The hour of triumph had come at last. Away with the forebodings of Willet! Here was the might of England and the colonies, and, brave and cunning as St. Luc and Beaujeu and the other Frenchmen might be their bravery and cunning would avail them nothing.

They marched on all the morning, a long and brilliant line of red and blue and brown, and nothing happened. The forest on either side of them was still silent and tenantless, and they expected in a few more hours to see the fort they had come so far to take. The heavens themselves were propitious. Only little white clouds were to be seen in the sky of dazzling blue, and the green forest, stirred by a gentle wind, waved its boughs at them in friendly fashion.

About noon they approached the river, and Gage leading a strong advance guard across it, found no enemy on the other side, puzzling and also pleasing news. The foe, whom they had expected to find in this formidable position, seemed to have melted away. No trace of him could be found in the forest, and to many it appeared that the road to Fort Duquesne lay open.

"They've concluded our force is too great and have abandoned the fort," said Robert. "I can't make anything else of it, Dave."

"It does look like it," said the hunter doubtfully. "I certainly thought they would meet us here. The ford is the place of places for a defensive battle."

Gage made his report to Braddock, confirming the general in his belief that the French and Indians would not dare to meet him, and that the dangers of the wilderness had been overrated. The order to resume the march was given and the trumpets in the advance sang merrily, the silent woods giving back their echoes in faint musical notes. The afternoon that had now come was as brilliant as the morning. A great sun blazed down from a sky of cloudless blue, deepening and intensifying the green of the forest, the red uniforms of the British and the blue uniforms of the Virginians. Robert again admired the sight. The army marched as if on parade, and it presented a splendid spectacle.

The head of the column entered the shallows, and soon the long line was passing the river. Robert had a lingering belief that the bullets would rain upon them in the water, but nothing stirred in the forest beyond. The head of the column emerged upon the opposite bank, and then its long red and blue length trailed slowly after. Robert and his comrades crossed in a wagon. They had wanted to go into the woods, seeking for the enemy, but the orders of Braddock, who wished to keep all his force together, held them.

The entire army was now across, and, within the shade of the forest, the general ordered a short period for rest and food, before they completed the few miles that yet separated them from Fort Duquesne. The troops were in great spirits. They might have been held at the dangerous ford, they thought, but now that it had been passed without resistance the woods could offer nothing able to stop them.

"What has become of your warlike Frenchmen, Mr. Willet?" asked Grosvenor. "So far as this campaign is concerned they seem to excel as runners rather than warriors."

"I confess that I'm surprised, Mr. Grosvenor," replied the hunter. "Beaujeu, St. Luc and Dumas are not the men to make a carpet of roses for us to march on. There is something here that does not meet the eye. What say you, Tayoga?"

"I like it not," replied the Onondaga. "In war I fear the forest when it is silent."

Near them a small circle of land had been cleared and in it stood a house, lone and deserted. It had been built by a trader named Fraser and in it Washington, who had visited it once before on a former mission, and one or two others sat, during the period of rest and refreshment. The young Virginian, despite his great frame and gigantic strength, was so much wasted by fever that, when he came forth to remount, he was barely able to keep his place in his saddle.

Now the merry trumpets sang again and the red and blue column, lifting itself up, resumed its march along the trail through the forest toward Duquesne. The river was on one side and a line of high hills on the other, but the forest everywhere was dense and in its heaviest foliage. Braddock, despite the safe passage of the ford, was not reckless. A troop of guides and Virginia light horsemen led the way. A hundred yards behind them came the vanguard, then Gage with a picked body of British troops, after them the axmen, who had done such great work, behind them the main body of the artillery, the wagons and the packhorses, while a strong force of regulars and Virginians closed up the rear. Scouts and skirmishers ranged the flanks, though they were ordered to go not more than a few hundred yards away.

Robert, Tayoga and Willet were with the guides at the very apex of the column, and they continually searched the forests and the thickets with keen eyes for a possible enemy. But all was quiet there. The game, frightened by the advancing army, had gone away. Not a leaf, not a bough stirred. The blazing sun, now near the zenith, poured down fiery rays and it was hot in the shade of the great trees that grew so closely together.

Robert and the other scouts and guides in the apex marched on soundless feet, but he heard close behind him the tread of the Virginia light horsemen, behind them the steady march of the regulars under Gage, and behind them the deep hum and murmur of the army, the creaking of wheels and the clank of the great guns. Despite the following sounds he was conscious all the time of the deep, intense silence in the forest on either side of him. The birds, like the game, had gone away, and there was no flash of blue or of flame among the green leaves.

"There's a dip just ahead," said Willet, pointing to a wide ravine filled with bushes that ran directly across the trail.

They continued their steady advance, and Robert's heart fluttered, but when they came to the ravine they found it empty of everything save the bushes, and the scouts and guides, plunging into it, crossed to the other side. The light horsemen of Virginia followed, after them Gage's regulars and then the main army drew on its red and blue length, expecting to cross in the same way.

Robert, Tayoga and Willet, leading, entered the deep forest again. Some chance had put young Lennox slightly in advance of his comrades, but suddenly he stopped. A short distance ahead a figure bounded across the trail and disappeared in the thicket. It was only a flitting glimpse, but he recognized St. Luc, the athletic figure, the fair hair and the strong face.

"St. Luc!" he exclaimed. "Did you see, Dave? Did you see?"

"Aye, I saw," said the hunter, "and the enemy is here!"

He whirled about, threw up his arms and shouted to the column to stop. At the same moment, a terrible cry, the long fierce war whoop of the savages, burst from the forest, filled the air and came back in ferocious echoes. Then a deadly fire of rifles and muskets was poured from both right and left upon the marching column. Men and horses went down, and cries of pain and surprise blended with the war whoop of the savages which swelled and fell again.

Robert and his comrades had thrown themselves flat upon the ground at the first fire, and escaped the bullets. Now they rose to their knees, and began to send their own bullets at the flitting forms among the trees and bushes. Robert caught glimpses of the savages, naked to the waist, coated thickly with war paint, their fierce eyes gleaming, and now and then he saw a man in French uniform passing among them and encouraging them. He saw one gigantic figure which he knew to be that of Tandakora, and he raised his reloaded rifle to fire at him, but the Ojibway was gone.

Surprised in the ominous forest, the British and the Virginians nevertheless showed a courage worthy of all praise. Gage formed his regulars on the trail, and they sent volley after volley into the dense shades on either side, the big muskets thundering together like cannon. Leaves and twigs and little boughs fell in showers before their bullets, but whether they struck any of the foe they did not know. The smoke soon rose in clouds and added to the dimness and obscurity of the forest.

"A great noise," shouted Tayoga in Robert's ear, "but it does not hurt the enemy, who sees his target and sends his bullets against it!"

The soldiers were dropping fast and the bullets of the French and the savages were coming from their coverts in a deadly rain. Robert, Willet and Tayoga, with the wisdom of the wilderness, remained crouched at the edge of the trail, but in shelter, and did not fire until they saw an enemy upon whom to draw the trigger. Then a deeper roar was added to the thundering of the big muskets, as Braddock brought up the cannon, and they began to sweep the forest. The English troops, eager to get at the foe, crowded forward, shouting "God save the King!" and the cheers of the Virginians joined with them.

"We'll win! We'll win!" cried Robert. "They can't stop such brave men as ours!"

But the fire of the French and the savages was increasing in volume and accuracy. The bullets and cannon balls of the English and Americans fired almost at random were passing over their heads, but the great column of scarlet and blue on the trail formed a target which the leaden missiles could not miss. Continually shouting the war whoop, exultant now with the joy of expected triumph, the savages hovered on either flank of Braddock's army like a swarm of bees, but with a sting far more deadly. The brave and wily Beaujeu had been killed in the first minute of the battle, but St. Luc, Dumas and Ligneris, equally brave and wily, directed the onset, and the huge Tandakora raged before his warriors.

The head of the British column was destroyed, and the three crept back toward Gage's regulars, but the fire of the enemy was now spreading along both flanks of the column to its full length. Robert remembered the warning words of St. Luc. Every twig and leaf in the forest was spouting death. Gage's regulars, raked by a terrible fire, and in danger of complete destruction, were compelled to retreat upon the main body, and, to their infinite mortification, abandon two cannon, which the savages seized with fierce shouts of joy and dragged into the woods.

"It goes ill," said Willet, as the terrible forest, raining death from every side, seemed to close in on them like the shadow of doom. Braddock, hearing the tremendous fire ahead, rushed forward his own immediate troops as fast as possible, and meeting Gage's retreating men, the two bodies became a great mass of scarlet in the forest, upon which French and Indian bullets, that could not miss, beat like a storm of hail. The shouts and cheers of the regulars ceased. In an appalling situation, the like of which they had never known before, hemmed in on every side by an unseen death, they fell into confusion, but they did not lose courage. The savage ring now enclosed the whole army, and to stand and to retreat alike meant death.

The British charged with the bayonet into the thickets. The Indians melted away before them, and, when the exhausted regulars came back into the trail, the Indians rushed after them, still pouring in a murderous fire, and making the forest ring with the ferocious war whoop. The Virginians, knowing the warfare of the wilderness, began to take to the shelter of the trees, from which they could fire at the enemy. The brave though mistaken Braddock fiercely ordered them out again. A score lying behind a fallen trunk and, matching the savages at their own game, were mistaken by the regulars for the foe, and were fired upon with deadly effect. Other regulars who tried to imitate the hostile tactics were set upon by Braddock himself who beat them with the flat of his sword and drove them back into the open trail, where the rain of bullets fell directly upon them.

Robert looked upon the scene and he found it awful to the last degree. The bodies of the dead in red or blue lay everywhere. Officers, English and Virginian, ran here and there begging and praying their troops to stand and form in order. "Fire upon the enemy!" they shouted. "Show us somebody to fire at and we'll fire," the men shouted back. The confusion was deepening, and the signs of a panic were appearing. In the forest the circle of Indians, mad with battle and the greatest taking of scalps they had ever known, pressed closer and closer, and sent sheets of bullets into the huddled mass. Many of them leaped in and scalped the fallen before the eyes of the horrified soldiers. The yelling never ceased, and it was so terrific that the few British officers who survived declared that they would never forget it to their dying day.

Among the officers the mortality was now frightful. The brave Sir Peter Halket was shot dead, and his young son, the lieutenant, rushing to raise up his body, was killed and fell by his side. The youthful Shirley, Braddock's secretary, received a bullet in his brain and died instantly. Out of eighty-six officers sixty-three were down. Washington alone seemed to bear a charmed life. Two horses were killed under him and four bullets pierced his clothing. Braddock galloped back and forth, cursing and shouting to his men, and showing undaunted courage. Robert believed that he never really understood what was happening, that the deadly nature of the surprise and its appalling completeness left him dazed.

How long Robert stood at the edge of the circle of death and fired into the bushes he never knew, but it seemed to him that almost an eternity had passed, when Tayoga seized him by the arm and shouted in his ear.

"It is finished! Our army has perished! Come, Lennox!"

He wiped the smoke from his eyes, and saw that the mass in red and blue was much smaller. Braddock was still on his horse, and, at the insistence of his officers, he was at last giving the command to retreat. Just as the trumpet sounded that note of defeat he was shot through the body and fell to the ground where, in his rage and despair, he begged the men to leave him to die alone. But two of the Virginia officers lifted him up and bore him toward the rear. Then the army that had fought so long against an invisible foe broke into a panic, that is what was left of it, as two thirds of its numbers had already been killed or wounded. Shouting with horror and ignoring their officers, they rushed for the river.

Everything was lost, cannon and baggage were abandoned, and often rifles and muskets were thrown away. Into the water they rushed, and the Indians, who had followed howling like wolves, stopped, though they fired at the fleeing men in the stream.

As the retreat began, Robert, Tayoga and Willet, whom some miracle seemed to preserve from harm, joined the Virginians who covered the rear, and, as fast as they could reload their rifles, they fired at the demon horde that pressed closer and closer, and that never ceased to cut down the fleeing army. It was much like a ghastly dream to Robert. Nothing was real, except his overwhelming sense of horror. Men fell around him, and he wondered why he did not fall too, but he was untouched, and Willet and Tayoga also were unwounded. He saw near him young Stuart who had lost his horse long since, but who had snatched a rifle from a fallen soldier, and who was fighting gallantly on foot.

"Who would have thought it?" exclaimed the Virginian. "An army such as ours, to be beaten, nay, to be destroyed, by a swarm of savages!"

"But don't forget the Frenchmen!" shouted Robert in reply. "They're directing!"

"Which is no consolation to us," cried Stuart. He said something else, but it was lost in the tremendous firing and yelling of the Indians, who were now only a score of yards away from the devoted rear guard that was doing its best to protect the flying and confused mass of soldiers.

Robert discharged his bullet at a brown face and then, as he walked backward, he tripped and fell over a root. He sprang up at once, but in an instant a gigantic figure bounded out of the fire and smoke, and Tandakora, uttering a fierce shout of triumph, circled his tomahawk swiftly above his head, preparatory to the mortal blow. But Tayoga, quick as lightning, hurled his pistol with all his might. It struck the huge Ojibway on the head with such force that the tomahawk fell from his hand, and he staggered back into the smoke.

"Tayoga, again I thank you!" cried Robert.

"You will do the same for me," said the Onondaga, and then they too were lost in the smoke, as with the rear guard of Virginians they followed the retreating army.

Robert and his comrades, swept on in the press, crossed the river with the others and gained the farther shore unhurt. Willet looked back at the woods, which still flamed with the hostile rifles, and shuddered.

"It's worse than anything of which I ever dreamed," he said. "Now the tomahawk and the scalping knife will sweep the border from Canada to Carolina."

The panic was stopped at last and the broken remnants of the army, covered by the Virginians who understood the forest, began their retreat. Braddock died the next day, his last words being, "We shall know better how to deal with them another time." Washington, Orme, Morris and the others carried the news of the great defeat to Virginia and Pennsylvania, whence it was sent to England, to be received there at first with incredulity, men saying that such a thing was impossible. But England too was soon to be in mourning, because so many of her bravest had fallen at the hands of an invisible foe in the far American wilderness.

Robert, Willet and Tayoga followed the retreating army only a short distance beyond the Monongahela. They saw that Grosvenor, Stuart and Cabell had escaped with slight wounds, and, slipping quietly into the forest, they circled about Fort Duquesne, seeing the lights where the Indians were burning their wretched prisoners alive, and then plunging again into the woods.

Late at night they lay down in a dense covert, and exhausted, slept. They rose at dawn, and tried to shake off the horror.

"Be of good courage, Robert," said Willet. "It's a terrible blow, but England and the colonies have not yet gathered their full strength."

"That is so," said Tayoga. "Our sachems tell us that he who wins the first victory does not always win the last."

A bird on a bough over their heads began to sing a song of greeting to the new day, and Robert hoped and believed.